OF
INNOCENCE

Also by Tami Dane:

Blood of Eden

"Werewolves in Chic Clothing"
In
The Real Werewives of Vampire County

BLOOD
OF
INNOCENCE

TAMI DANE

KENSINGTON PUBLISHING CORP.

http://www.kensingtonbooks.com

KENSINGTON BOOKS are published by

Kensington Publishing Corp.
119 West 40th Street
New York, NY 10018

All Kensington Titles, Imprints, and Distributed Lines are available at special quantity discounts for bulk purchases for sales promotions, premiums, fund-raising, and educational or institutional use.

Special book excerpts or customized printings can also be created to fit specific needs. For details, write or phone the office of the Kensington special sales manager: Kensington Publishing Corp., 119 West 40th Street, New York, NY 10018, attn: Special Sales Department, Phone: 1-800-221-2647.

Kensington and the K logo Reg. U.S. Pat & TM Off.

ISBN-13: 978-0-7582-6710-8
ISBN-10: 0-7582-6710-X

First Mass Market Printing: June 2012

10 9 8 7 6 5 4 3 2 1

Printed in the United States of America

BLOOD
OF
INNOCENCE

Adopt the pace of nature; her secret is patience.

—Ralph Waldo Emerson

I

There are three things I would have gladly given my right arm—and leg—never to see.

How hot dogs are made (trust me, you don't want to know).

How Porta-Potties are emptied (ditto).

And this.

I'm Sloan Skye, summer intern for the FBI's PBAU—that's the Paranormal Behavioral Analysis Unit. You know how the BAU, aka the Behavioral Analysis Unit, profiles criminals? We profile criminals too. But our bad guys have fangs and fur.

At the moment, I was standing in a pretty neighborhood, in a pretty house, in a pretty bedroom . . . that also happened to be the scene of a horrific crime.

It wasn't that it was a grisly scene. There was no blood spatter. No sign of a struggle. The victim was lying in her bed; her blankets were tucked under her chin. She looked peaceful, as if she were sleeping, with the exception of her eyes. They were staring blindly. And she was grimacing. It was a creepy sight.

At my first crime scene—which happened to be on my first day on the job, which just happened to be last week—I threw up. I was determined not to do that again.

When a cool gust from the open window carried the scent of death to my nose, I gagged. It wasn't looking good for me.

I headed for the window, hoping some fresh air might help.

Special Agent Jordan Thomas—aka JT, aka the drool-worthy, heart-palpitatingly handsome man I'd kissed a couple of days ago—was standing next to the bed. I was guessing he was completely unaware of my struggle to keep my lunch where it belonged.

"Hmm. Looks like the killer punctured the femoral artery," he said.

I had to assume he'd uncovered the victim. There could be no other way for him to know that. "Is that so?" I said, sticking my face up to the screen and poking at a little hole in the corner. A big blackbird was perched on a tree limb outside. It snapped its wings, zooming into the early-morning sky.

Using gloved hands, I pulled the screen up and looked down. There was no way for a killer to get up here. Unless he was a really good climber. And small. The scraggly ornamental tree outside wouldn't hold the weight of a full-grown adult, by my estimation. "I don't think he or she came in this way."

"No sign of forced entry downstairs either," Gabe Wagner, another member of our team (who also happens to be just as good-looking as JT), said as he strolled into the room. "And look, jewelry sitting in plain sight on her dresser. Nice stuff too." My body bristled at the sound of his voice. It tensed even more when I realized he was coming toward me. "What do you have there?" He leaned in, close enough for me to smell his cologne and the subtle hint of warm summer air still clinging to his clothes.

Avoiding eye contact, I slid the screen back in place. "Nothing."

Before you get the wrong idea, let me explain something to you. Gabe and I have a bumpy history. We dated. A long time ago. He dumped me for another girl. We've been frenemies since. Actually, we've been more like enemies than friends. He even stole my dream job with the BAU. That was just last week. Then he had the nerve to request a transfer a couple of days later. To the PBAU.

So, of course, I was in full I-hate-him mode at that point.

But then, a few days ago—right after I was rescued from a kidnapper—he confessed he still had feelings for me.

I wasn't sure what to say or think about that.

Then JT kissed me.

And I didn't know what to say or think about that either.

It's all very messed up.

And it's pretty much all my fault.

At the moment, I just wished it all would go away so we could concentrate on our jobs. Someone had killed this woman. It was up to us to profile who did it and help the police stop him.

"Oh, damn," JT said.

Thankful for any excuse to get away from Gabe, I headed back toward the bed. As crazy as it sounds, the corpse was the lesser of two evils. "What is it?"

"I think this woman is—was—pregnant."

"Oh, damn," I echoed. "Is there any chance . . . ? The baby . . . ?" I couldn't say the words. They wouldn't come out.

"Based on the fact that rigor has begun to set in, I'm thinking . . . no."

The contents of my stomach surged up my throat.

Oh, shit.

I raced back to the window, shoved open the screen, and hung my head outside.

So much for my pride.

And my lunch.

"'A single white prince, with a passion for juicy steaks, good beer, and moonlit strolls on the beach, seeking single elf with similar interests for long-term commitment.'"

Katie, my roommate, best friend, and the closest thing to a sister that I'll ever have, spewed a mouthful of cola all over me. After hacking for about five minutes like a lifelong smoker, she said, "Sheesh. Sorry I spit in your face, but you can't post that."

Blinking away the droplets that had landed in my eyes, I scrutinized my personal ad for errors. I didn't see any, not a typo. Nada. "What's wrong with it?" I wiped a cheek with my sleeve.

"What isn't wrong?" Katie kindly went to the kitchen for some paper towels. "It's clichéd. It's misleading. Not to mention, you used the word 'elf.' You'll get a bunch of fruitcakes dressed like Santa's little helpers if you post that."

I ripped several towels off the roll and dabbed my face. "But I *need* an elf. That's the most important part."

Katie flopped next to me on the couch. She didn't pick up her glass of cola, thank God. This conversation clearly needed a spew warning. "Regardless, you can't put that in the ad."

"How else am I going to find an elf? Elmer needs a bride. And that bride must be at least half-elf, like me. If I can't find him a willing vict . . . er, wife, he'll be dragging me down the aisle. Again. Have you looked at him? That face." I shuddered. "Those creepy eyes—"

Sniffing the air, Katie patted my shoulder. "I know, honey. Scary."

"Scary doesn't even come close." I clicked delete.

So much for that.

This wasn't going to be easy.

I was no matchmaker. I couldn't even manage my own pathetic love life—at the moment, I was trying to figure out what to do with not one but two men. And here I was trying to hunt down a bride for the prince of the *Sluagh*?

If I'd had any choice in the matter, last week I wouldn't have promised Elmer, my so-called ex-fiancé, I'd help him. But I was desperate. He'd kidnapped me and was trying to force me to marry him. Besides, I sort of felt bad for the guy. Not only was he freakishly ugly, but he was also miserable. He can't eat. He can't drink. Being fond of food myself, I couldn't survive a single day walking in his shoes. Not to mention, he can only materialize after sunset. Supposedly, all his problems will magically disappear when he marries.

Being a cynic, I wanted to tell him that plenty of people had believed that over the years. Many had learned otherwise.

Staring at the keyboard, I sucked in a deep breath in preparation for a long, drawn-out sigh.

Mistake.

Smoke.

Putrid odor.

Gag.

"Katie." I pointed at the thick haze billowing out of the kitchen.

"Oh, shit." Katie jumped up. "I'm on it."

Katie is finishing up her master's in chemistry. I love her dearly. And I generally have no issues with her doing experiments in our kitchen. It would go unused, otherwise. But sometimes it got a little old, living with the constant stench of *eau de sewer.*

"Shitshitshit," Katie yelled.

Crash.

Thump.

A darker, more menacing cloud rolled into the living room.

Not moving from my cozy spot on the couch, I shouted, "The new fire extinguisher's under the sink." Reading some information about a dating site on my computer, I reached for my gas mask. Most people have framed photographs on their living-room tables. Or books. Figurines.

Not me. I have emergency gear on my living-room table.

"Where?" she shouted, sounding a little frantic.

"Under the sink." I clapped the mask over my mouth and nose and kept reading.

"Ah, thanks. Found it!" A second later, she said, "Everything's fine."

"Glad to hear it."

"What the hell is that stench?" someone else said.

I jumped, jerked so hard my knee slammed into my computer, sending it flying. Luckily, I caught it before it crashed on the floor. I gave the guilty party a glare. "You scared the hell out of me. I told you, you've got to stop sneaking up on me like that."

"I can't help it." Elmer, the sneaky prince of the *Sluagh*, blinked his beady little *Sluagh* eyes at me, and my glare evaporated. "I tried to think about someplace else at sunset, so I wouldn't zap here. But . . . well . . . magical transportation isn't exactly a science." He glanced at the computer. "What're you doing?"

"I'm writing your personal ad for an online dating site. Want to help?"

"Online dating?" he echoed, sounding less than enthusiastic.

I didn't want to point out the obvious, like how much easier it would be to charm a girl if he didn't meet her face-to-face right off the bat. Elmer had some pride. I wasn't about to shred it. "I thought we'd give it a shot, since you're sort of limited to socializing during nighttime hours."

"I was thinking we could try one of those speed-dating events."

"Speed dating?" I didn't see that working for him. But I didn't have the heart to say that.

"Yeah. I read about one in the newspaper. They take all types."

"Sure, even elves?"

"That I don't know."

"I think we should stick with online dating for now."

He looked disappointed. That wasn't a pretty look on a guy who already had the face that only a mother could love.

"If we strike out, we can try the speed dating next."

"Okay." He wilted.

"Doubting me already?" I was doubting myself, but I sure didn't want him to know that.

"Maybe."

"Remember, you've got nothing to lose. If I don't find your dream girl, you will still get married."

His wilt grew wiltier. "To you."

"Yeah, to you." I grimaced. "Since when wasn't I good enough?"

He grumbled something unintelligible. I decided to ignore it. Then he cleared his throat. "I'm the man of your dreams. Sexy. Rich. A genuine prince."

"What?"

"I'm dictating my personal ad. Why aren't you typing?" He poked at my computer.

I set my fingers on the keyboard. "I am now. What was that?"

Early the next morning—before sunrise—I dragged my exhausted body out of bed, stumbled into the shower, cooked myself in the scalding spray for as long as I could, and cut off the water.

Dripping wet, I grabbed one towel and turbaned my hair. I used a second towel to dry my face as I stepped out.

I ran smack-dab into someone.

"Aaaaahhh!" I screeched, jerking the towel away from my eyes. "Elmer!" I clasped the towel to my breasts, smoothing it down to cover my vitals. "What are you doing here?"

"Waiting for you."

"In my bathroom?" My ass was hanging out. I knew it. Elmer knew it too. I backed up, pressing it against the wall.

"Um . . . sure." He grinned. "I thought you might need someone to wash your back."

"Get out!" Flustered and irritated, I repositioned the towel to cover my butt as best I could, stomped to the door, wrenched it open, and motioned with my head. As Elmer took his time leaving, I said, "Don't you dare look at my ass."

"Too late."

"Urk!" The instant he was out, I slammed the door. "Wait a minute. I thought you could only materialize between twilight and midnight? That's what you said."

"Oh. Yeah. I did say that, didn't I?"

"Yes, you did. So what's the deal?"

"I . . . er . . . Actually, I can materialize any time between twilight and dawn. I kinda lied."

"Why?"

"Because I thought it made for a more convincing story."

"Elmer."

"But, Sloan, I need your help," he shouted through the door.

"Go lie to and ogle someone else for a while. Then see if they're in the mood to help you."

"But this is important. I need to talk to you about the personal ad we placed last night."

"I don't care. I can't deal with this now. I need to get to work." Actually, I did care. Kind of. But I cared more about having privacy while I took care of the essentials. First things first, I put on my clothes—just in case Elmer decided to sneak back in.

"Someone responded," he said.

"That's wonderful. Go write her." I combed my hair, slicking it back into a tidy ponytail. A ponytail wasn't exactly professional FBI style. But it was quick. And easy. And practical. Especially if I had to go to any crime scenes today.

"I can't write her," Elmer the Whiner said.

"Why?"

"I don't have a computer."

"Use mine. It's in the living room. All charged up." I smoothed on some moisturizer.

"I don't know what to say."

"Figure it out for yourself. You're the charmer. Charm her."

Ten minutes later, I rushed out to the kitchen, in search of caffeine.

The pot was empty. *Empty!*

Elmer, looking mighty comfortable on my couch, slurped.

I gave him an extra-harsh dose of mean eyes. "What are you *drinking*?"

"I was getting a little drowsy, sitting here by myself."

"But you told me you couldn't eat or drink. . . . You lied about that too?"

Elmer shrugged. The little lying weasel. "I can drink. But food is out. That's still bad. You try living on a liquid diet."

"What else have you lied about?"

Elmer shrugged again.

I glanced at the clock. There was no time to get into this with him. "No more lies, or our agreement is null and void. Got it?" He nodded. I pointed at the window. "What time do you vanish?"

"Sunrise." He burped. "Excuse me. That was some strong coffee. I'm feeling really alive right now. Oh, damn. Here comes the sun." And just like that, *poof,* he was gone.

"I think I hate you," I grumbled to the empty couch. "Okay, that's just caffeine withdrawal talking." Then I threw my laptop in the case and trudged to my car.

I shoved the key into the ignition.

Click. Clickclickclick.

Click. Click. Click.

Now what? Dead battery?

"Oh, hell." I rummaged in my laptop case for my cell phone and dialed JT's number.

"Hey, Sloan, where are you?" he said when the lines connected.

"At home. My car's dead."

"I'll pick you up in ten."

"Thanks."

Ten minutes was enough time to make some coffee. I burned the little energy I had dashing back inside. Dumped some grounds into a fresh filter, poured the water in, and paced the floor waiting for the first drips of liquid energy to pour out the bottom.

Katie came dragging out of her room as I was catching the black gold in a cup. "Why are you still here?"

"Dead battery. JT's coming to pick me up. Why are you up?"

"I heard voices."

"That was just Elmer. He popped in for an impromptu visit just before sunrise."

"Lucky you."

JT knocked.

Katie grinned. "Speaking of lucky."

"It isn't like that. We only kissed."

"And went on a date. Don't forget that part."

"I lost a bet. I don't think that counts as an official date. It was more of a . . . debt repayment."

"But you ended up being the winner."

"Dating a coworker is against bureau policy."

Katie shrugged. Clearly, she had no respect for the bureau's rules. JT didn't either. That was one thing they had in common. Me, I wanted to be a little more cautious. For both of our sakes. He was an agent. I was an intern. If we were to start . . . you know . . . and people found out, it would look bad for both of us.

The problem was getting that through JT's thick skull.

I opened the door.

"Hello, beautiful." He beamed at me as he strolled inside.

Like I said.

I grimaced. "We only went on one date, JT. That hardly qualifies you to graduate to endearment status."

"Hmm." He looked down into my mug. Or was he checking out my boobs? I couldn't be sure. "That coffee smells good."

"You don't drink coffee, remember? Besides, we should be going." I shoved him toward the door.

"Speaking of which, I'm going to jump in the shower," Katie said, beating a hasty retreat. She zoomed past the bathroom door.

"The shower's that way," I called.

"Good morning." JT grinned at me. His smile was lopsided, his eyes sparkly, and he was standing close. Way too close. He smelled scrumptious. "We have a few minutes, and I'm thirsty. It's already eighty out there. It's going to be close to a hundred today. Do you have some vitaminwater?" He brushed past me, letting a hand trail over my hip as he went by. I tried to ignore the little quivers shooting through my body that were sparked by the innocent touch. "You don't mind if I help myself." In the kitchen, he opened the refrigerator and dug through its contents. Finding a bottle, he twisted the cap off and leaned his hip against the counter.

"No, of course, I don't mind," I said rather belatedly as I sipped. If the damn stuff hadn't been so hot, I would have gulped it. "Do you have any idea what we're in for today?"

His grin upped to full wattage. It was one of his wicked smiles. My mood dimmed.

"What?" I said.

"We're heading to another crime scene this morning. Might want to stick with a liquid breakfast, just in case. . . ."

My face flamed so freaking hot, I think it was steaming. "Shut up. I was doing just fine until you told me that lady was pregnant. I mean . . . a baby?"

"I know. But about that. The ME called me last night,

confirming my suspicion. The victim was pregnant. But she wasn't when she died. Since she hadn't delivered the placenta yet, he estimated she'd died within thirty minutes of delivering."

"Really? Okay. So . . . where did she deliver? Where's the baby?"

"I don't know."

A shiver crept up my spine as the image of a child, lying helpless in a garbage can, flashed in my mind. "Did the police search everywhere? The garbage? The yard?"

"The lead, Riggleman, has a crew on it now."

"There wasn't any blood. No amniotic fluid. If she'd given birth in the house, we would have found something." I folded my arms across my body. "This case is getting worse by the second."

His expression sobering, JT set down the bottle and grabbed my hips, pulling me toward him. "It's terrible and tragic, but we'll figure it out. Come here."

I resisted. Or rather, I tried to resist. But JT is strong. And he smells good. And he looks good. And I was creeped out and could use some strong arms at the moment. And . . . okay, damn it, I'm weak. I did, however, manage to send him a warning glare, even though I was standing boob-to-chest with him.

Completely ignoring my unspoken warning, he slid his hands up, up, up, and back, until I was enfolded in his arms. Then the little creep kissed the top of my head.

Did he have any idea how sweet that was?

I swallowed a sigh of contentment and shoved out of his embrace an hour earlier than I would have liked to. "We need to go."

"When are we going on our second date?" An extremely persistent JT asked while watching me hurry toward the door.

"Never."

JT drained the bottle; then he set it on the counter. "We'll see about that."

"No, we won't." At the door, I turned to face him, thinking I'd squint my eyes at him and show him I meant business. Big mistake.

He was close enough to kiss. His lips curled up a little, into a ghost of a smile. I almost melted. "Were you going to say something?"

"No," I snapped, jerking back around to open the door. "Let's go." I grabbed my phone and dialed the auto club to schedule a tow. The sooner my car was fixed, the better.

He slapped his hand on the door, holding it shut. Bending over my back, he whispered, "Thank you for the water."

"You're welcome. Now, can we go? We'll be late."

He let his hand drop. I opened the door, grateful for the fresh air, and staggered outside.

Together, we roared off into the early morning.

I do not think there is any other quality so essential to success of any kind as the quality of perseverance. It overcomes almost everything, even nature.

—John D. Rockefeller

2

Once again, we were in a pretty subdivision, in a pretty Colonial, in a pretty bedroom, dissecting another crime scene. Walking into the room, I got a creepy-bad case of déjà vu. Today's victim, Katherine Jewett, was lying in bed, blankets tucked up to her chin, eyes open, staring at the ceiling.

JT made a beeline for the victim. I started at the door, checking out the clues. I right away noticed the money and jewelry sitting on the nightstand. Not that I'd ever thought these killings were robberies gone bad, but if the unsub could kill a victim without being detected, why wouldn't he take the money or jewelry? It was right there for the taking.

All around us, crime scene technicians from the Baltimore PD were still hard at work, shining lights and scouring the scene for minute fibers, footprints, and fingerprints.

One of them shook his head. "We live by the assumption that every suspect takes something with him and leaves something behind," he said. "But damn if we can find what that something is."

"You haven't found anything?" I asked.

"Not a fingerprint. Not a footprint—and this carpet is white. It rained last night. What the hell did he do? Take off his shoes at the door?"

I scrutinized the carpet. "You wouldn't think so. Maybe it's that special stain-resistant carpet?"

The technician stooped. "Stain-resistant or not, dirt should show. At least a little."

"Interesting. The body appears to be drained of blood," JT told me. To the medical examiner, who was still doing his preliminary examination, he said, "Any ideas about the time of death? Or COD?"

"Based on the level or rigor, I'd say it's been about five hours," the ME told him. "We'll be running a full autopsy, but looks like cause of death is exsanguination."

In plain speak, she bled to death.

Feeling brave, I headed over to the body.

The ME pulled the covers off the victim. Immediately one thing became clear. She was—or had been—pregnant. "I see no sign the victim has been moved after death. And she shows no defensive injuries. Her husband was asleep when she died."

"He was in the bed with her?" I asked, fighting a serious case of light-headedness.

"Yes, that's what I've been told." The ME pointed at the victim's legs, which were parted slightly. "I found only one small puncture wound in her groin. No blood on the sheets, on her clothing, or even on her skin. That makes no sense. Assuming this is the site of the blood loss, when that artery was punctured, there should have been arterial spray."

"Unless her heart was stopped before the puncture was made," I reasoned. "Without a heartbeat, there can be no spray."

JT nodded.

"No sign of trauma," the ME said.

"Drugs?" I offered.

"I'll look. May be tough to get enough blood to test for everything. She looks pretty dry. I can use tissue samples for some."

"Maybe the killer is removing the blood to cover evidence?" I suggested.

"It's possible." JT borrowed my camera to take a close-up of the puncture wound. It was small, roughly the size of pencil lead. "The wound is a puncture. No signs of tearing."

"Take all your photographs now," the ME said. "We'll be removing the body soon."

"Thank you." JT set about taking shots of the victim from every imaginable angle while I went back to searching the surrounding area for clues. Focusing the camera on her swollen stomach, JT asked, "The baby?"

The ME shook his head. "I'm not getting a heartbeat. We'll know more when I get her into autopsy."

My insides twisted. I scurried away and concentrated on breathing deep and slow. "Find anything yet?" I asked the crime scene technician I'd spoken to earlier.

"Not a goddamn thing." Standing next to a window now, dusting the sill and frame for fingerprints, he sighed, rubbing his forehead with the back of his hand. "We've checked every inch of this room. The only prints I'm finding belong to the victim and her husband. No sign of forced entry. No footprints. No foreign fibers. And at this point, we're not finding anything on the body either."

"Where is Mr. Jewett?"

"Down at the station, being questioned."

I set my hand on the sill. It was damp. "Was this window open?"

"Yeah, it was open about an inch. But we're fifteen feet

aboveground. And I checked for prints. Found nothing inside or outside."

"May I?" I motioned to the window.

"Sure."

I pushed up the double-hung window, lifted the screen, and hung my head outside. There were no trees or other means for an intruder to enter. "I'll be right back," I told JT, and headed outside. The grass below the window was wet. There were no indentations or marks. No sign that a ladder had been set there or anywhere else, for that matter. As it turned out, several windows had been left open a crack. No foreign prints were found on any of them.

Deciding all the evidence was pointing at the husband, I went back inside the house.

As I wandered through each room, one word kept playing through my head. Exsanguination. Exsanguination. Exsanguination.

How was this possible without any signs of blood spray?

Even if the unsub had somehow started the process of draining the blood while the victim still had a heartbeat—and somehow contained or blocked any blood spray—he wouldn't have been able to drain it all without some sort of mechanical aid. Not if that puncture wound, situated on the front of the body, was the site of the bleeding. It was a simple fact, that only so much blood would escape a wound before the heart stopped.

I knew a mortician used a pump to draw blood from a body after death. Assuming the killer had removed what he could before the heart stopped, and somehow drained the remaining blood from the victim after death, he would have needed to use some kind of pump. Once the heart stopped, blood was moved by gravity, from the higher points of the body to the lower. In this case, the lower was the victim's back—away from the puncture wound.

Following the path of my logic, I had to conclude the pump would have collected the blood into some kind of container. And that container would have had to be emptied somewhere.

I checked the en suite bathroom upstairs.

It was pristine. And it smelled like bleach.

I stumbled upon a second technician out in the hallway. "Did you check the bathroom with luminol?"

"Found only trace signs on the sink and a little in the shower. Nothing out of the ordinary. Everyone nicks themselves once in a while when shaving."

"What about the toilet?"

"It was clean."

Clean. Damn.

"Basement?" I asked. I'd yet to be in a basement that didn't have a utility sink.

The technician shook his head. "Nothing."

"What about other bathrooms?"

"We've checked everywhere. There's nothing more than trace signs of blood in this house. And all of them were in that bathroom." He indicated the master en suite.

"Okay. Thanks."

JT joined us. "I'm done here for now. Ready to head back to the unit?"

"Sure." In the car, I asked him, "What do you think? Was it the husband?"

"All the evidence seems to point to him." JT snapped his seat belt on.

I sensed he was holding something back. "But . . . ?"

"But the MO is the same as yesterday's killing. Exsanguinations aren't common. At least, not this brand of them. The modus operandi says it's definitely the same guy. And, nearest we can tell, he came out of nowhere.

We need to find the connection between Katherine Jewett and our first victim, Victoria Sprouse—besides the obvious. We also need to see if there are any other possible victims out there. Is this guy a new killer? Or has he just hit our radar?" He cranked the car; it started and angled away from the curb.

"This guy is good. He left nothing behind. He can't be new."

"That's what I'm thinking. And I'm thinking something else too. He's not done. I know guys like this. He won't stop until we stop him."

Imagining lying in bed, helpless, some guy draining the blood from me, I shuddered. "I was afraid you'd say that."

When we got back to the PBAU offices, JT headed toward Brittany Hough's techie-geek lair while I made a beeline for my cubicle. If anyone could find a traceable connection between the two victims, Brittany could. She was absolutely genius at mining the Internet for those precious little nuggets of information. Me, I was a genius too. But my strength lay in other areas—like memorizing facts. Statistics. That kind of thing. Not very useful in this job. But you never know.

As I made myself comfortable and dug out my laptop, Gabe paid me a visit, resting his butt on the spot on my desktop where I had intended to put my computer.

I squinted at him.

He grinned back. "Hey, Skye. What's up?"

"I'm trying to get some work done." I shoved his hip. It didn't budge. "Move it, Wagner."

"I'll move. In a minute."

My squint got squintier.

He scooted over a little. "I need to talk to you. About the case."

I set up my laptop and powered it up. "What about the case?"

"I found out Victoria Sprouse had a little secret."

"Yeah? What kind?" I asked, waiting impatiently for Windows to boot up.

"The kind that might've gotten her killed," he said, his voice sounding like that guy who does voiceovers for movie trailers. Gabe was a dork. Then again, so was I.

"Sheesh, you and the melodrama. What was it?"

"What can I say? I have a flair for the dramatic." He cleared his throat. "All right, I'll get down to business. Sometimes, Skye, you're so stiff. Mrs. Sprouse was not only having an affair, but that kid she was carrying wasn't her husband's. At least, that's what the neighbor said."

"Interesting. Did her husband know that?"

"I haven't found out. Yet. I told the chief what the neighbor said, and she wants me to check it out. I was about to head over to ask him. Want to go with me?"

I glanced at my notebook. Nothing pressing. I powered it down. "Sure." Standing, I slid my computer in the bag and looped the strap over my shoulder.

Gabe motioned for me to precede him out. Behind me, he said, "We can grab some lunch while we're out."

"Now you're pushing it, Wagner." I stopped in the hallway, waiting for an elevator.

"You know me." He stood next to me, looking big and devious and untrustworthy. He leaned close, closer, and whispered, "I'm always pushing it."

I elbowed him in the gut. It wasn't a serious elbow. It was sort of playful. Still, it was firm enough to let him know I didn't appreciate his "pushing."

The elevator door opened and I stepped inside the full car. I wriggled between a lady, who looked annoyed, and a man, whom I recognized from the BAU—my dream unit. This was the guy who told me I had been fired. On my first day. Before I'd even made it into the office. I smiled at him. "How are things in the BAU?" I asked.

"Going well. Thanks," he said stiffly. He glanced at Gabe, and I swallowed a chuckle. Gabe had been hired by him. And then Gabe had requested a transfer. Seems he wasn't quite over it.

The door slid open and out we all rushed. Gabe and I headed to his car. I threw my computer bag in the back-seat and then plopped in the passenger-side front. We drove maybe two miles before Gabe finally spoke, "Listen, about Thomas—"

"Wagner, there's no need to go there," I interrupted. "There's nothing going on between us. Promise. Not that you have any right to ask."

"I know. I'm sorry if I'm stepping over the line. But we've been friends for a long time, and I think that gives me the right to be concerned."

"First, *friends?* Really?" I asked, making sure he heard the sarcasm in my voice.

He shrugged.

"Second, my personal life is none of your concern. It hasn't been for a long time. And just because you told me our breakup had nothing to do with Lisa Flemming, and you've really had feelings for me all this time, doesn't mean suddenly we're BFFs and you can poke your nose in my business."

"Got it."

"Good."

Not another word was spoken the rest of the drive. I was oh-so-glad to get out of the car when we finally pulled up in front of Sprouse's house. I don't think Gabe had even shifted the vehicle into park yet, and I already had the door open. He caught up to me after I'd knocked on the front door.

The man who answered was knotted up for work.

Standing behind me, Gabe said, "I'm Gabe Wagner. Thank you for agreeing to talk to me."

The man stepped to the side. "You said you're criminal profilers with the FBI?"

"Yes, sir," Gabe said. "We study the behavior of the unsub—that's short for unidentified subject—and generate a profile for the local police departments."

Gabe left out the part about how we were actually interns and profile *paranormal* "unsubs." The subject in our first case was an *adze*. That's a vampire from Africa that changes into a firefly and preys on children. Up until I joined the PBAU, I'd been of the mind-set that vampires and their ilk didn't exist. Hell, even as I was chasing the *adze*, I was sure the killer was just your run-of-the-mill psychotic Homo sapien.

I was wrong.

Now with this case, we didn't have a clue yet whether we were dealing with a homicidal human being or something else. Alice Peyton, our unit's chief, aka the boss, explained that our department would be given any case that *might* involve a paranormal creature—be it a demon, vampire, ghost, whatever. The cause of death in this case was the trigger. The BAU tossed our unit the bone. Now it was up to us to figure out what was really going on.

The man looked at me.

I offered a hand. "Sloan Skye. I work with Wagner. Profiling."

"Pete Sprouse." The man shook my hand. "I'm happy to help. Tell me what you need."

Gabe pulled a small notebook from his shirt pocket and flipped to a blank page. "Sir, can you tell me about your wife's friendships? Do you know who she was interacting with on a regular basis?"

"Um, sure. But what's that have to do with profiling her killer?"

"As we investigate a crime," I explained, "we not only profile the killer, but we also profile the victim. In order to find your wife's killer, we need to understand why he picked her."

The man's expression darkened. "I understand."

"Let me assure you, anything you tell us will be held in confidence. None of it will be shared with anyone not directly involved in the case."

He didn't speak right away, and I wondered if he was going to shut down for good. But, thankfully, he didn't. "My wife doesn't have much of a social life. She's a quiet person. Prefers being home. But she does have one friend, Shannon Kersey. She lives two doors down. The two of them do a lot together. They were even going to the same obstetrician. Shannon just had her first child a couple of weeks ago. We were . . ." His lip quivered.

His pain stirred me, but I did my best to remain professional. With plenty of sympathy in my voice, I said, "I'm truly sorry for your loss. It was a terrible tragedy. Which is why we are so determined to catch this guy."

Sprouse took a couple of seconds before continuing. "There's something else the two of them were doing together," he said quietly. "They were both having sex with Shannon's husband. I found out the day before she . . . I found out, and I was so fucking mad. So hurt. I slept on the couch part of the night. Maybe if I hadn't—if I'd slept in our bed the whole night—maybe she'd still be alive."

"Was she dead when you joined her?" JT asked.

"I don't know. She might have been. I didn't check. Then again, who would? I assumed she was sleeping."

"You can't blame yourself for this," I told him.

"I can't *not* blame myself. It was my fault. The affair. Everything. I was pushing her too hard, blaming her for our problems." He dropped his face into his hands. "None of that matters anymore—now that they're gone. I lost them both."

You are not a pawn in the chessgame of life, you are the mover of the pieces.

—White Eagle

3

After Sprouse melted down, Gabe and I quietly thanked him and excused ourselves. We said very little during the drive and retreated to our separate cubicles to do some more digging into Victoria Sprouse's and Katherine Jewett's lives. The rest of the team was nowhere to be seen.

By six o'clock, I was hungry, grumpy, frustrated, and ready to call it a day. After hours of searching the Internet, I had nothing to tie our two victims together. And I just knew, deep in my gut, that we were working against a tight deadline. This guy was prolific. I was not looking forward to hearing he'd killed again.

But there was some good news. My car was ready, thank God. I would be self-sufficient, with my own mode of transportation—none too soon.

JT came strolling into the unit as I was dialing the number of a taxi company. He gave me a just-a-second index-finger lift, told me he'd drive me to the dealership in a few, and hurried toward Brittany's "Cave of Wonders." Less than a minute later, he emerged with a huge grin on his face. Of course, I was hoping that beaming smile meant he had good news.

"Did she find something?" I asked him when he eventually made his way over to me. I was packing up for the night. He seemed to be ready to go; his laptop case was slung over one shoulder.

Standing with one shoulder resting against the edge of my cubicle wall, he shook his head. "Nope."

"No?"

"Not yet. But she's still digging." He patted my shoulder. "Don't worry. She'll find something soon."

He was still grinning like a goon.

What was up with that?

"JT, this guy killed two women in forty-eight hours. 'Soon' isn't going to cut it." *And why are you so happy?*

"I realize that. Which is why I'm going to come back tonight after I drop you off. I'll work all night, if I have to."

"Well, okay." Still didn't explain why he looked as juiced as a kid who was going to Disney World. But maybe that was none of my business.

No, it definitely wasn't my business. If he wanted me to know, he would tell me.

"Are you ready?" he asked.

"Give me five."

"Will do." He strolled to his cubicle, which was kitty-corner from mine, and disappeared behind the half wall. I finished packing my computer. My cell phone rang just as I dropped it into the deepest pocket—of course.

I answered a fraction of a second before it clicked to voice mail. "Hi, Mom."

"Sloan. Where are you?"

"At work."

"Your father and I need to talk to you. Can you meet us tonight?"

"I suppose. But I need to go to the dealership first. I had to get a new battery. Give me about an hour."

"Fine. We can meet at Giovanni's."

"Giovanni's?"

Giovanni's was one of the finest restaurants in all of Maryland. And, of course, one of the most expensive. A couple of weeks ago, neither Mom nor I would have been in any position to have dinner at a place like that. Mom had been scraping by, living mostly on long-term disability—she's schizophrenic. I've been going to school for years, making ends meet by working some of the worst jobs imaginable.

Everything changed last week, when my father—who we'd thought was dead for the last twenty years or so—came back to life. Actually, he hadn't come back to life. He'd just come out of hiding. But that's another story for another time.

All that to say, Mom could tell her jerky landlord, who'd threatened to kick her out last week, to kiss her ass. And I wouldn't have to pay him off anymore to keep him from tossing her out on said ass.

"See you in an hour." I clicked off as JT rounded the bend to see if I was ready. He had me at the dealership within fifteen minutes. After thanking him, I watched him zoom away; then I went inside to pay the bill to get my car back.

The price of a car battery . . . ? Holy effing Jesus.

I cursed the entire drive to the restaurant. But before I went inside, I slicked on a little lipstick, tidied my hair, and pasted on a happy face. A polite hostess escorted me to my parents' table. Dad jumped up and gave me a fatherly hug. Mom's hug was jubilant too.

Something was up.

I sat before they dropped the bomb.

Dad's smile was bright enough to blind a girl. "Some wine?" He offered a bottle.

Sounded like a good idea. "Sure. Thanks." I held my glass as he poured. I resisted the urge to chug. "Nice place. What are we celebrating?"

My parents exchanged exuberant grins. They looked like a couple of little kids who'd just found out that Santa *was* real. That was twice today. JT had looked much the same way. What was with all this gleefulness? It wasn't natural.

"We're getting married!" Mom finally exclaimed. She thrust her left hand at me, displaying the ginormous rock sitting on her ring finger.

"Married? Aren't you already married?"

"Not legally," my father said. "James Skye is technically dead. And so, the marriage between James and Beverly Skye is null and void. My legal name is now Irvine."

"Oh, I guess that makes sense."

"I want you to be my maid of honor," Mom proclaimed.

I wasn't as enthusiastic about that as Mom was. After all, being maid of honor meant I would have to help her with all the planning. That would involve time. And work. And as much as I didn't want to disappoint Mom, because I really did love her, I wasn't in a position to do work now. I had a job. *A demanding job.* Our first case, last week, had me working undercover, around the clock. I had to assume that wasn't a fluke. There would be no time left for china shopping or wedding rehearsals.

But . . . but I couldn't break her heart.

"Sloan, you will be my maid of honor, won't you?" Mom asked.

"Sure, Mom."

My mother actually squealed like a girl. Then she

flung herself at me, giving me a bouncy hug. "It'll be so much fun, Sloan! We'll be like BFFs. We can go cake tasting, and dress shopping, and pick out stuff for my registry. Oh, and you get to plan my bachelorette party!"

"Sure. Fun." *Not.* Just the thought of it made my head spin. Once I extricated myself from my mother's tight embrace, I went about draining my glass. Dad refilled it. "So how big of a wedding are we talking here?"

"I'm estimating we'll have a private ceremony, with maybe two hundred guests," Mom said.

"But the reception will be bigger," Dad said. "The queen will be expecting an invitation, of course." That was the queen of the elves. Dad was 100 percent elf. And he also happened to be the head of the queen's security force and army.

"The queen?" I drained my wineglass a second time.

"Yes, and all her family will expect invitations too," Dad said. "You know, she has a fairly large family. She herself has birthed almost a hundred offspring."

"That many?" I forced down a few curse words and turned to my mother. "Have you thought about hiring a wedding planner?"

"Oh, yes. All fae are fertile, of course." Dad slid a glittery-eyed leer at my mom, and I tried to pretend I didn't see it. "So all of her kids of childbearing ages who are married have also birthed children. And their children too. And, naturally, there will be media. The fae community just loves this kind of thing—"

"But I thought you fairy type like to keep that hush-hush," I said, grasping at straws.

"We like to keep the fairy stuff quiet. That much is true. But Her Highness is a celebrity among the humans too, for very different reasons."

This was just . . . wonderful.

"Here's a thought," I said to my two extremely giddy

parents. "Why don't the two of you run off and elope? It would be romantic. Exciting."

Mom scowled. "Absolutely not."

"The queen would never forgive me," Dad said. "Oh, and money is no object."

Mom beamed.

As I drove home, images of my mother stuffing dollars into strippers' G-strings and an insanely overdone reception—Mom wanted a horse-drawn carriage, like the British royals had—played through my mind.

What a freaking nightmare.

But it was Mom. And Dad. And even though they were both on the quirky side, I loved them both very much. I would do my best to make sure they had the wedding of their dreams.

Step one: enlist Katie's help.

Step two: find a qualified wedding planner *yesterday*.

When I let myself into our apartment, I called out to Katie, "Hey, girl, we need to hire a wedding planner."

Dark? Why were the lights off? The shades drawn?

Rustle, rustle.

Click. The living-room lamp snapped on.

A rumpled-looking Katie was partly reclined on the couch. A strange man was sort of leaning over her. It would seem neither was wearing clothes. Thank God there was a blanket covering most of them.

"Oh," I said, shielding my eyes. "Sorry I interrupted."

Katie giggled. "We weren't having sex, Sloan. We were just watching a movie." Katie motioned to the man draped over her. "This is Jesse. Jesse, this is my roommate, Sloan. She works for the FBI."

He greeted me with a tip of the head. Maybe because his hands were busy. I couldn't see them. I didn't want to know where they were or what they were doing. "Cool. I've thought about joining the FBI. Heard training is a bitch, though."

"I'm just an intern at this point, so I couldn't say."

"Oh."

I could tell by the flatness in his voice that he wasn't all that impressed. Whatever. I wasn't impressed by him either.

"What was that about a wedding planner?" Katie asked.

"Nothing. We can talk about it tomorrow."

"Okay. We're watching *Scream*. Want to watch with us?"

"No thanks. I think I'll do some work in my room. Have fun." On the way to my bedroom, I served myself a big dish of ice cream. And I grabbed a bag of barbeque chips too. I hadn't eaten much of my dinner. The whole wedding thing had shot my appetite. Now I was regretting leaving the leftovers with my mother.

In my room, I powered up the laptop and flopped on my belly on the bed. While I was poking around the Web, researching local wedding planners, I emptied the ice-cream bowl. And the bag of chips. I checked the clock. It was eleven. Maybe for once I'd go to bed early. I shut down the computer, set the dishes on my nightstand, set my alarm clock, and headed to the bathroom to take care of my before-bed ritual. I tried—really, I did!—to ignore the sounds of lips smacking and low moans coming from the living room. It would seem Katie and her new friend were doing more than watching the movie. Good for her! After being dumped by her ex-boyfriend, she'd sort of fallen apart. I was glad to see she was moving on.

I wasn't glad to see I had a visitor when I returned to my bedroom.

"It's over." Elmer was slumped on my bed, his ugly little face a mask of misery.

"What's 'over'?"

"My relationship." He sighed. "With the woman of my dreams."

"Relationship?" I hadn't known he was in a relationship. I thought I was supposed to be helping him find the woman of his dreams. "Who is this woman? What happened?"

"You remember, I told you I was going to try speed dating?"

I bit back a retort. "Yes."

"Well, I met someone there. She was perfect."

"Elf?" I asked as I pulled a detangling comb through my hair. The extensions I'd had put in last week, when I went undercover, made for a nightmare when I washed my hair. To be honest, I couldn't even remember if I was supposed to wash it. But I wouldn't complain if they all fell out. I was tired of them already.

"One hundred percent. Pure-blooded. And beautiful. And absolutely breathtakingly gorgeous. And intelligent."

"So . . . ?"

"She said she wasn't ready for anything serious."

"Hmm. How did the topic of a long-term relationship even come up? You get what . . . two minutes with each person?"

"I asked her to marry me," he said.

I swallowed a guffaw. "You didn't."

"Sure. I knew she was perfect. Why wouldn't I?"

"Elmer." I couldn't help it—I heaved a heavy sigh. "You broke the first cardinal rule of dating. You don't ever, under any circumstances, mention the 'm' word on your first date."

He crossed his lanky, skinny arms over his chest. "That's a stupid rule."

"Is it? You chased away 'the woman of your dreams.' You still want to tell me it's a stupid rule?"

"Well . . ."

"We need to stick with online dating. At least that way, I can keep an eye on what you're doing."

"Or you could come with me tomorrow night. I found a speed dating just for people like you and me."

"Like you and me?"

"Yeah, not human. You know."

"There's such a thing?" At his nod, I shook my head. This would lead to nowhere good. I could see it already. "I'm allergic to speed dating."

"Come on! You don't know. Maybe you'll meet someone too."

"You don't want that," I pointed out. "I'm your backup bride."

"Good point." He thought about it for a few minutes. "I still think it's worth a try. You can sit next to me and watch what I'm doing. If I start making an ass of myself, you can stop me."

Ugh. "Why are you so dead set against the online dating?"

"I prefer to meet women face-to-face. So will you go with me?" He lifted pleading eyes to mine.

I was a sucker.

I sighed. "Okay. I'll go. Once. Only once."

Before I could stop him, he grabbed me and planted a kiss on my mouth. "Thank you!"

I bit back a curse word and grumbled, "Don't you ever do that again."

"Sorry." Looking very un-sorry, he vanished.

One often hears of a horse that shivers with terror, or of a dog that howls at something a man's eyes cannot see, and men who live primitive lives where instinct does the work of reason are fully conscious of many things that we cannot perceive at all. As life becomes more orderly, more deliberate, the supernatural world sinks farther away.

—William Butler Yeats

4

The following morning, the team met in the conference room to talk about the case. It was the usual crowd—the chief, JT, Gabe, Brittany, Chad Fischer, who was officially the unit's media liaison, but he also doubled as an agent, and me. We were short-staffed. Sadly, there weren't hundreds or thousands of wannabe vampire profilers, like there were criminal profilers. The members of the FBI who knew what our unit was really all about thought we were a joke. It didn't help that the bureau had done a nice job of concealing the fact that the first killer we profiled was an *adze*, an honest-to-God, genuine, blood-sucking vampire.

At any rate, we still had some of the sharpest minds in the bureau on our team. And because of the lack of manpower, this intern got to spend the majority of her time out in the field, chasing murdering vamps, rather than fetching coffee and lunch.

This morning's meeting started out with a little pep

talk by our chief. As bosses go, Chief Peyton is the best I've ever had, even though she dragged me to a morgue on my first day. I've had bosses who've done worse. That said, the chief tended to be a little formal, stiff. She was the boss. Not a friend.

Today she was as serious as ever. Of course, we were talking about an extremely serious case.

The chief cleared her throat. "Another fact has come to light," she said solemnly. "Our second victim, Katherine Jewett, who we suspected was pregnant, also delivered her child within an estimated hour of her death. Her infant is also missing."

Horrible.

I hated this case already.

What kind of monster were we dealing with? Or were the mothers delivering somewhere, returning home, and then being . . . punished for what they'd done?

"I know you all are anxious to get this case solved," she said. Of course, we all nodded in agreement. "Once news of this gets to the media, which it will, it could blow up. Somehow we've got to keep a lid on this one. We don't want to chase the unsub away. I have a feeling he's been doing this for a long time. He's just been moving on when the heat gets too hot. We must keep him here, if we're going to catch him. So what do we have?"

"MO," I said. "The killer appears to be selecting pregnant women, or women who have just recently delivered, as his victims—though that can't be confirmed yet, since we've only had two victims. His mode of killing is to somehow drain the victims' blood. Puncture wounds have been found in the groin of both adult victims, suggesting he's either a vampiric creature or a Homo sapien using some kind of pump, similar to what a mortician uses to drain the blood in preparation for a funeral. He's killing at night, while the victims are asleep. And he's killing them in the victims' own homes, rather than removing them to a location he can control."

"We've found no defensive wounds on either victim," JT added.

"No signs of forced entry," suggested Gabe.

"He's leaving no trace evidence. Nothing," I contributed.

"At this point, we see no sign that his killing is for material gain," Gabe mentioned. "Jewelry and money were left untouched at the scenes."

"However, there is the question of the missing children," JT pointed out. "If he is delivering them and then killing the mothers, the children could be sold on the black market."

"Damn," I muttered.

"Still, cash is untraceable. And it's easy enough to sell jewelry on the street," Gabe said. "If he's out for material gain, why not take what's right in front of his face?"

Good question.

"Here's another scenario," I said. "It's far-fetched, but still worth mentioning. What if the mothers are delivering the children and then abandoning them somewhere, and the killer is then killing them as a form of punishment? That would make him a mission-oriented killer. He would see his actions as a service to society."

"Excellent point," the chief said. "But that raises a lot of questions, like where are these women delivering, how they are able to leave their homes and then return undetected, and finally why they would hide the birth of their children from their husbands and then dispose of the child?"

"In Victoria Sprouse's case, her motivation could be to hide the paternity of the infant," I offered, already doubtful that the scenario I had sketched out fit the evidence.

"What does all this tell us about the unsub?" the chief asked.

"Assuming the missing children weren't taken to sell, and taking into account the money and other valuables left at the scene, our unsub is more likely male than female," I said. "Women more commonly kill for material gain. And they historically use poisoning. They also tend to kill husbands, their own children, and relatives. On the other hand, if the unsub is delivering the infants, and the children are being sold, we could be dealing with a female unsub."

"Good. What else?" the chief asked.

"If our killer is organized, which the crime scenes support, then the victims would tend to be strangers, unknown to the killer," JT suggested.

"Excellent. However, we must keep looking for a connection between Sprouse and Jewett," the chief said, writing notes on the whiteboard behind her. "Because we've found no evidence of a break-in, defensive wounds—and because our unsub is killing in the victims' homes—we can't rule out an unsub that is familiar to the victims. Husband. Friend. Someone who would have access to them when they were sleeping. In our investigation, we're going to focus on victimology. We need to know why the unsub chose these women as his victims." She pointed at Fischer. "I want you and Wagner to go back to each crime scene and interview both husbands again. Find out if anyone was in their house the day of their wives' death. Thomas, I want you and Skye to dig into Sprouse's and Jewett's backgrounds. See if you can find any concrete connections between the two. Also see if there would be a motive for them to give birth and then abandon or kill their own children. Life insurance policies, that kind of thing. Hough can help as needed."

When the meeting was over, we headed back to our cubicles. I was powering up my laptop when JT came rolling up on his wheeled office chair.

"So . . . ," he said.

"So," I echoed. "What now?"

"Two pregnant victims." He scooted his chair closer to mine, so he could see my computer screen. My skin warmed a little. "What do you think?"

"I think . . . I hate this case."

"Yeah." His jaw clenched. "I do too. Do you believe the punishment theory you presented at the meeting?"

"No, not really. It seems to rely upon too many coincidences."

"Yeah, I have some serious doubts about that theory too. I think the unsub is taking the kids."

"Then how is he able to deliver them without leaving any evidence? Without alerting the husband? How is he getting the children out of the house?"

"I wish I knew. What I do know is this—the thought of anyone out there hunting pregnant women . . ." He looked angry, furious, more emotionally invested in this case than how I'd seen him before. And the first case involved the kidnapping of an innocent child. That was nothing to sneeze at either.

"We'll get him . . . right?" I asked, sounding doubtful because I was, a little.

"You know we will." He motioned toward Brittany's Cave of Wonders. "I have Hough digging into the victims' medical history, looking for a common thread, like a doctor."

"That was my first thought."

"It's better to leave that to her. With the HIPAA Privacy Rule, she's better equipped to navigate those waters."

"Where does that leave us?"

"Let's map out where they live, where they work, see

if, or where, their paths cross." Scooting forward, he set an arm on my desktop, next to mine. This brought him even closer than before. Now I could smell the scent of his aftershave; and when he shifted positions a little, his arm brushed mine.

Skooching sideways, to put a little distance between us, I said, "Okay." I opened a window and typed in the first address.

He inched closer again.

So much for that.

Two hours later, we had nothing earthshaking on either victim. Nada. Nil. I was stiff, sluggish from sitting in one position for so long, and a little warm from being in such close proximity to JT for two hours. I had no doubt he was sitting so close on purpose—the twerp—which was why I'd pretended it didn't bother me. I stretched as he finally rolled back to his cubicle. Minutes later, I watched him head toward Brittany's Cave. I wondered what they might dig up with her superpowered search engines. It seemed she was our last hope.

Gabe came strolling into the office just as I was about to go to the Cave of Wonders to take a peek. "What's up?" he asked while dumping his laptop case on my desk.

"Absolutely nothing. That's what. Tell me you got somewhere today."

"Oh, I got somewhere. Plenty of somewhere." He went to his cubicle, grabbed the back of his chair and wheeled it up to mine. He sat, kicked an ankle up on his opposite knee. "I'm learning something about people."

"What's that?" I asked, entering another term into a Google search.

"Everyone has secrets."

"There you go with the drama again. That's a bit of an overgeneralization, don't you think?"

"Absolutely not. I have secrets."

"I don't."

"Of course you do. You just don't want to admit it."

Time to get this conversation back on course. "So . . . what kind of secrets are we talking about, in regard to our case?"

"First there was Victoria Sprouse and her kinky three-somes. And then there's Katherine Jewett. Let me tell you, her secret makes Sprouse look like an angel."

"Yeah? Are you telling me she's not the innocent sub-urban wife and soon-to-be mother that we thought?"

"Far from it. Jewett was running a call girl service."

"No way."

"Yes way. Let me tell you, her girls were . . ." His face turned five shades of red, each one brighter than the last. "They were very nice."

"Shocking." This conversation was making me feel a smidge weird. "So, do you think her unusual career had anything to do with her murder?"

"Not sure."

"Is that all you found out?"

"That was the most interesting thing we found out. Fischer's following up on some other stuff. A neighbor thought she saw someone snooping around the Sprouses' house a few hours before she was killed. She swore it was a woman. Well-dressed. Attractive. Maybe a salesper-son. Or a Mormon doing some mission work. Doesn't fit our profile, but Fischer said we have to check it out, anyway. Oh, and get this, that couple Sprouse was in-volved with were wanted in ten states for at least a dozen charges each. They skipped town. Vanished."

"Doesn't exactly make them look innocent, does it?"

"Nope, though none of the crimes were violent.

They've been running a bunch of phony businesses, scamming people. Mostly real estate, though they've also recently gotten into the psychic and life-counseling business too. It amazes me how many people fall for these kinds of things. But they do."

"Maybe Sprouse caught on to what they were doing, so they decided to silence her?"

"Maybe." He checked his watch. "But then, what about the baby? It's getting late. I think I'm going to call it a night. You?"

"Yeah." I glanced at JT's empty cubicle. "I guess I'm ready to quit too." I poked the power button on my laptop. My stomach growled. Slightly embarrassed, I clapped a hand over my belly.

Gabe stood but didn't leave. "Hey. Do you want to go get something to eat?"

"I don't know. . . ." When my computer powered off, I closed it and tucked it into its case.

"It's only food."

"I know."

"I swear, I won't make more out of it than that."

My stomach growled again.

He pointed. "I think your stomach said yes. My treat."

"No, absolutely not. I won't let you buy me dinner."

"Your treat?"

"How about we pay for our own?"

"Fine by me." He rolled his chair back where it belonged; then he came sauntering back with the trademark Gabe Wagner swagger that both annoyed me and made me feel a little breathless. "Where should we go? Somewhere quiet? Intimate?"

"Intimate? No, absolutely not."

"Fine. I've got the perfect place in mind." He took

my laptop case from me and then motioned for me to proceed out to the elevators.

"We'll drive our own cars."

He shrugged. "If you insist."

"I insist." I gave him a warning glare. "And you'd better keep your word. This is a casual meal with a coworker. Nothing more."

"You got it. Nothing more."

Twenty minutes later, we were sitting in a noisy restaurant, where model airplanes, piloted by birds, swooped and zoomed over our heads. All around us, clamoring children were happily munching on French fries and slurping shakes while their parents nagged them to eat their burgers.

Intimate, it was not.

Lesson learned—next time I would expect Gabe to take my suggestion in the most literal sense possible.

While we were waiting for our burgers and fries, we gobbled up yummy potato skins slathered in melted cheese and sour cream.

Gabe said, "Okay, now that I've got you here, and you've had a little bit to eat, I feel I need to confess something."

The mouthful of potato, cheese, bacon, and sour cream suddenly felt a whole lot bigger as it slid down my throat. "What?" I croaked.

"I had an ulterior motive when I invited you out to dinner tonight."

"Which was . . . ?" I guzzled half my glass of cola while I waited for Gabe to admit why he'd asked me out to dinner. I hoped it wasn't because of what he'd said last week, but I had a feeling it was.

"I wanted to get a chance to talk to you about Thomas."

"What about him? I've already told you, it's none of your business."

"I know. And I'm sorry if it seems like I'm getting too pushy. But I overheard him talking to Hough yesterday and I felt you should know about it."

I wasn't going to ask.

I didn't want to know.

No. Absolutely. Didn't want to know.

Oh, hell. "Okay, so tell me."

We learn the rope of life by untying its knots.

—Jean Toomer

5

Gabe had stopped eating. He was looking at me with the kind of serious expression I rarely ever saw. I had no doubt he meant business. This time, he wasn't over-dramatizing.

"Okay. You got me. What were JT and Hough talking about yesterday?" I asked.

"I heard Hough say, 'I need you. I can't do this alone.' And then Thomas said, 'I'm here, Britt. I love you. I'm not going anywhere.'"

"That could be interpreted a million different ways."

"Yeah. But the most obvious is . . . ?" He gave me one of those you-know-what-I-mean looks. "They're having an affair and she's planning on leaving her lesbian wife."

I gave him back a you're-full-of-bunk look. "She's happily married. And she and JT are just friends. Good friends."

"Says who?"

I shifted in my seat. "JT."

Gabe gave me a sure-right eyebrow lift. "And you believe him?"

"Yes, of course. He's given me no reason to suspect him of lying." This conversation needed to end.

"That you're aware of. You haven't known him long. All men lie. Sometimes."

"Yet another generalization. *All* men?"

"It's the truth. If you don't believe it now, you will someday."

"Which means you lie too, since you're a man."

"Sure. But I'm not lying now. Not about this."

"Okay."

The waiter brought our burgers and fries, asked if we needed anything else, then hustled away to serve his next table. While I ate, I mulled over what Gabe had told me.

Assuming he heard what he thought he'd heard, and it meant what he thought, it was a damn good thing I'd decided to keep JT at arm's length. Yes, a damn good thing.

Now I was glad Gabe had picked this insanely noisy, chaotic place for our dinner. We ate, paid our tabs, and headed out to the parking lot.

I was about to make a clean getaway when Gabe grabbed my arm. We were standing in between two parked cars, midway between my car and his. It wasn't quite dark yet. The sky to the west was purple, with some puffy salmon clouds. The east was already cloaked in deep indigo. Fireflies were flitting around us.

"Skye, I didn't tell you about Thomas because I expect something to happen between you and me."

I thought I understood what he meant by "something." I nodded.

"You keep telling me you and he aren't . . . Well, anyway, I can tell you like him." He released my arm. More softly he said, "I've seen the way you smile at him. The way you look at him."

I didn't respond right away. I wasn't certain what to say. I mean, here he was—obnoxious, irritating Gabe—being so honest. Vulnerable. Looking into his eyes, I could see the spark of something. Sadness? Pain? I didn't have the heart to brush off his feelings.

"Sure. You're right. I do think he's attractive. But the fact is you and I are interns. We have to be careful. How bad would it look if it got around that I was sleeping with him?" I sidestepped to a nearby light pole, leaned against the concrete base, and folded my arms over my chest. The wind was picking up, and it was actually getting a little chilly. "I guess I need to do a better job at setting aside my personal feelings and acting like a professional, if it's as obvious as you say."

"I'm not saying it's obvious to everyone. Only to me. But that's because you once smiled at me like that."

Shit.

My phone rang.

"Um, sorry. I should check to see who it is." I dug my phone out of my purse. The display was glowing but blank. Strange. I shrugged and slid it back into my purse. Then I looked up at Gabe.

"I should let you get going. It's getting cold." He glanced at the western sky. "And it looks like we're in for some rain."

"O-okay." I still hadn't responded to his last comment. I didn't know what to say, honestly. This was beyond complicated. He was a nice-enough guy, when he wasn't intentionally trying to antagonize me. I didn't want to hurt his feelings. On the other hand, I didn't want him thinking I had any warm, fuzzy feelings for him. Because I didn't. At least I didn't have *a lot* of warm, fuzzy feelings for him. Maybe there was a little something there. A spark. But I was hell-bent on not traveling back down that road again. Once in a lifetime was enough for this girl. Besides, I technically still had one annoying and demanding would-be fiancé to contend with.

"See you tomorrow, Skye," Gabe said, shooting me a smile.

"Yep." I waved and then scurried to my car. I jumped in, buckled my belt, and then I just about peed my pants when someone tapped me on the shoulder. "Holy hell!" I screeched, jerking around.

Elmer. My so-called fiancé. "It's just me."

"I—I . . ." Whatever I was about to say completely vanished from my mind. *Poof,* gone. I was rendered speechless as my gaze took in Elmer's clothes. "W-what are you wearing?"

Elmer grimaced as he checked his nonreflection in the rearview mirror. (The *Sluagh* cast no reflection, like your typical Western European vampire.) "What's wrong? Don't you like my speed-dating look?"

I took in the goofy hat, the polyester shirt with the 1970s-style collar, and the really tacky vest on top of it before I responded. "It's a lot of look. Where do you shop?"

"Salvation Army. I like their prices. And their selection."

"I see." I briefly considered his problem; then I made a decision. As much as I didn't want to get Gabe or JT involved in this situation, I needed some help—or rather, I needed some decent clothes. "What time does the speed dating event start?"

"Nine o'clock."

"Good." I checked the clock. "We've got time." I dug my phone out of my laptop bag. After a quick struggle, trying to decide which guy to call first, I dialed.

JT picked up on the second ring. "Hey, Skye."

"Hi, JT. I need a favor." I slid a sidelong glance at my companion and fought a shudder.

"Sure," JT said.

"Where are you?"

"I'm on my way home."

"Good. Um. Can I have your address?"

"Sure. It's 626 West Elk Avenue, Unit 2."

"Thanks." I punched the address into my GPS. "I'll be at your place in ten."

"Okay. What do you need?"

"I'll explain when I get there."

"Fair enough. See you in a few."

Ten minutes later, Elmer and I were standing at JT's front door. When JT opened it, he smiled at me; then he scrunched his eyebrows at Elmer.

"We need to borrow some clothes," I explained, pointing at Elmer.

"Sure." JT's lips quirked. I could tell he was having a hard time holding back the guffaw. JT led us up to his bedroom. I marveled at his place as I followed. It was masculine. Clean. Contemporary. Very JT. His bedroom was nice. An enormous flat-screen TV hung on one wall. A ginormous bed was positioned against the opposite. Television. Bed. What more could a guy want in his room, right?

After shooting me an amused look, he motioned for Elmer to follow him. "This way. I'll hook you up."

I tested the chaise lounge facing the TV. I pointed the remote toward the television and was rewarded with the vision of a woman's tight ass, bigger than life.

No question what JT had been doing the last time he'd watched television. I clicked to a more PG channel, finding a thriller movie about a forensic psychiatrist. As a general rule, I'm not much of a television watcher. I prefer reading. But I do love a well-written thriller, especially when it's about the FBI.

I was just getting caught up in the story when JT came out of the walk-in closet.

"Whatcha watching?" he asked.

"Some movie about a forensic psychiatrist."

"Ah, Pacino. Seen it. The killer's his student, the lawyer."

"Thanks," I said flatly. I clicked the button, surfing the channels.

JT gently took the remote out of my hand, killed the TV, and then placed the remote on the table sitting off to one side. He made himself comfortable on the chaise; his butt was resting next to my hips. I felt my body stiffen slightly. His brows scrunched together. "What's wrong?"

"Nothing." I forced a smile. "How much longer do you think Elmer will be?"

JT shrugged. "Don't know. It isn't easy finding clothes in my closet to fit him. He's a foot shorter, and at least fifty pounds lighter."

"Yeah, I knew it would be tough, but you saw what he was wearing. I wasn't going out in public with him in that."

"Where are you heading?" he asked casually.

"Speed dating."

His neutral expression vanished for a split second. In a blink, it was back. "Speed dating, eh?"

"Sure. You remember, I need to find him a wife."

"Yes, I remember."

"I told him I'd go along."

"You're not . . . participating, then?"

I didn't want to feel that little happy-heart flip-flop at the sound of jealousy in his voice. But I did. And that worried me. "Actually, I was thinking about it."

"Really?"

"Sure."

His lips thinned. But he said nothing. Instead, he stood, grabbed the remote, and started clicking through channels. After burning through fifty channels, more or less, he powered off the TV and stared at me. "Why?"

"Why what?"

"Why are you doing the speed-dating thing?"

"Isn't it obvious?"

"No."

"People go to these things to meet people," I told him.

"Well, of course, that much is obvious. But I thought . . . We . . ." He sighed and powered on the TV again.

He was really taking this news hard. It made me feel all warm and fuzzy inside. That was not good.

"JT, we've talked about this before. You're an agent. I'm an intern. It wouldn't look good for either of us, if we were to start . . . you know . . ."

His jaw clenched. "I told you, the chief doesn't give a damn about our personal lives."

"But I care about my reputation. Remember, JT, the PBAU wasn't my first choice of units. Maybe someday I want to move on. What would a bad reputation do for my chances?"

He seemed to be listening. At the very least, that little muscle along his jaw stopped popping out. He nodded.

"Besides," I said, tossing out what Gabe had said before I could stop myself, "I've heard rumors you're involved with someone else, anyway."

There went that little muscle again. Two narrow, slitted eyes squinted at me. "Who told you that?"

"Are you denying it?"

"Who was it?" he snapped.

"Does it matter? Especially if it's true?"

"It isn't true. It's a lie. Who am I supposedly screwing?"

"Hough."

His face paled. He went back to hitting the button on the remote, but I had a feeling he wasn't actually seeing what was displayed on the television.

"Well, are you still going to tell me it's a lie?"

"She's a lesbian," he reminded me, still staring at the TV. "And she's married."

"So you said. But you and she were overheard having a very intimate conversation. How else am I supposed to take that?"

He clamped his lips together. His jaw flexed, but he didn't respond.

So it was true.

My heart dove to my toes. Before I said or did something totally humiliating, I pushed off the chaise and raced from the room.

JT followed me. "Sloan!"

I actually sprinted down the stairs. He caught up to me just as I yanked open his front door. He reached over my shoulder, using his flattened hand to slam it shut. That left me trapped between the door and his bulky body.

"There's nothing more to talk about," I said to the door.

"Yes, there is." He leaned closer, totally invading my personal-space bubble.

It was my turn to grit my teeth. "Stop being such an ass and let go, JT. This conversation is done. Over. Kaput. We're coworkers. And maybe friends, if you let me leave with my pride intact."

He moved his hand. "Fine. But . . . it's not what you think."

"It doesn't matter what I think." I went out to the car and waited for Elmer. Thankfully, it took him a while. I needed the time to collect myself, which I did. After indulging in a brief pity party, I freshened up my makeup and fluffed my hair.

When he returned to the car, Elmer looked a million times better. He grinned, showing off a set of pointed teeth that would make a piranha green with envy. "How do I look?"

"The clothes are a vast improvement. You might want to tone down the smile, though."

"Too much teeth?"

"Too much."

Nothing weighs on us so heavily as a secret.

—Jean de La Fontaine

6

Elmer played with the radio while we drove to the hall where the speed-dating event was being hosted. It wasn't the nicest place, but it wasn't the worst. The parking lot was jammed.

"This is going to be great!" Elmer said as a pair of long-legged women hobbled by on stilettos.

"Yeah, great," I echoed, scanning the parking lot for males.

I saw plenty of women. Not one man.

Then again, considering my frame of mind (*men suck!*), that was probably a good thing.

"We shouldn't walk in together," Elmer mumbled. "Wouldn't want anyone thinking we're a couple."

Ditched by my former-sorta-officially-still fiancé. What a loser I was. "Good point." I slumped into the car to wait. While I was killing time, I continued to scan the area for anyone with a Y chromosome.

Not one.

Things were looking pretty damn good for Elmer. Me, not so much.

Fully expecting this to be two to three of the longest hours of my life, I straggled inside and followed the sign, heading down the set of wide steps to the Gold banquet room. I signed in at the entry and wandered inside.

"May I please have your attention?" a fairly attractive woman was saying. Standing at the far end of the room, she waved her arms. The room went still and silent. "I'd like all the gentlemen to stand over here, please." She pointed at a corner. "Ladies, I would like you to take a seat at a table, please. We'll begin shortly."

There were dozens of tables, each with one chair on each side, facing each other. Within minutes, every table in the place was occupied. And I was still standing, after losing an impromptu game of musical chairs with the other women.

Oh, well. I'd sit this one out.

I backed myself toward the exit.

"I'm sorry," the hostess said, rushing up to me. "We have a big crowd tonight. Much larger than normal."

"Not a problem. I can come back another time."

"Oh, absolutely not. You're here. You must stay." She took my hand in hers—her skin was cold, clammy—and yanked me toward the far end of the room. "Wait here." She scurried off like a little mouse.

Feeling like I was being stared at, which I was, I glanced around nervously. Elmer gave me a toothy grin and a thumbs-up. I almost made a break for it; but before I got anywhere, the hostess was back. Two men—two gorgeous men—followed her, each one carrying a chair.

One set one behind me. The other set his in front of me. I thanked them both, wondering if they'd stick around for the fun.

They didn't.

"Okay, we'll begin in five minutes," the hostess shouted over the rising din. "We'll rotate the gentlemen every five minutes," she said as she escorted the first man to my chair.

It was hard to imagine, but this guy made Elmer look like Gerard Butler.

He leered.

I fiddled with my purse and watched the hostess point the other men toward a table for the first round.

"Okay. Your time starts"—the hostess hit a button on her watch—"now!"

Tall, dark, and creepy sat. "Hi." His voice was a low rumble. You know the old television show *The Addams Family*? Lurch. "I'm Adam. Troll. You?"

Adam? Fitting. "My name's . . . Sue. *Half*-elf."

"Oh," he said. "Half?" Then, nothing. He stared.

This was hell.

"What do you do for a living?" I asked, wondering how long five minutes could possibly last. I swear that five hours had passed.

"Butcher."

Ew. And ew. "I'm thinking about becoming a vegetarian."

A little chime sounded. I was so happy that I almost jumped out of my seat and did a little dance.

"Time's up," our hostess announced in a singsong. "Gentlemen, please move one table to the left."

A short, squat man took Adam's place. "Greg," he said, his voice a whiny, weaselly, nasally sound that made the hairs on the back of my neck stand up. "Goblin."

Apparently, Elmer wasn't kidding. This was speed dating for the otherworldly. I hadn't realized there were so many of them around the DC area. I supposed I shouldn't have been shocked.

"Sarah," I said. "*Half*-elf." I emphasized the *half* part again, hoping that would squash the interest I saw glittering in his freakish rodent-like eyes.

"Very glad to meet you," he began. Then, "I've-never-been-to-one-of-these-events-have-you-I-have-to-say-this-isn't-what-I-thought-it-would-be. . . ." And on. And on. And on.

He filled every excruciating second of the next five minutes with one long, rambling, horrifically boring run-on sentence that went nowhere and made my eyes water.

My next "date" was a zombie. Bob. Bob's ear fell off in the middle of our conversation. I almost lost my dinner. Things went south from there; blocks of five minutes spent with the weird, the scary, and the freakishly bizarre, culminating in my worst nightmare. At the very end of the evening, our hostess announced that the men were free to go and talk to any lady they might be interested in seeing again. Every one of them came back to my table.

Every. Single. One.

Gee, I was popular. With the undead. The living dead. And the soon-to-be dead.

Lucky me.

There was only one bright spot in this otherwise dreary evening. Elmer had his pick of all the other women in the room.

My alarm clock made some sort of bizarre noise, making me lurch upright. I smacked the snooze button. The noise didn't stop. I switched it off. The noise didn't stop.

"What the hell?"

"Sloan," Katie yelled from her room. "Would you answer your freaking phone?"

"Phone?" Blinking in the dark, I groped for my cell phone. Checked it. Sure enough, it was the source of the noise. But I hadn't changed the ringer. Strange. I hit the button. "Hello?"

"I apologize for waking you, Sloan," Chief Peyton said on the other end. "But there's been another murder. I'd like you to head over to the crime scene before the victim's cleared away."

"Oh. Sure." I took down the address and then stumbled my way into the bathroom. Glad I'd managed to escape the speed-dating thing relatively early (never again!), I took care of the essentials. A scorching hot shower partially woke me. The huge cup of coffee-to-go finished the job. By the time I'd arrived at the residence of Laura Volpe, I was feeling downright perky.

Until I saw JT.

Of course he'd be here. The chief liked to pair the two of us together.

"Hey," he said as I strolled toward the house.

"Good morning." A weird moment passed between us. Awkward silence. I motioned toward the door. "Are we clear to go inside?"

"Not yet."

I nodded.

He motioned toward a huddled circle of people. "They're questioning the husband."

"Another married victim?" I asked.

"I heard he was in bed with her. Just like the others."

"This is too weird. How could he not have woken up?" Then an idea flashed in my head. "Has anyone tested the husbands?"

"For what?"

"Drugs."

"I don't think so. I see where you're going with it. Let's see if we can get him to submit voluntarily to a quick blood screen." He motioned for me to follow him as he headed toward a pair of men standing on the porch. "I don't think you've met Detective McGrane yet," he told me. "He's the lead on this one. Detective, this is Sloan Skye. She suggested we might want to ask the husband if he'll submit to a blood screen."

"What're you looking for?" the detective asked.

"GHB? Any kind of amnesic or central-nervous-system depressant," I answered. "This is the third kill by this unsub. And every time, there's been someone in bed with the victim during the attack. And yet none of them have been able to recall anything."

"Damn." McGrane nodded. "I'll see what we can do. Thanks. We were looking at the husband."

"Never a bad idea," JT said. "But so far, the others have checked out."

"Got it. Who are the leads on the other kills?"

"Just one. Riggleman."

McGrane nodded. "I'll call him. Get all the details. I'll be taking over the case from here."

A member of the crime scene team interrupted the conversation. "We're set."

"Find anything?" McGrane asked.

The tech shrugged. "This is the cleanest scene I've ever seen. We got nothing. Not a drop of blood. No fibers. No fingerprints."

"Just like the other two," I said.

McGrane shook his head. "There must be something. We're not looking in the right places."

The tech said, "We scoured the place, top to bottom."

"If it's okay, we'd like to head inside," JT said to McGrane.

"Sure."

I followed JT after thanking the detective.

JT inspected the door first. "No sign of tampering with the door. How the hell is he getting in?"

"Maybe he's sneaking in when the door's unlocked,"

I suggested. "He could be hiding until the victim goes to bed."

"Hiding. Hmm . . ." He headed up the stairs, following the sounds of voices toward the bedroom.

I trailed behind; my gaze scrutinized everything as I walked. The steps. The banister. The walls. The framed black-and-white photographs that were hanging there. They looked so happy, Mr. Volpe and his wife. The last photo, at the very top of the stairs, made my blood run cold. She was wearing a white button-down shirt. The buttons were open from just under her ample breasts down, exposing a very round belly.

"Please tell me she wasn't pregnant too."

At the door, a uniformed cop looked at me funny. "She was. How'd you know?"

JT and I exchanged looks.

There could be no doubt. This was our guy.

Inside the bedroom, the ME looked to be finishing up his preliminary investigation. JT went straight to him. "Do you have a COD?" he asked.

"Exsanguination."

"The fetus?"

"No heartbeat. Looks like she's already delivered."

"Did you find the puncture wound?"

"Groin."

A bird chattered outside, drawing my attention. A dark shadow flashed across the window. I went to it, checked it. It was shut but unlocked. I opened the window and a black feather floated into the room on a soft breeze. A branch of the sickly maple tree outside, blown by a stronger gust, swayed. The black-red leaves rippled.

"What do you see?" JT asked.

"Nothing. Just a shadow. Must have come from the tree." I closed the window. "This was unlocked. But that tree outside is half dead." I pointed at the leafless limbs closest to us. "There's no way the limbs nearest to the window could support a grown adult." As if to support my theory, one snapped off and fell to the ground.

"So we still have no idea how the unsub is getting in," JT summed up.

"I'm still thinking a door. It's the most logical."

"Let's go talk to the husband. We'll see if he can tell us anything."

"Okay. Did you get anything from the victim?" I asked.

"Not a damn thing."

We found Volpe sitting in his living room, looking miserable and confused and overwhelmed. He had an elbow bent and was holding a piece of gauze against his arm. I was hoping that meant he'd agreed to the blood test. JT introduced us, as I'd come to expect.

"Mike Volpe." The man gave us each a nod. "I've told the police everything I know. I even gave them some blood."

"I'm sure they're grateful for your help," I said.

Volpe checked his arm. "I just don't understand. It's so strange. It almost doesn't feel real. It's like I'm going to walk upstairs and she'll be there, sleeping. And I'll learn it was all a sick joke." He wadded up the gauze.

Shit, there was nothing to say to that. "I'm sorry."

"Would you mind answering a few questions?" JT asked.

"No." Volpe stared at the ball of gauze in his hand.

"Do you keep all your doors locked at night?" JT asked.

"Of course."

"Windows?" I asked.

"The windows on the first floor are locked every night. When I was a kid, we had a break-in one night. Scared the shit out of me. I always lock the doors and windows. Don't worry about the second floor so much. There's no way for anyone to break in up there."

"Did you notice anything unusual before you went to bed last night?" I asked.

"No." Volpe crossed his arms over his chest and raised his gaze to me. "Unusual? Like what?"

"Like, was anything out of place? Did anything feel wrong?" I asked.

"Was your wife acting normal?" JT added.

Volpe's eyes narrowed. "Of course she was acting normal. Why would you ask a thing like that?"

"I don't mean to offend you, sir," JT said. "We're just trying to find out what we can, to help the detective solve the case."

Volpe's narrowed eyes widened. His gaze dropped to the floor. "Nothing stands out. We watched the news, like we always do. Then we went to bed. Together. It was a nice night."

"Did she leave you at any point?"

"Probably. To go to the bathroom. She's always complaining that she has to pee every half hour. But she was never gone for long. I wake up really easily, every time she leaves and every time she comes back. I would know."

"Was your bedroom window open last night?" I asked, jotting some notes.

"Sure. It was cool enough to cut off the air. But I can tell you for certain nobody got in our window."

I nodded. "Of course."

"Anything else?" Volpe asked, looking—and sounding—worn-out and shutdown.

"No. Not at this point," JT said. "Thank you." We excused ourselves and went back outside.

"I wonder what this victim's secret is?" I asked, recalling what Gabe had said yesterday as we strolled down the sidewalk toward our parked cars.

"What?" JT asked, hesitating in front of the house next door.

"Gabe told me he's learned something, working this case. Everybody has secrets."

"Oh, yeah? What's yours?"

"I don't have any."

"Well, then, that shoots his theory all to hell." He motioned toward the neighbor, who was standing on her front porch, a coffee cup in her hands. JT waved at the woman; she waved back. Turning on the charm, he headed toward her. I followed.

"Hello, ma'am, Agent Thomas. This is Sloan Skye. FBI. Do you have a few minutes to answer some questions?"

"About what?" she asked, peering toward her neighbor's house. "What's going on?"

"Your neighbor was found dead early this morning," JT told her.

The woman's face turned white. "Really? Mike is dead?"

"No, his wife," JT told her, after shooting a glance over his shoulder at me.

Maybe the Volpes had a dirty little secret, after all.

"Oh." The woman's brows drew together. She didn't speak for a moment, just glanced at the house periodically while staring down into her coffee cup the rest of the time. "That's . . . awful."

"You look very shaken," I said. "Were you friends?"

"No, not really." The woman looked at me. "She was pregnant."

"Yes," I said. "She was."

The woman gnawed on her lip. She glanced at the house again.

"Why did you assume it was her husband who was found dead?" I asked, keyed in to her pensive reaction.

She jerked her gaze back to me. "Oh. Um. His hobby."

"What kind of hobby does he have?" I asked.

"Well, he sort of likes to . . . test computer security systems . . . and then he . . . Oh, hell, he loves hacking into company's computers and messing with them. But it's not as bad as it sounds. He's doing the companies a favor, in a way. He's letting them know there's a vulnerability."

"And this has what to do with his wife's death?"

Her gaze flicked to her neighbor's house. "Last week, he told me he nailed some little company in Scranton. A few days later, he found a package on his front porch. Inside was a fake bomb. The note said if he so much as logged on to the Net, the next one would be real."

I shook my head. I'd known a hacker or two in college. For the most part, they were like this guy, harmless. But the fact was, they sometimes hit the wrong person. Then things could get ugly. "I'm hoping he realizes it's time to take up a new hobby."

Genius—to know without having learned; to draw just conclusions from unknown premises; to discern the soul of things.

—Ambrose Bierce

7

Three dead women.

Three missing babies.

I was convinced that their being pregnant was no coincidence. Despite all the other ugly secrets we'd dug up—the affairs and shady careers and so-called hobbies—the pregnancies were the unifying factor.

"What do you think?" I asked JT as we walked toward our cars. Both were parked a few houses down. JT's car was in front of mine.

"With a 'hobby' like that, it's a miracle something hasn't happened to him sooner."

"But it has nothing to do with the case," I stated.

"Right. Nothing."

We stopped next to my car. JT watched me get in.

I rolled down the passenger-side window and asked him, "What do you think? Check Laura Volpe's medical records next?"

He opened the passenger-side door and made himself comfy. "Makes sense."

"I don't suppose it'll be so simple that we learn all three women were going to the same doctor. . . ."

"That would be nice." He motioned to my phone,

which I'd set in the cup holder. "Why don't you go ahead and call Hough? She can have the physicians' names in a few minutes. In the meantime, we could grab an early lunch somewhere."

I checked my phone. It was early all right. More like breakfast time. But I was starving. "Sounds like a plan." I called Brittany, asked her to get us the names and addresses of all three victims' OB-GYN doctors. By the time I'd ended the call, JT was in his car and I was following him out of the subdivision. Twenty minutes later, we were pulling into the parking lot of one of my favorite little deli restaurants.

"Is this okay?" he asked in the parking lot.

"Sure is." I grabbed my laptop bag and headed inside. JT fell into step beside me. I reached for the door, but he beat me to it, opening it so I could step through.

Inside, we were escorted to a table in the back. I multitasked, ordering a cola while setting up my laptop. JT did the same. We pecked at our keyboards in silence for a few minutes.

"Hough e-mailed the doctors' names to me," JT announced, just as the waitress was returning with our drinks.

"Doctors, as in plural?" I asked.

"Yep."

"So much for things being simple."

We ordered our food. JT shut his laptop after the waitress hurried off to turn our order in to the cook. "Sloan, are you going to hide behind that computer screen the whole time we're here?"

"I'm not hiding. I'm working." I hoped he wouldn't look at my screen. I'd already checked my e-mail. Now I was on Facebook, reading my mother's latest rant. It was about me. Evidently, I was the world's worst maid of honor.

JT gently closed my computer. "Sloan?"

"Hey, I was doing something important."

He raised his eyebrows in a classic yeah-right expression.

I shrugged.

"Okay." He removed his hand. "I'll let you get back to your 'important' work." He drank half a glass of water. He fiddled with his napkin. He cleared his throat about a dozen times.

"Are you okay? Need another glass of water?" I asked.

"Nope. I'm fine." He blinked big eyes at me.

I swallowed a sigh. Yes, I had been hiding from him. That was rude. And childish. Immature. Unprofessional too. "My work can wait." I put my computer back in the bag. "So you said there's more than one doctor?"

"There are three."

"I don't suppose they all practice in the same building?"

"Doubt it. Their office addresses aren't the same—though they're relatively close. All in the Baltimore area."

"Well, that's something." I paused while our waitress gave us our food and asked if we needed anything else. When we indicated that we didn't, she set the tab on the edge of the table and thanked us. "This case is a tough one. We have so little to go on. And there's so much at stake, since the victims are—were—pregnant. What do you think the unsub is doing with the babies? They're all theoretically old enough to survive outside of the womb if they were delivered. But you never know. There's always some risk when a child is delivered."

"I think we'll have his motivation for killing when we

figure out what he's doing with the babies." JT took a big bite of his sandwich and chewed.

"I agree," I said. "But as far as gender goes, I'm second-guessing the assumption we're looking for a male. Historically, infants have been commonly murdered by women, going back over two hundred years to the practice of infant sweating in Victorian England. If those babies have been killed, I'm thinking our unsub is a female. Female with some kind of medical training."

"Do you have a statistic to support your theory? Or is it based on conjecture?" JT asked.

"I haven't found any hard numbers, but I can look for some."

"Don't bother. I'm only kidding." He flashed one of those insanely adorable grins, and I felt myself going soft. "You make a good point."

"What I don't like is how often the unsub is killing. Not only is he or she locating a new victim very quickly, but she is progressing through all seven psychological phases—aura, trolling, wooing, capture, murder, totem, and depression—within forty-eight hours, sometimes faster. To go through such extreme highs and lows in such a short time . . ."

"Someone has to be noticing," JT said, shaking a fry at me.

"Good point."

"When we find her, we'll know it."

"I hope you're right."

We ate for a few minutes in silence, but then our gazes locked. My heart lurched. My mouth went dry. I knew what was coming.

He said, "Sloan, about that conversation we had—"

"Please don't, JT. Let's keep things like this, friendly but professional. It's better for both of us."

"But I'd like to explain."

"There's no need." I'd eaten all I was going to. I pushed my plate away, dug out a ten-dollar bill, and put it on top of the bill. "Where to first?"

"I guess we'll pay Sprouse's doctor a visit first." He dropped his wadded napkin on his empty plate.

"I'm ready to go when you are."

"Okay." He tried handing my ten back to me; but when I refused to take it, he slid it under the candle centerpiece, placed a twenty on top of the bill, and grabbed his laptop bag.

We headed out into a bright, sunshiny morning. As I inhaled the scent of freshly mown grass, I thought that somewhere, out there, our killer was already hunting his or her next victim.

The drive to Sprouse's doctor's office was quick and relatively painless. Rush hour was winding down and the roads were passable.

In the lobby/reception area, JT introduced us to the young woman manning the front desk. She took our names and informed us someone would be with us soon; then she slid the little glass partition closed.

We waited among a dozen or so visibly pregnant women. A couple of them smiled at me after flicking their eyes at JT. I could only imagine what they were thinking. As tempting as it was to explain we weren't patients, I didn't bother. Several patients were called before we were. I was getting antsy by that time and had skimmed every *Parents* magazine in the lobby. Finally I heard my name.

As we strolled through a doorway, following a cheerful nurse dressed head to toe in scrubs (who, ironically, could be a cold-blooded killer), I peered into the bustling center of the practice. The office was staffed by at least a half-dozen women who were working phones and computers. Any of them could be the killer too. I nearly bumped into a woman pushing a cart full of sonographic gear—yet another suspect—as I rounded the corner, following the nurse down a crowded hallway. Our eyes met. Then hers flicked to my flat stomach. She smiled and apologized.

Numbered examination rooms were positioned at regular intervals along one wall. We were ushered into a teeny, tiny room by the nurse and asked to wait there.

JT sat on the chair pushed into a corner before I could. He grinned and pointed at the bed—the one with the stirrups.

"If you were a gentleman, you'd give up the chair," I pointed out.

"I guess that cinches it then, huh?" he joked. "I'm no gentleman."

I bit back a smart-ass retort and climbed up on the bed, leaving my legs swinging over the side. The paper crinkled under my ass. It was such a precious, wonderful, delightful moment.

Not.

JT's eyes glittered. "If you're sleepy—"

"Don't you dare." I crossed my arms over my chest and crossed my ankles too. "This is bad enough as it is. Do you really need to make inappropriate comments?"

His eyes sparkled. "No, I don't 'need' to. But it's kind of fun."

"Stop it."

"Done." His lips quirked for a split second.

I stared at the wall, trying to pretend I wasn't shut in a room the size of a closet with a man my body thought was the next best thing to chocolate. My mind knew better, thankfully. And my mind was in control.

What felt like an hour later, I checked the time on my phone. It had been fifteen minutes. "Sheesh. How much longer is this doctor going to make us wait?"

"Don't know. Should I poke my nose out and check?"

"Sure."

JT sauntered to the door, opened it. "Hmm," he said just as the sound of a woman's scream echoed down the hall. "I think something's wrong."

I slid off the table and rushed toward the open door. Several nurses were all dashing toward the same room, down at the end of the hall. Another shriek came from that direction.

"Great timing," I mumbled.

The nurse who ushered us into the room caught sight of us and sprinted over. "I'm sorry. Dr. Rosenstein is going to be busy for a while. Is there any chance you can come back later?"

"What's going on?" I asked, having some notion, but knowing my assumption could be wrong.

"A patient's delivering."

I wasn't wrong.

JT pulled a card out of his pocket and handed it to the nurse. "If you'd please let him know we'd like to talk to him as soon as possible? It's regarding one of his patients."

"I'll deliver the message." Off she ran.

And off we headed, to doctor number two.

Dr. Patel's practice was much like the first. The waiting room was packed with women sporting swollen bellies. The nurses bustled around, escorting patients to rooms, checking blood pressures and weights. Roughly twenty minutes after we arrived, a nurse called out JT's name and asked us to follow her. As we walked past the administration area, I eyeballed the huge wall of file drawers. There were perhaps a half-dozen people working back there, several nurses and maybe three administrators.

None of the faces looked familiar, not that I expected them to be. I figured it was safe to assume there was no way for the same person to work at all three offices.

This time—thank God!—we were taken to a small office. Not an examination room. We sat in the chairs facing the desk and waited for Dr. Patel to find his way back to us.

"I have a feeling we're wasting time here," I said.

"We don't know that yet."

"We can pretty much rule out the doctors—" I cut myself off as the man I presumed to be Dr. Patel came strolling in. I stood. So did JT.

After exchanging pleasantries and introductions, we all three sat down.

"How can I help you?" the doctor asked with a mild accent.

"We'd like to talk to you about one of your patients," JT explained. "Katherine Jewett."

His expression remained unreadable. "You realize her medical files are protected."

"We're not interested in accessing any private medical information," JT told him.

The doctor leaned back in his chair. "Then what kind of information are you looking for?"

"First, I'm sorry to tell you that Mrs. Jewett is dead," JT said. "Murdered."

The doctor's reaction was expected. He looked surprised and saddened. "This is very unfortunate news. Surprising too."

"Yes, it is." JT gave the doctor a moment before continuing. "We're working with local police to profile her killer. To do that, we need to gather as much information about both the killer and the victim as possible. Which leads us to why we're here. Mrs. Jewett is the second victim in a series of recent killings. All three women were pregnant and within weeks of delivery. We're trying to find a common thread among them. They weren't all your patients, but I'm wondering if you employ personnel who might work in multiple locations?"

The doctor's eyes widened. "You think the killer may be one of my employees?"

"Or perhaps an employee contracted by another company to provide some kind of service?" I offered.

"Hmm. Let me think. There's the ultrasound technician. She travels from office to office and would be the only one who might have contact with my patients. There's also the cleaning crew—we contract an outside company for that. And some administration tasks, such as billing."

"That's excellent," JT said. "Is there any way you could provide a list of the companies you contract, along with contact information?"

"Absolutely. Anything I can do to help. Agents, should I be warning my other patients about the danger?"

JT leaned toward the doctor, resting an elbow on the desk between them. "We'd like to ask you to please keep this information to yourself for the time being. We wouldn't want to cause a panic. And at this point, we don't know if there is any connection between your practice and the crime."

"We will keep you posted, however, and if we get something more substantial, we'll let you know," I added, hoping to ease his worries somewhat.

The doctor stood. Extended a hand. "Thank you. I hope you catch whoever did it."

"We're doing our best," I said, shaking his hand.

The doctor gave a short nod and headed toward

the door. "Please wait here. I'll get the information you need."

Almost three hours later, we were back at the PBAU. We'd visited the third doctor and made a second trip back to the first. JT was lurking around my cubicle. I was reading—or rather trying to read—the handwritten notes the doctors had given us.

"I thought my handwriting was bad. What they say about doctors' handwriting is definitely true. I can't make out a word of this chicken scratch."

"I'll take a look, if you like."

"Be my guest." I pointed at the scribbles. "I think we may have something here. If I'm reading this right, all three use the same ultrasound company. At least an ultrasound technician would have some medical training. More than someone doing billing."

"Or running a vacuum," JT finished. "I'll call all three practices to confirm the company's name. You can call the company itself and get a list of technicians. Bonus points if you can get the locations each one travels to."

"I'll do my best."

A plan of attack in place, we wasted no time. JT dashed back to his cubicle. I did a quick Google search for the ultrasound company, to make sure I had read the phone number correctly. Then I placed the call. After speaking to three people, including two managers, I came to the conclusion that I wouldn't get the information we needed without paying them a visit in person.

I headed back to JT's cubicle to tell him. He wasn't there. I checked a few places, including Chief Peyton's office and the conference room. Not there either.

Deciding I'd head over to the ultrasound company on

my own, I tossed my computer back in its case and zipped it shut.

"Where are you going?" Gabe asked as he strolled through the unit's main entry.

"I need to visit a company that provides ultrasound services to OB doctors in the area."

"Cool. Want some company?"

"Sure." I glanced around. Still no sign of JT.

My cell phone rang as we were heading out to my car. Mom. I considered ignoring it but decided that would only make things worse. I answered.

"You have exactly two hours to get over here," Mom said.

"Hi, Mom. It's good to talk to you too! How have you been? I've been busy. We're working an important case—"

"I don't want to hear about your case. I don't want to hear about stupid queens or assassination plots or anything else." Then she broke down and sobbed in my ear.

"What's wrong?" I started to slide into the driver's seat, but Gabe nudged me away, mouthing I should ride shotgun so I could talk to my mother. I didn't put up a fight.

"Your father is driving me nuts. He's been gone for three days. Three! Fricking! Days! I haven't heard a word. Not one."

"Mom, I'm sure he's okay."

"I hate him right now."

"Of course, you do. I would too."

She cried in my ear for ten more minutes while I tried to console her. It wasn't working. If anything, I think she was getting more worked up. Finally I said, "Mom, I'll come over as soon as I can. Can you hang on for a little while?"

"I." *Sob.* "Don't." *Sniffle.* "Know." *Snort.*

"Okay. Give me a minute. I'll call Katie and see if she can go over to your place until I can get there."

"No." *Sob. Sniffle.* "You don't have to do that."

"It's okay. I'm going to hang up now. So I can call Katie. Okay?"

"Okay," she blubbered.

I hung up.

I sighed.

"What's going on?" Gabe asked.

I gave him an index finger response and dialed Katie's number. "Just a little domestic situation," I told him. "Nothing big."

Katie answered on the fifth ring. "Hello?"

"Are you busy right now?" I asked.

"Um. Kinda. Why? Jesse's here. We're not watching a movie this time."

"Oh."

"What's wrong?"

"Mom's a wreck, and I'm in the middle of something. I can't get to her for a while. . . ."

"You want me to go over and calm her down?" Katie asked.

"If you don't mind?"

"Sure."

"You're the best."

"Just remember that the next time I do something annoying," she said, her voice bubbly with laughter.

"Like fill our apartment with toxic fumes?"

"Yeah, like that."

We hung up. I looked at Gabe.

"Problems at home?" he asked.

"What's new, right?" I grumbled. He seemed to be suppressing a grin. "Go ahead, laugh."

"I wouldn't laugh. That would be rude. And immature."

"A few weeks ago you would've laughed."

"That was before."

I didn't touch that comment. To do so would be like waltzing into an emotional minefield. Lately, Gabe was going out of his way to remind me that we'd once dated. This was in stark contrast to how he'd treated me the last few years. He'd been an ass. I'd hated him. He'd appeared to hate me. It was all so simple then. Who would've thought I'd miss it?

At least our mutual hating had been comfortable. Predictable. This new . . . whatever it was called was far from comfortable or predictable.

I could tell he was trying his hardest to make me see him as a new-and-improved Gabe Wagner. And, of course, he was also doing his damnedest to make me see JT as a jerkwad. The former was working to a point; the latter . . . well, I couldn't see JT as a jerkwad, as much as I wished I could.

"Want to talk about it?" Gabe asked as he maneuvered the car into a tight spot between a Hummer and a semi-truck, both traveling at least eighty miles per hour.

"What?"

"The problem. At home."

"Not really."

"Okay."

"I'd rather talk about the case," I said. "There are three dead women in the morgue and three missing infants out there somewhere. That's what we need to focus on."

"Of course."

"Did you get anywhere today?"

Eyes focused on the road, where they should be, Gabe shook his head. "Not really. I can tell you what the victims' favorite foods were, their routines, their relationships with their husbands, neighbors, and friends. But nothing's connecting. Nothing's making sense. We're missing something. Something big."

"I'm hoping we're onto that 'something' here."

"I hope you're right. Because at the rate this guy's killing, we're soon going to have dozens of dead women in the morgue."

Anyone who stops learning is old, whether at twenty or eighty. Anyone who keeps learning stays young. The greatest thing in life is to keep your mind young.

—Henry Ford

8

Sano Health Services was housed in an attached brick structure, flanked on either side by two light-industrial companies—a package delivery service and a medical sales office. Gabe pulled the car into the packed lot around the side and we walked in together.

A young woman with a cheery smile greeted us as soon as we stepped inside. The reception desk was neat and orderly, but not new. And not fancy. I was guessing they didn't get a lot of walk-in traffic. "Hello. How may I help you?"

Gabe and I flashed our IDs—the ones that provided access to the military base upon which the PBAU's office was located. They didn't say FBI, but it was the best we had.

"We work for an FBI unit that investigates local violent crimes. We need to talk to someone about getting a list of employees who have provided ultrasound services at a few local OB-GYN practices," I explained.

"Hmm." The woman held up an index finger. "One moment, please, if you don't mind waiting over there."

She pointed to a couple of well-used metal-framed chairs positioned along one wall.

"Sure," I said.

We sat.

The young woman disappeared behind one of the three doors that exited off the small lobby area.

"I hope I don't have to call in JT," I mumbled.

Gabe didn't look worried. "We'll get what we need."

The woman returned. "Do you have any identification that specifies you're with the FBI?"

"No, we don't," I said. "We're . . . interns. Hired for the summer."

The woman scowled. "I'm sorry, but we can't help you."

"We can provide the name and phone number of our superior," I offered as I pulled one of Chief Peyton's cards out of my pocket.

She took the card and disappeared again.

This time, she didn't return for a while. I was sure we would be leaving empty-handed. If only the FBI would provide their interns with some kind of official-looking ID, but I could appreciate why that might be a bad idea. In our case, however, because we were doing more than making lunch and coffee runs, some kind of ID would have come in handy. Thus, we were usually paired with an agent. And that agent, in my case, was almost always JT.

Finally she returned. "I'm sorry, but the information you requested is private. We can't give it to you."

Damn.

"However," the woman said, "we've spoken to your superior, Agent Peyton. She's coming in to pick up the list in an hour."

"Okay. I guess that's the best we can do. Thank you."

Feeling defeated, and slightly irritated, I headed out to the car.

* * *

A few minutes shy of an hour later, I was standing on the front porch of the new house my father had just purchased for my mom. She'd moved in a few days ago. I hadn't been inside yet. She took me on a drive-by the day before they'd closed.

This . . . mansion . . . was beyond words. It was huge. It was grand. It was everything Mom's old apartment wasn't. And Mom deserved every last square foot. That was because "dear old Dad" pulled a fast one on her twenty-something years ago, faked his death, and then disappeared. Mom was devastated. I grew up believing he was dead, until a week ago when he just reappeared, gave us a half-assed explanation about why he'd stayed away so long, and bought Mom this house as an apology.

Even before he'd bought the house, Mom had decided to forgive him. Me, I'm on the fence. I don't buy his nonexcuse. And I don't trust him.

After this call about him pulling another disappearing act, I had even more reason to distrust him.

A strange man answered the door. He was beautiful. Face. Eyes. Perfect hair. And even though he was fully clothed, I could tell his body was lean but overly muscled, perfectly proportioned for some woman's fantasy inspiration. But not mine. Maybe it was the cocky leer that killed it for me.

I forced a smile. "Hi, I'm Sloan."

"I'm Sergio. Your mother's expecting you. She's on the back patio."

"Thanks." I paused in the foyer. There was a waterfall on the wall. A waterfall. Insane. I looked toward Sergio for some help finding the back patio.

He obliged, leading me through the main floor of the house, past furnishings that had to cost more money than

I would probably earn in a lifetime, to a set of French doors. I stepped out onto a brick patio covered with a wood pagoda. Directly in front of me was an inground swimming pool. I located my mother, lounging on a chaise watching the flat-screen TV that was mounted on a brick wall.

A television outside. More insanity.

"Mom?"

"Sloan." Mom motioned to the lounge next to hers. "Come sit with me."

"Where's Katie?"

"She had to go." Staring at the huge color screen in front of us, Mom channel surfed.

"Are you okay?" I plopped my butt on the chaise.

"I'm fine."

"But—"

"Your father called. It was another emergency with *Her Majesty.*" Mom rolled her eyes. "I'm telling you, the woman is a drama queen. No doubt it was another false alarm." Her eyes sparkled. "Ooh. *House Hunters International* is on. I'm thinking about buying a house in southern France. Or maybe Spain. . . ."

"France?" I echoed, standing.

"Where are you going?"

"Home. I'm hungry. And tired. I haven't had any dinner yet. I've been on the run all day—"

"Why don't you eat with me? We can order anything you like."

"Well . . ."

Finally Mom looked at me. She gave me one of her trademark pleading pouts. "Your father won't be home until sometime tomorrow. I'm lonely. We can have a nice dinner out here by the pool. And then we can work on my wedding registry at Neiman Marcus."

Neiman Marcus. Mom was really enjoying the being-rich thing. But after spending over twenty years struggling to pay her rent, I could hardly blame her. She deserved to enjoy a little indulgence.

"Fine."

Mom's face lit up. "Oh, Sloany, thank you." She grabbed her cell phone and dialed. "What would you like for dinner?"

"I don't care. Surprise me."

Mom called in an order for some kind of vegetarian-whole-grain-organic something. Hung up. Then she turned her attention back to the couple on television who were touring a two-hundred-year-old stone farm-house in Aveyron. "Oh, just look at that view! I would love to wake up to that."

"I think I'll go out to my car and grab my computer," I said to her profile.

"Okay." She waved me off.

I headed back inside, slightly sunblind from the out-side glare. Blinking, I backtracked through the house, heading to the front door. I caught Sergio coming out of a room not far from the foyer.

He shut the room's door behind him, gave me a smile that would make a lesser girl swoon, and asked, "Are you leaving already?"

"No. I need something in my car."

"Good." Looking pleased, he nodded, then accompanied me to the front door. "Do you need any help carry-ing it in?"

"Oh, no. It's not big or heavy. It's just a laptop."

"Okay." He moved to let me pass, holding the door open for me. As I walked across the front porch toward the stairs, I sensed that he was watching me. Unable to stop myself, I glanced over my shoulder to check.

He was.

My face probably turned ten shades of red as I

rounded the corner toward my car. While I grabbed my laptop case, I found myself doing a quick mirror check. I smiled to make sure there was nothing in my teeth. Then I fiddled with my hair a little. As I strolled back toward the house, I reminded myself why I didn't need to encourage any attention from my mother's household staff members. Particularly ones who had inflated muscles and an ego to match. Men who looked that good were trouble. Always. I had two in my life already. I didn't need a third.

Sergio was waiting for me at the door. Before I'd made it to the top of the steps, he had it open and, with a stunning smile, was inviting me inside.

I thanked him politely and headed back to the patio.

Mom was right where I'd left her.

I spent the next half hour or so talking to the side of her head while she watched her television shows, and Sergio cleaned the pool—shirtless. He reached. He flexed. He skimmed. He flexed some more.

The ego was really getting to me. Not impressed. Nope.

I set up her registry on the Neiman Marcus Web site. Then, because she was being so irritating, not actually wanting to look at things so I could add them to her list, I started picking stuff for her.

A House Blessing Box by Jan Barboglio. No, Mom wasn't religious. That was the point. I also added a 150-dollar paper towel holder, a butt-ugly vase, and some plates printed with a huge, busy floral pattern. Our food came before I could find any more useless items for her list.

Mom's pool boy/butler had put our carryout on plates and had set them on the nearby dining table.

Mom crinkled her nose. "I can't see the TV."

Seriously? This was a woman who had taught me that television was akin to crack. It would fry my brain.

"I'll bring some trays," Sergio said.

"I'm good right here." I made myself comfortable in a chair and reached for the pitcher he'd just set down.

"I'll get it." He beat me to it. Our fingers brushed. A tiny, minuscule touch. But that little bit of contact made me flinch.

I was such a child when it came to men. But that was because I had so little experience with them. I didn't date in high school. That was mostly because the boys all thought I was a brainy geek, which was true. And also because I was years younger than most of them. But it was also because I'd done everything in my power to keep them at bay, including dress and look the part of a brainy geek.

Same thing in college.

There'd been one. Only one. Gabe.

Of course, that hadn't turned out well. A broken heart put me right back onto the path of man-avoidance. I'd been traveling that road pretty much since then. And men seemed to be willing to let me.

But lately . . . I couldn't say whether it was the stupid extensions I'd had put in last week—they were for work, I'm not that vain—or something else. But suddenly it seemed I was getting a lot more attention from men.

At any rate, I knew my life was out of balance. I was intelligent. I could translate a passage of text into at least a dozen different languages. I could recite statistics for hours. And my brain housed enough information to fill a set of encyclopedias. But when it came to social situations, I was an infant. Awkward. Self-conscious. Inept.

This was why I jerked my hand back like I'd touched a live wire.

If Sergio noticed—how could he not?—he didn't

react. Moving with fluid grace, he poured some ice water into my glass and set the pitcher back in place. "Is there anything else I can get you?"

"No. Thanks. I'm good."

He responded with another smile. "Are you?" he asked, not waiting for my answer before disappearing in the house.

It was a good thing—for him. After that little remark, I was tempted to throw something at him.

Men.

All the adversity I've had in my life, all my troubles and obstacles, have strengthened me. . . . You may not realize it when it happens, but a kick in the teeth may be the best thing in the world for you.

—Walt Disney

9

"I give up."

Speaking of men . . .

Blinking into the darkness, I leered at the shadow next to my bed. It was late, sometime between sunset and sunrise. I hoped it was closer to the former than the latter. I *needed* it to be closer to the former than the latter. "What's the matter now, Elmer?" My voice was scratchy, rough.

"We may as well get married and get it over with," he said with a sigh.

"Doesn't that sound romantic?" I stretched and blinked at the glaring red numbers on my clock. Was that . . . two-thirty? No, twelve-thirty. Thank God.

"Yeah, yeah. I know. But I'm getting tired of living like this. And I can't find a decent elf to marry, instead."

"You haven't been looking for long." I fluffed my pillow, hoping Elmer would get the message. It was a silly hope, I realized that.

"Yes, I have. I've been looking for *twenty years.*"

"No, you've been *waiting* for twenty years. For me," I corrected. I snapped on the bedside lamp and blinked at him. "Or were you looking for something better the whole time you were supposedly engaged to me?"

"Well . . ." His gaze flew to the floor.

My ego took a blow there. "Well?" I echoed.

"I stopped looking at least a year before I started contacting you, if that makes you feel any better," he said to the floor.

"Hmm." I went back to pillow fluffing. The pillow was flat. Very. It needed a lot of fluffing.

"Don't pout now. It was nothing personal."

"I'm not pouting."

"Coulda fooled me. You're beating your pillow to a pulp."

"It's flat. And as far as you go, you didn't have me helping you before. Now you do. And I'll find you the perfect wife." Next I shook out the covers and smoothed them down.

"I've heard that before. So far, your results have been less than impressive."

"You haven't taken my advice." Abandoning my nesting, I wagged a finger at him. "You can't hold anything that's happened against me, when you're still doing everything your way."

"I see your point."

"Then you'll agree to try it my way?"

He shrugged. "I may."

"I won't marry you unless you give it an honest try."

"Very well." He sighed. His shoulders dropped at least three inches. "What do you want me to do first?" he grumbled.

I reclined against the headboard for a moment and gathered my thoughts. Meanwhile, Elmer started pacing nervously.

"Women are impressed by power. Money. Do you have either of these?"

"I'm a prince. What do you think?"

"Right. How could I have forgotten?"

I took in tonight's ensemble. His pants were three inches too long, and his polyester shirt was roughly thirty-five years outdated. "You need to capitalize on your royalness. We're going to focus on online dating for a while. Let's see what that does for us."

"Online dating is a waste of time, I'm telling you."

I squinted.

He sighed. "I know, I know."

"Okay. Let me think. Hmm . . . you're a prince. You need a wife. We need to find the perfect woman for you. I know! I remember a while back a television network ran a show called *Who Wants to Marry a Millionaire?* It was a total train wreck. But there were some very attractive, interesting women who took a chance and auditioned for the show."

"Did the millionaire get married?" Elmer asked, his little, beady eyes glittering with hope.

"Um, no."

This time, he squinted.

"We'll find you a wife. I promise." The gears were turning already. I needed to find a production company that would be willing to take care of all the casting and filming. Then I needed to find a network willing to air it. This wasn't going to be easy. But if it worked, I'd have women lined up at my door, waiting to meet Elmer.

I had to find a way to make it happen.

My first thought was to talk to my father. As much as I didn't trust him, when it came to having contacts, particularly among elves and fairies, he was the go-to man. Who knew? Maybe he'd have some contacts in the press, since he did have regular interaction with them in his work for Her Majesty.

"Elmer, I have a plan."

He perked up. "You do? Already?"

"Yes. Now get lost. I have to get some sleep tonight. I have a day job, remember?"

"I'm outta here." *Poof.* He was gone.

After checking the time, I went ahead and called my father's cell phone. When he didn't answer, not that I'd expected him to, I left a message, briefly summarizing what I needed to talk to him about. Then I did what most any girl in my position would do.

I went and had a bowl of ice cream, to help me get back to sleep.

"Good morning." Chief Peyton looked downright chipper as she motioned all of us into the meeting room. She paced while we sat and gathered pens and paper for notes. When we were all ready, she announced, "Finally we've caught a break in our case."

I shifted to the edge of my seat and lifted my pen.

She announced, "Yesterday, with Skye's help, I obtained a list of contract workers for Sano Health. After reviewing the list, I noticed a pattern with the traveling ultrasound technicians they employ. In particular, there's one individual who not only worked at all three doctors' offices our victims were visiting for care, but she had provided hands-on services to them."

This had to be the big *something* we'd been looking for! And, I noticed, Chief Peyton had referred to the ultrasound technician as a *she*. I'd been right.

"What's next?" I asked.

"Unfortunately, this connection isn't enough in itself for the Baltimore PD to obtain a search warrant. So they're bringing her in for questioning this morning. Skye, Thomas, I'd like you two to be there for the questioning. JT, I've watched you in interrogation. I'd like to see if you can get anywhere with her." Turning to Gabe, she said, "Wagner and I will be digging up anything and everything we can on this individual, along with Hough, who will remain here at the unit as a liaison." She crossed her arms over her chest. "Let's stop this monster before she kills again. No mistakes. We can't have her walking."

I hurried to my cubicle to gather my laptop and purse. JT caught up with me there.

"I hope we can get her to talk," I said as I hurried through the process of powering down and packing up my computer.

"I'm going to do my best." JT wound the power cord up and handed it to me.

"Thanks." I shoved the cord into the zippered compartment and then added the computer to its padded pocket. "Almost ready. I didn't know you were a master of interrogation techniques. I'd like to learn more about it." I zipped the case shut; then I grabbed my purse. JT carried my computer bag with his free hand and together we headed for the elevators.

Out in the hallway, I poked the down button.

JT said, "You should study interrogation techniques. Having a woman interrogate female suspects would be helpful. Especially since the point of the first stage in interrogation is to develop a rapport with the suspect, make him or her feel a little at ease. Common knowledge says that once a person starts telling the truth, and the more he or she tells us, the more difficult it becomes for him or her to lie. It's breaking through that initial resistance that can be tough."

The bell rang. The doors slid open. We stepped into an empty car.

"I don't suppose you'd let me try?" I asked meekly.

"Not this time, Skye. You have no experience. Plus, I

don't like the idea of leaving you in a room alone with the suspect."

"What if I went in with you?"

"I don't know. If you make a mistake, what she says could become inadmissible. I'll talk to Peyton and McGrane. In any event, you'll be able to observe."

"That's good enough for me."

The car gave a little bouncing stop and the doors opened.

As we stepped out into the main lobby, JT said, "Remember, we don't have a lot to go on at this time. Part of interrogating a suspect is being able to develop a believable explanation of how and why she committed the crime. That's going to be almost impossible."

We headed outside.

A half hour later, through a one-way mirror, I was watching a young woman who looked no older than myself. The woman, our suspect, was sitting in a tiny white-walled room by herself. She had been asked to take the chair facing a table and the wall with the one-way mirror. Two empty chairs were positioned on the opposite side of the table, which would place the detective and JT with their backs to me. At this point, no detectives had gone in to question her yet. After waiting for ten minutes, she was already starting to look anxious. Her gaze was shifting from one part of the room to the other, occasionally flicking to the door. Twice she looked directly at the mirror. I knew she couldn't see me, but I still felt funny when she looked my way.

Finally McGrane went in, along with JT. They introduced themselves and then sat.

"Your name, ma'am?" McGrane asked.

"Terry Pietrzak. Why am I here?" she asked, folding her arms over her chest. That was a clear defensive sign.

Everyone knows how to read that one. "Am I in some kind of trouble?"

"No, no," McGrane said. "We're hoping you can help us with a case."

Pietrzak's shoulders visibly dropped. "Ah, okay. How can I help you?"

"Are you employed by Sano Health?" the detective asked.

"Yes, I am."

"What do you do for them?" he asked.

"I'm an ultrasound technician. I travel to doctors' offices and perform ultrasounds on their patients."

"That sounds very interesting. Do you enjoy your job?" McGrane asked. So far, JT hadn't said a word, outside of his name.

"Most of the time, yes. I specialize in obstetrical sonography. So nine times out of ten, the patients are looking forward to the procedure. I take measurements to determine how the fetus is growing, print photographs for the soon-to-be parents, and tell them the gender of their baby, if they want to know."

"Sounds like a great job," JT said.

Pietrzak smiled. "It is."

"Do you have any children? Have you had an ultrasound yourself?" JT asked. I wasn't sure where he was going with that question.

"No, not yet," she said. "I'm not ready for kids. I'm just getting my career going, and my wedding is a long way off."

"You're getting married?" JT asked. It seemed as though he was stepping in and taking over.

She nodded. "Yes, next June."

JT returned her smile. "Congratulations."

"Thank you. I'm very excited. We're planning a big wedding. Though, if it were up to me, I'd be happy with something small and private. But I doubt you care too much about that."

Ah, he was doing a great job getting her to loosen up and talk. I had to assume that was his intention.

JT shook his head. "No need to hold back. We're just having a friendly chat."

"Sure," Pietrzak said, crossing her arms again.

Looked like JT had said something wrong. I wondered what it was.

The detective continued. "You said part of your job is to travel to doctors' offices. Do you generally visit the same ones on a regular basis?"

McGrane was moving things back to the business at hand.

"Generally. But I also cover for other workers sometimes, when they're sick or schedule vacations."

The detective scribbled down some notes. JT didn't.

"Would the following doctors be on your regular schedule?" McGrane asked. "Dr. Patel, Dr. Rosenstein, and Dr. Yokely?"

"Yes. All three."

The detective once again took down some notes. "And how long have you been working for Sano?"

"Since I moved to Baltimore, in late May."

It was late June. Pietrzak had been in the area for about a month. The timing was a little off.

The murders had begun only this week. And there'd been three in rapid succession. Our assumption had been that our unsub had been killing for some time. Certainly more than a week or two. If that was the case, it wasn't likely she could have gone for three weeks without killing. Unless she had just recently escalated her killing for some reason.

Had some kind of trigger tripped something?

This was a killer who knew exactly how to cover her

tracks. She knew how to get into a home undetected. She knew how to kill without waking someone sleeping next to the victim. There was no way that kind of precision, and confidence, could be developed overnight.

"Where did you move from?" JT asked.

"Michigan. I finished up classes in May and was immediately hired by Sano."

"Do you have friends or family in the area?" JT asked.

"Nope."

"And your fiancé . . . ?" JT asked.

I think I had some idea where JT was going with this. He was looking for that trigger.

"He's still in Michigan."

Looking fairly sympathetic, JT shook his head. "It must have been hard moving out of state. Alone. With no friends or family to help."

"I was ready for a change. I've never been afraid to move. In fact, I moved to Michigan from Ohio on my own, to go to school. And as far as my fiancé goes, he's joining me as soon as he can find a job. He's made a few trips out here, and has gone on some interviews. I'm hopeful he'll get something soon."

Interesting.

I was still on the fence about Terry Pietrzak. She clearly wasn't lying about her job. She wasn't trying to hide the fact that she'd been at those doctors' offices; and thus, she wasn't making any effort to deny she'd had some kind of contact with the victims. For that reason, I wanted to believe she was innocent.

But . . .

She'd also just moved. Out of state. Alone.

She'd left behind a fiancé.

Why? For a job that paid a moderate wage? To me, that seemed highly suspicious.

She glanced at the detective, then at JT. "Can you tell me what kind of case you're working on?"

"We can. If you'd just answer a few more questions . . . ," McGrane said.

"Sure." Pietrzak glanced at her wristwatch. I leaned closer to the mirror.

That was one heck of a watch. Sparkly stones surrounded the black rectangular face. And the band was actually made of oblong links of jewel-encrusted white metal. It was flashy and yet sophisticated. Awfully expensive for a recent college graduate working an entry-level job.

Of course, it could also be fake.

"Do you keep some kind of log or written record of the patients you see every day?" McGrane asked.

"Yes, I do. I have to, for insurance-billing purposes."

The detective nodded. "Of course. So it wouldn't be difficult for you to give us a list of the patients you've personally seen over the past few weeks?"

She shifted in her seat a little. "I'd have to check with my supervisor, to make sure it's okay. You know, the Medical Privacy Act."

"Sure. But we're not asking for any diagnoses or medical information. Just names."

She shrugged.

Silence.

Looking a little more uneasy, she glanced back and forth between JT and McGrane. "Will this take much longer? I need to be at work in an hour."

"I think we're just about through," JT said.

Pietrzak visibly relaxed. "Okay."

"What sort of personal information do you have access to in the paperwork you're provided by your employer? Name? Birth date? Address?"

"Sure. All of those." Her eyebrows scrunched together.

"But so would anyone else working for the doctor, doing medical billing or any other contracted services. I'm not sure what you're trying to get at."

"Just a few more questions," McGrane said. "Have you ever visited a patient, for either personal or professional reasons, in her home?"

"No, never. I'd have no reason to."

One thing I'd learned while reading up on interrogation on the way here was the relationship between eye movement and truthfulness. According to several studies, a subject's eyes will shift up and to their right when they are asked to imagine something, to construct an image—aka, something that isn't real. In contrast, that same subject's eyes would shift up and to their left when they are asked to recall or remember a visual image of something that is real. I'd read that the technique wasn't foolproof. But it was useful.

This is why I'd been watching Pietrzak's eyes throughout the interview. If Bandler and Grinder's research was accurate, Terry Pietrzak had been honest in answering all but one question.

I'm convinced that tragedy wants to harden us and our mission is never to let it.

—Unknown

10

An hour later, I was still sitting on the other side of the mirror. Things hadn't changed much from my perspective, but they sure had from Pietrzak's.

The interview had taken quite a turn. Detective McGrane confronted her with both the facts she'd supplied and some lies he'd constructed to make her look guilty. He interrupted her every time she started to deny guilt, suggesting several different scenarios that were completely plausible, while continuing to cut off every denial. He twisted her objections into justifications. He expressed empathy. He offered a couple more scenarios, which were more socially acceptable, hoping she'd confess to one of those. It was a textbook study in police interrogation techniques.

When she still held out, refusing to confess, he continued to ask the same questions over and over.

The woman never once admitted guilt.

She never once asked for a lawyer.

She only appeared to be lying once. As it turned out, that was because she had visited a patient's home—though not one of our victims. To purchase some Vicodin. She had a twenty-pills-a-day habit.

JT and McGrane excused themselves from the room.

Out in the hallway, JT shrugged. "We need more evidence to go on. She's not biting."

"She has motive. Selling infants on the black market would certainly help support her addiction. And she has some medical training. But she looked genuinely shocked when you told her about the murders," I told him. "I've been watching closely. The only possible sign of dishonesty I caught was when McGrane asked her if she'd ever visited a patient at her home."

JT's phone rang. He checked it, then answered.

Based on his end of the conversation, I knew we were leaving. He ended the call. "Shannon and Scott Kersey are in custody in Michigan. We're flying out in thirty."

"Okay. What about Pietrzak?"

"McGrane's going to keep working on her. But if he can't get anything, he'll probably release her."

We both had our overnight bags with us. All agents are required to keep a packed bag with them at all times—a go bag—in case they're called out of town at a moment's notice. We headed to the airport together. Anticipating a long night, and hoping to avoid any further problems with JT, I closed my eyes and pretended to take a nap. While I supposedly dozed, I was aware of JT sitting in the seat across the aisle from me. He was doing something on his computer. I didn't bother looking.

The flight was short. I took the time to sort out the few facts we had in the case and the many questions that were left to be answered.

We knew:

Three women had died.

All three had been killed in their homes.

The killer had most likely delivered their babies and then drained their blood.

The children were missing.

The killer was targeting pregnant women.

Our one and only suspect—Terry Pietrzak—had recently moved from Michigan. And here we were, winging our way to Michigan.

And the killer had managed to deliver the infants and kill the mothers without leaving any signs of a break-in, no signs of the missing children, and no forensic evidence on the scene.

We suspected:

The unsub had killed before.

The unsub was a female.

We didn't know:

How the unsub was finding her victims.

What, if any, connection there was between Pietrzak and the Kerseys.

What the unsub's reason for killing was. (Monetary gain, perhaps. Or, in the case of a vampiric creature, sustenance. Or both.)

How the unsub was able to break in to her victim's home.

How she was killing her victim, delivering the baby, and removing all evidence without being seen or heard by anyone else in the home at the time.

Nor did we know what the unsub was doing with the babies.

In summary, we had more questions than answers.

I was hoping, by some miracle, the Kerseys would give us at least some of those answers.

A few hours later, we were standing in the Grand Rapids Police Department, talking to an officer named Beasely. He said, "Want the good news or the bad news first?"

"Bad," I said.

"Scott Kersey's already lawyered up. Wouldn't even give us his name."

I heard JT mutter something that I would rather not repeat.

I sighed. Had we just traveled all this way for nothing? "Now . . . the good?"

Beasely grinned. "His wife hasn't."

JT clapped his hands together. "Let's talk to her before she changes her mind."

We followed Beasely down the hall to the interrogation room.

"Got an observation mirror?" JT asked as we walked.

"Nope. Been wanting one, but our budget's tight. We'd rather spend the dollars on safety gear."

"I hear that," JT responded. He glanced at me. "Promise you won't say a word and you can come in the room with me."

"You bet. I promise."

In we went.

Shannon Kersey's eyes tracked my movements as I made my way to an empty chair. We measured each other up across the table. Yesterday, back at the PBAU, I'd taken a look at her rap sheet. It wasn't the longest I'd seen. Wasn't the shortest either. She'd lived a rough life, spent a good number of years in and out of jail for prostitution. Only recently, after marrying Kersey, had she graduated to scamming people.

I took a chair set off to one side, reserving the other two—both facing Kersey—for Beasely and JT.

They sat.

Right away, Kersey started talking. "I'll give you anything you want on my husband. I want to make a deal."

Could it be that simple? I doubted it. For one thing, I doubted Scott Kersey was our killer. He was the wrong gender, if our initial profile was right.

"What can you give us?" Beasely asked.

"Names. Dates," she said.

Beasely and JT exchanged glances. Then JT took over. "What do you know about Victoria Sprouse?" he asked.

"I know she's dead. I know she's my neighbor. And I know she was carrying my husband's child."

"What do you know about her death?" JT asked.

"Nothing, that's what I know." The woman's eyes never left JT's. If she was lying, she was a damn good liar.

"Are you sure?" JT asked.

"Positive. We were . . . busy that night."

"Can anyone else testify to your activities?"

"Yeah, Angie Feder."

"Who's Angie Feder?" Again, JT.

Shannon Kersey's smile was seductive and sickening all at once. "A *friend*. Let's just say none of us left our bedroom until well after dawn."

If her claims could be verified, that cleared both her and her husband from our short list; though, in truth, they hadn't been on our list, anyway. I was more hoping they'd heard or seen something.

As if JT had read my mind, he asked, "Can you tell us if you heard or saw anything out of the ordinary that night?"

"I told you, we were busy. Maybe we got a little noisy too."

"Got it." Beasley slid JT a sidelong glance. I had a feeling I knew what the two guys were thinking.

"Had Mrs. Sprouse told you she'd noticed anything out of the ordinary recently?" JT asked. "Had she heard or seen anything suspicious, felt uneasy about anyone, noticed someone following her?"

"No." For the first time since the questioning had

started, Kersey's gaze flicked to the table. "Well, there was one thing. But it couldn't be anything important."

"What's that?" JT asked.

"She said this ugly bird kept hanging around outside her window. It gave her the creeps. But a bird couldn't have killed her. That's silly. Oh, now that I think about it, there was something else. She'd said one of her husband's buddies was giving her a hard time."

"Did she say exactly what was going on?" JT asked.

"No. But when she told me, she got really emotional."

"What about a name?" JT asked.

The woman thought about the question for several seconds. Her eyes lifted to her left. "I don't remember. Maybe it was Joe. Or was it Jack?" She shook her head. "Sorry, my memory for names is shit."

"If you remember the name, we'd appreciate a call," JT told her.

"Sure." She turned her attention back to Beasely. "Is that it? Don't you want to ask me about the other stuff? Do I get my deal?"

"We're not through yet." He motioned to JT. "You need anything else?"

"Actually, yes. Does the name 'Terry Pietrzak' mean anything to you?"

Kersey echoed the name. "No. Who's Terry Pietrzak?" Shannon Kersey's lips thinned. "Who is Terry Pietrzak?" she repeated, her voice a tiny bit sharp. She mumbled something under her breath. I think it was along the lines of, "I'm going to castrate the bastard."

Clearly, Shannon Kersey had no idea who Terry Pietrzak was.

"Did Mrs. Sprouse ever mention the name?"

"No."

He pulled a picture of Pietrzak from his bag and slid it toward her.

Kersey's eyes flashed. "Oh. I know her. That's the woman who did my ultrasound before my baby was born. Why?"

"Did Mrs. Sprouse mention having an ultrasound recently?" JT asked.

"Sure. She had one last week. Found out she was carrying a boy. She was so happy. So was her husband. At the time, he didn't know . . . you know."

JT nodded. "Did she talk about anything unusual happening during the procedure?"

"No. Nothing."

"Did she mention talking to the technician, or knowing her?"

"No. All she did was show me the photographs. I couldn't see a damn thing in them. I never can. Not even my own. But she said she could. Never said a word about the person who did it. Nothing good or bad. I can tell you this, that woman did my ultrasound too, and she didn't do or say anything strange or suspicious to me."

"Okay. Thank you." To Beasely, JT said, "I think we're done."

We left the room.

Kersey got to stay.

Evidently, Beasely had plans for her.

I was disappointed, frustrated. We'd flown all this way for that. For a friend's name she couldn't recall and an ugly bird.

JT thanked Beasely and we both shook his hand before leaving.

In the rental car, I snapped on my seat belt. "So much for that. We're no closer to solving this case than we were earlier."

As he started the car, JT flicked his eyes at me. "This one's bugging you."

"Sure. There are babies involved. Infants. Isn't it driving you nuts too?"

JT shifted the car into drive and steered out of the parking spot. "Yes. But I've been at this longer than you. I've learned to keep my emotions under control. At least to a certain extent."

"Maybe I don't want to get to that point."

"Yeah. And maybe sometimes I wish I could feel more. Let's head back to Quantico. I don't think there's any reason for us to stay the night here. Maybe by tomorrow we'll catch another break. We haven't talked to Peyton and the rest of the team yet."

"Let's hope they've done better than we have."

We got back in town in the wee hours of the morning. Even after sleeping during the flight, I had to fight to stay awake during the drive home from the airport. After brushing my teeth and stripping out of my clothes, I fell into bed. My alarm rang five minutes later, or so it seemed. I hit snooze twice before finally summoning up enough energy to get out of bed.

My cell phone rang while I was in the shower.

JT.

"There's been another killing," he said in his message. He left the address and asked me to meet him there. I dosed up on caffeine and ran out of my apartment with a travel mug, my laptop case, and a couple of prewrapped muffins that came out of a box. I munched and slurped on the way. Thanks to the sugar and caffeine, I was feeling pretty much human by the time I'd parked.

JT met me in front of the house. "It's the same as the others. Puncture wound in the groin. Blood drained. But we might have caught a break with this one. The husband woke up and said he saw something weird. McGrane isn't buying his story, since the husband admitted he'd been drinking heavily last night."

"What did he think he saw?" I asked, feeling a little tingle of hope.

"I don't know. I haven't interviewed him yet. I was waiting for you."

"Let's go."

We found the victim's husband, Ben Townsend, sitting in the living room, talking to McGrane. Townsend looked exhausted, mentally and emotionally spent, and overwhelmed. I could only imagine how awful he actually felt.

"Sloan Skye," I said when McGrane introduced us to the husband. "I'm very sorry for your loss."

"It was like something out of a Stephen King movie. I'm telling you," Townsend said, his glance flicking toward the window, "I don't know what the hell it was, but I gotta believe it was what killed my wife."

"Sir, would you mind describing what you saw, from the beginning?" JT asked, pulling out a notebook.

I grabbed my phone and put on the audio recorder.

"It was just after one. I'd had a lot to drink and was feeling like shit, so I got up to go to the bathroom. Since my wife became pregnant, I've been sleeping on the far side of the bed. Natalie gets up a half-dozen times every night. It made sense. Anyway, as I was coming around the end of the bed, I tripped over something. It was . . . long, pale, a tube of some kind. It was coming from the window, stretching across the floor, and disappearing under the bed. I thought about grabbing it. But I had to get to the bathroom in a hurry. You know how it is, right? Anyway, when I went back to bed, I looked for it, but it was gone."

JT and I exchanged looks.

JT wanted to believe the husband's testimony.

So did I. Even though he'd been under the influence of alcohol. This was the first time a husband had possibly been awake and alert around the time of the killing.

"Sir, is there any possibility that you might have been under the influence of a drug that could have caused a hallucination?" I asked. "It's not so much that we care what you were taking than it is that we need to make sure you really saw what you believe you saw."

Townsend's bloodshot eyes widened as he nodded. "It was real. I'm telling you. As real as you and me. I drink too much. I'll admit that. But I don't do drugs. Never have."

"How much would you say you drank last night?" McGrane asked.

"I had twelve beers. And half a pint of vodka"

That was a lot of alcohol.

"How often do you drink?" I asked.

"Well . . . every day," he admitted reluctantly. "But, I swear, what I saw was real."

"Have you ever hallucinated after drinking alcohol?" JT asked.

Townsend sighed. "Yes. But it was years ago. I'd been drinking really heavy back then. More than now. Every day. And I ended up in the hospital after having some problems. They called it"—he visibly searched for the words—"'alcohol-induced psychosis,' I think. Yeah, I'm pretty sure that's what it was. I went through rehab and stopped drinking. Stayed sober for almost five years. I just started drinking again."

"How long ago did you start drinking again?" JT asked.

"I started again when I was laid off work. I mean, who wouldn't? I lost my job. The bills were piling up. That was right after Christmas."

That was over six months ago. If he'd been drinking twelve beers and half a pint a night since then, he had built up a pretty hefty tolerance. It was a known fact that alcohol tolerance could impact the effect of certain drugs, such as painkillers and anesthesia. If the unsub was dosing the husbands to give her time to kill, that could be why he woke up and the others hadn't. Then again, there was also a good chance he was having another bout of alcohol-related psychosis.

But something in the back of my mind told me he might have seen what he thought he saw.

"Would you consider providing a blood sample for testing?" I asked.

His eyes narrowed. "For what?"

"We suspect the killer may have drugged you."

He didn't answer right away. Finally Townsend nodded. "Sure. Okay."

"Thank you. I'd also like to take a look at the room," I said.

"Sure," Townsend said.

JT tapped my shoulder. "I'll get Townsend to an EMT. Then I'm going to see if any neighbors are available for questioning."

"Okay."

McGrane followed me upstairs. Like the other victims, the Townsends lived in a two-story Colonial. The bedroom was at the end of the hall, facing the backyard. I looked at the bed first—Natalie's body had already been moved—then went to the pair of windows on the opposite wall.

"Did Townsend tell you which window the tube was coming from?" I asked McGrane.

"This one." He pointed at the one closest to the front of the bedroom.

It was shut. "Do you know if the window was open last night?"

"I don't know. I can check with the crew. Maybe someone shut it."

"Thanks." I stooped down to inspect the frame and sill closer. "And could you ask Townsend to come back up after he's done with EMS? I have some more questions for him."

"Sure." McGrane left.

I concentrated on inspecting the window. It was vinyl-framed, double-hung. Outside the glass pane was a metal-framed screen for keeping out insects. And beyond that, there was no tree, no structure that an intruder could climb. I pulled some gloves out of my pockets and lifted the window; then I slid the screen up to look directly below. There was an evergreen bush planted under the window. It would be tough but not impossible for someone to get a ladder close enough to reach the window. From my vantage point, I saw no signs of damage to the bush or the grass in front of it. No nicks or scrapes or dents on the siding below the window either.

Maybe I had been wrong about this. I hooked my fingers over the screen frame and pulled down to close it. My left pinky poked through a little gap between the screen and metal frame.

Yes!

"You had some questions for me?" Townsend asked as he stepped through the doorway. He hung back, standing just inside the room.

"What was the diameter of the tube you saw?" I asked, wriggling my finger in the hole.

"Oh, I'd say . . . about the diameter of a pencil. Maybe a little thicker."

I tugged my finger out and looked closely at the metal

mesh. From the looks of it, it had been cut. With just the slightest pressure, the mesh gave way, creating a hole big enough for a tube the diameter of a pencil to fit through.

But if the window had been closed, would it matter? I took a look at the frame again. Was it possible the unsub closed the window from the outside? I pushed the screen halfway up; then I reached out and tried to pull the window down in place. Sure enough, it slid, as far as it could with my arm in the way.

But that still left one very troubling question. How the heck had the unsub gained access to the window?

I snapped a few pictures of the screen, the window, the sill, and the outside siding right under the window; then I turned around.

Townsend was sitting on the bed now, glaring at the vodka bottle in his fist. Tears were dripping from his chin. His face was red. His eyes were red. "I never thought it would cost me so much." He lifted the bottle. "I never thought it would take away the one, the only, person in the world who gives a damn if I live or die. And our child. My son." His hand tightened. His lips thinned.

"Vodka didn't do that." Fearing he might do something crazy, like hurt himself, I gently pulled the bottle out of his hand. "Alcohol didn't take your wife away. Her death isn't its fault. Or yours. This was a horrible tragedy, with only one person to blame. We're going to do our best to catch her. I promise. But will you promise me something in return?"

"What?" he asked, sniffling, lifting bloodshot eyes to mine.

"Promise me you'll go right now and check yourself into rehab. Please."

He didn't answer right away. With gritted teeth, he glared at the bottle in my hand. Finally he said, "Okay. I'll do it."

*You have to take risks. We will only understand the
miracle of life fully when we allow the unexpected to
happen.*

—Paul Coehlo

II

A few hours later, after spending the rest of the day re-
tracing Natalie Townsend's movements yesterday, I
headed over to my parents' place. I found my father
sitting in the living room; his feet were kicked up on
an ottoman. A bowl of chips were on his lap. He
looked like Joe Average sitting there, not like the head
of some supersecret security force for a queen. More
than once, I had wondered if the whole elf queen thing
was all a big, fat lie. If my parents' upcoming wedding
didn't bring the truth out in the open, I supposed my
special project just might.

My father smiled and patted the couch. "Sloan, come
sit with me."

I sat, but not where he wanted. I made myself comfortable on the love seat. He noticed, I'm sure, but he didn't
make a big deal out of it.

"What's this about a television show?" he asked.

"You know Elmer, right? The prince of the *Sluagh*. The
one you promised me to?" I had some very strong feelings about anyone who promised a child as a bride to a
grown man, but that was a topic for another day.

"Sure. I remember. Did you change your mind? Did

you decide to marry him, after all?" he asked, with one hand in the chip bowl.

"Hell no."

That gained a reaction. My father's lips twitched. He didn't smile. "You shouldn't judge a book by its cover." He delivered a handful of chips to his mouth and crunched.

"Easy for you to say. You're marrying Mom. And she might not be a sexy young thing anymore, but she's still very beautiful."

That was the truth. Sometimes I was so focused on what was wrong with her—in particular, her tendency to see things that weren't there . . . and build dangerous contraptions out of scavenged parts . . . and short-circuit entire buildings . . . and wear the most ridiculous outfits imaginable—that I didn't see what most people saw when they looked at her. She was classically beautiful.

Sadly, those beautiful genes didn't get passed down to me. I was nowhere near gorgeous on the looks scale. Being honest with myself, I'd have to say I was sitting smack-dab in the middle. More attractive than some girls. Less attractive than others. I generally described myself as "ordinary."

"That's true. Beverly is beautiful," my father agreed. "But so is Elmer—handsome, not beautiful—if you can look past the surface."

Elmer was much, much, much farther down on the beautiful-people scale, hovering very close to hideous.

"You're really reaching there," I told him.

He shrugged. "Someday you'll see what I mean."

"Anyway," I said, steering the conversation back toward the direction it needed to go, "I'm helping him find a wife."

"Interesting."

"And we've run across a few issues."

"I see."

"So I decided we need to get creative, tackle it in an unconventional manner."

"Is this where the television show comes in to play?"

"Yes. I'd like to do a *Who Wants to Marry a Prince?* program, where women vie for a chance to become his wife."

"Fascinating concept." His tone belied his words. *Doubter.*

"I think it'll work. But I need some help finding a production company to handle the casting and filming. And then I'll need help pitching the series to networks."

"And that's why you called me?" he asked as he crammed another handful of chips into his mouth. The man was either ravenous or just an overgrown child.

"Do you happen to know anyone in television?"

"I do," he said around a mouthful of deep-fried potatoes.

"Do you think you could arrange a meeting with me so I can pitch the concept?"

"Maybe."

"Really?"

He swallowed. "I'll put in a few calls. See what I can do."

"That would be great! Thanks."

"You're welcome." He turned off the television, giving me his full attention. "But I want to make sure you've thought this through. You realize what you're giving up, Sloan?"

Giving up? "Sure. Marriage to a man who doesn't love me."

"Are you certain he's not for you?" he asked, eyes leveled at mine.

"Yes. Positive. I have no doubt. Absolutely none."

"Okay. If that's the case, I'll do my best."

I could almost hug the man. But I didn't. "Thank you."

He nodded, giving me a small smile. "I know you're having a hard time accepting me, trusting me, but I mean it when I say that I only want what's best for you. I've always wanted what's best for you."

I believed he believed that. In some ways, he was probably as delusional as my mother.

"Thank you again for helping me," I said.

Mom's timing was perfect. She came prancing into the room, sporting a hot pink jogging suit with the word "pink" printed across her ass. Her face was the shade of her pants; her hair was gathered into a messy ponytail; she was breathing heavily.

Oh, and she had a lit joint as thick as my father's thumb pinched between her lips.

Exercise, an organic, vegetarian diet . . . and marijuana.

Oxymoron.

"Mom?" I pointed at the joint.

"It's homegrown. One hundred percent natural. Did you come to work on the wedding?" she asked as she bounced up to my father and gave him a little kiss.

"Actually, no."

Mom let me know, under no uncertain terms, that she was unhappy with that response.

Thus, I changed it. "I guess I have a couple of hours."

She beamed. "I'll go change my clothes. We can go dress shopping. You can try on dresses too."

Nifty. "Okay."

Mom scampered off to find something more presentable to wear, leaving me with my father. Thankfully, he'd turned the television back on when Mom and I had been talking. He was watching a baseball game. Not my cuppa. But that was okay. If he was involved in the game, we wouldn't have to talk.

He cut off the TV again. Turned his attention back to

me. "Listen, Sloan, while I've got you here, I want to talk to you about your mother."

"Sure."

"I'd like to buy her a wedding gift, but I don't know what to get her. Can you give me some suggestions?"

"Oh. Um. I don't know." If someone had asked me that question a few weeks ago, I would've had some ideas. But recently my mother had changed. She seemed to have become so much more materialistic. Take this freaking house, for instance, with its overpriced furniture, enormous rooms, and ridiculous square footage.

My father scowled. "I was hoping you'd have some ideas."

I shrugged. "Her whole life has changed in a short time. She went from having so little to this." I swept my arm, like Vanna White, in a wide arc. "What more could she need?"

"I see your point. But I still want to give her something special, something meaningful."

"Sorry I'm not being much help. But if something comes up today while we're shopping, I'll let you know."

"Good enough. Thank you."

"You're welcome."

"Sloan, I'm ready," Mom said, prancing into the room, wearing a very nice dress and sandals. Sporting a pair of jean shorts and a T-shirt, I was feeling underdressed.

"You look great," I told her. "Maybe I should go home and change first."

Mom tossed a dismissive hand. "You look fine. Let's go." She looped her arm with mine and together we went out to my car. She inhaled. "Do you smell that?"

"What?"

"The air smells so good today."

I wasn't smelling anything out of the ordinary. "Yes, it does," I said, deciding it was easier just to agree.

As we took our seats in my car, Mom said, "So what do you think of the house? I've never had access to an unlimited budget before. It's been so much fun shopping."

"I bet." I started the car and drove down the long, private driveway.

"I heard what your father asked you, by the way. Isn't he sweet?"

"He is," I said.

"I have the perfect gift in mind." She batted her eyelashes.

Another pool boy, perhaps? "So you want to tell me so I can give him a little hint?" I asked as I turned onto Maple Street, heading toward the freeway.

"No. That would be too easy. I want him to figure it out on his own."

That left me out of the equation. I liked that. A lot. "But what if he gets it wrong?"

She shrugged. "There won't be a wedding."

"Seriously?"

"Yes. If he can't figure out what I want, above everything else, then we shouldn't be married."

"Are you going to tell him this?"

"No." She smiled. "I can't wait to try on dresses. What do you think? Should I go with something traditional? Classic? Or should I go with something more modern? Of course, it must be white."

Nothing like an abrupt change of subject . . . and mood.

"Of course," I said.

"For the bridesmaids, I was thinking of orange dresses."

"Orange?" That was probably the worst color she could have picked. Naturally, I'd be smiling at my parents' wedding—if there was one—because it would be what they wanted. But . . . orange? Could she be so cruel?

We stopped at a light.

Mom poked the radio on and started station surfing. "You know it's my favorite color," she said over Alicia Keys. "Orange and white were my colors the first time we were married."

"That was a long time ago, Mom. Maybe you'd like to do something different this time."

She crinkled her nose. I wasn't sure if it was because of the music or my suggestion. "Why would I do that? We were happy back then. In love. Insanely happy." She hit the button, moving to the next station. The car filled with the nerve-grating sound of screaming guitars.

I sighed. "Well . . . I guess I can find a way to make orange work."

Mom smacked my shoulder, busting into a riotous guffaw. "I was just kidding. I have something else in mind. You'll love it." Then she started headbanging like a teenage boy at an Ozzy concert.

"I can hardly wait."

"Are you kidding? Please tell me this is another joke."

I've known for years that my mother's brain was wired differently from most other people's brains. After all, she is a walking, talking bundle of oxymorons and contradictions. Before I could speak a word, she was reading Kipling, Frost, and Poe to me, with a halo of pot smoke circling her head. She's a flower child. She's a wannabe inventor. She's delusional.

And she's clinically insane.

And I am not.

Which was why there was no way she was going to convince me to wear that awful . . . thing. Calling it a dress was stretching the truth too far.

"Please," Mom said, giving me one of her trademark

sad-eyed looks. "Try it on. That's all I ask. That you try it on."

I glanced at the tag. The price had to be wrong. There were far too many zeros in that number. "It's the wrong size."

"They run small. I had her pull the size according to your measurements."

"You don't know my measurements."

"Thirty-four, twenty-seven, thirty-six."

I gaped. Even though she had my hip measurement off by a couple of inches, that was scary-close. Then again, she'd borrowed my clothes plenty of times. My measurements weren't much different than hers.

She tipped up her chin in triumph. "I'm your mother. Of course I know your measurements." With a shooing gesture, she sent me toward the fitting room. "Hustle now. I can't wait to see you in that gown. It's going to be spectacular."

"Spectacularly horrific," I mumbled as I shuffled into a fitting room. A knock on the door interrupted my undressing. "Yes?" I called through the paper-thin wall.

"I've come to help you dress," a strange voice responded.

I stopped what I was doing, clutched the shirt I'd just shucked to my chest. "You have the wrong room."

"No, I work for Mizelle Designs. It's required we assist the customer anytime one of our gowns is tried on."

Lovely. I glanced at the strapless piece of crap I was supposed to be trying on and started putting my top back on. This just wasn't worth it. "I'll be out in a moment."

"Please allow me to help—"

"I'm not trying it on. No need for panic."

Silence.

I straightened up my hair and clothes and was about

to head back out to the lobby when there was another knock.

"Sloan? You promised to try the dress." It was Mom.

"Mom, I'm not trying it on today. I'm . . . not wearing the right kind of underwear."

"Sloan." Mom's sigh was audible.

I didn't let the disappointment I heard in her voice change my mind. I stepped out of the dressing room and handed the salesclerk standing behind her the dress. "I'll come back another time."

"This woman is a professional," Mom said.

"I'm sure she is. Like I said, I'm not wearing the right underwear. Now let's see what we can find for you." I headed toward the bridal gown section, intentionally blocking out my mother's guilt trip.

I grabbed the first gown I found in her size and shoved it into her hands. "Try this."

She looked at it. Frowned. Extended an arm. "This is far too . . . glittery. Look at it. I think it came out of Elvis's closet."

"And I think the dress you wanted me to try came out of Liberace's."

Mom looked at me. Blinked. Then laughed hard until she was crying. Once she had herself composed, she lifted her tear-filled eyes to me and said, "You're right. That dress was hideous."

"Why'd you insist I try it on?"

"Because it's a Mizelle. Anyone would be impressed with a Mizelle. Even the queen of the elves."

"Don't you worry about the queen of the elves. We'll impress her pants off. You'll see."

Six hours, and over a hundred dresses later, Mom still hadn't found *the* dress. My stomach was digesting itself.

My blood sugar was so low, I didn't dare move quickly, for fear of passing out, and Mom was nearly in tears . . . again.

"I can't believe I haven't found a dress here," Mom blubbered. "This is *the place to come* for a wedding gown. Everyone knows that."

"Maybe their inventory is low. We'll just have to come back another time." I gently coaxed my mother back to the fitting room to remove the last gown. It was a gaudy confection of tulle and lace that was so sugary sweet that it threatened to put my mother into a sugar coma. "Hurry up and change. I'll buy you some dinner."

Ten minutes later, Mom still hadn't come out of the fitting room. I didn't see the dressing-room attendant who'd been helping her, so I assumed she was in the room with my mother.

I knocked. "Mom?"

"Yes, Sloan."

"What are you doing?"

"I'm . . . stuck."

"Stuck?" I knocked.

The door swung open, and my fully dressed mother came ambling out of the room. The red-faced salesclerk followed her, making a beeline for the office.

"Whew! It's so good to be out of that claustrophobic closet."

"Why haven't you changed out of the dress yet?"

Mom tugged. Mom wriggled. Mom scowled. "We tried. We can't get it off without tearing it."

"If you got it on, you can take it off," I reasoned. "Taking it off should be the easy part."

"So you'd think. I guess I've swelled a little. It was a snug fit, going on."

I slumped onto a bench. "Great."

"You think it's bad for you," Mom said, doing a movement that looked a lot like a pee-pee dance. "I need to use the bathroom, and Gwen, the salesgirl, says I can't, since the dress costs eighty thousand dollars."

Gwen returned, with arms crossed over her chest. "I'm sorry. My manager said you can't wear that gown into the restroom."

"Well, if she peed, she might un-swell a little," I reasoned.

"I said the same thing." Mom gave the salesclerk a glare.

Gwen shook her head. "I'm sorry, but I can't let you go into the bathroom in the gown. It's against company policy."

Mom's face turned an interesting shade of pinkish white. "If I can't go to the bathroom in the next sixty seconds, it's pretty much a guarantee that the gown will be ruined. As will be the carpet."

Gwen's eyes widened. "I'll be right back."

"You'd better make it quick," Mom warned. The minute Gwen left, my mother chuckled. "She bought it. Now help me out of this thing."

"What?"

"She was doing it all wrong. Come on." Mom dragged me back into the room.

I shut the door behind me and went to work unzipping the gown. It stopped at around the middle of Mom's hips. "I'm thinking this mermaid look isn't for you."

"Believe me, I'm with you."

I tugged while pinching the fabric together. Finally the zipper gave. I put up a little whoo-hoo of victory.

"The battle's only half won." Mom wriggled while I cautiously pulled, trying to work the beaded fabric over her hips.

It wasn't budging. And a couple of seams along the sides were pulling.

"Mom, how the heck did you get into this thing?"

"I swear, it wasn't this tight when we put it on." She swiveled her hips. "Is that helping?"

I dug my fingertips into the fabric to try to get a grasp. "Not really. It's so tight! I can't get a good grip." I tipped my head to say something, but whatever I'd been about to say completely flew from my mind. "Mom, your face is swollen."

"It is?" Mom smacked both hands over her cheeks.

"Yes, it's puffy. It wasn't like that a minute ago."

"Oh, no. It must be an allergic reaction."

"To what? The dress?"

"I don't know." She twisted. A loud *riiiip* made her jerk. I jumped too. "What w-was that?" she stuttered.

I knew what it was. That was the sound of eighty thousand dollars going out the window.

A frantic knock cut me off before I had a chance to answer.

"Excuse me!" a harried-sounding woman shouted through the door. "I need to come in and assist."

I opened the door and stepped out. "Do you have any scissors?"

The woman's face turned the shade of the gown. "I think I . . ." She hit the floor hard.

Ten minutes later, we were in my car, speeding toward St. John's Hospital. The store manager had refused to let me call 911. I would've left her, but then she fainted again. I grabbed my phone and started dialing, but she came to and smacked the phone out of my hand. It slid across the floor and became lost under a rack full of gowns. So I did what any well-meaning girl would do, I dragged her stubborn butt out to my car and threw her in the backseat.

In return, she vomited.

"Sloan, you missed the turn," Mom said as we were speeding through an intersection on an orange light. My mother was looking a little like the Pillsbury Doughboy in drag.

"I'm sure it's this way, Mom."

"No, I'm certain it isn't."

"Ohhhh . . . ," the store manager moaned. She was sort of lying across the backseat now.

Mom glanced over her shoulder. "She isn't looking good. I think she may throw up again."

My car would never be the same. "Please make sure the bag is under her mouth."

"I'm trying." Mom's ass was in the air as she knelt on the passenger-side front seat and reached to the back.

"We should have used the store's phone to call an ambulance," I grumbled.

"They take too long," Mom said. "She'll be at the hospital much faster—assuming you can find it."

I mumbled something Mom wouldn't have appreciated hearing.

Our passenger threw up.

"Uh-oh," Mom said.

I knew what that meant.

I muttered something else she wouldn't have appreciated hearing as I turned into the hospital's driveway. I parked in front of the emergency entrance, and a guard approached Mom's window.

She opened it.

The guard peered inside.

"I have two patients for you. This one," I said, pointing at Mom, "is having an allergic reaction to something, and that one," I said, pointing at the backseat, "passed out and has vomited twice in the last half hour."

"I'll get some wheelchairs." The guard grabbed an

empty chair from the breezeway between two sets of sliding glass doors; then he hurried back to the car to help our backseat passenger out first.

A second guard, pushing another wheelchair, jogged out of the building for Mom. I parked, took a quick peek at my backseat, swallowed a sob, then called Dad to let him know what had happened.

No answer.

Next, I tried Katie. She answered.

"I'm at the hospital," I told her.

"I'll be there in an hour."

"No need. Mom's probably just getting a shot of Benadryl."

"Ah, okay. What happened?"

"She's allergic to wedding dresses that cost over fifty thousand dollars, I think."

Katie chuckled. "I think I would be too."

"I guess I'd better get in there. I'll talk to you later."

"Sure. You will tell me all about your dress-shopping experience when you get home, right?"

"You got it."

I ended the call, tried my father's cell phone one last time, left a message when it clicked to voice mail, dropped my phone in my purse, and headed inside. After checking in at the desk, I made myself comfortable in the waiting room and flipped through a magazine.

And another.

And another.

And another.

An hour later, I checked at the front desk again. After making a call, the lady informed me my mother was waiting for release instructions and the other patient was in radiology, getting a CAT scan of her head.

I went back to my seat and waited.

And waited.

Another half hour passed. Still no Mom.

Forty-five minutes after that, I headed up to the desk for another status check. I was getting concerned. It's not uncommon for my mother to have issues in the hospital. Last week, she started having hallucinations in the middle of the emergency room and ended up being admitted to the psych floor for a couple of days.

The woman reassured me that everything was okay. I went back to my seat, hoping for the best but expecting another long stretch of waiting.

Have I said how much I hate hospitals?

The doors slid open with a *whoosh* for the millionth time since I'd sat down. Once again, my gaze shot to the entry. This time, I saw someone familiar.

My father's long, hurried strides carried him to the desk long before I could get his attention. While he inquired into Mom's status, I rushed to his side and patted his shoulder.

"They said over an hour ago that she was being released."

He looked at me with concern-filled eyes and nodded.

"As I said, it was just an allergic reaction, nothing too bad. Only a little swelling."

"There's something you don't know, Sloan." He cupped my elbow in his hand and pulled me aside. "We were waiting to tell you. . . ."

A million possibilities flashed through my mind.

"Your mother's pregnant."

That hadn't been one of them.

"What?"

"We've suspected it for a few days, but we found out for sure yesterday," he said.

"What?" Pregnant? My mother? How?

"Sloan, are you okay?"

I staggered. Thankfully, the big, sturdy wall was behind me. It was holding me up. "Pregnant?"

"It wasn't something we planned, but now that we know, we're pretty happy about it."

"Sure." I did some math. My mother was forty-six years old. Not too old to have a child, granted, but certainly older than the average expectant mother. I did some more math. Dad hadn't been around for long. The odds of Mom getting pregnant were statistically low because of her age. Add in the fact that they'd been together for only a little more than a week, and the odds fell to the nearly impossible range. Talk about fertile. Or really damn lucky. "Happy."

"She had some problems with her allergies when she was pregnant with you too. I remember once she had a craving for strawberry shortcake. I bought her some. She ate it. And ten minutes later, she was covered from head to toe with hives."

"I had hives between my toes," my mother said. A man in a uniform was pushing her in a wheelchair. She was scowling, but otherwise looking much better. Definitely less swollen. She gave my father a great big grin, accompanied with a girly bat of the lashes. "Hello, dear." She lifted her head and puckered for a kiss, which my father dutifully supplied. "I'm assuming the cat's out of the bag?"

"It is."

Mom beamed and placed a hand on her flat stomach. "I'm okay to walk. Thank you, anyway." She pushed out of the wheelchair, sending the man behind it off with a wave. "Isn't it the most wonderful news?"

Did I really have to answer that question? "Um. Sure. Wonderful."

Of course, Mom caught on to my less-than-enthusiastic

response. "You're not happy to hear you'll have a baby brother or sister?"

"Sure, I am."

Mom wasn't buying it, but she let the subject drop with a little "hmpfh." That was followed by, "With our big news, I'm sure you realize we're going to have to bump up the wedding date."

"Of course."

"I don't want to be a fat bride."

"Who does?"

"So we're thinking we need to be married next month."

"Next month? Sure. No problem."

"I knew you'd understand."

Mom turned her attention back to my father. "I'm ready to go home. But can we make a stop first? I'm starving."

"Of course, dear, anything you want." Dad offered Mom a hand.

Mom tossed a childlike grin over her shoulder at me before taking my father's hand and practically skipping out of the hospital.

More than a little shocked, about the pregnancy, the bumped-up wedding date, the gushy, mushy "Yes, dear, anything you say, dear" display I'd just witnessed, I headed out to my car, wondering if Mars or Mercury was in retrograde. Something was up, the planets out of whack. They had to be.

Things are not always what they seem; the first appearance deceives many; the intelligence of a few perceives what has been carefully hidden. . . .

—Phaedrus

12

The next morning, JT loaded our computers and go bags into his car and headed out. My car was being left in the lot. With the windows open. Even though it had rained all night. And we were expecting more rain today.

Although I'd made my best attempt at cleaning up the mess in the backseat before I left this morning, the rancid odor hadn't cleared. I wondered if it might take at least a month. Maybe two.

After holding a quick powwow with the chief, we'd decided we needed to return to the first three crime scenes to inspect every bedroom window. Before leaving the PBAU, we called and scheduled appointments with each husband. The first one was in forty-five minutes, which left us plenty of time for a quick pit stop. I convinced JT we needed to stop at my fave bagel shop on the way out.

Recently, JT was clobbered over the head at this place. As far as I could tell, he hadn't so much as driven past the place since. He looked a little uneasy when we pulled into the parking lot.

"Nobody's going to knock you over the head and

toss you in the Dumpster," I reassured him. "No need to worry."

He cut off the engine and fisted the keys. His eyes flicked to the side of the building. "I know. It's just . . . bad memories, you know?"

"Sure. Would you rather stay in the car?" I opened my door and swung a leg out. I stepped smack-dab in a deep puddle left over from this morning's downpour. Just my luck.

"No, I'll go in with you." He patted his belly. "I could use a little something to eat too."

My shoes squeaked as we walked inside. I ordered the usual. He ordered a bagel breakfast sandwich, a donut, and a milk.

A *little* something?

When we hauled our take outside, we were stopped short by the sight of JT's car in flames.

JT's face went white. "That's it. I'm never coming back to this goddamn place again." He shoved his bag and milk into my hands and pulled out his phone. Dialing 911, he gave me a look, as if I'd known his car would burst into flames just because we stopped for bagels.

"I'm sure it's just a coincidence," I mumbled as my mother's voice echoed in my head. *"There's no such thing as coincidence."*

Figuring JT would be held up for a while, I called the chief to see what she wanted us to do. She told me she'd send Gabe over to pick us up as soon as possible; then she cut off the call.

JT said absolutely nothing while we waited for the fire department to put out the fire. He fumed. He gritted his teeth. He even did a little stomping. But he said absolutely nothing to me. I sat inside by myself and ate my bagel. Then I ate his donut. I couldn't help myself.

And, because milk only lasted so long before it spoiled, I drank that too.

As I was strolling outside a half hour or so later, I heard JT asking one of the firemen if they could tell where the fire had started.

"Under the hood. Definitely," the fireman said. The hood was open. They'd popped it to hose down all the hot parts. Everything was hissing and smoldering. And the unpleasant odor of burned rubber and plastic hung heavy in the air. The fireman pointed at a charred bit. "I've seen this before. We just had a heavy rain. Sometimes the wires get wet, causing a short. Computers overheat. . . ."

JT's expression went blank. "Well, hell."

"See, JT? It wasn't arson. Just an electrical short." I tried to give JT what remained of his food. He waved it away.

"I'm going to be tied up here for a while. You might as well go with Wagner. I'm sure the two of you can handle the interviews on your own."

"Of course we can. Fischer will probably be with him, anyway."

"Yeah, probably."

"Just look at it this way," I told him. "It's better that we weren't in the car when it caught fire."

Wagner rolled into the parking lot just as JT was sending me a not-very-friendly look.

I took my mostly empty coffee and JT's mostly full bag and climbed into Gabe's car.

"What the hell happened?" Gabe asked, gaping at what was left of JT's car.

"Electrical short caused by the rain."

"Well, that sucks."

"Yeah. JT lost his car and his go bag. My computer's crispy and my clothes are ash. Of course, my go bag was in the backseat. If we have to take off anywhere, I'm in trouble."

Gabe shifted his car into gear, and off we zoomed. "Eh, I don't see that happening."

"Sure, but wouldn't it be my luck that something comes up in say . . . California, and we have to fly out in thirty?"

"Not going to happen."

"Let's hope so. At least I'd taken my handbag into the coffee shop, or I'd have lost my license, my ID, my credit cards, everything."

"Yeah, good thing. Now," Gabe said, stomping on the brakes at the end of the driveway, "where are we headed first?"

"The Sprouses' house first." As we turned onto the street, I stared at the charred skeleton of JT's car. "Rain. Causing all that. Who would've thought?"

A couple of hours later, I had learned something useful. There were small holes in at least one screen in every bedroom window of our victims'. In one case, Sprouse's, the damage wasn't isolated to just one bedroom. I wondered if it was because she hadn't always slept with her husband in their bed. I was able to take out the whole frame in a couple of the houses, with permission, of course. Now we were on our way back to the PBAU with our loot in tow, hoping a look under the microscope might give us something.

Just as we pulled through the Quantico security checkpoint—our unit was located in the FBI's academy in Quantico, Virginia—my cell rang. The caller was JT.

"Hey," I said as I scrambled out of Gabe's car.

"Where are you?" he asked, sounding a smidge snappy, not that I could blame him.

"We're on base." I grabbed the metal frames from the backseat. "I have a couple of things for the lab."

"Good. We're flying to Cleveland in twenty."

"Seriously?" My gaze slid to Gabe, who was standing next to me.

"Yes. There's been a murder up there. Last night. Same MO."

Gabe mouthed, "What?"

"Are they thinking it's the same killer?" I asked JT.

"Maybe."

"Ohio? Do we know where Pietrzak was last night?"

"I've already put in a call to McGrane."

To Gabe, I said, "I'm flying to Cleveland." To JT, "Where are you?"

"Heading to the airstrip. Just meet me there."

"Okay." I ended the call, and then I gave Gabe a rundown. I wrapped it all up with a heavy sigh. "Just my luck. Called out of town, and I have no time to run home for essentials."

We got back in his car. Turning toward the airstrip, he gave me a grin. "I'd loan you my bag, but I doubt you'd accept."

"You know me so well. Thanks, anyway. But I wouldn't mind borrowing your laptop, if you don't mind lending it to me."

"Not a problem."

"Thank you." When he pulled up to the parking area, I said, "Call me if you get anything on the screens."

"Will do."

I opened the door, got roughly halfway out, when he grabbed my wrist.

"Sloan, you're doing a damn good job on this case."

"I'm trying. I hate this fucking case. Pregnant women. Missing babies."

"We'll get her."

"We have to."

Gabe nodded.

I walked down the drive toward the waiting plane.

JT was inside already, laptop open. His computer hadn't been in his car, like mine was. At least in that respect, he'd been lucky. He gave me a weary smile as I made my way to a seat.

"Sorry about your car," I said as I buckled myself in. The pilots still had their preflight routine to get through, so we wouldn't be leaving for a little while yet. But I still felt better buckled in.

"No reason to apologize," he said, sounding as tired and wilted as his smile had looked. "It was insured. I'll have a replacement in a few days."

"That's good."

"Yeah, it's just a temporary inconvenience."

"Still, I've been there. It's not a minor inconvenience."

"I'm working with my insurance agent on getting a rental until I get my new car."

"In that case, you'll probably be on the road again by the time we get back from Cleveland."

"That's what I'm hoping."

"So . . ." I studied his face, his body language. "If you don't mind my asking, why do you look so defeated?"

"It has nothing to do with the car. It's . . . personal."

"Ah. Okay." I didn't push. After all, I was trying to keep JT at arm's length. Prodding into his personal business wasn't the way to accomplish that.

I poked around on the Web with Gabe's laptop while the pilot went through his safety check. I Googled the phrases "missing infant" and "suspicious death of pregnant woman." Headlines popped up, most of them familiar. Another in Cleveland, published in this morning's *Cleveland Daily* newspaper. And one more from several years ago in Michigan.

"JT, you know how we're thinking this perp's been at this a while?"

"Yeah." He lifted his gaze to me.

"I think I found something. An old case. In Michigan."

"Looks like this trip might be longer than we thought."

Cleveland, Ohio, as I had already come to find out, was not the cultural or industrial Mecca I had envisioned. It was . . . tired, for lack of a better word. Neglected. Having probably been at its best back when manufacturing was the biggest segment of the United States' economy, it was now struggling to find its new identity in the twenty-first century. That's not to say it didn't have its charm. There were a handful of museums in the waterfront area, including the Rock and Roll Hall of Fame and the Cleveland Museum of Art. But for the most part, the city looked sad and forgotten.

Particularly Strathmore Avenue, with its poorly maintained early-twentieth-century homes parked on narrow, weedy lots. The house was a blue-sided Colonial, with a tiny garage huddled behind it. Stepping inside, I had the feeling of looking at the photograph of a woman who'd once been a rare beauty. Hints of her former glory remained, such as the beautiful staircase banister and handrail. But the years of neglect and disrepair had taken its toll.

At the door, we met Detective Fultz. As was standard, introductions followed. Standing at the foot of the staircase, Fultz gave us a brief rundown of what his people had found so far—or rather, what they hadn't. Then he welcomed us to take a look, now that the crime scene techs had finished up.

"We appreciate the chance to take a look around," JT said, testing the railing.

"No problem. I could use all the help I can get on this one. Our guys have gone over the scene with a microscope and they've found nothing. No fibers. No prints."

"Just like our cases," I whispered. I asked Fultz, "To verify, the victim, Renee Bibens, was pregnant, correct?"

"Yes, she was."

"The baby?" I asked, already knowing in my gut what I was about to hear.

"There's no heartbeat," Fultz said. "We'll know more after the autopsy."

JT and I exchanged a look, then headed up to the bedroom.

"Are we dealing with the same unsub here?" My gaze swept around the room. The bed sat centered against one cracked plaster wall. The sloping maple floor was littered with clutter, books, magazines, clothes. Opposite the bed was an old fireplace with what had probably once been a gorgeous marble surround and mantel. The surround was now stained. The mantel hidden under a coat of ugly blue paint. Not wasting time, I went straight to the window, on the far wall. There was only one window in the room, and it felt like it was nailed shut. Dozens of layers of paint was inhibiting the sashes from moving easily. I wondered how long it had been since the owners opened it.

"I don't know," JT said.

"It's so distant from the others," I pointed out.

"If everything else matches, I say we assume it's the same killer. At least for now."

"Okay." I curled my fingers around the handle and pulled. I strained. I silently cursed. Then I gave up. "I don't think the unsub got in this way," I told JT, who was inspecting the bedding.

"Hmm," he said. It was a weighted "hmm."

"Did you find something?" I abandoned my battle with the window, assuming it hadn't been open last night.

"Hmm," he said again. Then he shook his head. "No. Nothing."

"Why the 'hmm' then?"

"Because I was thinking."

"About . . . ?"

"When we get back home, I want to dig into your father's research again. We need to figure out what we're dealing with."

"'*What* we're dealing with,'" I parroted. "Then you're convinced the unsub isn't human?"

He shrugged. "Call it a hunch."

I had to admit, his hunch made sense. While I couldn't deny human beings could do some strange and terrible things—read a few history books and nobody could argue that point—this felt off. The pieces weren't fitting. Some were missing entirely.

Like motivation. Why drain the blood?

Like method. How was the unsub getting access to her victims, and exactly how was she killing them?

Turning a slow three-sixty, I scanned the room, searching for an access from outside.

My gaze settled on the fireplace.

Expecting an arm covered in soot as a reward, I put my hand up the chimney to check the damper.

Sure enough, it was open.

"I think we have our access point." As I withdrew my hand, something black fluttered down, landing softly on the empty log grate. A feather.

Risking a face full of ash, I decided to poke my head in and look up. The full length of the chimney was clear, no obstructions. But it sure was narrow.

I said, "If a human being were standing on the roof,

threading a tube down the chimney to drain the victim's blood, he or she would need someone in here to get it to the victim. There's no other way."

"Which is exactly why I'm thinking it can't be a human." JT came to stand next to me. As I withdrew my head from the filthy fireplace, he bent down, moving way too close to me for comfort. He picked up the feather and said, "Hmm."

"Another 'hmm'?"

"Birds can fly down chimneys." Holding the feather pinched between his finger and thumb, he smiled as he straightened up.

"And birds can sit on skinny tree limbs two stories up." I stood, dusting off my knees. "Then again, so can bats. And insects. That long tube Townsend saw could be a proboscis. Brings to mind an insect's mouth part. If you're going to go *there*—meaning, paranormal— we need to look at all the possibilities. Insects. Birds. And bats."

"Good point." He ran the feather between his fingers; then he lowered his hand, as if to let it fall. He didn't re- lease it, though. Instead, he handed it to me.

Accepting the feather, I said, "When we get back, I'll send this to the lab and see what I can find in my father's stuff."

"I think we're finally getting somewhere. Let's do a quick interview of the husband, Chad Bibens, then head to Michigan."

A little less than an hour later, we were back on the plane, waiting for the pilot to complete his inspection for the second time today. We'd already received a call from the ME. The Bibenses' infant was missing, like the others.

Although neither of us had said it, we were both assuming it was the same unsub. We still had no information on the whereabouts of our one and only suspect, Terry Pietrzak. But it was hard to imagine she would have traveled so far to kill Renee Bibens.

At the moment, JT was squinting at his laptop screen. I was pretty much doing the same thing with Gabe's computer. Though, by now, I wasn't so focused. The results of my search had proven to be far from satisfactory. According to the many Web sites I'd perused already, many varieties of vampires were known to shift into some form of animal, bird, or insect.

Knowing I would have to shut down the computer soon, I powered it down and closed my eyes. It had been a long day, and it still wasn't over. The flight to Michigan was short. We'd find a hotel for the night, catch a few hours of sleep, and then head over to the Canton Township Police Department in the morning.

The chime signaled that the pilot was ready to take off. I tightened my seat belt and put the seat back up. With my eyes shut, I listened to JT ready himself for takeoff.

"Sloan, are you sleeping?"

"No." I rocked my head to the side to look at him.

He had a book in his lap and was looking at me strangely, as if he was struggling with something. "Things have been strained between us lately."

"Not really."

"You don't think so?"

"No."

Silence.

The plane started backing away from the airport terminal.

"Are you upset about something?" JT asked.

"Upset? Should I be upset? You sound guilty."

"No, of course not. I just noticed you've been acting differently."

He was sounding a little like a girl. I found it charming. "I guess I've been a little stressed-out."

"About what?"

"About everything. The case. My parents—Mom's pregnant. They're getting remarried. Oh, and did I mention they want to have this huge wedding? And they're inviting a queen. Plus, I'm playing matchmaker for a certain prince who is hell-bent on getting married tomorrow. And if I don't find him a wife soon, he's going to force me to marry him."

"He can't do that," JT snapped, sounding far angrier than he should. "If that little bastard tries anything again—"

"Don't worry. He won't kidnap me again. No need for threats." I tried not to think about how sweet and protective JT was acting right now. One look at him and I could tell he wouldn't hesitate to act upon any threat he made.

"Oh, they aren't threats," he said. "They're promises."

"I know." Conscious of how vulnerable I was feeling, I shifted in my seat. "And I appreciate your concern, but I've got things under control. Well, I do with Elmer. My mother, on the other hand, is another story."

"Anything I can do to help?"

"Don't I wish. Unless you happen to know a wedding planner who's available." At his head shake, I sighed. "What about any contacts with someone at Maryvale Castle? My mother has her heart set on getting married there, but I'm having a hard time getting it booked."

"Sorry, can't help you there either. But if that falls through, I might be able to help you line up something else. My father's a member of a country club. It's a pretty decent place. I think they do weddings there."

"Thanks, I'll keep it in mind."

"Welcome."

We stared at each other for a moment. My heart did some little flutters. That was not good.

I faked a yawn. Yeah, I know, pathetic. "Wow, am I exhausted. As soon as we get to our hotel, I'm going to bed."

JT grinned.

I scowled. "Don't say it."

"Okay, I won't."

I closed my eyes.

He sighed. "Want some company?" he asked.

I slanted some squinty eyes at him. "You said you wouldn't say it."

"I couldn't help myself. I'm weak." His grin was 100 percent evil. And 100 percent adorable.

"That you are." I smiled to soften the blow of the insult and turned my head so he wouldn't see my cheeks burn.

How I despised the effect his smile had on me!

Keep looking below surface appearances. Don't shrink from doing so just because you might not like what you find.

—Colin Powell

13

I am on a beach, the sun blazing, a fragrant sea breeze tossing my artificially enhanced shoulder-length hair.

I'm lounging in a comfy chaise; JT is sitting in an identical lounge on my right.

Gabe comes strolling up, shirtless, droplets of seawater sparkling in the sunshine.

Life is so good.

"We're here," Gabe says in a soft voice. "Time to wake up."

I have no idea what he means by that. I am awake.

Or am I?

"Sloan, wake up."

It was JT's voice I was hearing now.

And someone was shaking me.

The sea was gone. The image of shirtless Gabe too.

I opened my eyes. "Damn."

"Sorry, but we have to get off the plane."

JT looked apologetic enough. If he'd known what kind of dream I'd been enjoying, he might have been even more apologetic. Then again, maybe not.

"Come on. Let's get to the room. We don't have far to go. The hotel's attached to the airport."

Pushing myself out of my seat, I coughed to clear my throat. "Wow, I was out." I grabbed Gabe's laptop case and checked around my seat, to make sure I hadn't forgotten anything.

"We've had a long day." JT led me out of the plane, down the stairs, and across the concrete tarmac to the airport's entry. It was cool outside for June. If not for the bright lights illuminating the runways, it would be dark outside too.

"What time is it?"

"A little after eleven."

We stepped inside. Having entered at a mostly empty wing of the airport meant we had a *loooong* walk to the hotel, which was located at the opposite end of the sprawling building. What felt like an hour later, the doors to the Westin *whooshed* open, welcoming us inside. We checked in—the bureau was paying for separate, though attached, rooms. I asked the clerk if they offered the basic essentials to guests and was rewarded with a little plastic bag containing a toothbrush, toothpaste, razor, and plastic comb. Up we went to our rooms. JT opened his door; I opened mine. We wished each other good night and didn't move.

I wanted him to kiss me. I was pretty sure he wanted to kiss me too. But, at the same time, I didn't want him to.

As if reading my mind, he ambled over to me and held my door open as I stepped inside.

It swung shut.

We were alone.

In a dark room.

The lights were out. He smelled so good.

"Sloan, I'm sorry, but . . ." His hands found my waist.

He firmly pulled me flush to him, cupped my cheek with one of his hands, and then he kissed me.

Stars exploded behind my closed eyelids. Heat crashed through my body. Huge bursts of electricity buzzed up and down my nerves. It was a kiss to remember. A kiss to savor. A kiss that should never end.

But then it did, and the synapses in my brain started working.

What the hell am I doing?

His hand still flattened against my cheek, he looked into my eyes. "Sloan, I've needed to do that since our date." His eyes flicked down to the general region of my breasts. The pad of his thumb caressed my lower lip.

A few bits of my anatomy decided they liked where this was going. I gulped a lungful of air.

"JT, still, we shouldn't."

"We're in a hotel. Alone. Who's going to find out?"

"Nobody. But that's not the point."

"What is the point, then?" He pulled me closer. A very prominent bulge, hard and long, was poking at my stomach. My breasts, which were a little on the sensitive side, were squashed against him. "I want you. You want me. We're adults. We're single. We can—"

"I can't." With great effort, I pushed against him while taking a step backward to put some distance between my flaming body and his. "I just . . . can't. And what about Hough?"

"We're friends. Only friends."

I wanted to believe him; really, I did. But something was standing in my way. Fear, maybe? His teeth sank into his lower lip, the one that had just been brushing over mine such a short time ago. He'd tasted so good, like mint and man and need. How I longed to taste him again.

You'll regret it.

"You're sure you can't?" he asked.

"Yes."

"If you change your mind . . ."

"I won't."

"I'll be next door. Just knock."

"Good night, JT."

After giving me one lingering look, he left.

I brushed my teeth, stripped out of everything but my undies, and dropped into the bed. What felt like five minutes later, someone was knocking on a door. I poked my head out from under the covers and followed the sound with my eyes. No, it wasn't coming from the door opening to the hallway; it was coming from the door leading to JT's room. No doubt he was going to try convincing me to change my mind about sleeping with him. I checked the clock.

Eight o'clock? In the morning? Could that be right?

"Sloan, are you awake yet? We need to get rolling."

"Hang on!" I shouted as I rolled out of bed and scampered to the bathroom. "I'll be there in a few."

"Meet me at the breakfast buffet," he shouted through the hollow door.

"Will do." I hurried through my morning routine. A five-minute shower woke me up. I did what I could with my hair and brushed on a little blush and lip gloss—at least those hadn't been lost in my go bag. Then I scurried down to the breakfast buffet, set up in a small dining area positioned off the lobby.

JT was sitting in the corner of the room, an empty plate on the table in front of him. He saw me right away and gave me a good-morning grin, which made my day.

I trotted over to him and slumped into the chair opposite his. "Sorry. I guess I slept in."

"We're fine. I called the lead detective. He's not available to meet with us until after ten, anyway." He motioned to the food, displayed on an L-shaped counter. "Hungry?"

My stomach rumbled. "Starving. Be back in a few."

JT pulled his laptop out of the case sitting at his feet. "I'll be right here."

I returned a few minutes later with a toasted bagel, some fruit, and a glass of orange juice. While I smoothed some cream cheese on the bagel, I asked, "Find anything interesting?"

"No. Your father's work is far and above better than anything I've found on the Net. You?"

"Nothing specific enough to be useful."

JT shook his head. "I put in a call to the chief this morning, asking her if she'd gotten anywhere in the search for the missing infants."

"Yeah?"

"Nothing. The bureau has some agents working on the infant black market trade, but so far they haven't seen any increase in recent activity in the area."

"What is she doing with the infants if she's not selling them?" I was still utterly confused about how the infants were being delivered and subsequently stolen without leaving a bit of evidence, or waking the men sleeping in the same bed with their wives. We were missing a big piece of the puzzle. A giant one. "Do you think they're still alive?"

"I hope so, but . . ." JT's expression darkened. He shook his head. "It's not looking good."

I set down my bagel. "We need to stop her."

"We will."

"How can you be so certain?"

"Because we have you on our team."

"I don't think that's enough in this case."

"Don't cut yourself short, Sloan. You're brilliant. You'll figure it out."

* * *

JT's words echoed in my head as we checked out of the hotel, picked up our rental car, and drove to the Canton Township Police Department.

JT had so much faith in me—more than I did, that was for sure. True, I'd helped track down the killer in our first case. But did that mean I'd be able to do it again? It could have been a fluke.

Oddly, for the first time in my life, I was having serious doubts about my own abilities. That scared me a little.

No, it scared me a lot.

At the Canton Township PD, we introduced ourselves to Detective Grigsby, and he led us to his cubicle up on the second floor. On his desk sat a single file box. It was labeled with a number on one end. He rested his hand on the top.

"This is everything we have. The case is old. There's not much to go on."

"Thanks." I eyed the small space. "We appreciate the chance to take a look."

The phone rang. It was sitting on Grigsby's desk, in the corner. We all stared at it.

As he eased past us to answer it, Grigsby said, "How about I set you up in a conference room where you'll have space to spread things out?"

"Sounds good," I said.

JT and I stepped outside his cubicle to wait while Grigsby took his call. Then we followed him down the hall to a conference room that boasted a big table and comfortable-looking metal-framed chairs, with cushy cloth seats.

After thanking the detective one last time, we dug into the box, pulling file folders out to inspect the photographs and reports.

The date on the box: August 7, 1984.

"Could it be the same unsub?" I asked. "That's almost twenty-eight years ago."

JT flipped through a report; then he handed it to me. "We did think the unsub had been at it for a while."

Right off the bat, we could see the similarities in the cases. The victim was found in her bed. There'd been a small puncture wound in her groin. There'd been no sign of forced entry, no blood spatter, no trace evidence. And it was confirmed, the victim had been pregnant. But that infant had died in utero. And there was no mention of damage to the window screens in the room. From the photos, I concluded there was no alternative entry to the room, no fireplace or skylight. Of course, it would make no sense whatsoever to go inspect the windows now, nearly twenty-eight years later.

"The baby . . ." I swallowed a hard lump in my throat.

"Maybe she hasn't always delivered the infants before killing her victims? Perhaps she's evolved?"

"Maybe. Other than that, it's all familiar," I said, summing up what I'd read.

"Keep reading." JT, currently inspecting a photograph of the victim's wound, handed me another folder. "Here."

I accepted the folder and flipped it open. More photographs. Of the floor, the door, the windows. I noticed something in the last picture. Something pink was sticking out, seemingly caught between the window and the frame.

"JT, look at this." I showed him the picture. "Could that be the proboscis?"

"Don't know. But somewhere in here's got to be an interview of the husband. Maybe he mentions something."

I dug through the remaining paperwork until I found the interview transcript. It was lengthy. Clearly, the detective on the case at the time had suspected the husband of the crime. By the time I'd read through the entire thing, my stomach was rumbling again. We'd been sitting in that little room for over three hours, poring over the details of a decades-old case.

Ah, the glamorous life of an FBI agent.

"There's nothing in here about the window or anything suspicious coming from it," I grumbled.

JT stretched and yawned. "Maybe the husband didn't mention it because he didn't think it was relevant. I'd like to go talk to him." He gave my noisy stomach a pointed look. "But we'd better stop somewhere along the way and get you something to eat. Or we won't hear what he's saying. He'll have to shout over that noisy stomach of yours."

My face probably turned ten shades of red. "Yeah, I could use a little something to eat."

After calling Fred Isbell, the victim's husband, to set up an appointment, making copies of some photos and documents, and calling Grigsby to thank him for giving us access to the files, we headed down to the lobby and stepped out into a sauna.

We dripped to our rental car. We zoomed up Canton Center Road, made a right at Ford, and considered our lunch options. I decided Burger King was as good as anything else, so JT maneuvered through the drive-through. Minutes later, I was munching on fries and a Whopper Jr. JT stuffed chicken fingers into his mouth as he drove.

Frank Isbell's house was only a couple of miles from the restaurant. Fortunate enough, he still lived in the house he'd shared with his wife so long ago. We parked in front of the brick-and-vinyl 1970s boxy Colonial and finished our lunches. I grabbed Gabe's laptop bag, looped the strap over my shoulder, and climbed out of the car. Right on time, we headed up to the front door and rang the bell.

Isbell answered right away.

We'd looked at pictures of him back then. Twenty-eight years ago, he'd been a young man in his prime. No longer youthful, but he still looked good for his age. His dark hair was now tinged gray at the temples. His body was thicker, and not nearly as sculpted. Otherwise, he hadn't changed much.

"I'm Special Agent Jordan Thomas," JT said as he offered Isbell his hand. "Thank you for agreeing to meet with us on such short notice."

"Not a problem." Isbell motioned us inside. "I was glad to hear someone had taken an interest in my wife's case. It's been such a long time. I assumed it had been forgotten." He led us into a living room, furnished with pieces that had to be original to the house. On the far wall was a fireplace. And above that mantel hung a painting of his wife. Isbell followed my gaze. "That's Evelyn. Beautiful, wasn't she?"

I nodded. "She was."

"Evelyn was pregnant with our first child when she died. I lost both her and the child that night."

"We're very sorry for your loss," I said.

Isbell cleared his throat. "How can I help you, Agents?"

Standing beside me, JT pulled out his little pocket notebook and flipped to an empty page. "We realize it's been a very long time since that night, but we'd like to ask you some questions."

"Sure, I'll do my best."

I pulled the picture of the window out of Gabe's bag. "Do you happen to recall whether your bedroom window was open or shut that night?"

"Open, I believe."

"It's shut in the picture." I handed him the copy we'd made.

"Yes, I shut it when it started raining, right after I discovered my wife. But I didn't think anything of it. Surely, nobody climbed up the side of our house and into the window."

He motioned for us to follow him. We went up the curved staircase to the second floor and turned in the first bedroom. He pointed at the window, which was narrow, maybe sixteen inches.

"This window looks out onto the attached garage's roof, so I guess someone could climb up there. But it's too small for an adult to fit through."

I inspected the window, noting the aluminum sliding frame, which looked exactly like the picture.

"And do you remember noticing anything strange or unusual about the window when you closed it?" I asked as I slid the pane to the left to open it.

He squinted at the photo for a moment; then he looked at the actual window. His lips twisted. "Well, I saw something move as I shut it. It was a strange pink thing that looked a little like a worm or an insect."

"Anything else?"

"Well, a few days later, I found a dead bird on my garage roof. But what would that have to do with my wife?"

"What did you do with the bird?" I asked as I poked my head out the window to check out the garage roof.

After twenty-something years, I had no hope that any evidence had been left behind, but I looked, anyway.

"Dumped it in the trash, of course."

"Of course." A rumble of thunder signaled an approaching storm. Just for kicks—the window frame was a little grungy, and there was a reddish smudge. I motioned to JT. "Swab?"

He pulled a swab out of the bag he was carrying and

ran it along the window frame; then he stuck it into a plastic bag. I shut the window and turned to face the bed. JT was standing next to Isbell, looking tired and ready to leave. I guessed he was ready to head back to Quantico.

"Finished?" he asked.

"I guess so." To Isbell, I said, "Thank you again for meeting with us. I appreciate it."

We headed out.

In the car, JT gave me a sidelong glance. "What do you think you're going to find on that window? That was over twenty-five years ago."

"It was worth a shot." I put the sample in Gabe's laptop bag for safekeeping.

JT maneuvered the car to the main road. "Any DNA you find after all this time is bound to be contaminated, not to mention degraded."

"Maybe. I've read very old DNA samples have been processed. Granted, under better conditions. The warmer and more humid the sample is kept, the faster it degrades. But what do we have to lose, right?"

"Sure." After a beat, he asked, "So what do you think? Are we dealing with one unsub? Or a whole species?"

"I wish I knew."

My phone rang. After a quick check, I answered.

It was bad news.

Confusion is a word we have invented for an order which is not understood.

—Henry Miller

14

Delivering bad news to Mom was always a dodgy prospect. She rarely ever took it well. Now she was pregnant. I'd never seen her pregnant. The last time she'd been pregnant *I'd* been the bun in the oven. All that to say, I had no idea how she was going to react to hearing the venue she'd chosen for her wedding was booked solid for the next year and a half. There was absolutely no chance she was going to be married at Maryvale Castle.

An hour after landing at the base in Quantico, I was standing outside my folks' place. JT was at the office, taking care of a few things. We were meeting later at my place to go over my dad's research.

I braced myself for a hysterical outburst and headed in, nodding to Sergio.

"She's in the media room, downstairs," he said.

"Thanks." I hadn't been in the media room downstairs, but I had some general idea of which direction I should be going. On my way toward the back of the house, I ran into my father. He was in the den watching a baseball game; or rather, he appeared, at first glance, to be watching a baseball game. Since his eyes were closed, I doubted that he was actually watching much of anything.

I didn't wake him, just kept going. I found the basement stairs in the kitchen, closed behind a white paneled door. I knew what she was watching before I'd opened the door. She was definitely testing the capability of her surround sound.

Not bothering to knock—she wouldn't have heard me—I headed down the narrow steps. At the bottom, I found myself in a full-fledged home theater, the kind with the fancy recliners set on risers. The TV/movie screen was positioned on the far wall. It wasn't the size of a full movie screen, but it was pretty damn big. Which made what Mom was watching all the more disturbing.

A woman screamed, blood spurting from her neck as the guy with the mask attacked her with a chain saw.

Mom was reclined in a chair up front, munching on popcorn.

I took advantage of a rare quiet moment to shout, "Mom!"

She jumped a little, then twisted to look my way. "Sloan? Is that you?"

The room was dark. I'd give her that. But who else would be calling her "Mom"? She pointed a remote at the screen and the movie paused.

"What are you watching?" I asked.

"It's some silly movie. I don't know why I'm watching it. What are you doing here?"

"We made plans. Remember?"

She looked at me as if she had no clue.

"We're meeting with the woman you'd talked to on the Internet about officiating the ceremony."

"Oh, yes!" Staring at the screen, Mom stuffed a handful of popcorn into her mouth. Chewed.

I checked my cell phone. "We're going to be late."

"I thought she was coming here."

"No, she couldn't," I said to her profile as I rounded the front row of chairs. I stood smack-dab in front of her. "Remember? She has a wedding later. She agreed to squeeze you in."

"Oh." She leaned to one side, looking around me, and crammed another handful of popcorn into her mouth.

"Mom, if you don't want to go—"

"Thanks! Let me know how it turns out." She shooed me away.

"That wasn't what I meant."

Mom acted like she hadn't heard me. She picked up the remote, made the volume higher, and resumed stuffing her face.

I was about to let her know I was not going alone, when someone tapped me on the shoulder.

My father.

"I'll go with you."

"All right."

My father motioned for me to head upstairs, which I did. I heard him say something to my mother before joining me in the kitchen. Upstairs, he said, "I'll drive. This'll give me a chance to talk with you."

"Is there something in particular you want to tell me?"

He motioned for me to wait, which I did. We headed out to the attached garage and boarded his black Lincoln Navigator. It looked fresh-out-of-the-showroom new. He didn't speak until we'd turned onto the road.

"I'm worried about your mother."

"Worried? Why?"

"Because of the baby, she's chosen to stop taking her medication."

I knew what that meant. I should've realized what was going on when I'd found her downstairs watching that movie.

"How long has it been?" I asked.

"A week."

"Really?" I would have expected a full-blown psychotic episode by now. Or at the very least, some tremors, nausea, pain and anxiety. It was actually shocking she was doing as well as she seemed to be. "Has she been hallucinating?"

"She says she's hearing some strange birdsong. She says it's talking to her."

"Hmm. Bird?" Ironically, I hoped it was a hallucination. With Mom being pregnant, though in the earliest weeks, she could be a target for our unsub.

"I've looked," Dad said. "There's no bird. It has to be a hallucination. But she insists on staying off the medications. She says it's too dangerous for the baby."

"It would be a good idea to talk to her doctor, see if there's something else she can take to avoid a full-blown episode. Then again, she's tried a lot of medications. Most of them haven't worked."

"What do I do, then?"

"Call her doctor. Tell him your concerns. And don't let her out of your sight."

"But I have to travel. It's my job."

"She's your wife, or rather, about to be your wife. She's the mother of one child. And she's pregnant with a second. She needs you now. Can't you let someone else take over those duties for a while?"

"I don't know."

"I think you'd better find out."

Allegra Love (the name had to be an alias) was a bizarre-looking woman, bedecked in head-to-toe beaded robes; a crown of daisies sat on top of a mane of frizzy red hair. She took one look at my father and me and something flicked in her eye.

My father extended a hand. "Jim Irvine. Good to meet you." He motioned to me. "My daughter, Sloan."

That something in her eye vanished. I realized then what it was and swallowed a chuckle. It seemed an apparent twenty-year or more age discrepancy between bride and groom made her a little uncomfortable. And she called herself "A Minister of the New Millennium"?

Reverend Love gave my father's hand a shake; then she took mine. "I was expecting your future bride."

"She's feeling a little under the weather," I explained.

"This could be a problem," she said, the slightest hint of concern pulling at her features.

"I'd be happy to answer any questions you may have for my mother. I will also relay any information—"

"That's not the issue." Reverend Love was walking as she spoke, leading us down a hallway to a closed door. "You see, my current success rate is one hundred percent. And I have no intention of losing it."

"One hundred percent of what?" I asked.

"One hundred percent still married." Allegra Love opened the door, revealing a room that was utterly, completely dark, with the exception of a single candle, sitting on top of what must have been a table covered with black material. It almost appeared to be floating. She moved into the room. "I must do a reading before I marry any couple."

"How interesting," my father muttered.

"I'm sorry, but I won't risk my reputation. Before I will agree to marry you, sir, I must do a reading."

My father and I exchanged glances. "Okay," he said. "I guess we'll reschedule for another time."

Reverend Love nodded. "How does next week look for you?"

"Well . . ." He slid a glance at me.

"He'll take whatever opening you have," I blurted out before he told her he would be out of town for work. I heard him sigh.

"If you have an unexpected opening this week, I'd appreciate a call," he said.

Birds sang, twittering and tweeting and chirping.

Reverend Love held up an index finger, pulled a cell phone out of her dress somewhere, and answered it. She said an "uh-huh" and an "okay," then hung up.

"It seems that you're in luck. I have an opening for to-morrow. At noon."

"Sold."

My father grumbled all the way out to the car. I didn't catch much, bits and pieces. But I got the gist.

JT was waiting for me in the parking lot as I rolled up to my apartment an hour later. He was out of his car before I had mine shifted into park. And by the time I had my car door open, he was standing next to it, offer-ing to take Gabe's laptop case.

I handed it to him, not because it was too heavy or any-thing, but because such an old-fashioned, polite gesture couldn't be ignored. We strolled up to the building; our steps were perfectly synchronized.

"How did it go with your mother?" he asked as I let us into my apartment.

I did a quick sniff test after cracking the door, to make sure it was safe to enter without a gas mask. "As well as could be expected, I guess. She's pregnant. And she's stopped taking her medications. So she's a hormonal, chemically imbalanced, ticking time bomb. My father has no idea what he's in for, I think." I motioned for JT to set Gabe's laptop on the coffee table and headed for the kitchen. "Something to drink?"

"Water's fine." JT made himself at home on the couch. I must say, he made our dumpy old couch look pretty darn good. As I approached with the water bottle in hand, his gaze swept up and down my body, and he gave me some hungry-man eyes. "Thanks." He accepted the bottle. Our fingertips brushed. The memory of that kiss in the hotel blasted through my mind. My brain short-circuited. "Hungry?" he asked.

"I was going to ask you the same thing."

"I'm starving," he said.

I wasn't 100 percent sure he was talking about food.

My face burned. A few bits of my anatomy sizzled. "I . . . I think I'll go see what I can dig up." I stepped away from him before I did something crazy, like fling myself at him.

This was insane.

This was dangerous.

Get yourself together, girl. You're playing with fire.

I wandered into the kitchen, stopped, then, forgetting what I was in there for, stared at the sink.

"Would you like some help?" he asked as he came to stand next to the refrigerator. He was leaning a shoulder against it, arms crossed. Thick arms.

"Um, no thanks. I can manage." I stared at the sink.

"Is something wrong?"

"Nope. Not a thing."

"Why are you staring at the sink?"

I remembered just then why I'd gone into the kitchen. It irritated me how brain-dead I became sometimes when

I was alone with JT. Particularly when he looked at me like *that.*

"I'm thinking. That's all. Thinking." I opened the refrigerator. A tub of margarine. A few slices of American cheese. A container of soy milk. And a mostly empty jar of green olives. I grabbed the jar. "Olive?" I asked, thrusting it toward him.

"No thanks."

I returned the jar to its place and shut the door. I opened the freezer. Ice. Lots of it. And not much else. There was one slightly crumpled frozen dinner. I checked it. "Tuna casserole?" I asked.

JT wrinkled his nose.

"Look, I never claimed to be Betty Crocker."

"It's okay. I didn't expect you to be." He stepped closer. Too close. No, not close enough. He slid his arms around my waist and pulled me toward him. "I'm thinking . . . Italian?"

"Italian what?" I asked, staring at his lips. Did he have the world's most perfect mouth, or what? Yes, he did. And a perfect face. And his eyes. And his hair. It was shaggy and a little messy, and I loved how that one wave swooped down over his forehead.

"Italian food." He lowered his head. "Or maybe we should go for French."

He went for French. But it wasn't food.

His French made me weak in the knees. It also made my head spin; so I had to fling my arms around his neck to hold on.

He took my desperate attempt at staying upright as a sign that I needed to be saved. While still kissing me, he scooped me into his arms, like a romance novel hero, and carted me to the couch. When he set me down, he climbed on top of me and kissed me until there wasn't a single neuron firing in my brain; plus, all the blood in my body had rushed to other places, where it didn't normally collect.

When the kiss finally ended, I stared up into his eyes and murmured, "Wow."

"Wow back." His lips curled into a seductive smile.

My hands took a little tour of his torso, starting at the sides of his waist and working up, over the top of his knit shirt. Even through the cotton, I could feel the deep lines cutting across his abdomen. It was the kind of stomach that made a girl drool a little.

He just stayed there, arms extended, holding himself up so he didn't crush me as I explored. "I'm getting warm."

"Me too."

He shifted his weight back, kneeling upright, knees trapping my legs between them. He took off his shirt and tossed it somewhere. "Your turn."

I got my shirt up to my bra when the doorknob jiggled. I yanked it back down just as Katie wandered into the apartment.

JT didn't budge, so I shoved him. He still didn't move.

Katie looked at me, at him, then back at me again. Without saying a word, she headed to her bedroom.

JT took that to mean it was time to get back to what we'd been doing. I took that to mean it was time to get something to eat and get to work. The gray matter had received a little oxygen, and I was thinking more clearly. However, a second look at that shirtless JT was threatening to whisk away all thoughts of work again.

He gave me a man-on-the-hunt look.

I reluctantly shook my head. "JT, we need to work."

He sighed. "Damn it, I knew you were going to say that." He flung his leg off me, allowing me to get up. I went for his shirt, tossing it at him. He didn't look happy as he tugged it over his head. When it popped out, his hair was all messy and sexy and I had to fight the impulse to grab a handful of curls and kiss him hard.

I pointed at his chest. "You order the food and I'll go get my dad's research papers."

"Okay." He pulled his phone out of his pocket. "What'll it be? Italian or French?"

"Italian. I think I've had enough French for a long, *long* time."

He mumbled something that sounded like "ntmrblsht" as he poked the buttons on his phone. I headed to my room to drag out the big box of papers that had once been down in storage. After they'd proven so useful in our last case, I decided it was a good idea to keep them accessible.

I dragged the box down the hall to the living room. Once JT saw me struggling, he dashed over, hauled it into his muscular arms, and set it down next to the coffee table.

"The food'll be here in about a half hour," he said as he pulled the top file out of the box.

My stomach responded. "Good." I wrapped one arm around my midsection to muffle the sound and grabbed a file out of the box. JT sat on the couch. I opted for the floor. I concentrated better with at least five feet of space between us.

Forty minutes later, when the food arrived, I'd done a ton of reading but hadn't found anything useful. I was ready for a break. I set the bag on the kitchen counter. JT pulled foam containers out while I gathered plates, forks, knives, and napkins. We dished out some salad and pasta, then carried our plates back to where we'd been sitting and dug in.

JT put on the television while we ate. We amused

ourselves by talking about how unrealistic the show *Criminal Minds* was. I managed, somehow, to avoid doing anything foolish, like flirting with JT, or kissing him.

Before I knew it, my plate was empty. I dumped it into the sink, shoved the leftovers into the refrigerator, and turned to find JT blocking me in the tiny kitchen. There was no way out, but one. I'd have to squish past him.

From the glitter in his eye, I was guessing he was happy about that fact. He set his plate on the counter. "That was delicious."

"It sure was. I'm ready to get back to work now." I clapped my hands together.

He caught my wrists. "But what about dessert? I provided dinner. So you . . ."

I could see where he was going with that.

But it wasn't going to work. Oh, no, it wasn't.

Staring at the counter to avoid meeting his lusty gaze, I reached blindly for the cupboard, knowing Katie had a box of chocolate graham crackers in it. I grabbed the box and smacked it against his chest.

"There you go." I shoved past him, trying hard not to melt at the sound of his low, deep chuckle. I went back to reading; JT's crunching and munching resounded in the background.

After a couple of hours spent reading, I started to get slightly frustrated. My father had researched thousands of paranormal creatures. And when I say "researched," I mean he wrote long, detailed descriptions of each. From what I could tell, there was no order to it at all, no classification system. So I'd read about a *Rakshasa* from India, then a *Leahaun-shee* from Ireland next.

I sighed. "We need to organize this stuff, create some

kind of system to classify the creatures. We're wasting time."

"I'm with you there."

I powered up Gabe's laptop, opened a new spreadsheet, and stared at the screen. "Now, where to begin? What categories should we have?"

While moving the files into stacks, JT suggested, "How about vampires, shape-shifters, noncorporeal—"

"Sure, but some vampires—many, actually—shape-shift too. And some creatures are noncorporeal at some times and corporeal at others, like Elmer, for instance."

A file in each hand, he glanced back and forth. "We could cross-categorize each creature."

"That'll take years. We don't have time for that."

JT set the folders down. "Here's a thought. It's your father's research, right? Why not ask your father to do it?"

"If I thought it might get done in a timely manner, I would insist he do it. He is, after all, the most familiar with the subject."

We both mulled over the situation for a few moments. JT started flipping through another file. "Why not just go to him with what we have and see if he can figure it out?"

"That's against bureau rules, isn't it?"

"It's a gray line, that one."

"Fine. I'll ask him." I started putting the dozens of files we'd stacked back into the box.

"Just don't tell him too much."

"Right. Not too much."

JT gave me a hopeful look. "Now that we're done working for the night—"

"Don't even think it." I gently pulled JT to his feet. Then I ushered him toward the door. "Good night, JT. I'll see you in the morning."

JT hesitated to give me a lingering, smoldering look.

I shook my head. "It won't work."

"It worked before."

"I was weak. Low blood sugar."

His adorable chuckle and glint in his eyes made my knees go a little soft, but I still managed to get him out of the apartment without throwing myself at him.

Most men lead lives of quiet desperation and go to the grave with the song still in them.

—Henry David Thoreau

15

On my way to work the next morning, I called my dad. No answer. As I was leaving the message, my call-waiting kicked in, but I missed the call. I left a message for Dad, telling him I needed to consult him on a case, and headed into work. When I got to the unit, the place was deserted, with the exception of Hough, who was hiding out in her techie-geek lair.

I poked my head into her cave. "Where is everyone?" I asked her.

"At the scene," she said. "JT just called, said he was trying to get ahold of you, but you weren't answering."

I checked my phone. "He called once and left no message."

"That's JT for you. Anyway, here's the address." Hough handed me a piece of paper with an address and a second one, with a map that had several virtual pushpins plotted on it. "JT asked me to map out all the victims' homes. Would you mind giving this to him when you see him?"

"Not a problem. I guess I'll head out then."

"Th-thanks." Suddenly Hough was looking a little green.

"Are you okay?"

"Yep." She burbled, grabbed the trash can beside her desk, and heaved.

"Are you okay?" I asked.

She gave me a wilted smile and a nod then stuck her head in the trash can again. I decided now was as good a time as any to head out.

I tried my father's cell phone several more times during the drive over to the home of Mr. and Mrs. Klinger. Still, no answer. When I arrived, it appeared I was the last to show. The meat wagon was already gone, and only a few police cars were angled at the curb. Inside, I found JT. No Gabe. No Fischer. No chief.

JT was talking to a man who looked like he'd been to hell and back, no doubt because he had.

"I didn't hear a thing," Gil Klinger said. "I just woke up, and there she was dead." His hands shook as he tapped a cigarette out of a pack.

"And you say your wife went to bed last night at what time?" JT asked, scratching notes in his notebook.

Klinger lit the cigarette, inhaled and exhaled a ribbon of smoke. "Right around eleven."

"And you didn't notice anything unusual?" JT asked.

"Nothing." The man inhaled another lungful of carcinogens. Exhaled. "We watched the ten o'clock news, then went to bed, like we always do."

"Thank you." JT gave me a nod. "Sloan?" He started toward the rear of the house.

I followed. "What's the story?"

At the staircase, JT motioned for me to go first. "This isn't like the others."

I clomped up the stairs. "Really?" At the top, I hesitated, waiting for JT to show me which room it was.

"Yes, really." Looking grave, he stepped into the first room.

I followed him. Immediately I noticed the huge stain on the mattress. The blood spatter on the wall, on the floor.

"Oh."

"I'm guessing whoever killed Madeline Klinger thinks they've copied our unsub's MO. Fischer's done a good job of keeping certain key pieces of evidence out of the press, though. So he didn't realize there should be no blood."

"This is awful."

JT motioned toward the bathroom. "He dumped the blood in the toilet after draining it."

"Please tell me she wasn't pregnant."

JT didn't respond.

"Bastard. Are you thinking it's the husband?"

"Everything points to him."

Angry and irritated, I swept my gaze over the horrific scene. "What's he still doing here?"

"He'll be taken in for questioning soon. We don't want him to know what we suspect. We want him to think we're pegging this on the 'Baltimore Vampire.'"

"'Baltimore Vampire'?" I echoed.

"Yeah, that's what the press has dubbed her. Oh, and they've also decided she is a he."

"That's interesting."

"At any rate, this is clearly not a case for us. So we'll be stepping aside on this one."

"Just for kicks . . ." I motioned to the window. "Should I check it?"

JT shrugged. "Sure, why not?"

I checked the screen. Intact. "Okay. I'm ready."

We thanked Klinger on our way out, and passed two

uniforms as they were heading in to escort him down to the precinct for a friendly chat.

With what that guy did to his wife, and the innocent unborn child she was carrying, I hoped the guy got what he deserved. And then some.

"Bastard," I muttered as JT walked me to the car. "What do you think it was? Money?"

JT stopped on the opposite side of the car, looking at me over the roof. "That would be my first guess. He has no priors. Lost his job recently. And the house was in foreclosure."

"So he decided his wife and child didn't deserve to live?" I slid into the seat, cranked the engine, and powered down the window.

JT shook his head as he ducked down to look in at me. Bent at the waist, he leaned his arms against the door. "Part of our job is to think like a killer, to anticipate their next move. But that doesn't mean we really understand their motivations."

"I don't think I want to try."

"I hear you."

My phone rang. I glanced at the display. Dad. I checked the clock on my dashboard. It was eleven twenty-eight. I lifted an index finger, letting JT know I was going to take the call, and answered.

"I need you to come with us. I'm not sure I can do this alone," he said in greeting.

This was a man who protected a queen. This was a man who commanded an army.

"I need to talk to you anyway, Dad. Your appointment's at twelve, right? You didn't change it."

"I didn't change it."

"Hang on, Dad." To JT, I said, "Where are you going now?"

"Back to the office for a while."

"I'm going to meet up with my dad, talk to him about the case."

"Good. Call me when you're done."

"Will do." After giving JT a farewell wave, I tucked the phone between my ear and shoulder and pulled away from the curb. "There's no chance I'll make it before twelve."

"Please. I need you here."

"It's physically impossible. I'm at a crime scene. It'll take at least a half hour to get—"

"I'll do anything."

"You'll tell your queen you can't travel for the rest of Mom's pregnancy?"

Silence.

"You said you needed to talk to me about something," he then said, trying to force me into backing down.

"I can't do that over the phone. Time's ticking," I told him, sensing I had him.

"Fine," he snapped.

"I'll be there as soon as I can."

And I was. It just wasn't at twelve on the dot. But I hadn't promised I'd make it on time. That's not to say I took my sweet time getting there. I broke a few laws, rolled through a few stop signs, and stretched the speed limits a bit when I could.

My father looked relieved when I eventually found him and my mother sitting on a bench outside of Allegra Love's mysterious black psychic reading room. "She's still in there with the last couple. I don't think things are going so well," he whispered. "I hear someone crying."

"You'll be fine," I said, sitting on the other side of Mom. "How are you feeling?" I asked her.

"Starving. Do you have anything in your purse to eat?" She eyed my handbag and licked her lips.

"No. I might have some gum."

"That'll work, I guess."

I pulled out the pack and started to take a stick out for her, but she snatched the whole thing and stuffed it in her mouth, foil wrappers and all.

Dad sighed.

I stared. "It generally tastes better without the wrappers."

She gulped. Smiled. "Delicious. Do you have more?"

I looked at Dad.

He shrugged. "She ate two Whoppers, a large fry, and an ice-cream sundae on the way here. That was twenty minutes ago."

"I can't help it if I get hungry," Mom said, sounding wounded. "It's the baby. She's doing it to me. I eat and a little while later, I'm starving again."

"I'm sorry, dear." My father patted her knee. "We're not trying to make you feel bad."

Mom smoothed her skirt over her thighs. "If you tell me I look fat, I'll cry."

The door swung open and a woman with bloodshot eyes, and a bad case of running mascara, emerged; a man was cradling her elbow. Her gaze was locked on the floor as she sniffled and snorted past us and out the main exit.

What the hell was that all about?

Allegra Love came out, gave my mother and father an assessing look, then asked, "Are you ready?"

I thought about telling my folks to forget the whole thing. But before I could get a word out, my mother shot to her feet.

"You bet," Mom said.

My father followed.

I stood, thinking I'd go in with them, but Allegra Love blocked the door with her ample body.

"No one but the couple is permitted in the room during the reading. It throws off my reception."

What a freaking quack.

"Reception of what?" I asked.

"Energy. Everyone casts off waves of energy at different frequencies. I sense those frequencies and determine whether the couple's energy waves are harmonious or discordant."

"I won't say a word."

She flinched as if I'd poked her or something. Shifting back, away from me, she said, "That won't make a difference. I'm sorry. You'll have to wait outside." She stepped into the room and slammed the door in my face.

Rudeness is so unnecessary.

Mumbling a few expletives under my breath, I pressed an ear to the door. I could hear voices but couldn't make out any words. They were too muffled.

I returned to my seat.

What seemed like six hours later, my phone rang. Thankful for a distraction from the monotony, I answered.

"Hey."

JT, the caller, said, "Hey back. Where are you?"

"At the house of some crackpot psychic minister. She's doing a 'reading' of my parents to see if their energies are harmonious."

"I need to talk to you."

"I'm stuck here for at least a little while longer. I'd leave, but if this thing goes bad, my father's going to need my help."

"Where's the house?"

I gave him the address, and he said he'd be there in ten minutes and hung up.

After what felt like an hour, he was being escorted back to where I was waiting.

"Are they still in there?" JT indicated the closed door with a tip of his head.

"Yes. They've been shut up in that room for quite a while. Not sure if that's a good sign or a bad one."

"Hopefully, they'll stay in there a little longer. I need to talk to you."

"What's so important? Is it the case?"

He shifted in his seat, turning so his body was angled toward mine. "No, it's personal."

"Okay."

JT fumbled with his laptop case. "You see, I've been wanting to tell you something—"

The door swung open and my mother, looking very cheery, came prancing out of the room. "Our energies are perfectly matched," she told me. "Of course, I never had any doubts."

My father, walking behind her, gave me a thank-God-it's-over look.

Mom swung around to address Allegra Love. "Then we'll see you in three weeks."

"I'm looking forward to it." Reverend Love slid a glance our way before smiling at Mom. "Good-bye."

Mom threw her a wave and half-danced/half-walked down the hall toward the exit.

Dad gave me another look. "Are you coming back to the house for lunch?" he asked. "You said you wanted to talk to me about your case."

"I had Sergio make your favorite too," Mom yelled.

I glanced at JT. "I guess I'd better, then."

JT didn't appear too happy about my response. "I really need to talk to you, Sloan."

"He can come too!" Mom shouted.

"I'd hate to make you drive all the way over to my folks' house when you have so much work to do."

Of course, he'd driven over here to tell me something. That meant he'd already gone out of his way. And he hadn't had a chance yet to tell me whatever it was that he'd come to say.

"How about we talk here? That way, you can get back to Quantico sooner?" I suggested to JT.

To Dad, I said, "I'll be over in a few minutes."

"All right. See you later." Dad left.

Allegra Love cleared her throat. She moved closer, extending her arms in front of her, fingers spread, hands held palm out toward us. She closed her eyes and smiled.

"I've never seen anything like this. It's . . . remarkable."

With absolutely no warning, she grabbed my arm and practically broke into a sprint, dragging me back toward her psychic reading room.

"I must get a clean reading."

At the door, she motioned to a very confused-looking JT. "Young man, please follow me."

He hesitated for a moment before following us into the room.

Allegra Love sat. I started toward the door. "If you leave, I'll have no choice but to call your parents and cancel."

Sneaky, manipulative woman!

"This had better be quick." I glared at her and plunked into the closest chair. JT sat in the chair next to me.

She lifted her hands again, holding them upright, palms facing us. She closed her eyes. "Oh, yes. My goddess, yes."

JT and I exchanged bewildered glances.

"Your energies are so harmonious. They produce the most amazing effect. I've never experienced anything like it. I feel almost"—she swayed—"intoxicated."

"'Intoxicated'?" I mouthed to JT.

JT grinned and shrugged.

"That's all fine and good, but we need to get going," I said to the intoxicated minister.

Love's eyes snapped open. "You two are lovers."

"No, we aren't," I stated matter-of-factly.

Reverend Love's gaze shifted to JT.

He shrugged. "We're coworkers. It's against bureau policy."

Love shrugged. "It doesn't matter. There's no way anyone could ignore such a strong natural force. Your energies are like two magnets, drawn toward each other. Like the pull of the Earth on the Moon. Nobody, not even your boss, will be able to stop it."

I'd heard enough. More than enough. Had JT paid . . . ?

I snapped a glare to JT. "Did you by any chance pay this woman to say these things to me?"

"I've never spoken to this woman before in my life. I swear."

I checked his face for any sign of deception. Seeing none, I checked Allegra Love's face next.

She shook her head. "I've never spoken to your friend. I don't even know his name. I'm telling you the truth. You two aren't merely compatible. You are soul mates. Your energies resonate on a level I've never seen before. It's beautiful."

Not completely convinced of anything, especially our magically resonating souls, I beat a retreat, with JT at my heels. I got as far as the door before remembering I had promised to let JT get off his chest whatever he'd come to tell me.

I rested against my car's passenger-side door. "Okay, you drove a long way to talk to me. Why? What's so important you couldn't wait to tell me later?"

"It's not that it's so important, but that it's personal,

and I know you'd like to keep our personal lives out of work."

"Fair enough." I motioned with my head that he should proceed.

"I can't keep this from you anymore. It's about Hough."

"Yeah?"

"She's pregnant. And I'm the child's biological father."

It took a few seconds for his words to sink in. When they did, something inside of me coiled into an excruciating knot. My lungs deflated. Thankfully, I had the car to support me. If it hadn't been there, I would have probably been lying on the ground.

"She's . . . pregnant. And you're the father," I mumbled.

"I am."

"Then it's true. You're sleeping with her. You said it wasn't what I thought."

"We had sex once. Only one time."

"Sure. Only once." I jerked open the door and tossed my purse on the seat before rounding the front end of the car.

JT stopped me just before I reached the driver's-side door. He yanked on my arm. "Sloan, let me explain."

"Explain? JT, I've known where babies come from since I was three. What's to explain? Sperm meets egg. They fuse. Twenty-three chromosomes become forty-six—"

"There's a whole helluva lot more to it than that."

"Oh, I'm sure there is!" Ready to kick JT in the noodle, thereby assuring his gametes would never again meet an ovum, I gritted my teeth. "You'd better let me go right now, or your baby-making days will be over."

He let go. Smart man.

I jerked open my car door and plopped into the seat. The second I had the door closed, JT was at the window, knocking. Ignoring him, I started the car, shifted into reverse, and pulled out of the parking spot.

As I drove away, tears of fury and hurt blurred my vision. I just kept blinking and driving until I couldn't see a damn thing. Then I pulled over and let it all out. I cried until my head felt like it might split in two and my tear ducts had dried up. Then I let my head fall forward. My forehead rested against the steering wheel.

A knock on my window made me jump.

I looked. "Are you kidding me?"

"Sloan, are you okay?" JT mouthed.

"I'm fine. Go away," I mouthed back.

He didn't go away.

I rolled down the window. "JT, I don't know what you expect me to say."

"I don't expect you to say anything. I just want you to listen."

"But I don't want to hear any more."

"I kind of got that when you just about ran me over."

"I didn't get even remotely close to running you over. Believe me, if I had wanted to, I could've run you over."

"The truth is, Hough—Brittany—asked me to be a donor."

"Yeah? So what's wrong with doing it the old-fashioned way? Shooting it into a bottle and then letting the doctor put it in there with a meat-baster thingy?"

He gave me a *really?* look. "Doing it the natural way was less complicated. And less expensive. I didn't want to make her pay a doctor to do what I can do for free."

What a freaking pathetic excuse. "Oh, and I'm sure you enjoyed every minute of it."

JT shoved his fingers through his hair, pulling it out of the low ponytail he'd slicked it into. I tried not to notice how incredibly hot he looked with his hair loose. That was the last thing I needed to be noticing.

"I really didn't enjoy it. It was . . . awkward. But I'm beginning to see you aren't going to believe that."

"If you managed to finish the job, which you clearly did, then you couldn't have found it too terribly 'awkward,' could you?" I waved him away. "Not that it matters, anyway. Not that any of this matters. After all, we're coworkers. We aren't lovers. We'll never be lovers. And I don't give a damn about harmonious energies or soul mates. That's all a bunch of bullshit." When JT didn't say anything else, I asked, "So, are you done explaining?"

"I guess so." He stepped back from the car.

I roared away, leaving him eating my dust.

If you can find a path with no obstacles, it probably doesn't lead anywhere.

—Frank A. Clark

16

I was not in the mood to deal with my parents, but I knew I needed to get over there. Hoping Mom might be preoccupied with a movie or something, I roared over to their place, parked the car, and dragged myself inside.

Sergio met me at the door with a sparkly-toothed grin. I grunted a greeting at him and shuffled past him.

"Your parents are out on the patio," he informed me.

"Thanks." I headed out to join them.

When I got outside, my father was staring at the huge outdoor television, while my mother was floating around in the pool.

"Sloan, why don't you come for a swim before you eat," Mom said, waving me toward the water.

"No thanks. I can't stay long. I'm on my lunch break. I need to get back to work."

She pouted, then went back to fluttering around. I took a seat by my father.

Sergio came out, bearing a plate and a glass of something. "Your lunch."

Salad.

Water.

I grimaced. "I thought Mom said she'd had him make my favorite."

My dad shrugged. "Lately she says a lot of things. Most of them make no sense whatsoever."

"Have you talked to her doctor?"

"I have. We have an appointment next week. I couldn't get anything sooner, since she's not a threat to herself or anyone else. What did you want to speak with me about?"

"I need some help identifying our unsub. We're pretty sure it's vampiric."

"Okay." His gaze didn't move from the screen, much like Mom's when she was watching that stupid movie yesterday.

"We believe it shape-shifts to some kind of flying creature, at least at night. And we believe it feeds through some sort of long proboscis."

"Uh-huh."

"So what do you think?"

"About what?" he asked.

"The unsub."

"I think you're on the right track."

Gah! "I was hoping you'd be able to identify its species."

"Sloan, that research is decades old. I haven't looked at it in a long time. Can you tell me you remember everything you read twenty years ago?"

I started to answer, but he interrupted me.

"Of course, you do. You're brilliant. I'm just your run-of-the-mill elf. A lot of muscle. Not a lot of brains."

"Bullshit. If you had no brains, you wouldn't be the head of the queen's army. And you wouldn't have a Ph.D. So what's the deal? Don't you want to help me?"

"The deal is . . ." He sighed. "I don't remember. I was sick a while back—right before I came home. I had a pretty bad case of meningitis. It seems to have affected my memory. I don't remember a lot about that time of my life. It's all a little hazy."

He looked genuinely sorry, and a little concerned and frustrated too. "I'd love to help you, but I can't."

"Well, damn. I thought you came home to protect us."

"I have. That's why I'm marrying your mother again. And why I'd like for you to move in here with us until . . ."

"Until what? I'm married?" I asked.

He nodded.

"That could be years."

He didn't respond.

"Is that why Elmer started coming around recently? The timing is a little suspicious."

"The timing is convenient. Sloan, when I told you there was a danger—"

"Back to the case," I said, turning the conversation to a topic I preferred, "I need to find out what this creature is. There are children missing."

"Children?"

"Every victim has been pregnant. And the infants are missing."

My father squinted his eyes and stared down at the floor. "Infants . . . ?"

I waited, breathless, hopeful. When he didn't supply the answer I was so desperate to hear, I said, "Anything?"

"You have my files still, right?"

"Yes, I do."

"Take a look at Malaysian folklore. I remember a creature . . . don't recall what it was called, though. I'm sorry, Sloan."

"Don't apologize. That's more than I had before. Thank you." I checked my phone. "I'd better get back to work. Thanks again." To Mom, who was reclining on a floating chaise in the middle of the pool, I said, "See you later, Mom."

"Six o'clock? Right?" she asked.

"For what?"

"We're going dress shopping tonight. You and me. Don't you remember?"

Of course, I didn't. "Oh. Okay. I guess. Unless something comes up at work."

"I'll see you at six." Mom gave me a cheery wave.

The minute I got back to the office, I made a beeline for my cubicle. I saw no sign of JT. That was a good thing. Gabe had reclaimed his laptop while I'd been out, but a loaner sat on my desk. I powered it up and Googled Malaysian vampire folklore. There were 1,360,000 results. I clicked on the Wikipedia article first and skimmed it.

I hit pay dirt. It would seem many of the Malaysian legends involved some form of a vampiric being that preyed upon pregnant women. The trick would be in determining which creature we were dealing with, and then finding out how to stop it.

I printed out the article for reference and checked in with the chief. Her door was shut. I knocked. Then, at her response, I stepped inside.

Sitting at her desk, she waved me inside. "Skye. Thomas and Wagner are on their way down to Jacksonville to check out another case. It's just you and me."

"That's okay. I think I'm onto something. But I need to go home and dig into some of my father's research before I can say for sure."

The chief raised her brows. "What can you tell me?"

"I'm looking at Asian vampire mythology, specifically Malaysian legends. There are several creatures that prey upon pregnant women in Malaysian myths, several that fly and feed through a proboscis, like our unsub."

"Interesting."

"But so far, I haven't found the exact creature we might be dealing with. The myths vary. I'm finding conflicting information. Which is why I'd like to check my father's research."

"By all means. Any mention of the unborn children in the articles you've read?"

"Yes. Unfortunately, I'm not finding any good news there."

"Damn. I was afraid of that." She stood and circled the desk until she was standing directly in front of me. "We need to stop this beast. Yesterday."

"I agree."

"What do you think about going undercover again?"

"Posing as a pregnant woman?" I asked.

The chief nodded. "We still don't know how the creature is finding his or her prey."

"Her," I said. "I'm pretty sure we're dealing with a female."

"Very well. What about it?"

"I guess we could give it a shot. I'm not sure if I can fool whatever it is we're dealing with."

"At this point, I'm willing to take that chance. I'll make the arrangements. Of course," the chief said, leveling a look at me, "you'll have to have an agent with you at all times. Especially at night."

Let me guess. . . .

"You don't have any objections to JT being that agent, do you?" she asked.

I forced a smile. "No, of course not."

"Good. I'll have everything ready for you by tomorrow. Let me know if you find anything in your father's research."

"Will do. Thanks, Chief."

"No, Sloan, thank *you*. You've done a remarkable job for

this unit. I hope you'll consider becoming a permanent member of the team once you've graduated."

"I'm flattered, Chief. I'll definitely think about it."

Several hours later, after I had dug through half of my father's research and had failed to find anything on Asian vampire legends at all, I met Mom at the dress shop.

To say it wasn't going well was an understatement. But at least she hadn't swelled up like a life-sized blow-up doll.

"This dress makes me look fat," she said for the eighty-ninth time.

"Mom, you don't look fat." I held up the last dress she'd tried on. "What about this one?"

"That was even worse." Mom sighed. Her shoulders slumped. "I've tried on close to a hundred dresses, Sloan. They all look horrible."

"They don't look horrible. Honest."

Mom headed back toward the changing room. Over her shoulder, she said, "Maybe I should give up and just go to the Salvation Army, buy some piece of polyester faux silk and then throw it away when it's over."

"Mom, really, you're being hormonal," I said, following her.

Through the door, Mom said, "I know. I can see myself acting like a whiny baby, but I can't stop. I'm just so tired."

"You need to sleep more."

"I'm trying. But I keep waking up in the middle of the night, and I can't get back to sleep once I'm awake."

"Maybe you should try drinking some warm milk."

"What I'd like to try is drinking some wine." Mom exited the room bedecked in yet another stunning silk gown. This one, I had to admit, was my favorite so far. It was simple but elegant, with a bodice that was draped in such a way to emphasize my mother's still-tiny waistline and an A-line skirt with a short train. She stepped up on the podium in the main viewing area and studied her reflection. "Hmm."

"It's perfect," I said.

Mom scrunched up her face. "I don't know." She ran her hand down the front of the bodice. "My stomach is protruding."

"Mom, since you stopped taking your medication, you've lost weight. There's nothing protruding. I swear to you."

"You just want me to pick one and be done."

The saleswoman brought a small, simple tiara with a veil attached and set them on my mother's head. "There you go, dear. You're a picture."

Mom stared at her reflection some more. "It isn't too over-the-top gaudy."

"Not at all, Mom. It's elegant and simple, yet very pretty. Just right for the venue."

With the pushed-up date, we'd had to change the setting, opting for an outside garden wedding at a local historical landmark, instead of the formal event she'd originally planned. Of course, that meant the weather would be a huge factor. In Maryland, July wasn't the rainiest month of the year, but we had our share of summer thunderstorms.

Mom sighed. "Okay. This is it."

I bit back a "wahooo" and prepared myself for what would come next.

It was my turn.

In view of the changes, Mom had altered her color palette. Instead of the dark colors she'd originally se-lected, she was now going with white, black, and daisy yellow. I was a little scared what that meant for my dress.

I wasn't overly thrilled about walking down the aisle looking like a giant bumblebee. But it beat looking like a jack-o-lantern.

While Mom changed back into her street clothes, the salesclerk went in back to pull some dresses for me. She returned a few minutes later with several gowns in tow. She stuffed them into my arms and shooed me into a fitting room.

Option one was absolutely hideous. Okay, maybe I'm being a little harsh, and perhaps the clingy, uber-tight scrap of yellow would look nice on someone—if that someone had absolutely no hips, no boobs, and no curves whatsoever. But that someone wasn't me.

Next!

"Sloan, aren't you coming out?" my mother shouted through the door.

"No. This one's not worth a second look."

"But I let you see every dress I tried on."

I heaved a sigh so big, I almost split the seam on the stupid dress. "Fine." I tromped out to the podium while yanking the back of the dress down so my ass didn't hang out, did a three-sixty, said, "I won't wear this in public. End of story." Back in the changing room, I went.

The saleslady helped me into something a little more appropriate for round two. This one was full-length and it didn't look like a hooker dress. Two things going for it. But the one-shouldered gown had this ugly bow on that one shoulder, and it kept smacking me in the face. If I had to wear it for more than ten minutes, I'd be tempted to rip off the dumb bow.

For the sake of keeping the peace, I let my mother get a look at it. She grinned.

"Mom, I can't handle this." I grabbed the huge bow and shook it.

"They may be able to change it a little." Mom looked at the salesclerk. The salesclerk shrugged her shoulders.

Next.

I went back in to put on option number three.

Bumblebee. Totally. Black bodice. Yellow skirt. What was the designer thinking?

Sadly, it was the best of the three.

I went out to do the required three-sixty. Mom, of course, raved about it.

My dress, it would seem, had been chosen.

As I stripped out of it, I told myself that it was one less thing to worry about. We'd killed two birds today and were well on our way to having the wedding fully planned. Next up: flowers.

I accepted the bagged gown on the way out and tossed it in my trunk while Mom made herself comfortable in the passenger seat.

She yawned. "Damned birds are keeping me up all night. I'm thinking of having your father call an exterminator."

I slid behind the wheel and buckled myself in. Again, she was talking about birds. If she was anywhere close to delivering, I'd be worried she might be hearing something a whole lot more dangerous than a sparrow. "Mom, I don't think an exterminator can kill every bird that comes within a few feet of your house. Keep your window closed. That should help. And maybe you'd be better off trying to cover up the sound somehow?"

"Like how? There's a tree right outside the window. They congregate up there like teen girls at a Justin Bieber concert."

"You could change rooms." I started the car and shifted it into reverse.

"I don't want to do that, but I suppose I could. Just for the time being." She yawned again.

"Why don't you close your eyes and take a little catnap?" I suggested as I maneuvered the car out of the parking spot. "It'll be a while before we're home."

"Yes, that sounds like a good idea." She closed her eyes. Before we hit the freeway, she was sawing logs.

Artistic temperament sometimes seems a battleground, a dark angel of destruction and a bright angel of creativity wrestling.

—Madeleine L'Engle

17

After dropping off Mom, I drove home. Katie was lounging on the couch, doing a fine job of emptying a half gallon of chocolate-brownie-chunk ice cream while hunched over a book the size of a small island.

"Exam?" I dropped my laptop bag on the table next to the door and headed into the kitchen to hunt down a snack.

"No, just a quiz. What's up?"

Finding nothing, I grabbed a spoon and joined Katie on the couch. I dug into the carton, extracting a big blob of chocolate ice cream. "I'm going undercover again." I dumped the cold dessert into my mouth and had a "foodgasm."

"Cool. I'm jealous. I'd love to have a summer job like that. Any chance the PBAU needs a chemist?" Katie handed me the carton. "I'm done. You can have the rest."

"Thanks. I'll check with the chief about the job." I spooned some more chocolate heaven into my mouth.

"The ice cream was yours, anyway. And thanks for checking with the FBI for me. For some reason, research and development isn't looking all that great anymore." Katie closed the book and leaned back. "I always knew what I wanted to do when I finished school. But now . . . I've lost the love. It's all just letters and numbers to me."

"Maybe you're burned-out."

"Maybe you're right. Maybe I need to take a step back from chemistry for a while, and take a look at what else is out there."

"You could realize chemistry isn't such a bad thing," I said as I dug another scoop out of the carton. "I'm telling you, there isn't much out there worth getting too excited about."

"I don't doubt it. But I need a change. I bet I'd be a kick-ass undercover agent for the FBI."

"Sure," I said around a mouthful of sin.

"Just like you. It would be so exciting. We could work together. Like Cagney and Lacey."

"Who's that?"

"I don't know. A couple of girl cops. I caught part of a show on TV the other night."

"Katie, I'm pretending to be pregnant. I doubt it'll be all that great. Not to mention, I'll have JT following me around all the time. Even at night."

"I would've thought you'd be happy about that." She gave me a nudge. "I mean, you two were swapping DNA here on our couch, weren't you?"

"No. There was no DNA swapping involved. And speaking of DNA, he told me he fathered a child recently. With another coworker."

Katie's expression went blank. "Oh."

"Yeah." I filled my mouth with more ice cream.

"Bastard," she muttered.

"Yeah."

"We hate him."

"Yes, we do." I set the carton aside and dropped my face in my hands. "And now, I think I have to sleep in the same bed with him. See? This undercover thing isn't all it's cracked up to be."

Katie gave me a pat of commiseration. "Still beats sitting around, injecting rodents with toxins, and then measuring their tumors."

I grimaced. "Okay, maybe it does."

"The wedding's off!" my mother said between blubbering snuffles and hiccups.

It was late, almost eleven at night. Mom had called me just as I was going to bed and threatened bodily harm—to my father, not me—if I didn't come over *right away*.

So here I was.

"The wedding's off? Why?" I asked her as I stood next to the door, tracking her frenzied motions with my eyes.

Ignoring my question, my mother threw a wadded pair of velour lounge pants into the open suitcase sitting on her bed. "I'm coming to stay with you."

"But—"

"What was I thinking? How could I be such a fool?" Mom emptied one dresser drawer in a single scoop and dumped its contents into the suitcase.

"Mom, what happened?"

"What happened? I'll tell you." She dragged her hand across her face, under her nose, and blinked bloodshot eyes at me. "You were right. He's a bastard. A two-faced lying bastard." She emptied a second drawer, dropping the armload into the bag. Then she smashed the pile down to make room for more. "I don't ever want to speak to that man again."

"Mom." I tried to still her by grabbing her by the shoulders and staring into her eyes. But it didn't work for more than a split second. She went back to her dresser for more clothes. "Please stop moving around, Mom. I'm getting dizzy just watching you. It would be better if we sat down and talked about this."

"There's nothing to talk about." She paused. She set her hands on her hips and gave me a funny look. "Why are you trying to change my mind? All along, you've said you didn't trust him. Here I am, saying you were right, and now you want me to talk about it?"

"I just want to make sure—"

"I'm not delusional," she finished for me. "That's what you're thinking, isn't it?"

"Well . . ."

Mom gritted her teeth, but at least she didn't go back to packing. She slumped onto the bed, yanking me down next to her. "Okay. You wanted to hear the whole story? I'll give you the whole story. In a nutshell, your father is a two-timing cheat." She stopped.

After about twenty seconds of waiting for the rest of the story, I asked, "That's it? That's the whole story?"

"In a nutshell, yes."

"Are you sure he's been unfaithful?"

"He admitted it."

"Oh."

"Yeah." Mom crossed her arms over her chest and gave me an I-told-you-so look. "You want to tell me now that I'm being delusional?"

"I guess not."

She went back to packing. "Don't worry. I won't stay with you for long. That bastard is going to pay through the nose." She patted her flat stomach. "None of us are going to want for anything." She flopped the top over the suitcase and zipped it shut.

I dragged it—oh, my God, heavy!—off the bed and wheeled it down the hallway to the stairs.

Ugh. Stairs!

Mom snorted and gave it a shove with her foot. Down it went, flipping end over end down the steps. It landed with a thump at the bottom, just as the object of my mother's rage rounded the corner.

He looked at the bag.

He looked at us.

His eyebrows squished together.

"Yes, I am leaving you," Mom yelled. "My lawyer will be in touch." Head held high, she stomped down the staircase. I followed her, watching my father watch her. A dozen expressions crossed over his face. I couldn't name them all. Didn't even try.

"Is it true?" I whispered. "Did you cheat on Mom?"

"I wish there were something I could say to make this better" was his response.

It was as close to an admission of guilt as I needed. I shook my head and followed Mom outside. When I caught up to her, I took the suitcase from her and hauled it to the car. It went into the trunk, Mom went into the passenger seat, and away we drove.

Mom cried all the way to my apartment.

By three in the morning, my head was pounding so hard I was seeing stars.

I could hardly walk from being so exhausted.

And all I wanted to do was climb back into my cozy bed and go to sleep.

But my mother was standing in the middle of the living room, prancing around in her wedding gown, and screaming obscenities at the top of her lungs.

The neighbors were all letting me know how unhappy they were about Mom's outburst. Some were banging on the adjoining walls. Others were pounding on their ceiling (my floor). Some had gone to the trouble of knocking on my door. I answered to find six furious men and women crowded in the hallway.

"I'm very sorry. I'll get her settled down immediately," I said, risking life and limb by poking my head out to deliver my apology. I closed the door, slid a help-me look at one stressed-out, sleep-deprived Katie, and then rushed to my mom's side.

"Mom." I waved my hands in front of her face.

"I don't give a fuck what you need," she shrieked in the general direction of the window. "You stay the hell away from me and my baby!"

"Mom, who are you yelling at?"

"The fucking bird!"

"Bird?" I checked the window.

There was a blackbird sitting on a tree branch. Had I been too hasty in dismissing the possibility that Mom could be a target of our unsub? I went to open the window, but Mom stopped me.

"It's dangerous," she warned.

"I'm . . . going to shoo it away for you." I wanted to get a look at that bird. I needed to get a look at it.

Mom literally pried my fingers off the window frame. "Don't open the window!"

"I'm only going to open it a little—"

"No. Not even an inch. Not even a half inch." Mom banged on the window; then she yanked the drapes shut. "That thing will get me. It'll take my baby. Just like it did to those other women."

"How could you . . . ?" My gaze wandered around the room. I'd left some files sitting next to the couch. She wouldn't have.

Yes, she would.

She spun in a circle, looking from one piece of furniture to another. Her gaze settled on the bookshelf. "Help me move this, Sloan."

"Oh, Mom, have you been reading my case notes?"

Struggling with the shelving unit, Mom nodded. Her gaze jerked to the pile of file folders. "I read everything. I know what's happening."

"Please stop that. It's too heavy. You're going to hurt yourself, and maybe the baby too." I gently pulled her away from the heavy piece of furniture. I steered her toward the couch. "You weren't supposed to see that stuff."

"Then you shouldn't have left it out for me to see."

I bit my tongue to keep from saying something I'd regret. "Since you know as much as you do already, you must realize that bird can't be what we're looking for."

"Why's that?" She narrowed her eyes at me.

"Because all the other women were close to their due dates." I pointed at her flat stomach. "You're not even remotely close."

She flattened both hands over her stomach and gave a little "hmpfh."

"Maybe that doesn't matter," my mother argued. "Maybe she just *prefers* mothers who are closer to their due dates. Maybe any expectant mother will do."

"That's possible. Sure. But for some reason, I doubt it. So far, the unsub's MO hasn't changed. You can check yourself. Every victim was within two weeks of her due date. Yours is months off. A serial killer doesn't generally change her MO after killing for so long. We think this one may have been killing for many years. Decades. Every single victim we have tracked down was at least thirty-six weeks pregnant." Figuring none of us would get any sleep until that big mangy blackbird outside left,

I went back to the window and knocked as hard as I could. It didn't budge. Even I had to admit, it seemed to be staring at us.

This was tough, discerning whether Mom's worries were a manifestation of her paranoia or truly worthy of concern. But the more I thought about it, the more I believed it was a matter of her psychosis than reality.

Mom pulled a blanket over herself and let her head fall back. "I don't believe you. I think she's waiting for me to go to sleep. She's going to suck out all my blood and steal my baby. We need to make sure all the windows are shut and locked."

"Okay, Mom," I said, deciding I'd get to bed a whole lot faster if I humored her rather than argued. "We'll lock the windows." With the help of Katie, I made the rounds checking and double-checking all the window locks. Meanwhile, Mom dumped lines of salt on every windowsill in our apartment. She also put one in front of every door.

"The salt keeps them away," she said.

"Did you read that in those papers too?" I asked, hoping maybe she'd stumbled upon something I hadn't, like the name of the creature we were trying to track down.

"No. It's something my mother told me when I was growing up."

Her mother, like mine, was schizophrenic. Along with the advice about the salt, which I'd never heard before, she'd also been the recipient of such sage counsel as, "Make sure you wear tinfoil on your head when you go outside, so that you're safe from space alien transmissions." That one, Mom had shared with me.

However, I'd long ago decided a bit of foil wasn't going to save me from aliens. But to this day, my mother has been known to wear a little scrap on her head some-where, usually hidden in her hair.

In summary, there was no convincing the woman of anything.

Finally, with great effort, I got Mom in bed. She in-sisted I sleep with her, so I did. She was snoring long before I fell asleep.

When the will defies fear, when duty throws the gauntlet down to fate, when honor scorns to compromise with death—that is heroism.

—Robert Ingersoll

18

Someone was following me. He was a he . . . at least, I was pretty sure of that. And he was driving a black sedan. That's all I knew at this point. It was early, predawn, too dark to get a good look at his face. When we stopped at a light, he managed to keep his face hidden in shadow.

I toyed with the idea of driving to the police station. Instead, I called Gabe.

"What's up?" Gabe asked, sounding awake and alert, and surprised to be hearing from me so early.

"Please tell me you're back in town."

"I'm back in town."

"And tell me you weren't sleeping."

"I wasn't sleeping. Why?"

"Good. I'm being tailed."

"Where are you?"

"Down the street from your place."

"I'll be waiting outside."

"Thank you." I kept checking the rearview mirror as I drove, wondering if my stalker would give up. He didn't. He followed me right to Gabe's place.

Gabe was standing on the porch when I pulled into his

driveway. Before I had the seat belt off, he was loping toward the black sedan, parked on the street.

I got out and started toward Gabe.

"It's your father," he said. "It's a good thing I met him last week, or he'd be on the ground right now. Unconscious."

Wow, did I feel stupid. "Oh, shoot. Sorry about that, Gabe. I didn't recognize the car. He usually drives a Navigator." I peered inside the open window. Sure enough, it was my father.

"Are you sure you're okay?" Gabe asked, looking uncertain. "I was going to head to work early."

"I'm fine. I'll be in shortly. I owe you for this one. Sorry." I shooed Gabe away with an apologetic smile.

Dad waved. "Didn't mean to cause any worry. But it's reassuring to see you're aware—"

"Oh, I'm aware, all right." When my father unlocked the door, I opened the passenger side and sat. "What's going on? Why are you tailing me at five-thirty in the morning?"

"I need to talk to you. About your mother."

"Now?"

Dad shrugged. "Why not? You'll be busy later. So will I. Can you think of a better time?"

"Fine. What do you want to talk to me about? I'm not thrilled to be in the middle of your problems."

"I just need one small favor." From the look on his face, I was guessing his definition of "small" would probably not coincide with mine.

"What 'small favor'?"

"I just need you to get her to come to the country club, where we're going to be married."

"You mean where you *were* going to be married. Past tense. You cheated on her. She's not going to marry you now."

"Please, Sloan. Bring her to the country club?"

"What am I supposed to tell her?"

"Tell her you're taking her golfing."

"Neither one of us plays golf."

"Then tell her you're taking her for lunch at the club."

I glared at him.

He gave me a goofy grin. "Please, Sloan? After everything, you don't owe me a thing. I realize that. But I'm asking you to do this for your mother's sake."

"Why?" I asked. "Why do you want me to take her there?"

"I need to talk with her."

"She's going to make a scene."

"I'm prepared for that."

Silence.

I thought about it for at least sixty seconds. Maybe longer. As much as I wanted Mom out of my apartment, I didn't like what my father had done. And I wasn't going to encourage Mom to go back to him. As the old saying went, "Once a cheater, always a cheater."

"To be honest, I don't want to be a part of this. I don't condone what you did, and I don't want my mother thinking I do."

He nodded.

He sighed.

He stared out the windshield. "I understand."

Assuming the conversation was over, I reached for the handle. But I hesitated for some reason. "You made a really big mistake. Do you realize that?"

He didn't speak, just nodded. Finally he said, "There's something else I need to talk to you about."

"What's that?"

"Your TV show. I found someone who loves the idea. I set up an appointment for you and Elmer to meet with her."

"Really?" Now that was good news. *Great* news. "Thank you." Naturally, I felt indebted to him after this.

He pulled a business card out of his pants pocket and handed it to me. "The time and date are on the back. She asked for you to call if you need to reschedule."

"Thank you." I fingered the card. Inside I battled with myself. A part of me wanted to smack the man in the head and scream at him for being such a fool. The other part could see the pain in both their eyes. Did I want my little baby brother or sister being raised like I was? By a single mother who periodically became lost in her own bizarre world? If nothing else, my father might provide some stability for the child—something I wished I'd had growing up. "I'll see what I can do about Mom. But I'm going to make it clear to her how I feel about what you did."

"Thank you, Sloan." He smiled, but it wasn't a cheerful expression. "I can understand why you don't trust me. But I swear to you, I have only your mother's well-being and safety in mind. She's all I think about. Your mom. The baby. You."

"If that were true, you wouldn't have cheated," I blurted out. Then, "I'll call you if she agrees to come. But I'm not lying to her. I'm not tricking her into going anywhere. If she comes, she'll know it's to meet you."

"Fair enough."

"Bye."

Feeling conflicted, I stepped out of the car. Gabe was there, at my side. I gave him one look and he tossed an arm over my shoulder and steered me toward his house.

"You look like you need a drink. Or three."

"It's not even six in the morning. . . ."

"Coffee, then. I'm not taking no for an answer." He half-walked/half-nudged me up his front walk and into his house. This was the first time I'd been in his place. It was bigger than the typical bachelor pad. Considering who his father was, Senator Wagner, that was no surprise. It was very nicely decorated, with modern furniture and tasteful but contemporary accents. The den he eventually led me to was slightly more cozy and inviting than the other rooms. The furniture was more substantial; the seating was cushy. "Have a seat." He turned on the ginormous flat-screen TV hanging on the wall, handed the remote to me, then went to the kitchen, which was open to the den at one end.

"What'll it be?"

"Coffee. Lots of it. I thought you were going to work early?"

"I was. But then an old friend of mine looked like she could use some help. So I decided I'd stick around, just in case." He filled a mug. "Sugar? Cream?"

"I think I'll go with black for the first round. Thanks."

"Black it is." He handed the full mug to me.

I sipped. Good coffee. "Delicious."

"Thanks. Do you want anything to eat? Bagel? Muffin?"

"No thanks." I sipped again while he poured a cup for himself.

He sat beside me, tossed an arm over the back of the couch, angling his body to face me. "Are you as frustrated and irritated by our case as I am?"

"Probably more," I said after taking another drink. "I can't help wondering where the babies have gone."

"Do you think they're alive?"

"They were all within a couple weeks of their due dates, meaning they would probably survive if they were delivered, as long as there weren't any complications. But unexpected things happen all the time. If one did need some support, it would require specialized equipment. IVs. Incubators. Respirators. Would our unsub go to such lengths to keep an infant alive or . . . ?"

"Assuming she would, because I don't want to think about the alternative, who would have access to those kinds of things?" Gabe asked.

"Only employees of hospitals. And we've already checked all the local hospitals." I sighed.

Gabe sighed too. He set his mug on the glass-topped coffee table. He took my hand in his.

Alarms started ringing in my head.

My heart started thumping against my breastbone.

My face started burning.

"Sloan, I've been waiting for this chance for so long—"

I tried pulling my hand away. "Gabe, please don't. We should get to work."

"We aren't kids anymore," he continued, ignoring my protest. "We're adults."

"Adults with complicated lives." I twisted my wrist to the right.

"Yes."

"Adults with responsibilities." I twisted it to the left.

"Of course."

"Adults with other priorities." I jerked my arm. Still, my hand didn't pull free.

"Adults with needs." With his other hand, he cupped my cheek and stared into my eyes.

"Adults with . . ." The words flew from my mind as Gabe's mouth inched closer. I knew what was happening. I had no doubt he was going to kiss me. And my brain was 100 percent sure it didn't want that. But my body, everything but the gray matter in my skull, decided to roll out the proverbial red carpet. My pulse quickened. Parts of my body tingled. My thoughts centered on the sensations buzzing and zapping along my nerves.

His mouth hovered over mine. His breath puffed over my lips, which felt too dry. I moistened them and let my eyelids shut out the sight of those amazing, mesmerizing eyes of his.

"Sloan, if I kiss you, I won't be able to stop," he whispered.

"Don't kiss me then," I answered.

"I want to."

I wanted him to. Maybe. No, I didn't. Yes, I did.

"Neither one of us needs this now."

"Don't speak for me. You don't know what I need," he said. Generally, you'd expect those words to sound defensive, maybe even angry. But not this time, not now, not coming from a man who seemed to be on the verge of losing control.

They sounded sexy.

I told myself to lean back, but I didn't listen. I lifted my hand, which he wasn't holding hostage, to his face, instead. I palmed his cheek and let his curls wind around my fingertips.

That was definitely a bad idea.

"Okay, I don't need this now. I need a friend," I said.

"Friends kiss."

"No, they don't."

His lips touched mine. It was a fleeting contact, hardly a touch at all. But oh, how devastating that not-quite-a-touch was.

All the air left my lungs.

The circuits in my brain shorted out.

My heart went berserk, thumping so hard I could count the beats.

And still I managed to do something smart. I jerked backward, away from temptation. My hand flew from his face. He caught my wrist before it had come to rest anywhere. Now he had both hands. He brought one up to his face; this time, he flipped it over. After releasing the other hand, he uncurled my fingers one at a time, exposing my palm.

"You want to know what I think?" he asked.

"No."

"I think you're scared."

"Scared of what?" I twisted my arm, trying to pull it out of his grasp. "I'm not scared of you, if that's what you think."

"I think you're scared of trusting people, trusting men. Though considering your close call with JT—"

I yanked my hand away, swinging it at his face. "Don't go there." I missed, intentionally, but I let him know he'd crossed the line.

I guzzled what was left in my coffee cup; then I handed it back to him. "It's time for me to go." I stood. "Thank you for helping me out. I appreciate it." I headed toward the front door as fast as I could.

Gabe followed me. "Sloan, I'm sorry. I'm an ass."

"Yes, you are. But we both knew that." Standing in his foyer now, I softened the blow my words might have delivered by giving him a smile. I grabbed the doorknob and turned to face him. "I'm not mad. Don't worry."

"You're a rotten liar."

"So I've been told." I was in an awkward position, thanks to my out-of-control, raging hormones. I'd sort of led him on by not shutting him down right away. And yet I was constantly telling him, "No, no, no." Mixed messages. I released the doorknob and crossed my arms over my chest, fully aware of the message my body language would be sending. "Look, since we've been working together for the PBAU, we've managed to turn what had been a somewhat hostile relationship into something close to a friendship. I'd rather not end up sliding backward."

"Got it."

"If we started . . . spending time together outside of work, we'd eventually end up at each other's throats again."

"What makes you so sure of that?"

"It's just a feeling I have."

Gabe shrugged. "Can't help a guy for trying, Sloan. You're a beautiful, intelligent, interesting woman."

"I'm a woman with a lot of baggage. Men don't like baggage."

"Some men don't."

Ready to leave, I reached for the knob again.

Gabe leaned over and grabbed it before I could. He stepped aside, pulling the door open. That left me no choice but to step past him to go outside. "Thanks again, Gabe. It was very nice—the way you looked out for my safety."

"I've always got your back, Sloan. Don't ever forget that."

Twelve hours later, after a frustrating day at work—both Townsend's and Volpe's blood work had come back inconclusive, and the lab analyzing the swabs I'd collected called to say they needed more samples—I was standing in the police department's parking lot, next to my car, being verbally assaulted by my mother.

"I hate you," she snapped as she stomped around the front of the vehicle.

"I love you too, Mom." I got in and buckled my seat belt. I powered down the window. "Come on, let's go."

"What you're doing is unforgivable."

"I know." I shoved the key into the ignition and gave it a swift crank.

"It's detestable." She sat, slamming the door.

"Absolutely."

"Then why are you doing this?" she practically shrieked after snapping on her seat belt.

"Because you're driving me, my roommate, and every single person living in our building nuts. Prowling the house day and night, checking, double-checking, triple-checking all the windows and doors. Shouting obscenities and threats out the window—"

"I swear, I didn't know Mrs. Heckel was outside, walking Daisy. She didn't have to call the police."

I twisted to face her. "Look, I'm tired. I'm exhausted. I have this huge, important case to work, and I need to concentrate on that right now. Women are dying. And nobody knows why. The answer may be sitting in my living room, buried in Dad's stuff. I'm sorry, but I can't deal with your bird phobia right now."

"It's not a phobia, Sloan. A phobia is an *irrational* fear of something. My fear is far from irrational."

"Well, regardless, it's causing huge problems for me and Katie too. If I take you back to our place, someone else will probably call the police again. And then what?"

"I'm sorry, but I have to protect myself, Sloan. And your baby brother or sister. Surely, you understand."

"Not every bird in the world shifts into a vampire."

"But that one does. It's evil."

"Mom." I gave her squinty eyes.

"It's the Devil in disguise."

"No, it's not. Most likely, it's just a bird." I crammed the key into the ignition and jerked it, starting the car.

"You're wrong."

I sighed.

Mom sighed.

We drove the rest of the way to the country club in silence. Mom took a little catnap. How I wished I could do the same! She woke up just as we turned onto the private drive leading up to the clubhouse.

She blinked. "Where is the bastard?"

"I'm guessing he's waiting inside, not out here in the parking lot."

"Chickenshit."

"A bird, again, Mom?"

"What can I say? Lately birds have been on my radar." Mom let herself out of the car. Still looking no more pregnant than me, she jerked her chin up and *click-clacked* up the front walk. I followed.

At the reservation stand inside, I stopped to give the hostess our name. We were led to an empty table in the very back corner of the dining room.

Mom complained as she slid gracefully into a chair. "He's late."

"I'm sure he isn't late intentionally. Something important must have—"

"More important than me," Mom interrupted.

"That's not what I meant." Slightly peeved, I searched the room with my eyes.

"You're on his side."

Where the heck is he? "I'm on nobody's side."

"Liar."

Why would he be late? "Okay, I'm on *my* side. I want my apartment back. I want my bed back. I want my peace and quiet back."

"What a way to make your mother feel loved."

Have I mentioned how good my mom is at guilt-tripping people into doing things they don't want to do?

"Mom, of course I love you."

"You don't want me to be safe."

"Of course I want you to be safe. And happy. Which is why I brought you here." *Where the heck is my dad?*

If he didn't show his face in one minute, I was going to leave one hell of a nasty message on his voice mail.

"You yourself said once a man cheats on you, he'll do it again."

I was regretting those words now. "Yes, I did. But maybe I was wrong."

Mom gave me a look that said, "Oh, really?"

"I don't suppose your sudden change in attitude regarding your father has anything to do with that silly idea you had for a television show?"

"He did help me with that, but there were no strings attached. He just did it as a favor." I pulled out my cell phone and scrolled down to his name.

"You know, you should really rethink that whole thing. A prince, especially *Sluagh*, is a real prize."

"Mom, I'm not discussing this with you." I hit the button, sending the call.

"Maybe I should make you sit down and talk to your prince, work things out? Would serve you right for meddling in my affairs."

She did have a point there.

One ring. Two.

"But I'm not wreaking havoc on your life," I said.

"Says you."

I laughed. Mom laughed too.

And then a man who looked vaguely familiar—in that I-think-he's-famous-but-I-can't-place-him way—strolled up to her, holding a cordless microphone. Behind him a handful of guys, maybe in their fifties, assembled into a semicircle, musical instruments at the ready. The man lifted the microphone. There was a moment of silence.

He said the first line of "The Power of Love" in a mellow voice.

Mom gasped. "It can't be. Frankie Goes to Hollywood?"

He sang another line.

"Our song." Mom thumbed her lower lashes.

The men behind the singer parted, and my father

stepped into view and joined the man singing. The lyrics were powerful. The love in his eyes was so true and pure and beautiful—I couldn't help crying too.

I had to give it to my dad. When it came to making an entrance, he knew how to make one that nobody would forget. Looking very dashing, extremely handsome, and confident, he sang out his heart as if every word were written by him, for him.

And at the end, when the last note played, he whispered, "'I'll protect you from the dark enemy. Keep the vampires away,'" and dropped on one knee.

The band guys silently retreated.

In a loud voice, my father said, "Beverly Skye, I made that promise once. A lifetime ago. I haven't forgotten. I can't ever forget." He visibly swallowed. "I made a terrible, unforgivable mistake. I don't make any excuses. And I am a fool—no worse, a complete and utter ass— to come here, asking for your forgiveness. But I can't live another day, another minute without you."

The surrounding area filled with muffled "aahs" and "oohs." Clearly, the crowd was on his side.

My mother looked at me. She looked at my father, who was grinning up at her like a lovesick teenager. She looked at the crowd of onlookers. They were all smiling and nodding. "You ass." She gave him a little whack on the shoulder. "Nothing like putting me on the spot."

Dad blinked. The innocent act wasn't fooling anyone. Not me. Definitely not Mom.

"Forgive him," someone shouted.

Mom scowled over her shoulder. "Do you know what this man did?"

"What?" someone else said.

"He cheated on me. And I'm carrying his child."

I could feel the energy in the crowd shift. My father

was in trouble. I think he sensed it too. He looked around, nervously, still on bended knee.

"I'm not denying I made a mistake. I screwed up."

Some people left.

Others grumbled among themselves.

Mom made a sweeping gesture. "You see? They're abandoning you, now that they know the truth. Those were beautiful words, Jim. But you didn't live up to them."

My father caught her hand between his. "Please, Bev. I'm begging you to give me another chance. I'll do anything you want. Absolutely anything, if you'll come back to me."

"Go to counseling?" Mom asked.

"Absolutely. Tomorrow, if you want."

"Give up watching sports for a whole year?" she said; the corners of her lips curled up.

"Not a problem."

Her expression turned serious again. "Quit your job?"

Dad lowered his head. He didn't answer right away. I wondered how he'd talk his way out of this one.

Mom tried to pull her hand from his. "See? You won't do 'absolutely anything.'"

His head snapped up. "Yes, I will. I'll quit my job."

"Really?" Mom said, doubt clear in her voice.

"Really. I'll quit right now, today."

"Really?" Mom perked up.

"Please, Bev. I love you. I need you. I swear I'll never betray you again."

Mom looked askance at me.

I shrugged. "He sounds like he means it."

Mom's lips curled into the slightest hint of a smile. "Well . . ."

"There's only one small hitch," my father said.

"What's that?" Mom asked warily.

"We get married in three days."

"Three days?" That hint of a smile vanished. "What's the hurry?"

"I love you. I lost you once. And I nearly lost you a second time, thanks to my own stupidity. I can't stand the thought of losing you forever. I want to stand in front of the world and promise to love you for the rest of my life."

"But . . . what about all of our plans? My dress. My flowers—"

"I can have it all set in time," he said, pleading with his eyes.

"Was that . . . really—"

"Holly Johnson. Frankie Goes to Hollywood," my father finished for her.

"Where did you find him? He hasn't performed in ages."

He smiled. "See? If I can get Johnson to serenade you, don't you think I can plan a wedding?"

"Oh, for crying out loud. Okay. You jerk!" Mom threw her arms around my father's neck.

The crowd that remained cheered loudly.

I cried.

"I hope a sunset wedding will do," my father said after giving my mother a kiss that made my cheeks flush.

"A sunset wedding will be perfect." Mom looked at me. "Sloan, I need your help."

The next morning, I was at the unit, bags packed with all the essentials needed for at least a week of undercover work. I had a bit of a challenge picking clothes, though, since my wardrobe was purchased to fit my current thirty-four, twenty-seven, thirty-eight figure. However, someone seemed to have anticipated my shortage of maternity wear. I discovered a box of clothes sitting on my desk when I arrived at the office.

Hough wandered out of her cave just as I was inspecting the contents. I didn't want to appear ungrateful, but the garments were hideous. My mood was sour. Her smile was sparkly. I wasn't in the frame of mind for sparkly.

"The chief told me about your assignment. I thought you could use those. They were my mom's."

Translation: too ugly and outdated for her to wear. But good enough for me.

With great effort, I produced a smile. "That's so thoughtful. Thank you."

"I figured you wouldn't want to buy any maternity clothes now, since you're not really pregnant and probably won't be for some time. They are so expensive," she said as she ran her hand over her nonexistent baby bump, currently clothed in a cute, flattering black-and-gray knit dress. "Who's to say when you'll get around to having children? The styles could change by then, right?"

Little Miss Sparkle Face seemed to be throwing my single-with-no-prospects status in my face, but I took the high road. I kept right on smiling. "You are so right about that. I'd like to concentrate on building my career before I even think of having kids, anyway."

"That's very smart."

I cleared my throat.

Her glittery happy-mother-to-be eyes lifted, focusing on something or someone behind me. "Good morning," she greeted with a singsong.

I knew, by the look on her face, who it was.

My heart did a little jump in my chest. My blood turned cold. My body tensed.

"Good morning," JT said.

I shoved the box off my desk, letting it free-fall to the floor, and set my laptop case where it had been.

"I loaned Sloan some clothes for her undercover assignment," Brittany announced.

"That's very nice of you." JT leaned a shoulder on my cubby partition.

I pulled out my secondhand laptop and fired it up.

"Just doing what I can to help," Brittany said. "I'll be here if you need anything else, Sloan," she said to me. "I tried to convince the chief to let me go undercover instead of you, but she said absolutely not."

JT scowled. "No way. It's much too dangerous for both you and the baby."

Googling the words "shape-shifting vampires," I tried to tune the two lovebirds out.

"I know it would be dangerous," Hough said, "but I feel like this could be my big chance. I mean, we're dealing with an unsub that's preying upon pregnant women. And here I am, pregnant. Besides, with you watching over me, I'm sure I'd be safe. You'd never let anything happen to me. Or the baby."

Considering it was *his child,* I had no doubt about that too.

"Still, it makes more sense not to risk it," JT told her. I wished they'd take their conversation somewhere else, so I could concentrate. "We have Sloan. She can do the job as well as you, and that's one less life at risk."

"Okay." Hough heaved a sigh of disappointment. "I'll stick with doing my usual thing."

"Your 'usual thing' is something nobody else in the unit can do. Which is why the chief brought you on board."

"Thanks, JT. You always know the right thing to say." Hough bounced back to her "Bat Cave."

JT turned to face me. "Ready to get started?"

"As ready as I'll ever be." I abandoned my search, which had proven fruitless, and powered down the laptop.

JT's eyes slid to the box. "You have a doctor's appointment this morning. Since the first victim was a patient of Dr. Rosenstein, we're focusing on his practice today. You should change your clothes before we leave."

"Fine. I'll change." I started digging through the box, finding one butt-ugly garment after another. The tops all looked like overgrown baby dresses, with huge bibs and bows. Many of them were stained. I'm not much of a fashionista, but these clothes were beyond unwearable. "What time's the appointment?"

"Ten," JT said.

I checked the time. It was already after nine. There'd be no time to stop at a mall and buy something better. I grabbed the best outfit I could find—a sundress with big yellow flowers all over it, and shuffled to the ladies' room to change. When I returned, JT and the chief were eyeing me.

JT shook his head. "I agree, Chief. We need the suit."

"What suit?" I asked, hoping it was a maternity business suit, something that looked more professional.

The chief escorted me to her office and handed me a bag. "Sloan, we all appreciate the sacrifices you're making." She patted me on the back.

I pulled out a white garment. Didn't look like a business suit to me. "What's this?"

Imagine a full-body girdle, the old-fashioned kind with wide shoulder straps and a padded cone bra. That was what I was holding. But this girdle had a huge, round protuberance sewn onto the front. And it weighed about ten tons.

So much for the somewhat decent sundress.

"It's a pregnancy suit. You can't expect anyone to believe you're nine months pregnant looking like that." She pointed at my midriff, which was concealed by ample yellow-flowered yardage.

I bit back a groan and hauled the pregnant bodysuit back to my cubicle. I selected another dress. This one looked like an enormous toddler dress. I went back to the bathroom for another change.

When I returned, JT, the chief, and Hough all looked pleased.

"Now that's a pregnant woman," the chief said.

Feeling slightly hormonal, I hurried back to my cubicle, flung my laptop case over my shoulder, and practiced my mother-to-be waddle as I headed toward the elevators.

At exactly ten o'clock, JT and I were standing at Dr. Rosenstein's check-in desk, registering for my first appointment. The kind lady at the desk took a look at my stomach and said, "Please take a seat and we'll call your name as soon as possible."

I didn't even have time to get comfortable in an empty seat before my name—or rather, my new undercover mother-to-be name—was called.

"Mrs. Thompson?"

JT gave me a nudge.

"Already?" I asked as my ass hovered over a chair.

He shrugged.

I met a smiling nurse, wearing scrubs with grinning cartoon baby faces, at a doorway.

She handed me a little paper cup. "Please write your name on the cup, collect a urine specimen, and leave it in the bathroom, on the metal tray."

I did as I was told, wondering how many of the employees at the doctor's office knew I wasn't really pregnant. A simple dipstick test and my cover would be blown. When I exited the bathroom, she steered me to a small area set off from the hustle and bustle of the main check-in counter. Stopping there, she had me stand on a scale. It was off. Way off. Even taking the extra pounds the fake belly added. Next she had me sit and then checked my blood pressure. Those numbers looked good. Then she sent me back to a room. JT was waiting there, sitting in a chair.

"Kind of reminds me of the last time we were here," he said.

"Do you think anyone recognizes me?"

"I doubt it." JT motioned to the bed. "Aren't you supposed to strip your clothes off or something?"

I glowered. "Don't you think you've seen enough women naked from the waist down?" Low blow, I realized. I regretted it the minute I said it.

A knock sounded before he could respond. That was probably a good thing. Our conversation was bound to go downhill from there.

Dr. Rosenstein came strolling in, all smiles. He took a look at me, eyes twinkling. "*Mrs. Thompson,* you're looking very good." Of course, he knew I wasn't pregnant. It was unavoidable. Not that we were too concerned. We'd pretty much eliminated him, and all the other doctors, in his practice. For one thing, he was the wrong gender. The purpose of my visit was hopefully to catch the eye of the unsub, *if* she was one of the contract workers the practice regularly employed.

"Thanks, Doctor," I said.

He shut the door. "How can I help you, Agents?"

JT said, "We'd like to make sure my *wife's* name, address, and phone numbers appear on all paperwork that would normally be processed for a new patient. We've concluded someone who contracts for several local doctors is either our killer or is somehow supplying a list of names and addresses to the killer."

The doctor's expression darkened. "I can't see anyone who works for me doing such a thing."

JT continued his explanation. "Because several of the victims aren't your patients, we have to assume it's nobody who works directly for you. We're following up on one person of interest, an ultrasound technician. Can you think of any other contract workers who have access to patient files?"

The doctor thought about it for a moment. "Could be billing."

"Billing," I echoed.

"Sure. I don't do any billing in-house. It's contracted out. Saves me over thirty thousand dollars a year, when you take into account benefits and taxes. I'm sure other doctors in the area do the same thing."

"We'd like information on that company if you can get it to us," I said.

"I'll be back in a few minutes." He left.

I sat on the edge of the examination table, legs crossed at the ankles.

JT stared at me. "I meant to tell you earlier, nice dress."

I shot him a gesture that was more biker chick than pregnant suburbanite. "We expectant mothers have ways of making you pay."

"I don't believe for a minute that Hough was trying to make you look like an idiot, if that's what you're thinking."

I kicked a leg, sending the lower part of the skirt fluttering. "But you agree, I do look ridiculous."

"Maybe not ridiculous. But . . ."

"Silly," I offered. "Pathetic. Laughable. Absurd."

"No. You could never look pathetic. Or absurd." JT pulled out his wallet, slid a credit card from a slot and waved it. "But since you feel so strongly about it, how about you do some shopping after we're done here? I can't have my *wife* walking around looking like an overgrown two-year-old."

My sour mood instantly improved. "Thank you, dear husband. I wouldn't mind picking up a few things."

The doctor returned, handed us a business card,

reminded me to take my prenatal vitamins, winked, then told me he'd like to see me in a week. And that was that. With any hope, my name, address, phone number, and fictitious due date were now in the hands of a bloodsucking killer.

As JT and I strolled out of the building, we passed Hough, on her way in. As would be expected, she pretended not to know us.

In the car, I stared at the building's entry. "Shouldn't Hough change doctors?"

JT buckled himself into the driver's seat. "We told her it would be a good idea, but she said she likes her doctor. She trusts him, and she's not going to change, unless it's absolutely necessary. I can't argue with her. She's still in the early weeks of her pregnancy, so her risk may be limited."

"True. I keep telling myself the same thing, when it comes to my mother."

"Exactly. The unsub's MO has been consistent. I agree, there's no need to get paranoid. Yet. Besides, in the end, it's her choice. Nobody at the bureau can force her to change doctors. But if we don't catch the killer soon, by the middle of her second trimester, you bet I'll be putting pressure on her to make a change."

"Good idea."

Strength does not come from physical capacity. It comes from an indomitable will.

—Mahatma Gandhi

19

The first thing I wanted to do when we returned to the unit was change my clothes. The pregnant bodysuit was heavy and hot and uncomfortable. My back was aching. My center of gravity and balance were out of whack. And I hated how my protruding stomach kept knocking into things. That thing seemed to have a mind of its own.

So, of course, when we strolled into the office, I made a beeline for my regular clothes, folded on my desk.

The chief stopped me. "Skye, I need you and JT to go to this address and interview a woman named Quaid." She set a piece of paper on the stack of clothes now cradled in my arms. "She claims to have seen something suspicious outside of her neighbor's house last night. Her neighbor is pregnant." Her gaze flicked down to the clothes. "You'll need to stay in the maternity clothes until we've either caught this killer or at least ID'd her."

"Even when I'm here in the office?"

"Considering the fact that none of us, with the exception of Hough, stay here long, I'd say yes."

"Okay." I dropped my normal clothes back on my desk, Google Mapped the address, and went in search of JT. I found him rummaging around in Hough's computer lair. He scurried out when he saw me.

"JT, the chief needs us to go to this address." I handed him the paper. "It's not far from our new rental home, so maybe we should drive separately. That way, we won't have to come back here later."

"Fine. Go on ahead without me. I'll be there in a bit."

"Sure." I started toward my cubicle, but JT stopped me with a tap on my shoulder. "Skye, leave the box of clothes. I'll take it down."

"But I can carry it. It's not that heavy."

"How do you think that would look, a very visibly pregnant woman hauling a huge box by herself?"

"Ah, good point. Thanks." I headed down to my car with just my laptop case. My other stuff—shoes, personal items, a box with some of my dad's research, etc.—were still in my trunk. I motored to the witness's house, parked at the curb, and, with notebook and pen at the ready, knocked on the door.

A woman in her early thirties answered. She opened the door just wide enough to peer out.

"I'm Sloan Skye," I explained. "I work for the FBI. Are you Tricia Quaid?"

"That's me." Peering over my shoulder, Tricia Quaid motioned me inside, then shut and locked the doors. We walked into the foyer of what seemed to be a nicely kept Colonial home. "I'm so glad you came so quickly. I'm absolutely petrified to leave the house."

"What happened?" I flipped to an empty page in my notebook.

A little dog yapped somewhere in the house. I love animals. Really, I do. But, unfortunately, they don't love me so much. I inched closer to the front door, readying myself for a hasty getaway.

Quaid launched into her story. "Mitzy had gotten out

of our yard last night. When I went looking for her, I found her standing under the neighbor's window, fighting with some gnarly-looking blackbird."

"Okay." I had no idea if it was a normal thing for a dog to attack a bird. Possibly. But it did seem to be an interesting coincidence that there'd been a mangy blackbird outside of a pregnant woman's house when a similar bird had been seen by other witnesses. Maybe my mother was right, about that bird hanging around outside my apartment. "Was there anything unusual about the bird? What made you call the FBI?"

"There was some kind of long pink tube coming out of its mouth. And when I say long, I mean, *really* long. I'd never seen anything like it. And it seemed to have been caught in my neighbor's window. I read the article in the paper, about the Baltimore Vampire. A black bat or bird was mentioned. This seemed suspicious enough to at least make a call."

"Can we go see where your dog attacked the bird?"

"Sure." Tricia Quaid led me out the front door and around the side of her house. "It was right about"—she looked up, at the side of the neighbor's house—"here." She pointed at an area of grass.

I stooped down; or rather, I tried to stoop down. It was no small feat. Neither was seeing the ground. The stupid belly was in my way. I duckwalked back a bit so I could search the area a little better.

From the general vicinity of the front of the house, a familiar male voice said, "Hello."

Tricia Quaid headed toward the voice, which belonged to JT.

I shifted forward, taking on a froglike crouching position to comb my fingers through the grass. I could just imagine what a freakish sight I was.

"How's it going, Skye?" JT asked.

"Oh, just fine. As you can tell, it's so easy for a pregnant woman to search for clues on the ground."

"Please let me." JT caught one of my hands in his, placed the other under my elbow, and helped me to my feet. Instantly I had a new respect for all pregnant women around the world. "I noticed the neighbor's car just pulled in."

"Thanks for the help. Sheesh, I'll never again take certain things for granted." To Tricia Quaid, I said, "This is Special Agent Jordan Thomas. He's going to finish up the search here while I go talk to the neighbor."

"Okay." Quaid said, taking a step back. "Is Mitzy going to be okay? Is it safe for me to let her out?"

I didn't answer right away. These things had to be handled carefully, to keep people from panicking, jumping to conclusions, or spreading rumors that could hamper our investigation.

JT responded, "Ma'am, the best advice I can give you is to take your dog to a veterinarian if she appears ill, or you have any concerns for her health. Otherwise, I believe she should be okay."

"That's a relief." Quaid visibly exhaled. "But what does the bird have to do with the murders? I read an article in one of those newspapers in the grocery store. They're saying it's a bird-monster. That's just silly, right? You don't believe that there's some freakish bird-monster out there killing people. I mean, nobody believes in monsters."

"Of course not," I answered.

"Then why are you here?" she asked.

"We're merely doing our jobs," JT replied. "With the Baltimore Vampire on the loose, we've been told to investigate any report of suspicious activity near the home of a pregnant woman."

I pointed at the neighbor's house. "I'm going to talk to your neighbor. What's her name?"

"Paula Wahlberg."

"Thanks." I rounded the front of Paula Wahlberg's house and rang the bell.

A pretty women who was very pregnant answered the door. Her gaze dropped to my belly, and she smiled. "Hi, may I help you?"

"My name's Sloan Skye. I work for the FBI. We're checking out a report of some suspicious activity outside your home last night."

Paula Wahlberg's perfectly plucked brows scrunched together. She looked confused. But for some reason, I wasn't buying it. "Suspicious activity?"

"Yes. Did anything unusual happen last night?"

"Well . . ." Paula Wahlberg looked at me. She blinked a few times. "Did someone say something about a rope?" Her gaze flicked over my shoulder, outside, as if she was expecting someone to be out there.

"Rope?" I echoed, wondering if she'd mistaken the creature's proboscis for something else.

"My husband and I have been experimenting lately. He tied me up last night. But I swear, he didn't hurt me. And the baby's just fine." A blushing Paula Wahlberg ran a hand over her stomach, as I was beginning to notice so many pregnant mothers did.

An image—bizarre and a smidge disturbing—flashed in my mind. "I don't believe that's the suspicious activity that was reported."

"Oh." Her cheeks turned the shade of a cherry.

I reassured her with a smile. "No worries. Your secret is safe with me."

"Thanks. So, if it wasn't . . . that . . . what was it?" Paula Wahlberg asked.

"When you were falling asleep, did you happen to feel or hear anything unusual?"

Her eyes lifted as she visibly searched her memory. "No, not that I can remember."

"Would you mind if I went up and took a look at your room? I promise it'll only take a minute."

"Well . . ." Paula Wahlberg's face turned an even deeper shade of red. "Are you sure it's necessary?"

"It would be a big help."

"Okay." She led me upstairs, hesitating at the top of the staircase before opening the door. Finally she opened it.

And I could understand why Paula Wahlberg had hesitated.

My gaze swept the room. It was my turn to falter and blush. The room looked like something from one of those bizarre bondage porn sites. There were several pieces of wood and leather bondage furniture lining one wall. The bed had four thick posts, and chains were hanging from huge metal rings bolted to them.

Trying to pretend like I saw this kind of thing all day long, I wandered over to the window. It was open now. If the Wahlbergs had central air-conditioning, they weren't using it. The weather had been unseasonably cool the last week or so. But there was a window fan shoved in the window, held in position by the sliding frame. After cutting off the motor, I moved the fan out of the way.

I used a flashlight to look for traces of blood and tissue on and around the window. "Was this window open last night, by any chance?"

"Yes, for a while. But when it started to rain, my husband shut it. Why?"

Pulling out a swab, I ran it all along the edges of the frame and sash, then dropped it into a plastic bag. Next I checked the screen. My finger slipped into the small hole at the corner of the frame. Goose bumps prickled my skin. My stomach turned.

How close had this woman come to being the killer's next victim?

It had been only a matter of sheer luck that we hadn't been called to this house this morning, to investigate Paula Wahlberg's death.

"Do you have central air-conditioning?" I asked.

"Sure. But with it being so cool at night, I prefer sleeping with the window open. Fresh air is so much healthier for the baby."

"I strongly recommend you use the air-conditioning." Turning to face her, I stared at her stomach. "Until after you deliver."

In an attempt to avoid answering the flurry of questions that were sure to follow, I thanked her and headed downstairs. Outside, I found JT sitting in his car. He waved me over. I climbed into the passenger seat and shut the door.

"I picked up a few specimens. What did you get?" JT asked.

I handed him the plastic bag. "Some tissue from the window. The screen has a hole, like the others. Paula Wahlberg doesn't know how lucky she is that it rained last night." I glanced up at the window, which was visible from my vantage point. It was shut now. I hoped that meant she was taking my warning to heart.

JT waved the bag. "I'll take these in, if you want to go to the rental and make yourself comfortable."

"I could do that. But I want to pick up an outfit or two. I refuse to wear any of these overgrown baby dresses in public again. And I should probably stop at the grocery store while I'm out. Any special requests?"

"Buy whatever you like. I'm easy." He winked.

I ignored it and went about the complicated business of extricating myself from his car.

JT grabbed my elbow to stop my retreat; then he

shifted to face me directly. "Look, Sloan, I realize you don't like me very much right now. I understand this is awkward. But are you sure you're okay with this assignment? Because if you're not, we can get someone else to stay with you."

"I can handle it."

"I'll need to stay with you at night."

"I figured as much."

"But I promise not to do or say anything inappropriate anymore."

"Well, that would be a welcome change."

JT nodded. "I deserved that."

With a little extra effort, I got out of JT's loaner car and went to mine. Feeling a little crappy after that sarcastic dig—I'm so much better than that—I cranked the engine and pulled away from the curb.

This thing with JT was turning me into someone I didn't like very much. It was time to do something about it.

A handful of hours later, JT came home to a house filled with smoke, a smoke detector squealing, and a flustered, irritated make-believe, pretending-to-be-pregnant wife. When he strolled into the kitchen, his eyes were the size of grapefruits, and he was fanning his face with his hand.

I took a break from disaster cleanup duty to welcome him home with a cold bottle of vitaminwater.

"What's this?" he asked, accepting the drink while perusing the mess.

"It was supposed to be an early dinner, but things got a little out of hand."

Focusing on the torched black blobs smoldering on the stove, he said, "A *little* out of hand?"

I plopped onto the stool, pushed up against the kitchen island. "It was supposed to be a peace offering."

"For what?"

I slid a sideways glance his way.

He grinned.

"Do I get points for trying?" I asked.

"You do." He patted my shoulder. "It wasn't necessary, you know. It should be me making a peace offering."

"Maybe, but I felt I've been a jerk lately too. Here I am telling you, over and over, that we need to be professional, that we must set aside our personal feelings and act like coworkers. Yet, I've been acting like a little whiny bitch. And all because of something that's none of my business. You've fathered a child. That's wonderful."

JT unscrewed the cap on the water bottle. "I think you're being a little hard on yourself."

"I don't. The FBI is no place for whiners. It's also no place for flirting or fooling around. So no more screeching tires. No more sarcastic slams. No more kissing either. We're coworkers and nothing more. Okay?"

JT thought about it for a moment.

I gave him a jab. "Okay," I answered for him.

"If you insist. Though we may have to act like we're more than coworkers while we're undercover. To make it believable." He winked.

I gave him my best mean eyes. "You're impossible."

We ate turkey sandwiches and fruit for dinner. Then JT hauled in the box with my dad's research first, so I could keep searching for information on Malaysian vampires, while he brought in the rest of my stuff.

An hour or so later, JT joined me. "I put most of your stuff in the second bedroom, the one that faces the front. Do you think you brought enough?" He winked.

I did the mature thing; I stuck out my tongue. "Maybe next time I'll pack *more*. I think I forgot some things."

"All joking aside, how are you doing?" He motioned to the files.

"It's going slowly." I glanced around the piles of folders spread around me. "But I'm classifying them as I go. I'm assuming we'll be digging through this stuff all summer long. Might as well organize it so we'll know where to find things."

"Good idea. Can I help?"

"Sure. I'm creating piles, based on creature type and then geographical region. Vampires are over here. Shapeshifters are there. Ghosts and other spirit beings are there."

"Got it."

I rubbed my temples, feeling the start of a tension headache coming. "My father was thorough—I'll give him that much. It's just sad that he doesn't remember most of it."

"He doesn't?"

"He told me he had meningitis recently and he's had some memory loss."

"Really?" JT's tone was doubtful.

"You don't believe him?"

JT shrugged. "I guess I have no reason to doubt him."

That was the conclusion I'd come to as well.

We worked together until just before midnight. And we managed not only to get a lot done, but we did it without JT flirting with me, or me getting snarky or sarcastic. Overall, despite the fact that we hadn't come across the files on Malaysian vampire legend yet, I could only classify the evening's work as a major success.

Even so, I dreaded what was about to happen next.

I showered before bed; then, wrapped in a towel, I barefooted it to the spare bedroom. I put on as much clothing as I could stand, considering the weather had changed and a muggy feeling had crept in while we'd been working. To provide the killer with her opportunity to attack, the window would have to stay open. The air-conditioning would have to stay off. But as a safeguard, to avoid becoming her next victim, I would have to sleep with JT. The more barriers to his wandering hands, the better.

Wearing the pregnant bodysuit, a pair of shorts, and a T-shirt, I shuffled back to the master bedroom. JT was already tucked in. He wasn't wearing a shirt.

I hoped he had on some pants.

I went to the window.

"It's all set. Open. The screen's intact." He grinned and patted the mattress. "Come to bed, *wife.*"

Ugh was all I thought.

You gain strength, courage, and confidence by every experience by which you really stop to look fear in the face. You are able to say to yourself, "I lived through this horror. I can take the next thing that comes along."

—Eleanor Roosevelt

20

Something was touching my leg.

Creeping.

Crawling.

Oh, God, it was moving up, up, up.

I jerked upright and ripped the covers off myself.

I nudged JT.

He grunted and rolled over, seeming to be in a deep sleep.

A pink slithery thing wriggled on the mattress.

I shrieked like a girl and scrabbled away, crawling right on top of him.

That woke JT up. He clamped his arms around me and whispered, "I knew you'd change your mind."

I smacked him, then flung myself on the floor. "It's here! The thing!"

"Oh. Shit!" JT lunged forward just as I snapped on the lamp.

The pink proboscis slithered right out of JT's hands.

"Shit, it's slimy," he cussed. "I can't get a grip."

I dashed to the window and slammed it shut just as it slid out.

Outside, I heard a strange clicking sound, and then the flap of wings. I saw absolutely nothing.

Leaning back against the closed window, I sucked in a lungful of air. "Oh. My. God. Why didn't you wake up?"

"I didn't expect it to find us so soon." Lips curled in disgust, JT inspected his hands. "It's what . . . three A.M.?"

I checked the clock. "A quarter after."

"Just goes to show how desperate it is."

"I don't know about that." He waved a hand at me. "We should collect a specimen of this slime." While I went in search of swabs, JT continued, "Think about it. You just went to Dr. Rosenstein's office yesterday. And within hours it's got you in its sights? Why is that? Why isn't it hunting one of the many other patients who have been seeing the doctor this whole time?"

"Like . . . Hough, for instance?" Finding a swab in JT's laptop case, I went to work, collecting the sample.

"Like Hough, yeah."

"I don't know. Maybe it already visited all the other patients and couldn't get in." I sealed the swab in a plastic evidence bag and set it on the nightstand.

"I suppose that's possible." He went to the bathroom and washed up. When he returned to the bedroom, he said, "We need to set a trap. So that next time, we catch it."

"That's right up my mother's alley," I said as I stared out the window. My skin was prickling all over with the creepy-crawlies; and my heart was still thumping so hard, I could hear every beat in my ears. "I'll call her later, at a decent hour, and ask her if she'd like to help."

"But you can't tell her what we're trapping," JT reminded me as he smoothed the covers back in place.

"Sure, I know." I wasn't about to tell him about Mom

reading all my case notes. I figured it was better for both of us if he didn't know.

He motioned to the bed. "Come on, Sloan. You should try to get some sleep. We'll leave the window closed until we're ready for it."

"I'm not sure if I'll be able to sleep." I checked the window one last time, to make sure it was closed and locked. Then I paid a visit to the bathroom. While I was peeing, JT took the sample downstairs to put it in the refrigerator for safekeeping.

JT was in bed, his back to me, when I returned.

I settled in.

I rolled onto my back and stared up at the ceiling.

Then I flopped onto my right side.

Then I rolled onto my left side.

"If you don't stop flopping around like that, I'm going to tie you down," JT grumbled.

"I'm a stomach sleeper. I can't get comfortable." I tried my right side again.

"You didn't have any problem falling asleep earlier."

"Yeah, well, that was before some vampiric thing tried to suck every drop of blood from my body."

"It's gone," he pointed out.

"I know."

"You're safe." JT set a hand on my arm.

"Yeah."

He gave my arm a soft shake. "Sloan, I promise I won't let anything happen to you."

"You said that before. You almost failed to keep that promise."

"It won't happen again." He rolled over to face me. "No excuses. I shouldn't have assumed she wouldn't find you so quickly. Now I know better. I swear, I won't fail you."

I nodded and closed my eyes.

I tried to fall asleep. I really did. I pretended to fall asleep, for JT's sake, so he wouldn't feel worse than he already did. But slowly the hours dragged by. Birdsong signaled the arrival of dawn.

I sat up.

JT stretched and yawned. "How'd you sleep?"

"Okay. You?"

"I didn't. But don't worry, I'm okay."

I left the bed, all rumpled and cozy and smelling like a certain sleepy, cuddly man, and went into the bathroom to take care of a few essentials. When I came out, JT had the bed made and was already dressed. His hair was freshly damp.

"Took a quick shower in the other bathroom," he explained, sitting on the bed to tie his shoes.

I'd been in the bathroom all of . . . ten minutes. "How did you accomplish so much in such a short time?"

"I was in the army. In boot camp we had three minutes to shit, shave, and shower." He grabbed his phone, sitting on the nightstand, and started poking buttons.

"And that was how long ago?"

With his attention focused on his phone, he shrugged. "The habit kind of stuck with me. But it comes in handy when I'm in a hurry."

"Are we in a hurry?"

"We are." With his phone held to his ear, he motioned toward the door. "The chief called while I was cleaning up. It seems our unsub left here and found herself another target last night."

My insides twisted into a knot. "Damn it. If only we'd been able to stop her, that woman would be alive right now."

"We tried, Sloan. We can't blame ourselves. It won't do us any good," he said as he punched the keys on his phone.

"Yes, it will. It'll make me that much more determined to get her next time—if there is a next time."

"I have the feeling there will be." He scowled. "The victim's house is about three miles from here."

Together we stomped down the stairs and made a turn toward the kitchen. I went for the instant coffee—filling a travel mug to the top—and a S'Mores-flavor Balance bar. JT grabbed a vitaminwater out of the refrigerator, a banana, and a protein bar. Out we went. JT rammed his breakfast-to-go down his throat while he drove. I did the same while I navigated for him. We were both still chewing when we pulled up in front of the scene.

JT heaved a sigh as he cut the car's engine. "We've been to way too many of these scenes."

"I completely agree. Which reminds me . . ." I dialed my mom's phone while I scrabbled out of the car. JT was way ahead of me. His long legs carried him up the front walk at a brisk pace that I couldn't meet in my current condition. My mother's line rang five times. No answer. After the sixth, it clicked over to voice mail. I left a message, ended the call, then followed JT into the house.

It was swarming with people. Crime scene techs. Detectives. Uniformed cops. I located JT upstairs, at the top of the staircase, talking to a man who looked like he might be the victim's husband.

The man had a bewildered, confused look on his face. He was still wearing his pajamas. His feet were bare, and his hair was sticking out at odd angles.

"I don't understand. Cassie was fine when we went to bed. I didn't hear a damn thing. Nothing. I saw nobody. I felt nobody. I normally wake up when she gets the hiccups," he lamented. "How does someone get in our home and kill my girlfriend, and steal our child, while I'm fucking asleep? Can you tell me that?" His hands were clenched, shaking; his face and neck were the shade of a nude sunbather on the planet Mercury.

"We are doing everything in our power to find out who is doing this and stop them," JT said.

"It makes no sense. None whatsoever!" the man shouted. "Cassie shouldn't be dead. We should be eating breakfast, talking about how she spent too much money yesterday on baby stuff, and arguing with me about what color the fucking nursery will be." The man's eyes watered.

Mine sort of did too.

I blinked a bunch of times and turned toward the wall to collect myself.

My phone rang. It was Mom.

I hit the button and shuffled back down the stairs.

"Sloan, it's early. What's wrong? Why did you call me?"

"Nothing's wrong. I'm okay. I just need a favor," I said as I wedged myself into a quiet corner of the living room.

"What sort of favor?"

"You know how you love to create inventions?" Before she had a chance to respond, I continued my pitch. "Well, I need you to make something for me. A trap. A very special kind of trap. Are you up for it?"

"Will you be using this trap for work?"

"Yes, I will be."

"Then I'd be essentially working for the FBI?"

"In a sense."

"I'll do it!"

"Great. I'm busy right now. I need to go. But I'll get in touch with you later to give you the specifics."

"Okay. I'll talk to you later, then. Bye."

"Bye." I shoved my phone in my pocket and went in search of JT. He was still upstairs, though he'd made it into the bedroom and was checking out the window. "Is the screen cut?"

"Just like the others." He was shining a flashlight at the

edge, where the screen was affixed to the metal frame. "I don't see any signs of tissue."

"Was the window still open?"

"Yeah, the victim's boyfriend, Nick Ellanson, said he hadn't touched the window."

"If only he had." I sighed. "I wonder if we should contact all three doctors and tell them to recommend their patients sleep with their bedroom windows closed and locked until we can catch the unsub?"

"If we did that, chances are she'll move on, and we'll have to wait for her to kill again before we could find her. In the long run, that could cost a lot more lives."

"I know, but this is killing me." Reluctantly, I turned toward the empty bed. The ME had already taken Cassie Crause away.

JT nudged my arm. "We'll get her."

For some reason, my hand went to my artificially swollen belly. "How close was she to delivering?"

"A few weeks," JT mumbled.

A shudder swept through my body. "I hate this case."

JT looked at his notes. "Here's something interesting. She had a doctor's appointment yesterday."

"So did I."

"Yes, you did. But she doesn't go to Rosenstein. She's a patient of Patel's."

"What about the other victims? Were they killed within twenty-four hours of their appointments? I don't remember looking at that variable."

"I don't know. I'd have to take a look at our notes. In fact, I'm not sure if that's a question we've even thought to ask."

"We should have, if we didn't."

"Yes, we should have."

After talking to a couple of neighbors, JT and I agreed it was time to go. First on our to-do list was reviewing the notes on the other victims, to see if any of the others had visited their doctors within twenty-four hours of their deaths. If we were lucky enough to have found a concrete variable, that would help us eliminate a substantial number of pregnant women from the potential victim list every night.

If not, we were hoping Gabe, Fischer, and the chief were getting somewhere.

When we stepped into the PBAU, the chief waved us over.

"Status meeting in five," she told us.

We dumped our stuff on our desks, grabbed pens, paper, and our notes on the case, and headed into the conference room.

"I know all of you are horrified by the tragedy of this case," the chief began as she took her position at the front of the room. "And I hate to add pressure, but I need to tell you that it's getting increasingly difficult to keep a lid on this one. The media is all over it. Because it involves pregnant women and infants, they aren't backing off. If anything, they're getting more aggressive. Fischer's doing his best to feed information to the right people, and to keep what needs to be kept quiet from leaking out. However, if we don't get some movement on this case soon, one of them is going to bust through, and then it'll be panic. I'm sure you all can imagine where that'll lead."

I had a vivid imagination. All sorts of possibilities played through my mind.

The chief continued, "We need this case wrapped up yesterday. But we have a problem." She paused; and once again, all sorts of possibilities played through my mind. Surely, the FBI wouldn't shut us down already? While we were in the middle of such a horrific case? "It's something of a good problem. We have a second case, this one in California. I need to split up the team." She looked at me. "Skye and Thomas will stay here and keep working the Baltimore Vampire. Fischer is needed here, to keep the media out of the way. And Hough's out on medical for a few days. That means I'll be going to Los Angeles with Wagner." She stood. "Wagner, wheels up in a half hour. Fischer, Skye, and Thomas, I'm counting on you to handle things here."

I hoped we wouldn't let her down.

"We'll do our best," Fischer promised.

"That's all I can ask." She looked at me one last time. "Skye, do you need anything from me before I head out?"

"No, Chief, I don't think so."

"Very good." She gave a little nod and left.

Wagner glanced my way and grinned. A couple of weeks ago, he would've made a smart-ass comment about my new, rotund physique. Not today. He just said, "Good luck, Skye," and left.

I turned to JT. "What's wrong with Hough?"

"Nothing serious. She just needed some rest."

Sitting on the opposite side of the room, Fischer moved closer. "We've got one hell of a job to do."

"That we do," I agreed.

"When the chief was talking about the press, she wasn't exaggerating. We're days from a huge media shit storm. We need to get a profile to the Baltimore PD before that, or we'll lose her."

"We're trying," JT said. "We're just hitting a lot of brick walls."

"Let's talk through what we have," Fischer suggested. "Maybe we're closer to the answer than we realize."

"Wouldn't that be nice," I said, flipping open my notes.

"First, I think we can all agree, this killer is showing no signs of any thrill-seeking or power-and-control behaviors in her killing," JT began.

I added, "She's a female. Killing for personal gain. Possibly material too, depending upon what she's doing with the infants. The babies could also be taken as trophies. She's organized. She's selecting her victims with some care, determining whom she'll choose by some criteria we haven't completely figured out yet. And she's leaving the crime scene with very little evidence. That means she's intelligent."

"Her MO," JT said, "is to hunt at night, taking advantage of an open window or chimney to gain access to the victim. She is adopting the form of some kind of flying creature—we think it's a bird—and uses a long, flexible proboscis to drain the victim's blood and somehow extract the child from the deceased mother. We've recently noticed a pattern that could be helpful, but we haven't verified whether it applies to all of her victims yet."

"I think you should take your preliminary profile to the Baltimore PD," Fischer suggested.

I wasn't sold on that idea. "But we haven't identified the species of the unsub yet, which makes it difficult to know how to stop her."

"It's enough to be helpful, especially if you can verify that pattern you discovered," Fischer said.

"I'll get on that today." JT scratched some notes down; then he pointed at me with the end of his pen. "Meanwhile, Skye, I think you should dig deeper in your father's research and come up with a list of possible matches."

"Okay."

Fischer grabbed his cell and started dialing. "I'm calling McGrane and setting up a meeting tomorrow. We'll present what we have then. That gives you roughly twenty-four hours to finalize what you can."

Knowing what we had to do, we split up. On the way back to the rental house, I called my mother. She answered on the first ring.

"Sloan, I'm ready. What do you want me to make?"

I sketched out what I needed; then I thanked her and hung up.

Determined to find the answer to the fifty-thousand-dollar question, I headed into my home away from home.

This Malaysian vampire was going down.

Several hours later, I'd sorted through roughly three-quarters of the files I'd brought over from my apartment. I'd found some interesting stuff about the Brazilian *lobishomen,* the South African *impundulu,* and the *Yara-ma-yha-who* from the "Land Down Under," but nothing about Malaysian vamps. I was beginning to question whether he'd researched them.

Stiff and slightly headachy, I checked the time. It was almost eight. I hadn't heard a peep from JT since I'd left the unit, and I was starving. Just as I was about to call JT to see how much later he would be, my phone rang. It was my father.

"Sloan, I just received a call from Dale Nessinger, the television producer. She said you hadn't canceled tonight's meeting. Did you change your mind?"

"Oh, shit!" I glanced at the clock on my phone's display. "I can be there in an hour, if she cares to wait. Please, please tell her I'm sorry. We've been working this case—"

"Not a problem. I'll let her know."

"Thanks, Dad. I owe you one."

"I say we're even, after everything you did for your mother and me."

"Fair enough. Gotta go. Bye."

"Um, Sloan?"

"Yeah?"

"I . . . love you."

The words sat on my tongue, but I just couldn't spit them out. "I . . ."

"Don't say it until you mean it. Bye, Sloan. Good luck tonight."

I ended the call, feeling a little guilty, a little confused, and very pressed for time.

We can be knowledgeable with other men's knowledge, but we cannot be wise with other men's wisdom.

—Michel Eyquem de Montaigne

21

Dale Nessinger was nothing like I'd imagined. Because she was a television producer, I'd expected her to be tall, movie-starlet beautiful, and bedecked in the latest fashions from New York, Los Angeles, or Paris.

In reality, she was as Jane Average as me. This immediately put me at ease.

"Thank you for meeting with me." I shook her hand. "I'm very sorry I was late."

"My pleasure. It's not a problem." She glanced around. "Where's our prince?"

"He should be joining us at any moment." I glanced at the window. "The sun must be completely set."

"Ah, of course." She followed my gaze. "I guess we can start without him."

"Sure. I can get him caught up when he arrives."

Nessinger flung one leg over the other. "Your idea for a television series intrigued us."

"I'm very glad to hear that, but I have a question."

"Of course."

"Do you work for a network? Or do you produce the program and then shop it around? See if you can get a taker? My father didn't specify."

"I work for WIMM. It's a network that airs and produces programming for paranormal, fantastical, folklore, and supernatural creatures."

"No kidding? I had no idea there was a network for supernatural creatures."

"Absolutely. We're the only one. WIMM is a subscription-only network, available through cable and satellite providers. And we only accept paranormal and supernatural subscribers."

"Interesting. How would you know if your customer is either?"

Dale Nessinger opened a drawer, pulled out a color brochure, and handed it to me. "We work a little differently than most subscription channels do. Take HBO, for example. A mortal customer who wishes to subscribe to the network simply contacts his cable provider, letting them know he would like to add the channel to his lineup, and the cable company adds it, then handles billing. To subscribe to our channel, the customer must enroll with us and then *we* contact his cable or satellite provider and have the channel added to his service."

"I see. So you're able to pick and choose who subscribes." I flipped through the brochure, skimming its contents.

"Exactly."

"Is it fair to ask how many subscribers you currently have?"

"We currently have twenty million subscribers."

My heart did a little hop in my chest. I hadn't realized there were that many supernatural beings out there, walking the streets, living the lives of the average mortal Joe and Jane. Suddenly the likelihood of finding Elmer a wife didn't seem so remote. "That many? Twenty *million*?"

"That's just in the United States. We're in negotiations with several cable and satellite providers in Europe, Asia, and South America, which could potentially increase our subscriptions to over a hundred million."

Taking a look at the programming, I noted a distinct lack of reality-type shows. "You think your viewers would have an interest in a reality dating program?"

"They'll eat it up, pun intended." She winked.

I forced a chuckle and closed the brochure. "So what's the next step?"

"Our legal department has already drafted a contract."

"Oh." This bothered me for some reason. Call me a skeptic, but when anyone is that eager to shove a contract under my nose, I get a case of the what-the-hells.

She withdrew a folder from her desk drawer, opened it, and handed a bundle of pages to me.

I accepted it with a thank-you.

"What's this? Did you ladies start without me?" Elmer, the soon-to-be star of a reality television show, said behind me.

Dale Nessinger beamed, stood, and extended a hand to him. "Dale Nessinger. Glad to meet you at last."

"Your Royal Highness Elmer Schmickle the Third, at your service."

Schmickle? I swallowed a guffaw. He'd never told me his last name. It was no wonder.

His Royal Highness Elmer Schmickle slid a raised brow glance at me, flicking his eyes at my fake belly before turning his attention back to Nessinger. He asked, "Are you really going to put me on TV?" He gave Nessinger's hand a hearty shake before taking the chair beside me. He set the briefcase he'd been holding between our chairs.

"I'm hoping to. I gave a copy of the contract to your . . . partner? Agent?"

"Manager," I said.

"Manager," she echoed.

"We'll need some time to look this over," I told her as I skimmed the first page.

"Of course," she said, staring at Elmer with glittery goggle eyes. "You are really the prince of the *Sluagh*?"

He nodded. "Yes, I am."

I swear she did a happy-girl sigh. What the heck was she seeing that I wasn't? Dollar signs, perhaps?

"I'll need verification of your identity."

"Not a problem. I figured you'd ask." Elmer pulled the briefcase onto his lap and fished several documents out of it before snapping it shut. He handed the papers to her. "If you don't mind, I'd prefer it if you kept these documents private?"

"Not a problem. Let's see what we have here." Nessinger glanced down at them. "I'm sorry to have to ask for documentation, but we've had similar offers before and in every case the individual making the request wasn't what he claimed."

"If you need more proof, I'd be happy to provide it." Elmer motioned toward the pages in her hands. "Those copies are yours to keep."

"Thank you." Nessinger set them aside. "Now, just to summarize what we were offering, WIMM Productions will be doing all the writing, casting, directing, filming, and distributing of the show. In return, you will be paid one hundred thousand dollars for each episode filmed."

Elmer wheezed. So did I.

"In addition, we are willing to offer a substantial bonus if you conclude the season with an engagement that leads to a wedding." She tittered like a bird, flipping her hand in the air. "Our viewers just love their happy endings."

"Hey, I'm in this for real. I want to find a wife as much as the next guy. And the cash would come in handy. But you understand all applicants must be full-blooded elves," Elmer said.

"Yes, of course."

"Then we have a deal." He shot to his feet.

I jumped to mine. "Wait a minute. We should read this contract over first—"

"What for? I have nothing to lose in this deal." He snatched the contract out of my hands. "Where do I sign?" he asked, flipping through it.

"The last page," Nessinger told him, sliding a look at me.

I tried to stop him. "Elmer, you don't know what you're signing."

"It'll be fine," he said. "What are you worried about? Afraid I might actually find someone I like better than you?"

"Of course not. I want you to find a wife. If I didn't, I wouldn't have set this whole thing up—"

"There you go." He handed the signed contract to Nessinger.

Nessinger slid a somewhat chilly glance my way. "I'll go ahead and sign now, and then my office will send your copies to you tomorrow."

"Perfect." After waiting for her to finish up, Elmer offered her his hand, which she shook.

"Here's to the success of *So Who Wants To Marry An Undead Prince?*" Nessinger said excitedly.

"That title's a little long," Elmer said, grinning from ear to ear. "What about *The Bachelor: Dark Prince?*"

Nessinger bounced excitedly. "I like it!"

To me, he said, "If this doesn't work, nothing will. Thanks, Sloan. I owe you."

I had a sick feeling he was in for a whole lot more than he bargained for. "Don't mention it," I grumbled.

After thanking Nessinger, and giving Elmer one last farewell, I headed back to the rental house. I'd been worn-out and ready to quit plowing through my dad's stuff before I'd rushed out to this meeting. However, I was ready to give it another hour or two before turning in, once I returned home.

No doubt because I was petrified to go to sleep.

When I walked inside, JT was sitting where I'd been, bent over a file. He gave me a questioning look as I joined him.

"I forgot I had an appointment to handle a personal thing," I explained. "How's it going? I left a stack that looked promising off to the side."

"It's going good. Here." He handed a file to me. "Tell me what you think."

I read it in minutes and smiled. "That's it."

"And I've also verified the link between the doctor's office visit and the victims' deaths. Tomorrow you'll present the profile to the Baltimore PD." He reached for me but then pulled back. "You're damn good, Sloan."

I grabbed my protruding faux belly and gave it a shake. "Does this mean I can ditch the pregnant suit? It's hot and uncomfortable."

"Not if you want to catch her. I'm recommending you remain undercover and work with the Baltimore PD on apprehending her."

"Sure. But should I be seen going into the police station, then? And what about tonight? We don't have a trap yet. I'd give just about anything to sleep on my stomach. . . ."

"Just about *anything*?" JT echoed.

I shot him some mean eyes.

JT shook his head. "This marriage stuff is for the birds. Okay, I'll give you one night."

Upstairs, I double-checked the window locks, then shut the drapes. Confident there'd be no nocturnal visitor, I went into the bathroom to shower and change. By the time I had sudsed up, rinsed off, toweled off, and dressed, JT was lounging in bed, reading.

I gave him a what-are-you-doing look.

"She's still out there somewhere. I'm not making the mistake of assuming anything again. So, whether you like it or not—don't tell me—I'm spending the night in this bed. Even with the windows shut."

"Fine." I flipped the covers up and climbed in.

I closed my eyes.

The gears in my mind started spinning.

What if . . . she comes back?

What if . . . she finds my window locked?

What if . . . she kills some other, unsuspecting woman?

I rolled out of bed.

"Where are you headed?" JT grumbled.

I barefooted it across the bedroom, toward the door. "I'm putting the suit back on. Open the window."

When I returned to the bedroom, JT was situated next to the window, in a chair. He was holding a set of barbeque tongs. He waved them. "It's the best I could come up with. I made a promise. I'll sit awake all night, if that's what it takes."

Now that was one determined, dedicated bodyguard.

"Thanks, JT."

"It's nothing. Sweet dreams, Sloan."

After rolling from my left side to right and back again, I slipped off to dreamland.

The next morning, JT looked like death. Although I was still sporting my pregnant belly, and I hadn't been able to sleep in my favorite position, I looked fresh and rested.

Yes, I most definitely felt guilty about that.

"You need a nap," I told him as we drove to the Baltimore PD.

"There's no time. I'll sleep after this bitch is caught."

My phone rang while we were on the road, and I answered. "Mom, we're heading to a meeting. What's up?"

"I caught a piece of something. It's pink. I told you it was after me! Now you believe me, don't you?"

"I guess I owe you an apology." Of course, I couldn't know for certain she'd caught the unsub in her trap. Not without taking a look. Depending upon what sort of trap she'd created, she might have caught the toe of a squirrel, or the tail of a mouse. There was no saying. "Where did you catch it?" I motioned to JT, and pointed at the phone.

"I set it in my window, thinking I'd give it a test run before handing it over to you. I'm a little disappointed that the little beast somehow got away, though. I'm going to make some adjustments today. What do I do with this . . . piece?"

"I'll be over to pick it up in a while."

"Okay. I'll have a tweaked version of the trap ready for you when you get here too."

"Thanks, Mom."

"You're welcome. I'm glad you're finally letting me help. I hate feeling so useless."

"You're not useless. You've never been useless."

The call ended abruptly when my mother clicked off. JT gave me an inquisitive, raised-brow look.

"Mom tested her trap last night. If what she believes is true, and the pink thing sitting in it belongs to our unsub, it was a damn good thing she set her trap. Or she might be dead now."

"Your mother? She doesn't fit the profile of our other victims," JT pointed out.

"I know. She is pregnant. But not anywhere close to

delivering. It's possible the sample she caught in her trap belongs to your run-of-the-mill mammal or bird. But . . . what if . . . ?" My eyes started tearing. I dragged my hand across my face and took a few deep breaths. This case was getting to me. "All this time she's been telling me something was after her. And I've been completely dismissing her fears, basically calling her paranoid. If she really has caught a part of that thing, then I owe her a huge apology. And there's Hough. You should call her right away."

"I will." JT extended his arm, weaving his fingers through mine. "We'll stop her. We know what we're dealing with now."

We were silent for the rest of the drive, until we'd parked. Then JT looked at me and asked, "Ready?"

"Yes."

I'd done this once before. Not long ago. That time, I'd been very nervous. I was certain I'd get laughed right out of the room. But that wasn't the case then. And I knew it wouldn't be the case today either.

Feeling fairly confident, though a little emotional because of my mother's possible close call with the unsub, I headed inside with JT at my side. We checked in at the desk and were escorted to a large meeting room where Commissioner Allan, Detective McGrane, a large shift of uniformed officers, and several detectives had gathered.

Commissioner Allan gave me a friendly wave before coming over to shake my hand. "Good to see you again, Ms. Skye. Can't tell you how much we appreciate the help with this case." His gaze flicked south, to my belly, which hadn't been anywhere near that round when he'd last seen me.

I patted it. "I've gone undercover."

"Ah, I see." Commissioner Allan motioned to the attendees, who were sitting in chairs arranged to face the front of the room. "They're ready for you, whenever you are."

"I'm ready to go. I'm as anxious as you are to catch this creature. She's dangerous. And she won't stop, can't stop, until we make her stop." I stepped up to the podium and wished them all a good morning. Then I went right into the profile.

"We're looking for an intelligent, charming, organized killer who appears as an attractive female by day and a blackbird by night. She is hunting only pregnant women, gaining information about her victims through her job. Most female serial killers kill for personal gain. This one is no exception. However, she's hunting for physical gain, for nourishment as well. Although I have no proof, I believe she's possibly selling the infants she's stealing for profit. At this point, the aspect of the missing children is a departure from classic *aswang* legend. According to legend, the infants would be killed as well."

One of the officers raised his hand. "How do we stop her?"

I had my response written out. After skimming my notes, I said, "This creature is an *aswang*, a shape-shifting vampiric species. Fortunately, she can be caught and detained. We will be setting up a trap tonight, and I have high hopes that we'll catch her. In her bird form, she extends a long proboscis into a sleeping victim's room to feed. If we are able to snag that part of her, we'll have her detained for a short time. We'll then need something that will contain her in both her human and winged forms. And should you need to know, salt burns the skin of an *aswang*. Also, according to Malaysian legend, you can identify her in her human form by looking into her eyes. Your reflection will appear upside down."

Questions and answers continued for some time. A

plan was made for that night: McGrane, the lead, would continue on the trail of the missing children. JT and I would focus on identifying her human form and capturing her.

When we left the building, JT beamed. "Well done, Sloan."

"Thanks."

At the car, he asked, "Where to now? Your mother's place?"

"Not yet. I'll call her and tell her to put the specimen on ice for a DNA match later. It's bugging me that we don't know yet *who* we're dealing with, only what. I mean, what if the trap fails? We've got nothing. We've been focusing too much on trying to capture the unsub and not enough on trying to identify her. That's our job."

"Good point." JT started the car.

"Do you think I could get into Hough's computer room?" I asked, adding, "Since she's out on medical leave?"

"I don't see why not."

"Let's head to the office then. I want to do some good, old-fashioned detective work."

"You got it."

JT drove us to Quantico; and within the hour, I was sitting in Hough's Cave of Wonders, trying to decide what I wanted to look up. JT was in the room with me, manning his laptop. It was close quarters, but better than having to run in and out with printouts. I decided to start with companies contracted by all four doctors' offices first. That took a phone call to each one. I learned there were four companies they all contracted. The ultrasound provider was the first. I hit print, sending the list to the printer. JT took it from there.

The second was a small cleaning company. All but one of the employees of that company were male. I gave JT the name of the only female in the bunch and moved on to the third, a medical billing provider. That company had just over a dozen employees, all of them contract workers, most of them female. The owner provided a list of contract workers and addresses, which I handed over to JT so I could check out the last company, ABC Delivery. As it turned out, there was only one person who provided delivery service to all four practices. And the driver was a male.

That left us with two companies that had multiple possibilities, and one with only one possible suspect. Our list of persons of interest was getting smaller.

Now it was time to do some digging.

JT said, "I've sent the list of all possible persons of interest to McGrane, but it's still a little long, if he's going to pay every one of them a visit today to check whether they have a sensitivity to salt."

"I get it." I was Googling the first name on the medical billing company's list, hoping to get lucky.

"We can eliminate Terry Pietrzak from the list. Not only was she in custody for questioning during the night Natalie Townsend died, but McGrane had someone watching her since she was released. There hasn't been a minute that her whereabouts can't be accounted for. Since she's the only ultrasound technician who travels to all of those doctors' offices, that means it's probably either someone from Pro-Ex Cleaning or MDS Billing."

Keys *tap, tap, tapped.*

JT said sometime later, "No priors on any of them. That surprises me. With a need for blood as strong as our unsub's, you'd think she'd be like a junkie—so desperate, she'd do anything."

"Good point. But I think she's too smart, too controlled, to let it get that bad."

"Hmm."

More Googling followed. Hours flew by. Before I realized it, my stomach was making obscene noises. I checked the clock. It was almost four in the afternoon. We'd been sitting in the Cave for nearly six hours.

JT rolled his head from side to side. "I need to take a break."

"One more," I said as I typed one final name into a Google search engine.

Seconds later, I was looking at the photograph of a very attractive woman—an abnormally, *supernaturally* attractive woman. I clicked. It was a newspaper article about a local store's grand opening. She'd been the first customer.

JT leaned over my shoulder. "Wow, who's *that?*"

"I think she's our killer." I circled her name and address on the employer's list. Then I said, "Let's go invite her out for dinner."

*Courage is not the absence of fear, but rather the judgment
that something else is more important than fear.*

—Ambrose Redmoon

22

On the way over to Onora Dale's house, I called
McGrane. He would meet us there, just in case we were
right about our hunch. When we stopped in front of
her house, he was already standing on the porch.

We joined him.

"I've knocked a few times. There's no answer," he said.

"She works from home." I stepped to one side to try to
peer in her window. "Maybe she ran an errand."

"I'll try her phone," JT offered before he headed back
to the car.

Disappointed, I glanced up and down the street.
"Looks like our timing stinks."

"Yeah. That's Murphy's Law for you." McGrane backed
away from the door. "I have a lot of work to do, so I'm
going to head back."

"No problem. I guess we'll hang out here and wait for
her to return."

"All right." McGrane clomped down the front steps.
At the foot of the stairs, he said, "Give me a call if she
shows."

"Will do."

I returned to the car. JT was frowning, listening to his phone.

He clicked a button and turned to me. "No answer. I tried both her landline and cell numbers."

"Chances are she's at the grocery store or something."

"Sure."

I twisted around, grabbed my laptop bag off the backseat, and dragged it onto my lap. "Let me see if I can dig anything else up about our new friend." I Googled while JT watched her house. Two hours later, all I had was a sketchy history and a full bladder. There'd been no sign of Onora Dale.

"I need to pee," I announced.

"Hold it."

"I have been, but I can't hold it much longer. For one thing, this stupid stomach is pressing against my bladder. Really, do you think I need to wear this thing? I mean, I'm running all over town with it on. I've been to the Baltimore PD. If she's following me . . ."

"I don't believe she's following you at all." JT slid a sideways glance at my protruding faux stomach. He cranked the key and pulled away from the curb. "There's a submarine sandwich shop up the road. I'm hungry, anyway. I'll grab some sandwiches while you take care of business."

"Great. I'll take an Italian sub and a bag of Doritos." My all-time favorite road food was Doritos. Don't ask me why, because I couldn't say.

Inside the restaurant, we parted ways. When I returned a few minutes later, JT was holding a bag and a tray with two paper cups. He handed me the bag and we headed back out to the car.

We parked down the street from Onora Dale's house and ate our meal. We said very little to each other, which was weird. The energy in the car was tense, but not the same kind of tense as it was a couple of days ago. I think we were both focused on just getting this case wrapped up, before another woman was found dead and another infant came up missing.

In the meantime, JT called Onora Dale's employer, to make sure she wasn't on vacation. He was told no. In fact, she'd been in touch that day, via e-mail, letting them know she'd be taking some time off *next* week. JT asked for a copy of the e-mail to be forwarded to him.

Next JT called Hough to tell her about my mother's apparent close call and to ask her for a favor. He wanted her to trace the e-mail Onora Dale had sent to her employer. He thanked her, warned her to keep her windows shut and locked, and hung up; then he asked me to log in to his e-mail account.

Then, for the next several hours, we stared at the dark, empty house. Sometime around eight, my mother called, asking where I was. I told her we'd be by to pick up the trap no later than ten. Gradually the eastern sky darkened.

For the zillionth time, I checked the clock. "She isn't coming home." At exactly nine-fifty, we pulled away from the house.

I came away from that experience having learned a couple of things.

First, going on a stakeout wasn't nearly as thrilling as you'd think, if you believed what you saw in the movies. And second, drinking a big glass of anything while on a stakeout was incredibly stupid—no matter how hot you are, or how much you need the caffeine.

After making another pit stop, this time at a bakery, where I decided I needed to buy some cupcakes, we headed to my parents' place to pick up the sample and the trap. Mom had frozen the chunk of pink flesh she'd caught in the trap, just as I'd asked.

She smiled proudly as she handed over what would be the very first (assuming it worked) invention of hers that I'd ever used.

"There's no way that thing'll escape from this trap," Mom said proudly.

"Thanks for both. And remember—"

"To lock the windows. Yes, I know, Sloan. Remember, I was the one who told you about the bird."

"Yes, you did. And if this sample is a match, then I owe you a huge apology."

JT and I headed back to our rental, stuck the sample in the freezer, and set up the trap. Once we turned in the sample to the Baltimore PD, it would take weeks to get back results. It would be a long time before we would know whether Mom had caught a bit of our unsub or just your run of the mill creature.

JT's phone rang just as I was getting ready for bed. I sat on the bed, next to him, and listened as he said, "Sure, uh-huh" and "Okay" a bunch of times. Then he ended the call and shoved his fingers through his hair. "That was Hough. She needs me to come over to her place." He stuffed his phone in his pocket and grabbed his shoes.

"Why?"

Sitting on the bed, he rammed his feet in his shoes; then he kicked one ankle up on the opposite knee to tie it. "I couldn't really understand her. She was crying."

"Oh."

His gaze zipped up and down my body. "Would you mind getting dressed? I'd like to get over there right away."

"But I can stay here."

"Hell no. I'm not leaving you here alone." He tied the

opposite shoe; then he went to the closet and started pawing through the maternity clothes I'd just purchased. "Here." He pulled out a pair of stretchy pants and oversized T-shirt and thrust them at me.

I crossed my arms over my chest. There was no way I was going anywhere.

I didn't want to be a third wheel. I'd been in that position more than a few times. It was never pleasant. "I'll lock the windows. You can call off the troops for tonight."

"No."

"JT."

"Sloan." Again he thrust the garments at me. "Look, I understand this situation is awkward for you, but Hough is our coworker, and she's my friend. I can't ignore her call."

"We're undercover. Doesn't work trump everything? Especially when we're working a case like this? We're so close to catching her now."

"Damn it, you make a good point." JT's shoulders sagged. "Maybe I can send a car over to pick her up and bring her here?"

"I guess that's better than the alternative." I sat on the bed.

JT closed and locked the windows; then he left the room to make the arrangements. He returned a little while later and opened the window; then he flopped next to me in the bed.

"Is she on her way?" I asked.

"She'll be here in a few." He sighed. "I feel bad that things are so uncomfortable between the two of you. Of course, when she and I . . . When the baby was conceived, you weren't working for the unit yet. So I hadn't realized what kind of fallout I'd be facing when she'd asked me to help her."

A little twinge of something hit my gut, but I tried to ignore it. "Do you regret what you did?" I asked.

"No, I don't."

"Well . . . I guess that's a good thing." I gnawed on my lip.

Silence.

I yawned.

"Go ahead, get some sleep," he said, motioning toward the bed. "One of us needs to be well-rested."

I lay down and closed my eyes.

I slowed my breathing.

I tried everything I could to relax.

Didn't work. I couldn't sleep.

I heard JT's phone buzz—he'd set it on vibrate to avoid waking me. I felt JT roll out of bed. I heard him shut the window. A little while later, I heard him return. He opened the window; then he climbed back into bed.

"Is everything okay?" I whispered.

"Brittany's here. She's settled in the spare bedroom. She and Whitney had a fight."

"Ah. Sorry to hear that."

"They love each other very much. I'm sure they'll work it out, after they've had a chance to settle down and think things through."

"Sure." I actually got the vibe that he wanted them to make up, which was a little surprising. After all, if they didn't, he might have a chance to wiggle his way into Brittany's life. With a child in common, he might even convince her to marry him.

He sighed, crossing his arms over his chest.

I went back to pretending I was asleep.

He rolled around for a while. He got up and paced. He checked the trap a few times. He went to the bathroom and peed. Finally he settled back in bed.

I lay there for a lifetime, next to a man who loved to flirt with me, who drove me absolutely crazy in lust sometimes, but who seemed to be struggling with his feelings for another woman.

And I was bait. For a freakish vampire creature.

Really, was there any hope I'd sleep? Of course not.

I got up.

"Where are you going?" JT asked, shifting positions.

"I need a drink. And something for my headache. I'll be back in a few."

JT flopped back down.

With the full intention of returning as quickly as possible so that the *aswang* wouldn't be disappointed, should she return, I crept down the hallway, down the stairs. In the kitchen, I helped myself to a bottle of JT's vitaminwater. Next I went in search of some over-the-counter pain medications. I remembered having packed some in one of my suitcases. JT had put some of my stuff in the second bedroom, where it would be out of the way. Water bottle in hand, I went back upstairs, opened the door, and paused. Brittany was sleeping. I didn't want to wake her.

That put me in a very tough position. A that-time-of-the-month headache was coming on. I could feel it. If I didn't start taking medication now, when the pain was still manageable, I'd be in absolute misery for the next twenty-four to forty-eight hours. I flipped on the hall light, hoping it would illuminate the room well enough for me to see; then I tiptoed inside.

It was then that I saw it.

The pink proboscis.

It was about a foot from the bed and inching closer by the second.

Knowing I had mere seconds to act, I searched the

room for something to trap it, grabbed a curling iron that I'd thrown into the top of my suitcase, clamped it around the slimy pink tube, and started twirling it up.

Then I started screaming, "JT! Help me!"

The pink thing was strong, like a snake. It writhed, threatening to break my grasp on the makeshift weapon. As I was fighting it, I got a pretty decent look at the very end of it. A series of concentric little sharp teeth circled the inside of what looked like a mouth. It reminded me of a long, skinny leech.

"JT! Help!"

Just as he pounded into the room and flipped on the lights, the pink snakelike projection slipped free from the curling iron, traveled across the floor, and exited out the window before either of us could catch it.

"Damn," I said.

"Damn," JT echoed.

"Holy shit!" Hough said behind us. "What the hell was that?"

JT turned to me. "You saved her life."

My face flamed. "It was dumb luck. I came in here for some Tylenol for my headache."

"Sloan, if you're that lucky, you should be playing the lottery." JT spun around. "Hough, are you okay?"

Hough's eyes were bulging from her head. "Sure. I wasn't the one wrestling with that . . . creature. It was the creepiest thing I've ever seen, and I can't believe it was about to bite me."

"Why did you leave the window open?" JT asked, plopping down on the bed next to her. "I warned you. You know what we're dealing with."

Hough shrugged. "I didn't realize it was open. I wasn't paying attention. Besides, I don't fit the profile of the other victims. I'm still very early in my pregnancy. The others were all much further along."

"Except my mother," I piped in. "We don't know for sure yet, but there's a small chance it also tried to attack her. Or she could have thought you were me."

"I told you about the danger," JT said.

"I know. I . . . I . . ." Hough looked at JT and blinked; then she started shivering and crying.

I decided to make a quiet getaway while JT struggled through the aftershocks of Hough's near miss. But he stopped me and grabbed my wrist when I passed the bed.

"Sloan, we both owe you."

"Yes, we do," Hough said through sniffles.

"No, you don't owe me anything. I just happened to have a headache, so I came in here for some medicine. Speaking of which . . ." I went to my suitcase, grabbed the bottle of Tylenol and the water. "Now I think I'll head to bed. JT, I'm pretty sure Onora Dale won't be coming back here tonight. Don't feel like you need to return to the room."

"Of course I'll be back. Please close the window until I can figure out what to do to keep you both safe."

I shut the window, even though I had no doubt that Onora Dale had been scared off—which meant she'd be hunting elsewhere—and crawled back into bed.

Even with one ear muffled by the pillow, I could hear JT and Hough talking. As I recalled the way JT had looked at Hough, my insides twisted into a knot.

I gave myself a mental head slap.

That was it. No more pining for a man.

He was the wrong man for me, anyway. I'd said that from the start.

Yes, the wrong man.

And the wrong time.

No reason for tears.

That just meant I was free to find the right one . . . when the time was right.

Sure.

Right.

I grabbed JT's pillow and crushed it over my other ear. Immediately his scent enveloped me.

Bad move.

No man is worth his salt who is not ready at all times to risk his well-being, to risk his body, to risk his life, in a great cause.

—Theodore Roosevelt

23

I woke up sometime later curled up against JT's hard bulk. Irritated that I'd snuggled up to him while I was asleep, I pushed myself upright.

It was then that I discovered I'd been part of a three-some.

JT and Brittany were still sleeping, and JT was looking mighty comfy settled between the two of us.

I bet he'd love it if that became a permanent thing.

I headed to the bathroom first and took care of a few essentials; then I trotted down the stairs in search of caffeine. When I rounded the corner downstairs, I discovered JT and Brittany had gotten up while I was busy. They were now in the kitchen, talking, sipping vitamin-water, and munching on protein bars.

We all exchanged good mornings.

And I fired up the coffeemaker.

"Coffee, anyone?" I knew JT didn't drink coffee. But I didn't know about Hough.

"No thanks," Brittany said as she ran her hand over her stomach. "My doctor told me I should try to stay away from caffeine."

Waiting anxiously for the first drops of coffee to fall

into the carafe, I patted my fake belly. "It's a good thing I'm not pregnant for real, then."

Hough chuckled. "Oh, JT, I have something for you."

"Yeah?" he said as he unwrapped a second PowerBar.

"I did some digging on your suspect last night. She has an ex-husband who doesn't live far from here. I've got the address upstairs."

"Excellent. Thank you." JT's eyes sparkled as he beamed at her.

I tried hard not to notice the sparkles. Or the beaming. They were making me a little ill.

"I'm going to get dressed," I announced before escaping upstairs. I dug out a cute black maternity dress from the closet and shimmied into it. I picked out some cute kitten-heeled shoes. Then I curled my hair and put on some makeup. I was admiring the end results when I heard JT and Hough come up the stairs.

It was safe for me to go down now. I hustled past them in the hallway.

"I'll be down in a few," JT told me.

"I assume we'll be interviewing the ex-husband?" I *click-clacked* down the steps.

"You assumed right."

"I'm ready to roll when you are," I said when I reached the landing.

While waiting for JT, I guzzled a couple cups of coffee. The caffeine kicked in, killing the little, niggling headache that had remained. It was a glorious thing.

"Ready?" JT asked about ten minutes later. He was alone.

"Sure."

"Hough's staying here until we've got Onora Dale in custody. She needs to get some sleep. There've been some complications. She's supposed to be resting."

"I'm sure she'll get plenty of rest here. After all, she'll be safe during the day."

JT and I headed out to his car. "You know, I'm still grateful for what you did last night. You saved her life."

"Anyone would've done the same."

"Maybe."

We didn't speak the rest of the drive. I think we both knew things had changed between us, and that change was a permanent one. And necessary.

Lucas Dale lived in a nice home on a quiet street in a tidy subdivision not far from our rental. A man in a gray suit was strolling out to the Lexus parked in the driveway when we rolled up.

With any luck, that man in the nice suit would be Lucas Dale.

JT wasted no time getting out of the car and approaching the man in the suit. "Lucas Dale?"

I waddled behind him.

"Yes, that's me," Lucas Dale said, his gaze shifting back and forth between us. "What's this about?"

JT flashed his badge. "I'm Jordan Thomas, FBI. This is Sloan Skye. We'd like to speak with you about your ex-wife, if you have a few minutes."

"Sure." Appearing slightly confused, he turned back to his house and ushered us into his foyer. "How can I help you, Agents?"

"We'd like to know if you've seen or spoken to your ex-wife recently," JT asked.

"Yes, I have." Lucas Dale tugged on his tie's knot, loosening it. "Why?"

"When was the last time you spoke with her?" JT asked, intentionally avoiding responding to the man's question.

"Last night." His gaze flicked to one side.

"Is she here now?" I asked.

"No."

"Was she here last night?" I asked, following a gut feeling.

The man's neck turned red. "Yes, she was. Why? Is she okay? Did something happen?"

"We'd like to ask her some questions, but we haven't been able to reach her," JT said. "It seems she hasn't been home in a while. If she wanted to get away for a few days, do you know where she might stay?"

"Well . . ." Lucas Dale looked at JT, then at me, then back at JT again. He visibly swallowed, and then he crossed his arms over his chest. An expression flashed across his face. "Let me think." He shook his head. "No, I don't have a clue where Onora would go."

He was lying. I had a feeling. But I had no proof, at least no solid proof. Profiling criminals involved the study of human behavior. One of the first things I'd learned during my first course in criminal justice was how to detect signs of lying.

To me, Lucas Dale's body language was screaming, "I'm lying!"

JT pushed him. "You said she was here last night. Did she mention why she wasn't staying at home?"

"No."

"Did she mention anything about her work?" I asked.

"No."

"Has she ever spoken to you about her work?" I asked.

"No." Lucas Dale cleared his throat and looked at his watch. "I'm sorry, but I need to go."

"If we could ask you just a few more questions," JT insisted.

The man's jaw pulsed. "I'm going to be late for work."

"We'll make this quick. I promise," JT reassured him. "If you answer each question to your best ability, it will make things go a lot faster."

Lucas Dale's lips thinned. "I *am* answering to the best of my ability. Are you trying to suggest I'm lying?"

"Have you ever seen your ex-wife in possession of an infant?" I asked.

"What the hell is this about?" Lucas Dale glared at us. He searched our faces. We didn't give him the answer he was looking for. "Wait. I've heard something about some missing infants on the news. You don't think my ex-wife has anything to do with those children, do you?"

"No, not at all," I lied, hoping to reassure him. If I was to believe his body language, he was very close to shutting us out. "We're trying to collect some information on the victims. We're hoping your wife—ex-wife, sorry—can help us."

The man's shoulders visibly dropped. "Ah, okay." He shoved his fingers through his hair. I could tell he was feeling conflicted, confused. "Onora is a wonderful woman. She'd never hurt anyone."

"Of course not," I said. To my ears, my tone was convincing. I hoped it would be to Lucas Dale's ears too.

His lips twisted.

I tried to give him the friendliest please-help-us look I could muster.

Lucas Dale glanced at his watch again. He fiddled with his tie. Finally he said, "I'm sorry, but I've got to go. And I have no idea where Onora might be staying. Nor am I aware of any reason for her to stay away from her home." He opened the door, using his body to shepherd us outside. When we were all out, he turned and locked the door; then he headed down the walk toward his parked car. "I'm sure she'll return your phone call if you leave a message."

"We'll do that. Thank you," I said.

Lucas Dale roared away in his Lexus. We got into our car.

"Obviously, he was lying," I said.

JT was reaching for his cell phone. "I'm going to let McGrane know what's up. Maybe he can get someone to tail him."

"What about a phone tap?" I asked as I buckled myself in.

JT shook his head. "We don't have enough evidence on him for that."

"Urgh." I sighed. "Search warrant?"

"Not a chance."

I knew he was right, but damn it, it sure was frustrating. I heaved an exaggerated sigh.

"I know."

"Onora Dale is our killer," I told JT. "I know it."

"I have a good feeling you're right. Maybe the Baltimore PD will get lucky."

"Or maybe she'll move to Florida. Or Ohio. Or Massachusetts. Or Texas—"

"I hear you, but there's nothing we can do."

I mulled the situation over as JT called and waited for McGrane to answer.

Thirty seconds later, JT left a message; then he dropped his phone into the cup holder. "I guess we're in a holding pattern until McGrane calls back." He shoved the key into the ignition, but he didn't start the car.

"Maybe there is something we can do in the meantime."

"What?"

"We could break in." I couldn't believe I was actually suggesting we commit a crime, but I was desperate. And I was mad. And desperation and anger was a bad combination.

JT jerked the key and the car's engine cranked over. "No way. Anything we find will be inadmissible in court. That could kill our case. I know you know that."

"You're right. I do know that. But . . . this case is pissing me off." I took a few seconds to brainstorm in silence. An idea popped into my head, and I blurted it out, "What if *someone else* broke in? And what if that person sort of . . . left any evidence she found outside, where we could find it? Or called in an anonymous tip?"

"No way. If a judge caught wind of anything like that, we'd not only risk letting Onora Dale walk, but we'd lose our jobs. The PBAU could be disbanded. . . . No, we can't take those kinds of risks."

"*Gah!*" I covered my face with my hands. "I can't just sit by and wait for something to happen."

JT shifted the vehicle into gear and turned the steering wheel, angling the tires away from the curb. "You're still undercover. We can pay a visit to Dr. Patel today, and then leave the window open—"

"And hope for the best? How many other patients are in danger? She may be widening her circle of potential victims to include newly pregnant women. And after her close call last night, she'll probably avoid our house like the plague."

He punched the gas, and we zoomed away from Lucas Dale's house. "It's still better than your plan. Mine is legal."

"Legal but reactive. Being proactive is *so* much better."

At a stop sign, JT stomped on the brakes. "Think of a way to be proactive without breaking the law, and, I assure you, I'll be glad to hear it."

"Okay. Just give me a few minutes to think."

"Fine. In the meantime, we'll pay a visit to Dr. Yokely for a—"

"Headache. I have a raging headache." I pressed on my temples, which were throbbing. "But first we should swing by my mom's place. I need to get some advice from my father."

* * *

The minute we arrived at my folks' place, my mom started shooting questions about the case at us nonstop. Both JT and I did our best to be evasive, but Mom was like a hound on the trail of a rabbit. She wasn't about to let up.

Thankfully, she gave up after only about five minutes of that. But sadly, the direction she took her questioning made me even more uncomfortable.

"So, Agent Thomas, have you slept with my daughter yet?" she asked.

JT turned the shade of a glowing neon stoplight. "You know, I need to make some important phone calls. I think I'll go out to the car—"

"No, you won't, young man." Mom smiled, but her eyes were not smiley.

"Okay. I guess they can wait." JT slid me a beseeching glance.

I excused myself to go find my father.

"He's down in the basement, tinkering around with something," Mom informed me when I asked her where I might locate him.

He was exactly where she said.

"I need your help," I told him, wasting no time. Better to make this brief. Otherwise, Mom would have more time to make things even worse with JT.

"Sure. What is it?" He was fiddling with the cables going to the big TV in the movie room. The TV's screen was black.

"I need help calling Elmer."

He stopped tinkering and turned his full attention to me. His eyes twinkled, telling me he was happy to hear I was looking for Elmer. "Does this mean you've changed your mind about marrying him?"

"No." *Hell no. Absolutely not.* "I need to ask him for a favor."

The twinkle vanished. "Hmm. Before you do that, I should warn you, the *Sluagh* are notorious for demanding a high price for their help." He went back to fussing with the wires. "They make damn good spies, though. I've employed one or two in the past."

"What kind of price?" Considering how frustrated I was about this case, I was willing to pay a pretty hefty amount. Elmer was the only one I knew who could pull off what I had in mind. "Like cash?"

"Oh, no, nothing like that. It's different for each *Sluagh.* They love to collect things. Whatever Elmer would want to collect, that will be the price he'll ask you to pay."

"Things? Like old coins?"

"No, they generally collect things that are . . . unusual. Valuable. At any rate, to call a *Sluagh,* you need a slab of rotten meat, a pentacle summoning grid, some bat's blood—"

"'Bat's blood'?"

"Yes, or a cell phone. I have his phone number." My father grinned and chuckled.

"You are impossible. I have no idea how Mom is going to live with you. What's the number?" I asked, giving him a playful scowl. I pulled my phone out and readied my dialing finger.

He fished his phone out of his pocket and poked some keys. "999-551-6347."

"That's a strange area code," I said, dialing.

"It's the area code of the *Sluagh.*"

I checked the time. "Can he use his phone now, during daylight hours?"

"Sure. During the day, his powers are limited, but he can answer a phone."

"Okay, thanks." After checking in on JT, who was being grilled by my mother, I found a quiet room to make the call. Elmer picked up on the third ring. I gave him a run-down of my plan. He agreed to help me, asking for an un-named price (to be negotiated later), and then clicked off.

That was that.

Now I just had to hope His Royal Undeadness would find something useful.

And I had to pray that the price he would ask would be reasonable. Considering the trouble I was going to in an effort to find him a wife, I told myself it had better be reasonable.

JT poked his head in the door, startling me as I was shoving my phone into my pocket. "Whew, that was . . . fun. Ready to go to your doctor's appointment?"

"Yes." I adopted my exaggerated waddle, one hand resting on my pregnant belly. "If you ask me, this under-cover operation is getting us nowhere, but I'm willing to do just about anything to stop this creature."

"We'll get her," JT said.

"I hope so. I'm worried that by now her ex-husband might have warned her we're on her trail. She could be halfway to Timbuktu by now."

"Or she could be waiting just around the corner," JT said as he escorted me to the door.

Mom met us in the foyer. She and JT exchanged a weighted look. I was pretty sure I didn't want to know what that was all about. "Good-bye, Sloan. Be careful." She gave JT another sidelong glance.

When written in Chinese, the word "crisis" is composed of two characters. One represents danger and the other represents opportunity.

—John F. Kennedy

24

My phone rang as JT and I were leaving the doctor's office. I hit the button, answering the call, then slumped into the passenger seat. "Hello?"

"I think I found something," Elmer said, sounding quite pleased with himself. "You said you wanted me to look for addresses, somewhere Onora Dale might hide. I found some pictures of the two of them in a drawer. One was taken in front of a house. The address was plainly visible. And it says on the back, 'Our new home away from home. Ocean City.'"

My heart jumped. "Great! What's the address?"

My new handy-dandy *Sluagh* spy rattled off the address, and I jotted it down. Then he said, "Now, about my price—"

"Sorry, Elmer. I have to go. We'll talk about that later, after we catch this monster." I clicked off, slightly worried what that price might be. But I told myself it couldn't be too unreasonable. After all, I hadn't asked him to perform some miracle, only do a little illegal snooping.

To JT, I said, "We need to turn around and head toward Ocean City."

"Why?" JT's eyes turned squinty. "And how did you come by this information?"

I snapped my seat belt. "It's probably better if you didn't know."

He grimaced. "Sloan."

"All I got is an address. That can't get us into trouble, can it?"

JT gritted his teeth. "Hmpfh." He navigated through the thick traffic, exited the freeway, and then reentered, traveling in the opposite direction. "So what's going on?"

"My . . . er . . . secret informant has told me he has reason to believe our suspect is hiding out in the Ocean City vicinity. I'll put in a call to Hough, asking her if she minds doing a little work from home, see if she can identify the property's owner. I'm hoping it's Lucas Dale."

JT maneuvered the car into a tiny gap between a mini-van and a semi. "Then we're driving to Ocean City, all because of a hope?"

"No, more like a hunch. A strong one."

"It's a three-hour drive one way. That's a six-hour round-trip. If we're wrong, we had better hurry back. Hough's alone. . . ."

"I know you're worried about her. I am too. But I feel very strongly about this, JT. Onora Dale's our killer. And she's at this house. Besides, we have plenty of time to make it back before sunset. Oh, and we'll need to stop somewhere to pick up some salt. Assuming we see her, I'll just throw it at her and see what happens."

"Okay." After a moment, he said, "If salt burns her skin, she'd have to be mighty desperate to go to a seaside town to hide out. She's practically inhaling salt."

"She *is* desperate."

"Or she's not our unsub."

I said, "I'm thinking it's the first. I'm praying it's the first."

"I guess we'll see. After you talk to Hough, you'd better call McGrane and tell him everything you know. Just please leave out the part about how you got the information . . . unless he asks."

"What if he asks?"

JT hit the gas, pushing the car's speed up to eighty. "I'm sure you can think of something."

We rolled up to Lucas Dale's vacation home (Hough confirmed ownership) five *hours* later.

Five. Freaking. Hours.

It had taken us nearly twice as long to get there than it should have because there'd been an accident on the freeway and all lanes were shut down for two hours. We were caught between exits and had no choice but to sit and swelter in the car.

Feeling sticky, grouchy, and anxious to get this whole thing over with, I grabbed the plastic bag of salt I'd prepared—a bag was much easier to conceal than a big carton—and scrambled from the car.

Lucas Dale's Craftsman bungalow had a killer view of the canal across the street. Absolutely breathtaking.

"Could you imagine waking up to that every morning?" I asked JT as we both stood on the front porch, staring at the water with our mouths slightly agape.

He pointed at the FOR SALE sign in the front yard. "This place is for sale. Maybe your folks will buy it. You could come out here to chill out and relax."

I hadn't even considered that option. "Maybe they will. Then again, I wonder how much chilling out and relaxing I'll be doing this summer."

JT shrugged and knocked while I went down to the plastic-covered box nailed to the signpost to grab a color flyer.

"No answer," he said.

"She's here. I know it. Keep trying."

JT knocked some more. I walked across the front of the house and tried to peer inside some windows. "See anything?"

"The living room is very nice. I like the floors. I think they're bamboo."

"I mean, do you see any signs of Onora Dale?"

"No. Wait." I cupped my hands around my eyes, shading them from the glare. "I see a purse sitting on a table." I tried a few more windows before returning to JT. "I heard some movement inside. Somebody's in there. Somebody who doesn't want to answer the door."

JT turned around. "Let's wait to see if anyone comes out."

We went back to the car. I munched on the snacks I'd picked up at the store when we'd made our salt stop. JT called Hough to check in with her.

A while later, a black Lexus turned into the short driveway in front of the house. Lucas Dale got out, glanced at our car—we'd both ducked down and were peeking out the window—then ran inside.

"Did you see that?" I asked. "Could he look any more suspicious?"

JT dug into my Doritos bag. "He does look like he's nervous about something."

"We have to get to her somehow," I said as I stared at the bag of salt in my hand. "How do we get her to come out?"

"You mean, besides waiting for her to go hunting?"

I checked the seal on the salt bag. "I'd rather deal with Onora Dale in her human form."

"She might be easier to detain as a bird," JT suggested before he crammed the Doritos into his mouth.

Crunching loudly, he rummaged in the snack bag for more food. The man had already consumed two sandwiches, some grapes, a prepackaged salad, half a bag of Doritos, and a pack of Ding Dongs. And he was still hungry?

I moved the Dorito bag out of his reach. "Maybe. But she'll be a whole lot harder to catch in her bird form. And there's no way to follow her once she takes flight. No, we need to get to her now, before she's changed. But her ex-husband is going to be a problem. . . ." The door to the house swung open. Lucas Dale dashed to his car and pulled away. "Wow, could it be our luck is finally changing? We need to get in that house. Now."

"No way." JT ripped open a snack-sized bag of potato chips. "We can't break in. We have no proof, no search warrant, nothing."

"Darn it! I feel so helpless." I stared at the house; then I grabbed my phone and called the number on the sign. A sales agent answered and I gave her a fake name, telling her my husband and I were sitting outside and would like to see the house immediately.

Apparently, the property had been languishing for a long time. She was all too eager to accommodate us. After promising to meet us in twenty minutes, she clicked off.

I gave a little hoot. "Success. We're getting in the house within a half hour, and we're doing it legally."

As a reward, I helped myself to some more Doritos.

A half hour later, we were strolling through the front door. I had the bag of salt stowed in my purse, ready to go when I found Onora Dale, wherever she was hiding. JT had a second bag in his pocket. We toured the first floor. I marveled at the glorious views, the open kitchen, and the lovely original woodwork. When we headed upstairs,

JT quietly slipped away, pretending to be fascinated by the gorgeous mosaic tiles in the foyer.

He was actually waiting for Onora Dale to try to make her escape.

On the second floor, I oohed and aahed over the hand-painted mural in the media room at the top of the stairs. I gushed over the charming bedrooms and had a little moment of house lust when I stepped into the master bedroom's en suite bath, with its soaker tub and skylights. Despite snooping in every single closet and built-in cupboard, I found no evidence of Onora Dale. But I had noticed her purse was no longer sitting in the living room.

Just as I was about to give up, I heard a huge thud downstairs, then the sound of banging and thumping.

I wasted no time hauling my butt downstairs to help JT. He was on the floor, losing what appeared to be a pretty ugly wrestling match with a supernaturally beautiful blonde.

Then Onora Dale kneed him in the crotch.

I grabbed the bag of salt, opened it, and flung it at her.

She screeched.

She clawed at her skin.

She turned toward me with hatred in her eyes.

Behind me, I heard the real estate agent say, "Oh, my God!" Then I heard footsteps retreating up the stairs.

Onora Dale charged me, fingers curled into fists. Her beautiful face was a mask of fury; her eyes were narrow slits. An odd smell, like burned hair, wafted from her.

"Who are you?" she spat. Her gaze flicked to my fake stomach.

I took a couple of steps back and tried to think my way out of the pickle I'd just put myself in. Gauging from JT's defeat, I was guessing Onora wasn't just supernaturally gorgeous. She was also supernaturally strong. "I'm just here to look at a house," I said, lifting my hands, palms out, in the universal stay-the-hell-away-from-me sign. I knew JT had handcuffs on him, but until we had something—a confession, a reason to believe she was the killer—I didn't want to show her our hand yet, so to speak. "We were told the house was empty."

Onora Dale squinted at me. "You threw salt on me."

"You kneed my husband in the crotch. That pissed me off. I sort of need those bits to stay in good working order."

"But why *salt*?" She grimaced as she brushed some of the crystals off her arms, revealing tiny red marks that looked like little burns.

"I . . ." *Shit.* "I crave salt, now that I'm pregnant." My hand came to rest on my stomach. "I always carry some with me." I leaned closer, studying the marks on her skin. "Are you allergic?"

"Yes."

"I've never heard of a salt allergy."

Onora Dale sniffed the air. Her expression darkened. "You're not pregnant." Before I could react, she charged into me like a bull. The force of her blow sent me sailing backward. I slammed into something hard and saw stars for a brief second. I tried to blink them away, but I couldn't. By the time my vision was clear, she was gone.

So was JT.

More than a little shaky, I half-ran/half-staggered out the door.

I saw a large man-sized lump lying on the sidewalk in front of the house next door. I recognized the colors of the lump.

Sprinting on wobbly legs, I dashed to JT and knelt down. He was curled into a fetal position.

"Did she get you again?" I asked.

Red-faced, he whimpered and nodded.

I stood, took a look around, then accepted defeat. "We lost her."

JT groaned a second time. "Call McGrane. He'll send some men out here. I'm going home. Gotta protect Hough."

*Love takes off masks that we fear we cannot live without
and know we cannot live within.*

—James A. Baldwin

25

Mom was crying.

I was crying.

The lady we didn't know, who happened to be in the country club's powder room with us, was crying too.

Talk about estrogen overload.

"Your mascara's running," my mother pointed out to me. "You have the world's worst raccoon eyes."

"I'm pretty sure yours are worse," I said, leaning into the mirror, a tissue at the ready. I blotted at the black smudges.

Mom checked her makeup. "Damn, you're right."

We both cried some more.

Finally I said, "Enough of this damn crying. What are we bawling about, anyway?"

"I'm hormonal," Mom said. "What's your excuse?"

"I'm menopausal," the strange lady said as she dabbed at her eyes.

"I don't have an excuse," I said. "Other than exhaustion. And frustration. And . . ." I did a strange little laugh-sob thing. It sounded like I was choking. "We spent all night waiting for that damned"—my gaze shot to the stranger—"bird to come back."

"You'll catch it, Sloan. I believe in you." Mom took a few deep breaths. "Okay, I think I'm done. I'm ready. How do I look?"

"You look beautiful," I told her. That wasn't a lie. I swear, she was radiant. Unlike me. Her face was flushed a pretty shade of pink. My face was a blotchy red mess. Her dress was absolutely gorgeous. Mine, a yellow-and-black disaster. She looked happy. Full of life. I looked half dead.

"You look lovely," the strange lady said.

"Thank you." Mom preened. I think she was surprised by how fabulous she looked. "Maybe it's the hormones," she said, checking her face more closely. "My skin looks smoother." She ran her fingers down her neck. "My jaw seems firmer." She raised an arm and shook it. "And look, no more triceps flop."

I was wearing a sleeveless dress. Wouldn't hurt to check my arms. Not floppy yet. But I could see some signs of future flop.

I made a mental note to renew my gym membership at the end of the summer. I hadn't stepped foot in the place since my first day with the PBAU, and I had a feeling I'd be too busy to work out until September.

"Whatever it is you've been using, can I buy some?" the lady asked. "Is it a cream? Or have you been exercising?"

"No, it's not exercise. I'm pregnant," Mom told the lady.

"You're pregnant?" the lady said, failing miserably at hiding her surprise.

"Yes, I'm five weeks today." Mom ran her hand down her flat stomach. "I haven't been exercising much since I found out. I don't think I should be."

"Congratulations." The lady took one last look at my mother, in her white wedding gown, then at me, and left.

Abandoning my efforts at fixing my makeup, I threw

away the tissue and stepped back from the mirror. "Mom, pregnant women work out all the time."

"Really?" She looked shocked. "Back when I was pregnant with you, the doctor told me no running, no lifting, no jumping . . . pretty much no doing anything."

I fluffed my hair. It was humid today. Humidity did nothing for my hair. "At my gym, there's a water aerobics class for pregnant moms. They all seem to like it."

Mom's brows scrunched. "Are you trying to tell me I need to exercise?"

I fluffed harder. "No, of course not. You look amazing."

"Then why would you say such a thing?"

Allegra Love came into the powder room, saving my butt. I'd have to thank her later. She had excellent timing. "Are we ready?" Dressed head to toe in gauzy purple material that was both translucent and opaque at the same time, her hair adorned with pink and purple feathers, Allegra Love gave Mom an exaggerated up-and-down look. "My, don't you look lovely! Something looks different. Did you do something with your hair?"

Mom flushed. "No, actually, I didn't. But thank you." She glanced at me. "Ready?"

"Sure."

Allegra Love said, "We didn't have a rehearsal. There was no time. But your future husband assured me you would know what to do."

Mom fussed with her dress. "Yes, we've been through this once before."

"Very good. Then I'll head out." After a quick mirror check, Allegra Love swooped out like a Broadway starlet preparing to take her place on the stage.

"That is one bizarre woman," I said, watching her grand exit. "Where did you find her?"

"Your father. Don't ask. I have no idea." Mom took

another deep breath and gave me a slightly strained look as she brushed past me, heading for the exit.

"What's wrong?" I asked, grabbing her arm to stop her.

"Nothing."

"Mom, are you sure you want to go through with this wedding?"

"Yes, I'm sure." She glanced down at my hand.

I let go of her arm. "You don't have to get married today. I mean, I know I sort of forced you to meet with Dad because . . . well, I felt you loved him. And that whole Frankie Goes to Hollywood thing was super romantic. But I don't want you to feel pressured to go this far so soon. Maybe you two should take some time to—"

Her gaze jerked to the floor. "I don't feel pressured. Not at all." Mom lifted her chin and took another step toward the door.

Liar.

I intentionally put my body between my mother and the exit. "We can leave right now. I promise I won't complain about your wandering around in the middle of the night, chasing away shape-shifting vampire birds. Or testing your inventions and short-circuiting my apartment building—"

"No. I should be with the father of my child. I don't want your little brother or sister to grow up . . ." Her words trailed off.

"Like I did?" I finished for her. "Without a father?"

Mom gave me a sad nod.

"I had a great upbringing. A wonderful childhood."

Mom's eyes started leaking again. Of course, mine did too. We hugged. She sniffled and snuffled. Someone knocked on the door.

"Yes?" I poked my head out.

"They're waiting for you." Katie shoved two bouquets

of flowers into my hands. "The white one's for your mother."

"Thanks." I handed Mom her flowers and out we went. Through the clubhouse and out into a pretty court-yard that had, by some miracle, been turned into the prettiest setting for a wedding that I'd ever seen.

I walked down the aisle while a small string quartet played Pachelbel's *Canon in D Major*. My father gave me a happy grin at the front. The music changed as I curved to the left to take my place. I turned and watched my mother walk down the aisle, and I couldn't help but marvel at how beautiful she looked, and how happy. I saw her gaze lock on my father. They exchanged a look of utter love.

Would I ever know what it was like to be that much in love? So much in love that everyone could see the sparkle in my eyes?

So much in love that some man would be willing to give up what meant the most to him to be with me?

It seemed impossible. Or, at least, improbable.

Certainly, I didn't have anything that special with JT. Nor did I have it with Gabe.

Would there be that once-in-a-lifetime love for me?

This whole wedding thing was turning me into a girly, mushy romantic. That was so not me.

As the sun hung low over the western horizon, the sky stained pink and blue, I watched my parents say their vows, exchange rings, and, eventually, kiss. The guests, including the woman I surmised was Her Majesty, all ap-plauded politely. And as the new Mr. and Mrs. James Irvine pranced back down the makeshift aisle, the guests tossed white daisy petals into the air.

I gotta say, it was quite an event. Especially consider-ing the fact that we hadn't had time to make any of the arrangements. My father had handled every detail. I never would have thought any man capable of planning such a pretty, elegant event. I was impressed.

"Hopefully, that'll be me very soon," Elmer said as he *poofed* in front of me. He moved to the side, so I could continue to watch the crowd slowly file toward the building, where a reception dinner was being set up.

"Yes, hopefully soon," I echoed.

"Who is this?" Allegra Love said, eyeballing Elmer and me.

"A friend," I told her. To Elmer, I said, "This is Allegra Love. She has a very unique way of determining which couples should be married."

She was staring at us. I'd seen her look at me like that before. "Remarkable."

I didn't like the sound of that. In the interest of avoiding a calamity, I tried to steer Elmer away from her.

"Are you hungry?" I asked him.

"Your energies resonate so beautifully!" Allegra Love shouted.

"What's that mean?" Elmer asked, looking at me for an explanation.

"I told you, she has a very unique way of determining which couples are compatible. Resonating energies are bad. Very bad." I gave him a nudge forward.

"No, it's quite the opposite!" Allegra Love corrected from a widening distance.

Elmer stopped dead in his tracks, turned, and then asked Allegra Love, "You mean we're compatible?" Elmer motioned between us. "Sloan and me?"

"Very compatible. Perfectly compatible."

"Perfectly?" he echoed.

I groaned. "She said the same thing about me and JT."

She seemed to float toward us. "It's very unusual for

one person's energy to match more than one other person's."

"Yeah, it seems mine matches every man I know," I told Elmer.

Elmer gave me a second look. "Why's that?"

I gave him a confused shrug.

Allegra Love motioned to me. "Sloan does seem to be unique."

"Too bad none of them are perfect for me," I mumbled.

"What was that?" Elmer asked.

"Nothing. This is all nonsense. We both know we're not compatible." I gave Allegra Love a warning glare and escorted Elmer to the clubhouse. "Let's go inside. I'm willing to bet there are some single elf bachelorettes in there, just waiting to meet you."

Katie waved me down when we stepped into the ball-room. She had a drink in her hand and a great big smile on her face . . . until she saw who was standing next to me.

"Look who popped in for some cake," I told her, motioning to Elmer.

"You know me, never one to turn down free food *I can't eat*," he said. "Sloan and I need to have a little chat. About a certain favor . . ."

"Elmer." Katie gave him the kind of empty smile someone does when she's trying her damnedest to be nice but failing. "Good to see you again."

"Thanks. What're you drinking?" His little squinty eyes settled on her glass.

"Champagne. You can get some over there." Katie pointed at the bar set up along the far wall.

"Great. I don't care for champagne." Elmer rubbed his hands together. "But I'd be happy to get you some, Sloan. What about it?"

"No thanks—I mean, sure, I'll take some champagne, thanks."

The minute Elmer was out of earshot, Katie said, "What is *he* doing here?"

"Being a pest, like usual."

"Why don't you tell him to go away, then?" Katie motioned to a pack of handsome, available-looking young men huddled on the opposite side of the room. "Check that out. Men. Single. There's not an ugly one in the bunch. But you're not going to get anywhere with any of them with Elmer here. They're going to think he's your date."

Doing my best to not be too conspicuous, I gave the man pack a second glance. Katie was right. Those were some promising-looking men. Especially the one on the end, in the corner, reading a book. The fact that he was reading at a wedding reception made the geek in me swoon. "I need to ditch the *Sluagh.*"

"Bribery usually works," Katie suggested.

"See, that's the problem. I already owe him for one favor." While trying to think up a proper bribe for a desperate *Sluagh,* I took a roundabout way to the bar to find him, figuring I'd avoid being seen with him any more than possible.

I located him standing next to the bar, chatting with my mother.

Mom beamed. "Sloan, there you are. Wasn't the wedding lovely?"

"It was. But I should get going. We're still working the case—"

"Sloan, there's someone I'd like you to meet." My father stepped up from behind me and took my arm. "Your Royal Highness, Elmer, come with us."

Elmer said, "I'd be happy to."

My dad, Elmer, and I headed toward a table where the woman I had assumed was Her Majesty, the queen of the elves, was seated. She looked upon me with assessing eyes.

My father pulled me forward, stopping roughly five feet in front of the queen. He tipped his head in reverence. I didn't. "Your Majesty, I'd like to present my daughter, Sloan."

Her Majesty offered me her hand.

I've never met royalty. That is, outside of Elmer. I wasn't sure what I was supposed to do. Was I supposed to shake her hand? Kiss it? Genuflect?

Playing it safe, I did all three. Kind of. I did a little curtsey, bent my head over her hand, and gave it a tiny shake.

"Your Majesty." I took a half step backward.

"She's lovely," Her Majesty said.

"I assume you know who this is?" My father motioned to Elmer.

The queen looked like she'd seen the Second Coming of Christ or something equally magnificent. "Yes, of course." She offered Elmer her hand.

Elmer dipped into a low bow, showing a side of himself I'd never seen. He moved with regal grace. It was a total shocker. "It's good to see you again, Your Majesty."

"My daughter has decided not to wed His Royal Highness," my father informed her.

This surprised me. Why would the elf queen care?

"Really?" Her Majesty's eyes narrowed. "I'm very sorry to hear that." She stared at me. "Very . . . surprised."

And clearly unhappy.

"His Majesty deserves much better than me," I reasoned. "After all, I'm not even full-blood elf."

The queen considered my response for at least an hour, or so it seemed. "She makes a good point." She motioned to the man pack, the one Katie had been eyeballing. "Perhaps she would like to meet my sons?"

"I would be happy to introduce her," my father said.

"Very good." With a nod, the queen of the elves dismissed us, calling Elmer to come sit by her side to have a talk.

Dad ushered me toward the center of the room.

"I can handle the introductions on my own," I told him, once we'd moved out of earshot of the queen. "No need to take you away from Mom."

"Very good. If you need anything, let me know."

"Will do."

I went in search of Katie, finding her in the bathroom, doing a makeup check. Our gazes met in the mirror. "Guess what? The men you were checking out are the sons of a queen. Real-life princes."

"Like . . . Elmer?"

"No, more like Prince Wills. But not exactly. Elmer's undead. These princes are elves."

"No way."

"Yes way."

"Are you kidding?" She gave me a goggle-eyed look of surprise. "Elf princes?"

"Not kidding."

"All of them?"

"That, I don't know."

"Oh, my God, I'm so glad you're my best friend." She gave me a bouncy hug. "But wait a minute. Weren't you leaving early?" She released me to turn back toward the mirror. "You wanted to get back to your case."

"Yeah."

"Are you sure you have to leave?" she asked as she brushed more bronzer on her cleavage. "I mean, you're just an intern. You're not an agent yet. And this is summer vacation. And it's your parents' wedding. *Your parents.* And—and they're freaking *princes.* Why would anyone hold it against you?"

"I know. But . . ." I tried to remind myself why I had to leave the wedding early. JT was watching Hough. He didn't need my help. I wasn't working undercover anymore. Onora Dale knew I wasn't pregnant. I'd already profiled the killer. McGrane had men watching Lucas Dale and their house in Ocean City. What was there for me to do? I motioned to the brush in her hand. "The queen herself suggested I introduce myself. Who am I to ignore a royal command, right?"

"Yes!" Katie gave a fist pump. "It's been ages since we've been out together. Tonight'll be like old times."

Actually, I hoped it wouldn't be. Because back then, Katie had men dropping at her heels. I stood in her shadow and watched. "Can I borrow some of that bronzer? Maybe I'll finally meet a man who isn't an ex-boyfriend, a coworker, or the walking dead."

"Here you go." Katie whisked a little more tinted powder on herself, then handed the brush to me. Next she dug out some pink lip gloss. "I can't believe this. Did you know there would be princes here?"

"Didn't have a clue." I scrutinized my reflection in the mirror and frowned. "If I had, I would've taken more time getting ready. I would have at least done something better with my hair. And my makeup is a nightmare."

"You look great." Katie painted some gloss on my lips. "There, now you look a little sexy."

I checked my reflection.

She lied. But whatever.

Maybe, with any luck, the geek reading the book in the corner was a prince. And maybe he'd like average girls like me.

And maybe our energies would resonate.

I pulled the bodice of my dress down a little, exposing as much cleavage as I could, brushed some fake tan onto the enhanced swell of my breasts (I am now a big fan of Victoria's Secret) and handed the brush back to Katie. "Let's go."

Katie led the battle charge. "Watch out, Princes, here we come."

When it comes to the future, there are three kinds of people: those who let it happen, those who make it happen, and those who wonder what happened.

—John M. Richardson, Jr.

26

An hour later, I was feeling a little like Goldilocks. As odd and inappropriate as it sounded, meeting the queen's sons was a little like tasting porridge. The oldest son in attendance had been my first choice. He was the one who'd been reading the book. Surely, I'd told myself, that meant he was intelligent.

Surely, I'd also told myself, that meant he would be capable of interesting, thought-provoking, stimulating conversation.

Lukewarm and bland as hell. That's what that porridge tasted like.

After being bored to tears by a never-ending analysis of last night's dream (and OMG, was it bizarre!), I excused myself to go to the bathroom, fluffed my hair, gave myself a pep talk, and sent myself back out there to sample the next porridge.

When I returned to the ballroom, I discovered Katie had abandoned her first choice as well, in favor of another prince—all I can say is thank God the queen's a very fertile woman. There were still plenty more for us to choose from, and it seemed we were two of an extremely small number of single women at the wedding.

While my mother and father danced the Macarena—a horrific sight to which no child should be exposed—I introduced myself to Bachelor Number Two.

"Nice to meet you," he said, giving me a sparkly-eyed smile. It was a good start. "I'm Taggart."

"Sloan, daughter of the bride and groom."

"So I've been told." Prince Taggart flicked his eyes around the room. "Are you here alone?"

"Yes."

Those eyes returned to me, settled on my boobs. "Care to go somewhere quiet?" he asked them. "Somewhere where we could get to know each other more . . . intimately?"

Holy shit, this man didn't play around. Or was he joking? I laughed, giving him the benefit of the doubt.

He looked confused. His gaze wandered up to my face. "So, is that a no?"

"That would be correct. Thanks, anyway."

His jaw dropped. Poor prince. Didn't know how to handle rejection, it would seem.

Time to move on.

Prince Number Three was standing at the bar, looking lonely. At least, that was what I told myself. I decided he needed some company.

"Let me guess, you hate weddings?" I said by way of a greeting.

"Detest them." Prince Number Three flagged the bartender.

"Not a fan myself." I offered my hand. "Sloan Skye."

"Damen." His handshake was firm. His gaze was friendly, with the slightest hint of a smile pulling at his lips. He didn't leer at my boobs. "I've known your father for years. I have a great deal of respect for him."

At this point, I didn't know if I could say the same. Especially in light of his most recent activities . . . despite helping me out with Elmer.

"That's very nice," I answered. To the bartender, who was now patiently waiting for me to give my order, I said, "I'll take a diet cola. Thanks."

"Your father saved my life," Prince Damen said after taking a drink from the glass sitting in front of him on the bar. Swiveling, he turned to face me.

"Saved your life?"

The bartender set my cola on a paper napkin in front of me. I grabbed it and sipped. Lukewarm. *Blech!*

Prince Damen studied me for a long moment, as if he was reading my body language, or my mind. "What do you know about your father?"

Some other wedding attendees stepped up to place orders. Damen reached a hand to my waist, coaxing me to move aside, out of the way. As it happened, we were now standing in a semidark corner of the room. Fairly isolated. It was sort of cozy. Intimate.

If only we could get off the subject of my father . . .

"I know very little about him, to be honest. He just recently 'resurrected' from the dead." I made quotes in the air with my fingers when I said the word "resurrected."

Damen gave me a doubtful, slant-eyed look.

"Let me clarify. He let my mother and me believe he was dead for over two decades. Then he just suddenly reappeared, got my mother knocked up, cheated on her, and then talked her into marrying him today." I bit my lip. "Okay, that was probably a little more than you wanted to hear." I determined it was a good time to busy my mouth with something besides talking. I was saying too much. I sucked on the skinny straw in my glass.

"Actually, I appreciate the honesty."

I shrugged, hoping to appear relaxed, confident.

"What's the point in lying, right? We don't know each other. I don't need to impress you."

He stirred his drink. The ice clanked against the glass. "I wish more people felt that way. Just about everyone around me lies. They're either trying to advance their career, or they're trying to get to my mother, or they're trying to push a political agenda. . . ."

"Must suck, being a prince." No, I didn't feel that way. I could think of a million reasons why being a prince or princess would be downright fabulous, but I felt he was looking for some empathy.

"No, it doesn't 'suck.'" He tipped his head slightly and studied me for a moment. Even though his gaze wasn't hard or assessing, I felt my face warming. "It would suck having to stay away from your family, from missing every major event in your child's life. From living day after day wondering what was happening to the woman you loved. Don't you agree?"

I lifted my chin. "I thought we were talking about you, not my father."

"I guess what I'm saying is I have it great, compared to some people."

I respected him for that. I lifted my glass to him. "Well played."

"I'm not trying to win a game, or a debate. I'm just trying to . . . connect with someone."

"I—"

Frankie Goes to Hollywood's "The Power of Love" started playing, interrupting what I was trying to stammer out. "My folks love this song."

Damen took my hand and led me to the dance floor. His arms enfolded my body and the beat thrummed through me. I closed my eyes and leaned a little closer. We swayed to the beat.

Now . . . this felt good. Better than good. It felt right.

When the song ended, I tipped my head back to thank him. He was looking down at me. His gaze locked on mine, and a current of sensual energy buzzed through my body.

It was a magical moment.

Until my freaking phone rang.

It was in my handbag, but I knew from the ring that it was JT. Bad, horrible, atrocious timing. I decided to ignore it.

"Are you going to answer it?" Damen asked as he released me and took a step back. It rang again. I gritted my teeth. "Sounds like someone is anxious to talk to you."

"It's a coworker, but I'm off the clock."

My phone rang a fourth time.

Damen and I exchanged a look. He took another step back and motioned to my purse. "I'll let you get that."

"Thanks." I dug my phone out and hit the button. "This had better be a matter of life or death."

"I need to talk to you. Now," JT said.

"I'm busy. Can't it wait?"

"No."

"JT, I'm at a wedding."

"It's a matter of life and death."

"Does this have to do with our case?"

He didn't respond right away. "I can't say for sure yet."

"What's going on?" I asked.

"It's Brittany. She's missing. And with our case . . . you know . . ."

I glanced at Damen, who was staring out at the dance floor and pretending not to listen. I grumbled, "Where are you?"

"I'm at home."

I heaved a heavy sigh. "I'll be there in a half hour."

* * *

"Nice dress." JT stepped aside, letting me into his house. Earlier, we'd packed up our things and vacated the rental.

"I told you, I was at *my parents'* wedding." I gave him some seriously evil eyes as I *click-clacked* into his entryway.

"No, actually, you said you were at 'a wedding.' You never specified." JT ushered me toward the living room.

I stood, arms crossed, next to the couch. "Whatever. So what's the story with Hough?" I gritted my teeth as I said her name. Then I reminded myself that I didn't have to be jealous of the woman who was carrying JT's child. After all, I had just danced with a gorgeous prince who had a traffic-stopping smile. Of course, I had no idea if I'd ever see said gorgeous prince again. Because JT had called me, interrupting my evening.

"She called me a few hours ago, but I'd left my cell phone in my car and missed the call. She said something about hearing a strange noise. Naturally, I got worried."

"Naturally."

"So I tried to call her back," he continued, pacing back and forth so fast he was making me dizzy. "She didn't answer."

I leaned against the side of the couch. "When did you call her?"

"About an hour ago."

I checked the time. "Maybe she fell asleep?"

"I went to her place. She's not at home."

"Isn't she married? Shouldn't her . . . wife . . . be worrying about her?"

"Whitney's out of town on business. And she is worried. I called her from their driveway, and she gave me permission to break in."

"And . . . ?"

"I found Brittany's phone and purse sitting on the kitchen counter. Her car's in the garage."

I had to admit, that sounded suspicious. "So she left, but she didn't drive. Have you checked local hospitals? Maybe she was taken in for some reason."

"No. Good idea." He gave me a wilted smile. "Thank you for coming. I'm sorry I made you miss the wedding."

"It's no big deal. The wedding was over. It's just a reception." I dug my cell phone out of my purse. "Let's find Brittany."

"I'm sorry I made you worry," Brittany told us an hour later. It was nearly midnight. We were at the hospital. Brittany was looking sleepy. I was feeling sleepy. JT had overdosed on caffeinated energy drinks. He would probably be up all night. He might even be up for the rest of the week. "You didn't have to come here."

"Of course we had to come. We're your friends," JT said, sitting on the edge of her bed.

Friends. Right.

He continued, "Besides, we weren't doing anything tonight."

Brittany glanced at me. "It looks like Sloan was. I doubt she puts on a full-length gown to watch *Criminal Minds* reruns."

"Actually, I do," I said, shooting her a grin.

I could tell by her reaction, she didn't believe me. I wouldn't believe me either.

"What's going on? Why did you call 911?" JT asked Brittany.

"It's no big deal. I heard something outside, so I went to check what it was. I tripped and fell then. The doctor told me I had to come in and be monitored for a few hours. My neighbor drove me in."

"And . . . ?" he asked, brows raised.

She pointed at the monitor sitting on the stand next

to the bed. "Everything's fine. I should be clear to go home anytime now."

"Thank God." JT patted her hand. "We'll wait until you're released. I'll drive you home."

"But maybe Sloan has somewhere to go? Did you two drive together?"

"No, I drove myself. It's okay," I reassured her. "The reception was over at midnight. Which is"—I checked the clock on the wall—"*was* five minutes ago."

Brittany grimaced. "I'm so sorry, Sloan."

"Don't worry about it."

"Just tell me it wasn't someone very close to you," Brittany said.

"It wasn't someone very close to me," I echoed.

For my lie, I received a grateful smile from JT.

"Sloan, you look tired," Brittany said. "You don't have to stay."

"I'm fine. Though I'd be more comfortable if I could sit down." I glanced around the tiny curtained-off area, looking for somewhere to sit. I found a chair shoved way back, against the wall.

I sat.

I closed my eyes.

What felt like five minutes later, JT was nudging me awake. "Sloan, it's time to go. Are you sure you're okay to drive?"

"Sure. Wow. I guess I'm more tired than I thought." I stretched and slowly pushed to my feet. Following JT, who was walking next to Brittany, riding in a wheelchair, I concentrated on getting alert enough to drive safely. At the hospital's exit, I gave JT and Brittany a clipped "See you on Monday," before heading out to find my car in the dark parking lot. As I walked, I powered up my cell phone, which I'd shut off while I was in the hospital.

Three messages.

The first was from my mother, who wanted to let me know how disappointed she was that I'd left her wedding reception without saying good-bye. I'd expected as much.

The second, however, was very unexpected.

"Hi, this is Damen. Your father gave me your number. I wanted to call to thank you for the dance and see if you'd maybe like to go out to dinner sometime."

The answer to his inquiry was hell yes.

After saving his cell phone number on my phone so I could call him during a decent hour, I checked the third message.

Katie.

"Sloan, you won't believe what happened tonight! I'm spending the night in the Presidential Suite at the Washington Court. Call me."

Deciding she was probably too busy to take my call, I headed to bed. The instant my head hit the pillow, I was in dreamland.

It is easier to find a score of men wise enough to discover the truth than to find one intrepid enough, in the face of opposition, to stand up for it.

—A. A. Hodge

27

The next morning, I lazed in bed until almost nine o'clock. It felt so good getting that much sleep. When I finally forced myself to get up, I was rested, alert, and more than a little giddy.

The dreams I'd had—all triple-X-rated—starred a certain handsome, polite, charming prince.

Yes, it was a good thing, stepping back from the stress and pressure of our case for a day or two. Now I could see how wound-up, how anxious, and how narrow-focused I'd become.

When we'd been working our first case, I'd barely slept. I was on the run constantly, and pushed myself to exhaustion, and beyond. I'd done a little better with this case. But I had still been pushing hard, taking personal responsibility for every new victim we found, for every infant who was stolen.

If I kept this up, I'd burn out before the end of the summer.

Making a vow to myself to keep my life a little more balanced—or at least make more than a halfhearted effort at doing so—I started the coffeemaker. That done, I showered and dressed. Katie came bouncing in just as I was making my way back to the kitchen for my first cup of caffeine.

"Oh, my God!" she said, hopping up and down. She was rumpled; her clothes were a wrinkled mess; her hair was a tangle of waves; and her makeup was totally gone. But she was practically glowing. She flopped onto the couch, grinning. "What a night! What an incredible, magical, unbelievable night!"

"That good?" I poured her a cup of coffee and sat beside her. After handing her the cup, I said, "Tell me everything."

"First, I did not sleep with him. Just so you know. But I wanted to!" Grinning like a goof, she closed her eyes and tipped back her head. "His name is Viktor, with a *k*. He's so polite, and charming, and funny. We just sat up and talked all night long. And then he kissed me, and, I swear to God, I saw fireworks."

"Fireworks, huh?"

"Yeah. Beautiful fireworks. Sparkling colors." She opened her eyes. "Wow, I sound like I've totally lost it, don't I? It's crazy, but I think I'm in love. Just like that. I've fallen in love in one night." She slurped her coffee.

"Katie, this isn't the first time. . . ."

She waved off my comment. "I know, I know. It's insane. And I know I've said that before. But this is different. Viktor's different." She sipped again, smacked her lips. "Great coffee." She took another sip. "Don't worry. I won't do anything impulsive, like run away to Vegas and become Mrs. Viktor."

"I'll kill you if you do."

"That's why you're my best friend." Katie took another slurp, then set the cup down and propelled herself off the couch. "Gotta get going. Viktor's taking me sailing today. On his yacht. He's picking me up in an hour. I don't know if I have anything yachtworthy. What does a girl wear on a yacht?"

"A hot bathing suit and a smile?" I suggested.

She grimaced. "The latter I can do. The former?" She glanced at the clock. "I wonder if I have time to run over to Macy's and pick up a new swimsuit? Maybe if I hurry . . ." She dashed into the bathroom and slammed the door.

While Katie readied herself for her sailing date, I sat down on the couch with my dad's research and started reading through it. While I had just made a vow to keep my life in balance, I was bored. I needed something to occupy my mind.

Twenty minutes later, Katie zoomed out the door.

A couple of hours after that, my phone rang.

It was Damen. I couldn't poke the button to answer the call fast enough.

"Hello," I said.

"Hi. It's Damen."

"What's up?" I hugged a sofa pillow to my chest. I swear, my heart was pounding so hard, it was bruising my breastbone.

"I was wondering what you were doing tonight?"

"Hmm. Let me think. I may have plans. To go out to dinner? With a certain man I'd met last night . . ."

He chuckled. I really, really liked the way that sounded. "Well, damn. I guess I'll have to try another time." After a well-timed beat, he suggested, "What about we get together tonight, then, around six or so. How does that sound?"

"Sounds wonderful."

He told me where he planned on taking me, and that we'd have a six o'clock reservation. "I'll see you tonight, at the restaurant."

"Okay. Bye." I didn't end the call. I waited for him

to hang up. Then I sat there stunned for a few minutes. Once the gray matter started functioning again, I decided I needed to run out and pick up something new for tonight's date. Something a little sexy, but also sophisticated.

I grabbed my purse and headed out.

At six-thirty, I roared into the restaurant's parking lot. Everything was messed up. I was late, looking like crap, and feeling like crap for wrecking Damen's plans. After a quick makeup check in the rearview mirror, I glossed up my lips and racewalked inside.

At the hostess table, I said, "Hi, my name's Sloan. I was supposed to meet a man named Damen here about a half hour ago. I don't suppose he's still waiting . . . ?"

"Let me check. I just started my shift." The hostess looked at her little grid of tables, then stepped away from her podium. She returned a minute later, smiled, and said, "This way, please."

I couldn't believe it. I mentally rehearsed my apology while I followed her through the main dining room to a quiet room set off to one side. There were maybe a dozen tables in the room. Only one was occupied.

Damen stood and greeted me with a smile that made my heart do a little flip-flop.

"I am so sorry," I said as I scurried up to the table.

He leaned into me, offering a quick, much-too-polite hug. "It's okay. I was late too. I just got here about ten minutes ago." He motioned to the chair across from his.

I sat, accepting his help with the chair. "Thanks for being so understanding. I can't believe how crazy things have been today."

"I'm sorry it was bad. I had a rough day too." He lifted

a bottle of wine, showing me the label. "I'm sure we could both use a drink."

I'm not much of a drinker. The label meant nothing to me. I wouldn't be able to recognize the difference between a five-dollar wine and a five-hundred-dollar bottle. But wine sure sounded good after my insane afternoon. I lifted the empty glass sitting next to my appetizer plate. "Thanks, I'll take a little." As he poured, I asked, "So what's a rough day for a prince like?" I sipped. Delicious.

"There's a brother you didn't meet last night," he said, looking grave. He set the bottle down, leaving his hand resting on the table. "The youngest. He's been in Afghanistan for weeks, serving in an MP unit of the U.S. Army. I don't have all of the details yet, but we received word that his unit was attacked during a training exercise with the Afghan National Army. He's missing."

"Oh, my gosh, I'm so sorry." Our gazes locked, and I was blown away by the worry and agony I saw in his eyes. My afternoon had been pretty crappy, but nowhere near as bad as that.

Damen looked down at the table; he fiddled with his napkin. "Of course, my first instinct is to get on the first flight out and go find him."

"Of course."

"My mother is refusing to let me go. There are some complications. I'm not a member of the U.S. military. As a civilian, I can't just fly out there and join the hunt." He shoved his fingers through his hair. "But my mother could make it happen, if she tried."

"She doesn't want you to go."

His jaw clenched. "She said she won't send two sons into a war zone."

"She wants to protect you."

He shrugged. "I know." He sighed. His lips twitched.

"Anyway, I don't want to dump all this on you. We don't really know each other."

I reached across the table and set my hand on his. "Don't worry about it. You needed someone to talk to, someone to listen. I'm flattered you trust me."

His glance slid to our hands. He flipped his over so that my fingers rested on his palm. "I thought about canceling tonight, but I thought a distraction would be good, since my hands are tied." Then he curled his fingers a tiny bit and his fingertips grazed the sensitive skin on my wrist. A tingle buzzed up my arm.

"Distractions can be good sometimes," I agreed.

The waiter came just then, left some appetizers for us, and disappeared.

"I hope you don't mind. I ordered for both of us while I was waiting." He gently pulled his hand away.

I set mine in my lap. "I don't mind at all."

"So tell me, what's a rough day for the daughter of Jim Skye, aka Irvine, like?"

"It started after I got your call. I wanted to buy a new outfit for tonight—"

"Nice, is that it?" He motioned to my top.

"Yes. Thanks. Anyway, I headed out to the store to find something nice. Everything went great until I was driving home and my car died. In the fast lane on I-95. It took forever to get a tow. And then I spent hours at the dealership while the mechanics worked on it. That was no joy. But on the bright side, my car was fixed, and here I am."

Damen's smile couldn't be more adorable. "Yes, here you are."

The next two hours flew by. We ate. We laughed. We talked about just about everything, including our childhood. It came as no surprise that they were very different. By the time dessert had been delivered, I was feeling very much at ease with Damen, and hopeful that something wonderful was happening between us. It was much too soon to make any snap judgments about our long-term potential, but things were looking promising.

When he took my hand as we walked from the restaurant, I felt a goofy smile spread over my face.

He held the door for me.

He walked me to my car.

He looked deeply into my eyes and asked, "Would it be okay if I kissed you?"

He asked permission? How easy would it be to fall in love with this man?

"It would be more than okay." I closed my eyes and held my breath.

He caged my head between his hands and gently tipped it. The kiss was a soft but not tentative seduction. My head spun. My knees quaked. It was a kiss that made stars explode behind my closed eyelids. I slid my hands up his chest. My fingertips dipped between planes of rigid muscle. An image of him shirtless flashed through my mind, and my body went instantly hot.

When the kiss ended, I nearly fell over. Thankfully, I had his scrumptious body there to help steady me. I stared up at him. Maybe I gaped a little. His smile made me wish he'd kiss me again, harder.

"Thank you for a wonderful evening, Sloan Skye."

"Thank you, Damen . . . ? You never told me your last name."

"My last name is Sylver. I'll call you."

Still a little tongue-tied, I nodded. "Damen Sylver."

The next morning, I floated into the office. Last night had been like a fantasy come true. I'd never had a more romantic date. I'd never felt so alive.

JT, on the other hand, looked half dead.

"Rough night?" I asked.

"You could say that." He scrutinized me. "You look different. Is it your hair?"

I smoothed my hand along the side of my head, hoping no wayward strands had sprung loose from the ponytail. "No, it's the same as always, though I'm about ready to ditch these extensions. They're a real pain."

He squinted. "There's something different."

I shrugged. "I don't know what you're talking about." I pranced over to my cubicle and got settled in.

JT paid me a visit a few minutes later. I brought a chair for him. Then he heaved a sigh.

"What's wrong?" I asked as I skimmed the search engine results for *aswang*.

"It's Hough. She called me ten times last night."

"Ah, ten times? That's rough. Why did she keep calling?"

"It was one thing after another." Leaning back in his chair, legs sprawled in front of him, he let his head fall back until it thumped against my cubicle wall.

I instantly interpreted Brittany's behavior as an attempt to get him to come over. That made me slightly uncomfortable, which irritated me. I had, after all, kissed another man last night. I had moved on.

If only my emotions were so easily shut off.

"Any news of another victim?" I asked, moving to safer territory.

"Since we lost track of Onora Dale, the deaths have stopped. I've come to the conclusion that she's moved out of state. I sent out a bulletin to all the FBI satellite offices, asking them to notify me if there is a similar murder in their area. As of this morning, there've been none reported anywhere in the contiguous forty-eight."

I grimaced. "She wouldn't just stop. I don't think she can. So where is she hiding?"

Looking extremely disappointed, JT shook his head. "If only I'd been wearing a cup that day."

"It's not your fault. She was much stronger than I'd expected. She caught us both off guard."

"I've got Hough watching her cell phone and credit cards. If she makes a call or spends money, we'll know. In the meantime, I think I'll tail Lucas Dale again today. I have a feeling he knows where she's gone. He's protecting her."

"I wish he'd believe us, if we told him how dangerous she is."

"It's like she has the guy caught under a spell." JT stood. "I guess I'll head out."

"Later."

JT left, which meant I was in the office by myself. Hough, evidently back from medical leave, was locked in her Cave of Wonders. I could hear her keyboard *tap, tap, tapping*.

With no clue what to do next, I powered up my loaner laptop and stared at the welcome screen.

What did we know about Onora Dale?

We knew she worked as a contract medical biller.

We knew she had been married but wasn't any longer.

We knew her age, her Social Security number, where she banked, and that she had a clean driving record and no criminal record.

But that was about it.

Oh, and we strongly suspected she turned into a blackbird-like creature after dark and drained the blood from pregnant women.

She'd need access to medical files to locate her victims. Thus, I felt it was safe to assume she'd probably look for the same kind of work she'd done in Baltimore, no matter where she lived. Taking that assumption further, I figured she'd probably held a similar job before moving to the Baltimore area. Maybe in Ohio. And Michigan.

I knocked on Hough's door.

"*Entrez-vous!*" she called.

I entered.

"What's up?" Hough asked while still staring at one of her monitors. White numbers flashed on a black screen.

"How much digging have you done into Onora Dale's personal life?"

"Not a whole lot. I'm watching her credit cards and have run her Social and her driver's license. Other than that, I think JT's been focused on finding her through her ex-husband."

"Can you do me a favor, then, and see what you can find out about her?"

"Sure," she said, her attention still focused on the screen. "Just give me an hour or so."

"Will do. Thanks."

"By the way"—Hough stopped working and looked at me—"about JT. If you think I'm interested in him as more than a friend, you're wrong."

I back-stepped toward the door. "It doesn't matter."

"Sure it does. Why wouldn't it? He cares about you. Like genuinely *cares.*"

I really didn't like talking about this here, at work. Especially with Hough.

I said, "First, how can he 'care' about me when we've only known each other for such a short time? And second, like I said, it doesn't matter. We can't get involved. It would look bad for both of us."

Hough leaned closer. In a soft voice, she said, "Do you really think there aren't other agents sleeping with each other, here in the bureau? It happens all the time. As long as you keep it out of work, you're fine. Hell, I can name three couples that have gotten married in the past two years. None of them have faced any disciplinary action."

"But I'm an intern. I'm not even an agent yet. I would hate to lose my chance at being accepted at the FBI Academy because of something silly, like an affair."

Hough dismissed my concern with a hand flop. "Honestly, the FBI isn't going to let you go. You're too smart. Too good. You could probably sleep with half the bureau and you'd still get in." She went back to staring at her computer monitor. "Anyway, I felt I needed to clear the air between us."

"Thanks."

I left her lair feeling a lot less floaty than when I'd first walked into the office.

I slumped into my chair, poked around on the Internet, doing my best to dig up some background information on Onora Dale. My cell phone rang about a half hour later.

Damen Sylver.

I answered, "Hello?"

"Where are you?" he asked.

"At work."

"Any chance you can get away for lunch?"

I glanced at Hough's door, then checked the time. "Shouldn't be a problem, but I'm on the clock. I can't go anywhere too exotic, like Fiji. I only get an hour."

"Well, damn. There goes that plan."

"Wait, were you really . . . ?"

There was that glorious, rumbling chuckle again, warm and adorable. I couldn't help smiling to myself.

"No, I was just kidding," he said. "I reserve trips to Fiji for special occasions, like one-week anniversaries."

"Sheesh, what do you do for a one-month anniversary?"

"You'll just have to wait to find out. Can I pick you up in twenty?"

"I'll have to meet you. Unless you have a military ID and can get on base. My office is in Quantico."

"Not a problem. See you then." He ended the call.

I stared at my computer for about thirty seconds, then raced to the bathroom to see how bad my hair really looked.

When I came out ten minutes or so later, makeup touched up, hair fluffed, there was a pile of papers sitting on my desk. And JT was leafing through them.

"I thought you were tailing Lucas Dale."

"Baltimore's got a man on him. I thought I'd come back and see what other angle we could take with the case. I see you've been busy." He gave me an up-and-down look. "Going somewhere?"

"Well, actually, I made plans for—"

Damen Sylver picked just that moment to come strolling into the unit. While I floundered a little, he headed straight toward me, his beaming smile in place.

"Sloan, I'm a little early. Would you like me to wait outside?"

JT visibly sized up the prince. Something flashed over his face.

The prince offered a hand to JT. "Damen Sylver. I'm a friend of Sloan's."

"This is Special Agent Jordan Thomas," I said. "We're going to lunch."

JT gave the prince's hand a quick shake before turning to me. "I'll see you after lunch."

"Okay." I grabbed my purse and started toward the door. Damen set his hand on the small of my back and fell into step beside me.

I could feel JT's stare drilling into my back as we left.

Hope begins in the dark, the stubborn hope that if you just show up and try to do the right thing, the dawn will come. You wait and watch and work: you don't give up.

—Anne Lamott

28

"Is there something going on between you and Agent Thomas?" Damen hadn't even waited until we'd gotten out of the building before asking me that question.

But I was determined to wait until after we were outside to answer it. "I've been told he cares for me." I strolled out the main exit into a blazingly bright afternoon.

"That much is obvious," he said as he escorted me to the limo idling in front of the building. "But that's not why I asked. It was more you. I get the sense that you have feelings for him."

The limo's driver got out, hustling to open the passenger door for us.

I didn't get in the vehicle. "Well . . ." How to handle this one? Here I was, about to go on a date with an incredible man—a man who wasn't an FBI agent; who wouldn't put my career in jeopardy. We had only gone on one date. He didn't have a right to dig into my personal life, any more than I had a right to dig into his.

Still, I felt he deserved an honest answer. "We went out once. But then, before things got carried away, I decided it would be a bad idea. I'm an intern. He's an agent. And

I'd like to get a permanent position with the FBI, once I graduate. Getting a reputation for sleeping with senior agents doesn't seem the best idea."

At Damen's tip of the head, I climbed inside, found a comfy seat, and waited for him to make himself comfortable too. "Now that I've answered your question, how about you answer mine?"

"Sure." Sitting next to me, he set an arm on the back of the seat and crossed an ankle over a knee.

"How is it you were able to stroll right into the FBI Academy? You're not military. You told me that at dinner. Is it the prince thing? I assumed that was kept hush-hush."

"It is kept quiet. Nobody in Quantico knows anything about my royal status. I can't tell you more, but suffice it to say, there are quite a few places I can access that the normal Joe Civilian can't."

"Are you an agent too? FBI? CIA?" The car started rolling. "I mean, if you're an FBI agent, I shouldn't be going to lunch with you. It would be a conflict of interest, like with JT."

"Don't worry, your reputation won't suffer."

Little warning bells rang in my head. Whenever anyone said the words "Don't worry," I did exactly that— I worried.

I made a point to return to work exactly one hour later. My lunch with Damen was nice. He knew exactly how to distract a girl. He'd arranged everything. Flowers were waiting for me at our table, which just happened to be tucked in a private banquet room. He'd ordered everything ahead of time, so our waiter paid us regular, but discreet, visits to deliver drinks, then salads, hors d'oeuvres, the main course, and finally dessert.

The food was amazing, the service outstanding, and the conversation—after a bumpy start—great.

But it was over. And it was back to reality. Back to JT.

Feeling a little uncomfortable, I strolled into the unit with the flowers kind of hidden in my folded arms. I saw JT working in his cubicle as I hurried to mine.

No sooner had I tucked the flowers into the corner of my cubby than he was knocking on my partition wall.

"How was lunch?" he asked, with his eyes glued to the flowers.

"Good, thanks."

"While you were gone, Hough and I did some digging. I found out Onora Dale has connections to an adoption agency in Columbia."

Adoption agency? That made sense.

I asked, "Are you thinking that she's funneling the stolen infants through the agency?"

"I'm hoping."

So was I.

But there were some problems with his theory. "First, how is she delivering them without leaving any traces of blood? How is she removing them from the scene if she's not even entering the premises? And, assuming she was somehow taking the children, how would she explain having so many?" I asked. "If she's feeding three times a week, that's over one hundred fifty children a year. You'd think that would trigger some suspicion."

JT shrugged. "I put in a call to the agency's director. She's agreed to meet with me in an hour and a half. Do you want to come with me?"

"Sure." As much as I dreaded the thought of being cooped up in a car with JT for hours—the drive was over an hour, one way—I needed to set our personal issues aside and keep working with him, just like I had been doing, up to that point.

He thumbed over his shoulder, in the general direction of his cubicle. "I'm just going to shut down my laptop and pack up. Then we'll leave."

"Okay." I did the same, leaving everything but my purse in my cubicle.

Now that we were no longer staying at the rental, I'd be driving my own car home later. I'd grab my stuff before going home.

We were on I-95, heading north, ten minutes later. From the moment we left, JT didn't speak a single word to me. To ease the uncomfortable silence, I turned on the radio and tuned it to a news station.

Twenty minutes later, he broke the awkward silence. "I know your personal life is none of my business, but I thought I should tell you. Damen Sylver is with the bureau. He's out of the WFO, the Washington Field Office."

I bit back an expletive and said, "Thank you."

"I thought you'd want to know."

"I do."

I spent the rest of the drive trying to decide how to handle Damen Sylver. I basically had two options: ignore his calls and end it now, or confront him about the lie. By the time we'd pulled up in front of the adoption agency's humble brick-faced building, I'd determined I wasn't the blow-him-off type. I didn't enjoy confrontation, but I was hurt and angry, and I wanted to let him know.

Oh, yes, *Agent* Sylver would hear from me soon.

That settled, I cleared my head, took a deep breath, and headed inside with JT. We needed to stop Onora Dale. That was where I needed to focus.

Men are trouble, Sloan. All of them. You should know that by now.

A smiling young woman sitting at a reception desk

greeted us as we came in. We told her we had an appointment with the director, and she asked us to take a seat in the waiting area, which was currently empty.

Two minutes later, a middle-aged woman dressed in a conservative suit and pumps stepped into the waiting area and introduced herself.

JT and I stood.

JT offered a hand. "I'm Jordan Thomas. This is Sloan Skye. Thank you for meeting with us on such short notice."

"It's not a problem. I'd been planning on working late, anyway. Fran O'Donnell. How can I help you, Agents?"

JT cleared his throat, then said in a low voice, "We'd like to ask about one of your volunteers, Onora Dale."

"What would you like to know?" Glancing over her shoulder at the receptionist, who appeared to be busy, Fran O'Donnell said, "Why don't we talk in my office?"

She escorted us through a door into a small but tidy and nicely furnished office. She invited us to sit in the chairs facing her desk.

"Can you tell us what kind of work she does for your agency?" JT asked, once we'd all gotten settled.

"Ms. Dale assists in many different capacities, and has been volunteering with us for quite some time. Why? Is something wrong?"

"Does she, by chance, bring a lot of infants to you?" I asked.

Fran O'Donnell's eyebrow twitched. "Well, yes, of course. She runs several homes for expectant teen mothers, after all." Looking nervous, she glanced at me, then JT, then back at me. "What is this all about?"

Neither of us had heard about any homes for teen mothers. Had we missed something? We exchanged glances.

"I'm assuming you're required to complete certain

paperwork on every child you place in foster care or adoption, correct?" JT asked.

The woman's lips thinned. "Of course."

"And Onora Dale has provided that paperwork for all the children she's brought to you?" JT pressed.

Fran O'Donnell nodded. "Yes. Absolutely. Every one."

"May we see your files?"

Something flashed in the woman's eyes. "No. Not without a court order. Those records are private. We share them with nobody, not even FBI agents. Now, if you'd please tell me what this is regarding . . . ?"

"One final question, if you please," JT said, again ignoring her question. "Do you know, or can you estimate, how many children Onora Dale has placed through your agency?"

"I'd estimate about fifty this year." Fran O'Donnell stood. "Now, I'm sorry, but I have a lot of work to do." She went to the door, opened it, and made it plainly clear she was done answering our questions.

We both thanked her, then headed outside.

In the car, I said, "At least we know some of the children are probably still alive, if Onora Dale is our unsub. Maybe there's more. Perhaps she's using another agency to avoid raising any red flags? I don't know how many expectant mothers your average group home houses, but I'm thinking more than fifty deliveries a year would probably raise some eyebrows."

"Could be. We need to see if Hough can locate which group homes Dale's affiliated with."

I glanced at the clock. It was a little after three in the afternoon. It had been several nights since the unsub's last victim had been reported. Would she hunt tonight? Would an innocent woman die before we could make the pieces of this puzzle fit?

"Now what?" I asked JT.

He let his head fall back and closed his eyes. Gone was the flirty, goofy, carefree man I was used to seeing. Beside me now was a guy who appeared defeated. "I don't know. We've done everything we can."

"Have we taken all our evidence to the prosecutor, including Onora Dale's tie to the adoption agency, to see if we can at least get a search warrant?"

"I think McGrane has."

"Maybe we should make sure."

JT studied me for a few moments, then nodded. "Okay. I'll put in a call to him. In the meantime, I say we call it a day and get some rest."

I was sort of okay with that plan.

"A new day. A new hope," I said, trying to cheer him up.

We are never deceived; we deceive ourselves.

—Johann Wolfgang von Goethe

29

Agent Damen Sylver was waiting for me in my living room when I got home. *Agent* Sylver was looking quite cozy, lounging on my couch. His feet were kicked up on the coffee table, an arm was slung over the back of the sofa, and he was chatting with Katie.

Katie grinned as I strolled in. "Hi, Sloan, you've got a visitor. And I have some reading to do." She scrambled to her feet. "I'll leave you two alone."

"Thanks." Hauling my dinner-in-a-bag, I offered, "Before you disappear into your cave, would you like a sandwich? They were buy-one-get-one-free at Como's."

"Sure. Thanks." Katie accepted a wrapped Italian submarine sandwich, then left.

Agent Sylver started to stand. "I hope you don't mind—"

"No, it's okay." I glanced at the empty glass sitting on the table. "Do you want something to eat? Drink?"

"No, thank you." He sat back down. But instead of leaning back and kicking up his feet, he sat forward, elbows on his knees. "I'm fine."

I stuffed the bag in the refrigerator. I wasn't in the mood to eat at the moment. Maybe after I got everything off my chest, that would change.

I sat as far from *Agent* Sylver as I could and narrowed my eyes at him. "I heard something interesting today."

"What's that?"

"You're with the bureau." There, it was out in the open.

The skin around Agent Sylver's eyes tightened. "I am."

"I asked you earlier today how you were able to gain access to the Academy. You intentionally avoided answering my question."

"I did. I'm sorry."

My stomach twisted. *Bastard!* "You lied. By omission."

"Once you told me about you and Thomas, I couldn't get myself to admit the truth."

Damn it. "You said my reputation wasn't at stake." My blood started pounding hot and hard through my veins.

"It isn't. I didn't lie to you about that." Agent Sylver's gaze searched mine. He knew how angry I was. I could tell. He visibly exhaled. "Sloan, you're an intern with the PBAU, which is part of the National Center for the Analysis of Violent Crime, the NCAVC. I'm a field agent out of DC. We don't work together, not directly."

"But we could in the future, if a case comes up in your jurisdiction."

"We can worry about that *if* it happens." He stood and my nerves started zapping. It irritated me how reactive they were to Agent Sylver, and to JT, and to Gabe, for that matter.

Since when had I become so insanely horny?

I backed away, giving him a come-no-closer glare. "You should have told me the truth."

"I should have told you the truth," Agent Sylver echoed. "You're right. That's why I'm here. I came to tell you."

I'd been expecting at least a little bit of a fight. His complete acquiescence did cool the fire from my anger a little. But my blood pressure was still probably in the stroke zone. Either he was a good man who'd made a mistake, and was willing to pay for it, or he was one heck of a manipulator. I had no way of knowing which.

He flipped his hands over, palms up. "I'm sorry, Sloan. I hope you'll let me make it up to you." I looked at those hands, a sign of capitulation; at his eyes, dark with concern; his face, a mask of guilt. How easy would it be to forget when he looked so genuinely sorry?

"I realize we've spent very little time together. We don't know each other yet. But I've never felt such a strong connection with a woman before."

Mirroring his posture, elbows on my knees, I dropped my face into my hands. I had such a hard time trusting any man—let alone one who was lying to me right off the bat.

"I need time to think."

Why were men so deceitful? Manipulating?

"Okay." Instead of trying to make me change my mind by hauling me into his arms and kissing me until my brain malfunctioned, Agent Sylver went to the door. Before he left, he turned to me. "I made a mistake, Sloan. I'm owning up to it. But I've never met anyone like you. I didn't want to kill our chances before we'd really gotten going."

Still sitting, I gnawed on my lower lip. "That's all fine and good, but you know what they say about honesty and trust. Without them, a relationship doesn't stand a chance."

He nodded and left.

Katie dashed out of her room no more than five seconds later. "What happened?"

I put my head down, pressed my palms against my forehead. "He lied. About his job. He works for the FBI. Now I don't know if I can trust him."

"Oh, Sloan. I'm sorry, hon." Katie hugged me, then went to the kitchen.

I lumbered to the bathroom, splashed some cold water on my face, and stared at my reflection in the mirror. Would this girl, the socially awkward brainiac reflected back at me, ever find a man who deserved my trust? Would I ever hear the words "I love you," spoken by a man whom I could believe in? Would I find a man whom I could trust with all I had and all I was?

After returning to the living room, I slumped, boneless, on the couch, right where Agent Sylver had just been sitting. If I inhaled really deeply, I could still smell his cologne lingering on the throw pillow. That scent made my nerves tingle.

I hugged it to my chest and let my head flop forward, burying my face in it.

Katie tapped me on the shoulder. "Chocolate ice cream always makes me feel better."

"I don't know if anything will help right now. . . ." I accepted a spoon.

"It's chocolate brownie chunk." Katie plunked down beside me and flipped off the lid. She tipped the carton toward me. "You first."

"Thanks." I dug a big clump out and deposited it in my mouth. The flavors of chocolate and fudge and almonds made my taste buds come alive. "I think I'd probably handle this thing with Agent Sylver better if it wasn't for JT. And for our case. We know who it is that we're looking for. But we can't find her. Get this, Damen strolled into the PBAU today to pick me up for lunch. JT was there. Things have been very tense between us now. Which is exactly why I kept telling JT getting emotionally involved was a bad idea in the first place. . . ." And on, and on I went, rambling in one long-winded, somewhat incoherent rant.

Throughout my soliloquy, Katie just kept nodding and gobbling ice cream. She offered no words of wisdom, only half-smiles of commiseration. Finally when I'd run out of words, she handed the carton to me. "Sloan, all I can do for you is what you've always done for me, tell you that you need to forget about everyone else—what they think, what they want, what you think they deserve—and do what is best for you."

"That's just it. I don't know what's best for me."

Katie shrugged. "Then you wait. You do nothing. With JT. With Gabe. With Prince Damen. Until you do know."

"If only it were so simple."

"Sloan, it can be that simple, if you make it so."

I woke up feeling like someone was watching me. I jerked upright, heart racing, and searched my dark room. It was silent, eerily so. No insects chirring. No birdsong. Just my pounding heart and the distant hum of Katie's window fan.

I went to the bathroom, then returned to bed. My skin was itchy; a creepy, crawly sensation tingled at the base of my neck. I settled in, cradling my head in the softness of my pillow. A breeze gusted in the open window, chilling my skin.

Maybe I was getting sick?

I thought about getting a thermometer and checking my temperature, but I was tired, weary, exhausted. My heavy eyelids fell shut. Slowly, gradually, my body relaxed.

Then I felt it, a tiny tickle, like a fly walking up my arm. I shook it, but the tickle didn't leave. I scratched. Within seconds, the tickle was back. I rolled over, wedging my arm between my body and the mattress. Images of glowing red eyes flashed behind my closed eyelids. Then the image of a slithering black snakelike creature. And tiny insects. Crawling on me.

All over me.

Arms. Legs. Chest. Face.

I jerked upright and rubbed my face. I broke out in a cold sweat. My spine tightened.

Something was wrong.

Terror gripped my throat, which made no sense. I was sick. Running a fever. Why was I so terrified?

Then I saw them—the glowing red orbs. They rose up, moved closer. They were floating in a deep inky shadow. As they drew nearer, I realized that shadow was corporeal.

I was frozen with horror.

"Who's there?" I whispered. My stomach clenched. My heart thumped in my ears.

No answer.

Move, damn it. Move!

"Elmer, is that you?"

Still, no answer.

Something inside me snapped. My frozen muscles jerked. I flung myself out of bed, hit the floor, then scrambled for the door.

An ice-cold band clamped around my ankle. I was hauled into the air, dangling upside down. I swung my fists; I thrashed.

The band around my ankle opened and I fell hard. Stars sparkled in my vision, but I hauled ass to the door a second time.

Out. Now. Escape.

I made it as far as the door, grabbed the doorknob, but the band snapped around my ankle again. Before I realized it, I was sailing through the air. I hit my dresser this time, then crashed to the floor.

Must escape.

How?

I was dead if I didn't get out. I knew it. A sick feeling swept through me. I gagged.

"My baby died because of you," a creepy, cracked voice said, sounding like a caricature of an old lady. "My sweet baby. Now you'll pay."

The cold vise closed around my throat this time. It didn't squeeze, but I struggled to breathe, anyway. Those frightening glowing red orbs moved closer. The stench of death hit the back of my throat. As the face of my attacker moved into the minuscule light leaking in my bedroom window, I gagged.

It was horrifying.

Huge, protruding teeth. Weird, glowing eyes. Its nose was very long, beaklike.

I was staring into the eyes of the *aswang*.

"I . . . I d-don't know what you mean," I stammered.

Air. I needed air. Not enough oxygen.

"I couldn't feed my babies because of you." The *aswang* tightened her grip on my throat.

Instinctively, I curled my fingers around her claw.

She was going to strangle me.

I was going to die.

She snarled. It was a sight I would never forget. Her wings flapped. A soft birdsong accompanied the *whoosh* of air as the wings stirred it. Instantly my thoughts coagulated. My body became heavy. I felt . . . peaceful. Then it stopped and the terror returned.

"Imagine what it feels like to hold your beautiful baby and watch her die."

I couldn't imagine that. I couldn't imagine anything. Not with her squeezing my neck.

Breathe, Sloan, breathe.

"I'm s-sorry," I mumbled, afraid to say too much, to

make her angrier. "P-please don't kill me. Maybe I can help."

"You are going to help me?" The creature's smile made my skin crawl. It made my insides twist too. "You owe me that much. But you won't."

Her claw tightened.

No air.

Pain. Terror.

Desperation.

This was it.

A blast of adrenaline charged through me. I fought. I kicked. Some strange, garbled noise filled the room. That sound was coming from me.

I couldn't breathe. I couldn't get free. I felt my energy slipping. I was losing. I felt the life draining from my body. My vision was dimming; sounds were muffled.

Stars.

Darkness.

And then a scream that made my sluggish blood turn to ice.

The pressure on my throat released. I gasped and choked and hacked, only vaguely aware of some kind of activity going on around me.

My vision was blurred; my eyes were full of tears. Still hacking and fighting to pull air into my oxygen-starved lungs, I looked up.

Katie was spraying something from a spray bottle at the *aswang*. "Leave her alone, you ugly bitch!"

The *aswang* fell to the floor, thrashing. Her skin was blistered and melted so badly from whatever Katie was spraying on her, it looked like she had been burned alive. There were feathers everywhere. Black feathers. She was writhing in agony in the middle of them, lying in a curled-up fetal position, clawing at the floor with one hand and covering her head with the other arm. An ear-splitting shriek cut through the room.

"Katie, wait!" I yelled.

"She's still alive, Sloan. She was going to kill you." Katie's hands were shaking. Her eyes were wild. Her face was the color of milk.

"The babies. I need to know what she did with the babies." Nausea clenched my stomach, but I forced myself to move closer. "Where are the infants?" I asked her.

The *aswang* lifted her eyes to me. They were full of agony and hatred; but for a split second, I felt a twinge of sympathy for her.

"I never hurt them. I couldn't. I love them all. I love all my babies."

"Where are they?" I repeated, watching breathlessly as she slowly changed from a bird-woman to just a woman. Onora Dale.

"They're gone," Onora Dale said. "I gave them away. To good families that deserved them. Loving families. I didn't keep any of them. I have two of my own. They needed me. My babies. So precious. So . . . beautiful." She visibly inhaled, exhaled. Her eyes were growing dim; her face and body were going lax. The *aswang* was dying. I had no doubt.

"Where are they?" I repeated, my concern for the ones she called hers growing. If she died, leaving them motherless, how long would they survive? At least the others were being cared for. For the moment, they were probably safe. "Where are your babies?"

"Hidden. They're mine. Only mine."

"They'll die if you don't tell me where they are."

She smiled. Licked lips that were so blistered they looked like they might burst. "By now, they're both dead, anyway. I couldn't . . . hunt. Couldn't . . . feed . . . them. My . . . sweet . . . babies."

She exhaled one last time.

I looked up at Katie.

I'd failed. To find out where the babies were. To find out if she'd attacked my mom, Brittany, Renee Bibens, Evelyn Isbell.

I'd failed to get so many answers.

"Sloan? Oh, my God." Katie glanced at the bottle in her hand. "It was just an SSC buffer solution. It shouldn't have burned her like that. She was hurting you. I . . . I killed her?"

She blinked once, twice . . . and fainted.

Within a half hour, our apartment was teeming with police and FBI types. We were sitting in the living room. Katie was being checked out by EMS, while I quietly told JT what had happened.

He scribbled notes, nodding a lot. Then, once I'd recited Onora Dale's parting words, he started making calls. A few minutes later, he told me, "McGrane's working on the warrant to search the adoption agency." He dialed another number. "And he has men in Onora Dale's apartment right now, looking for clues." He pocketed his phone and plunked his butt next to mine. His gaze searched mine. "Now that I took care of business, Sloan, are you okay?"

"Yeah." Even to my own ears, my response sounded hollow.

"Are you sure?"

I looked at him.

I inhaled.

I exhaled.

Then I started crying and shaking.

JT gathered me into his arms and held me while I fell apart. I made a mess on his shirt with all my tears. But slowly the sobs stopped. I snuffled, dragged my hand across my face, and licked my lips. Salt water.

"Tears killed her, basically. Ironic, isn't it? How many tears were shed because of her?"

"Yeah, it's ironic."

We just sat that way for a little while. It felt good, being held, feeling safe. Feeling grounded in reality again.

"Katie saved my life," I said at least a few times.

"Yes, Sloan," JT responded. This last time, he sounded a little sad.

I glanced up at his face. He looked sad too. Or maybe . . . guilty?

"It's not your fault, if that's what you think. You didn't know she would come for me."

"Yeah," he said. It wasn't a convincing "yeah."

"You can't protect everyone from everything," I pointed out.

JT's jaw clenched a little. The muscle twitched. "I promised."

"You're only human."

JT said nothing.

I said nothing.

I just sat there, soaking up JT's strength and warmth, and waited for the aftershock tremors to stop.

The attack was like a horrible dream now. It was still fresh in my mind, but it didn't seem real for some reason.

"The babies?" I asked.

"They'll find them." JT's phone rang. He let me go, checked the number. "McGrane." He answered it.

I listened to his end of the conversation. It sounded like they had found something. He clicked off.

"Lucas Dale called dispatch a few minutes ago. He found two dead infants in his marine storage unit in Ocean City. McGrane's team is on their way over to the scene. Do you want to go?"

Dead infants. I wasn't sure I could handle that. "I don't know, JT. Dead babies. That's awful."

"Okay."

"Are you going?"

"Later. I'll stay here for a little while longer."

"You can go. I'm sure you need to."

"In a bit." He put his arms around me again and held me tightly.

I wasn't trembling anymore, but I didn't mind. I had a feeling he was holding me more for his sake than for mine.

JT was a good man.

Maybe I could love him.

If only he weren't a coworker.

If only he hadn't tried to hide the truth about Hough's baby.

If only . . . I were capable of trusting someone, anyone.

We watched the ME take Onora Dale away.

I answered some questions. Lots of questions. And then people started filing out of the apartment.

JT's phone rang again. He looked. It was McGrane once more. He answered. There were a lot of "uh-huh" and "okay," and then "I'll be there as soon as I can." He clicked off. He met my gaze. "McGrane verified there were two infants. He said I need to get over there right away. They aren't normal."

"What does that mean?"

"It means, I don't think they belong to the victims. They're both female, Sloan. And they have fangs . . . and feathers. Coming with me?"

I looked at my shaking hands. An image of Onora Dale, half-bird, half-woman flashed through my mind. "No, I don't think I'm ready for that."

"Okay." He smoothed my hair away from my face. "Sloan, I'll see you tomorrow. Hopefully, by then,

McGrane will have his search warrant, and we'll get a bead on the missing infants. Sweet dreams."

I was hopeful about the former, doubtful about the latter. Donning the best smile I could muster under the circumstances, I said, "You too."

JT's call came in while I was driving to work the next morning. McGrane and his men were still in Ocean City, collecting evidence. Fran O'Donnell was in custody for questioning. JT was heading over to the Baltimore PD to interview her. He wanted me there too. So I changed directions, going north.

Rush-hour traffic was a killer, but I made the drive in two hours. I was escorted to a room adjoining the interview room and told to wait there. I had a clear view of JT and Fran O'Donnell through the one-way mirror on the wall between the two spaces. I surmised the interview had been going on for a while.

Right away, I noticed the woman was looking nervous. She was sitting on the edge of her seat, and her knee was bouncing. Her hands were splayed on the tabletop stretching between her and JT. In contrast, JT had his calm, friendly face on, trying to put her at ease.

The guy who'd escorted me back entered the room, whispered something to JT, then left. JT leaned back, crossed his arms over his chest, and said, "Maybe you'd feel more comfortable talking to a friend of mine. You met her when I visited the agency."

Fran O'Donnell shifted in her seat. "Um. Sure. I remember her."

The officer who'd been speaking with JT entered the room where I was sitting. "He'd like you to come in."

"Okay." Feeling a little nervous, I followed the officer

to the interview room, entered, glanced at JT, then at Fran O'Donnell.

Her eyes tracked my movements as I sat next to JT.

"Hello, Mrs. O'Donnell."

She muttered a stiff hello back.

I glanced at JT. He flicked his eyes at Fran O'Donnell, encouraging me to begin questioning her. Of course, everything I read about interrogation techniques flew from my mind.

I took a deep breath and smiled. "Sorry. This is the first time I've interviewed a witness. I'm a little nervous."

Fran O'Donnell gave a tight chuckle. "You're nervous? Try sitting on this side of the table. Am I in trouble?"

"Like I said, ma'am, we're just talking right now," JT said. "Asking some questions."

The woman's gaze flicked to me.

I smiled, to try to reassure her.

Remember, the more truths she tells you, the less likely she'll be to lie.

"I'm sure you're very nervous. After all, your agency does good work, doesn't it? Finding great homes for children," I said.

"Yes, absolutely."

Encouraged by her response, I continued. "I'm willing to bet you carefully screen every adoption applicant, to make sure they're the best choice for a child."

"Most definitely."

"And I'm guessing you feel very good when you see a child go to a loving, stable family, especially when that child would have had a very different life if you hadn't interceded."

She didn't respond right away. I thought I'd lost her. Then she said, "You have no idea what kinds of situations we've rescued children from."

"Yes, *rescued*," I said, catching on to her motivation.

Rescuing the children. That was one compelling motivation, for sure. "That's what you've done. Rescued the children from terrible fates. From parents who didn't deserve them."

"Yes. Exactly."

"That is a very noble thing, to give a child a good life, to rescue him or her from a situation that wasn't healthy." I indicated JT with a tip of my head. "I don't think anyone here would disagree with that statement."

The woman's gaze slid from me to JT, then back to me again.

"Take Victoria Sprouse's baby. Her marriage was in shambles. The child wasn't even the husband's. She was having an illicit affair with her neighbor. That child deserved so much better."

Fran O'Donnell's gaze flicked back and forth between JT and me again. She said nothing.

"And Katherine Jewett. She was a madam, running a prostitution ring. She had no business bringing a child into that kind of situation. I don't blame you for wanting to rescue that child."

No response from Fran O'Donnell.

"And what about Cassie Crause? She wasn't even married to the father of her child, Nick Ellanson. They were living together. In sin. What kind of a life would that innocent child have, if you didn't intervene?"

"I just wanted to help them," she whispered. "Someone had to do something."

We had her. We had her!

"Of course, you had to do something. Every child you took, you found good, safe, loving homes for. Now all we need to do is verify where they've all gone. Did you keep records?"

"Not exactly. I didn't file legal adoptions for all of them. It got to the point where I was getting so many, and so often. I didn't want to . . . raise any flags."

Flags were flying now, that was for sure.

"Did you at least keep a list of adoptive parents?" I asked.

"Oh, yes. Absolutely. And I followed up on every child I placed. Every single one. They're all doing wonderfully." She smiled, proud of her accomplishments. "I have a knack for selecting the right parents for a child. A special gift."

"I'm sure you do. Now, where is that list?"

"Why?" Her expression changed. "You need to leave well enough alone. Those parents all believe they've legally adopted their children. If you tell them . . . if you try to undo all of my work, you'll destroy lives. Hundreds of them."

"No worries." I forced a smile, when I felt like I wanted to throw up. "We just need to review the list."

"It's on my computer, under the name 'Gabriel.' Gabriel is the angel of child conception and adoption."

JT stood and, without saying a word, left the room.

"I have just one question for you," I said, ready to leave too. "How did you deliver the children without leaving any traces of evidence? No blood. No fingerprints. Nothing. Childbirth is messy business."

"The mothers always came to me to deliver."

"How? When?" I couldn't picture how this whole thing worked. It made no sense to me.

"I never hurt them. I only delivered their children."

"Where did you deliver the infants?" I leaned forward, anxious to understand.

"In my van. I converted it into a mobile hospital. They walked outside, where I was parked. After they delivered and had stabilized, they went back inside their homes."

That made no sense. Why would any woman wander outside in the middle of the night, meet up with a stranger, deliver, and then abandon her child?

JT had left a legal pad on the table and a pen. I grabbed them and started taking notes. "And you say they were alive and well when they came out to you?"

Fran O'Donnell nodded. "Yes. During delivery, I monitored their blood pressures and temperatures. I gave them IVs, when needed. They left in perfect health."

"Did you notice anything unusual about them when they came to you? Anything at all?"

"Well, there was one thing. They all had a mark. A tiny puncture wound in the groin. But the wounds looked healed."

"How . . . odd." I wrote down a few more notes. "How did you know who was delivering each night?"

"Onora called me to tell me who was ready to deliver every night. It was tricky. In many cases, I had very little time to get there."

The pieces were starting to fall into place.

"Did you see Ms. Dale while you were delivering the children?"

"No. Never."

"What about a strange-looking blackbird?"

The woman's eyes widened. "Yes, the bird. I'd even named her. She perched on the roof of my van every night. And she sang. It was the most eerily beautiful birdsong I'd ever heard. Almost . . ."

"Hypnotizing?"

"Yes, hypnotizing," Fran O'Donnell said. "After the women delivered, they'd return to their homes, and I would leave with the infant."

"Did you happen to notice that every time you delivered a child, the mother ended up dead the next day?" I asked her.

Her face paled. Her gaze slid to the table. "Yes, I did. But I knew it wasn't because of anything I'd done. The news called it serial murder. They implied someone was killing the women for their babies. That's not me. I had saved their children's lives by delivering them before the serial murderer got to them."

"That you did." I stood. "Thank you, Ms. O'Donnell. I have one final question, and then I'll be finished. Did you ever travel out of state to deliver any children?"

"Yes, once. I recently went to Ohio. The name was . . . Bibens."

Bibens. We were right.

With the exception of the old case in Michigan, and the attack on my mother and Hough, we had our answers, as bizarre and freakish as they were. It was a case of charity gone horribly wrong. Atrociously wrong. And hundreds of lives would be devastated, once the truth was revealed.

But at least the men who had lost the women they loved would have their babies back—once they all were tracked down. They would have closure and a small, precious piece of the lover, the partner, the friend, and the spouse they had lost.

It wasn't much of a happy ending, but it was the best we could give them.

Feeling a heavy weight lifting off my shoulders, I wandered through the Baltimore PD. Several officers, including Commissioner Allan, congratulated me on the way out. But my mood wasn't joyful. It was a bittersweet ending to a horrible case. For the most part, it had ended well. The *aswang* was dead. So were two future *aswangs*. The patients of Dr. Rosenstein, Dr. Patel, and Dr. Yokely were now safe from harm.

But . . . but so many lives would change when those infants were torn out of loving arms, to be returned to their rightful homes.

This case had been hell. I was almost afraid to see what we would face next.

My phone rang as I was strapping myself into my car. It was Elmer.

"Hello, Elmer," I answered. "What's up?"

"I'm ready," Elmer said, his voice sharp. "It's time I collect what's due to me. I've been patient up to this point. But not anymore."

A shiver swept up my spine. His tone was so cool, so evil. "What do you want?"

"You'll find out tonight. After sunset. Good-bye, Sloan Skye. I'll see you soon. . . ."

Helen Keller once said, "All the world is full of suffering. It is also full of overcoming." This has always been one of my favorite quotes. The perfect balance of stark reality and enduring optimism. Negative and positive. Dark and light.

But already, in such a short time, I'd seen too much death and sorrow in this job. So much darkness and so little light. I hoped by the end of summer, I wouldn't become cynical, callous. Because I don't want to only see the beast inside the man. I want to always see the man inside the beast.

GREAT BOOKS, GREAT SAVINGS!

When You Visit Our Website:
www.kensingtonbooks.com
You Can Save Money Off The Retail Price
Of Any Book You Purchase!

- All Your Favorite Kensington Authors
- New Releases & Timeless Classics
- Overnight Shipping Available
- eBooks Available For Many Titles
- All Major Credit Cards Accepted

Visit Us Today To Start Saving!
www.kensingtonbooks.com

All Orders Are Subject To Availability.
Shipping and Handling Charges Apply.
Offers and Prices Subject To Change Without Notice.